GADGET

GADGET

NICOLAS FREELING

COWARD, McCANN & GEOGHEGAN, INC.
NEW YORK

Grateful acknowledgment is made to Random House, Inc., for permission to use excerpts from *Collected Poems* by W. H. Auden, Edward Mendelson, ed., copyright © 1976 by Edward Mendelson, William Meredith, and Monroe K. Spears, executors of the estate of W. H. Auden.

First American Edition 1977

Copyright ©1977 by Nicolas Freeling

SBN: 698-10810-8

Library of Congress Cataloging in Publication Data

Freeling, Nicolas.
  Gadget.

  I. Title.
PZ4.F854Gad 1977   [PR6056.R4]   823'.9'14   77-24130
ISBN 0-698-10810-8

Printed in the United States of America

To Renée

CONTENTS

These are the five component parts of a classic fission bomb.   N.F.

Author's Note

A gadget is physicists' jargon for a nuclear device: a playful and harmless word for what we would call an atomic bomb.

This book is largely the work of a distinguished American physicist. He provided the theme, and built the gadget, and without him it could never have been written.

The personages in this book are imaginary, and so, at the time of writing, are the events. The gadget, though, is not imaginary, and every detail of it is true. The book cannot, however, be used as a blueprint. As a safeguard, one vital consideration has been omitted.

OBJECT

'The object of the project is to produce a *practical military weapon* in the form of a bomb in which the energy is released by a fast neutron chain reaction in one or more of the materials known to show nuclear fission.'

Paragraph One of
The Los Alamos Primer,
quoting Robert Serber

When the green field comes off like a lid,
Revealing what was much better hid . . .
        Unpleasant:
        And look, behind you without a sound
The woods have come up and are standing round
        In deadly crescent.

The bolt is sliding in its groove;
Outside the window is the black removers' van:
And now with sudden swift emergence
Come the hooded women, the hump-backed
    surgeons
        And the Scissor Man

        from *The Witnesses* by W. H. Auden

PART ONE

'The Casing'

'The green field comes off'

Jim came off shift at four in the morning; the accelerator at 'DESY' works around the clock and so do the men who tend it. 'DESY' is the acronym for the 'Deutsches Elektronen Synchroton' institute, a nuclear research station in Hamburg. The storage-rings are known as 'DORIS and PETRA'. The business is full of these names, and one would be forgiven for thinking that the men spend a lot of time around chorus-girls. To be told that Jim was a Wissenschaftlicher Mitarbeiter, and Stellvertretender Gruppensprecher, is perhaps not much help. It means he is the deputy group leader of his outfit, known as Gruppe F-45. The F stands for Forschung, which means research. What Jim is, in fact, is a medium-grade experimental physicist.

Ask Jim what he does: he might start twisting a lock of hair round his finger and say he was working on an experiment using the extracted beam from the main ring. This gets a dull thud. Is it a nuclear experiment? Yes, it is. And do you make bombs? Women sometimes ask, giggling, after three gins. Faint smile. No, we don't make bombs at Daisy. Not in Germany. True enough, say the men vaguely. Wasn't it forbidden, by a peace treaty or something?

Jim was tired and in need of a wash. He climbed into his Volkswagen beetle, which stood in even greater need of a wash. The night watchman raised the boom; he turned left into Luruper Chaussée, empty at this hour, gleaming with the damp of an autumn night in Hamburg. At the lights he turned right into the Stadionstrasse – a narrower, two-lane road which runs through the Volkspark. It is shaded by the park's trees, and those of the Altona Central Cemetery on the other

1

side. Jim was in a hurry to get home and sleep, but he drove slowly. The wet leaves made the surface dangerous, and he was a careful man. It was a goodish distance to home, past the Stadium, across the S-Bahn at the Eidelstedt station, across the northwest autoroute, past the Hagenbeck Zoo and up to the big Niendorf park, far enough from the airport to be quiet. Rather far from work, but 'nice for the children'. The Volkswagen made the contented noise of a car motor when there is plenty of moisture in the air.

The Stadionstrasse, with those dark trees, is definitely sinister and he was always glad to get it over with; he had an over-active imagination. The lights stayed red for a long time – unnecessary with no traffic. He shifted gears with a lurch, and sang a little song, mind far away. As at school, when the English master would catch him dreaming and say, 'Come out of the apple-barrel, you', while other children sniggered. 'Where's the treasure, Jim?' Been looking for treasure for thirty-seven years.

Some he had found, like his wife, Leora, an Italian girl who'd been a classics student. Could quote Latin and did, sometimes, apropos of bottles of wine or log fires. Or the refrigerator belt bust again.

Or his two daughters: Harriet old enough to wail crossly that being called Hawkins was too much to bear. And Cassandra so exceptionally beautiful at the age of nine. Not a prophet of doom in ruins of Troy. More like the poet Rostand's girl: he was going to lock the door to do serious work, but if she should turn up, 'Open up quick and don't keep her waiting.'

At work Jim searched for other treasures. One could scarcely hope for a new particle or a new planet, and sometimes physics was a bore, but more often it wasn't. And DESY was a good place. Better than being an associate professor at Lansing, Michigan, all among the Oldsmobiles.

Jim trundled, thought about Harriet (passing through a cheeky stage), about particles; sang his little song (he only knew one line and a half).

A glance in the rear-view mirror showed lights, another car, following at the same pace. Wrong time, wrong place, but maybe a belated whore. Jim's fantasy toyed with lecheries; Rosemarie Nitribitt, the Angel in the SL.

Another car – big BMW – came racing past them both, too fast. The driver seemed to notice this once past: the brake-lights showed suddenly. As though stimulated the creeping whore behind swung out and accelerated. Imprudently, for a car going the other way flicked its lamps, and the passing whore cut in precipitously, dazzled at the sudden beam or alarmed at the narrowness of the road.

Too precipitous, fishtailing Jim's beetle brutally, so that he cursed and braked, too late: her large behind scraped his front wing. Well; stupid bitch.

He stopped abruptly. So did she. Had the manners to apologize, at least. Jim, long of leg, got out laboriously, clumped forward to look at his scraped wing. A figure was coming back to see the damage. A hundred metres behind, the other car had stopped too, was reversing. Nice of him.

Only after several hours of sleep would Jim think how minutely timed and skilfully executed it had been. Even had there been passers-by – or even a cop car – who looks twice at a couple post-morteming a traffic scrape?

'Sorry,' said a dim individual in a hat, politely.

'Not very clever,' grumbled Jim.

'Fellow dazzled me.'

'Well – got a form to fill in?' Not the first time the beetle had got a dent. Jim stooped to cluck at the paintwork, got no further. He got a sack over his head. Have you ever had a sack over your head, pinning your arms? Not necessarily at four in the morning on the Stadionstrasse in Hamburg? You will be astonished, and also impotent.

Wehmerweg 45, half an hour later; Leora sleeping peacefully woke about ten per cent at a fumble and a thud of something dropping. Why can't Jim not open his own door and cross the living-room without dropping shoes?

Leora came awake with a jolt. That was Jim's time, and Jim's key in the lock, but not Jim's shoe or Jim's fumble. She sat up and opened her mouth to yell, not sure whether this was real or a nightmare. She did have nightmares, generally Dracula putting a pillow over her head, whether to rape her

3

or drink her blood she never did find out, because at that moment she yelled and woke up. Her yell came out a gurgle, because a hand not the least like Jim's compressed her jaw, painfully. Another hand ripped the bedclothes off. I am going to be raped, thought Leora, but had no time either to be indignant or to enjoy it because a wasp stung her thigh. She kicked her legs furiously and a heavy weight came down on them. Then a heavy weight came down on her mind and spread to the pit of her stomach, her fingers, the back of her neck, and she fell down wondering whether this was a new and nastier nightmare – a Dracula that picked her up and wound her in a blanket and bore her off to the pinnacled castle on the hill-top.

A gentler figure found the children's bedroom, turned the light on, lifted the blankets off, slipped a hypodermic needle through two sets of cotton pyjamas into two small behinds. Both small supple bodies thrashed at the prick. Harriet said, 'Get away' crossly and Cassandra said, 'Drawing-pin', before both fell again into deep sleep.

In the living-room a thin, youngish-looking man with a close beard stood in the light of the standard lamp. A good-looking man with a controlled face. Dark suit, white shirt. When he moved, and the light spilt sharply across his jacket, one shoulder seemed rather higher than the other, but he was not hump-backed: his face had not the dwarfish, suffering look associated with this condition. The expression was calm. He turned as a pretty girl with her hair in a braid came back from the children's room. Her face in the light had a whitish look, accentuated by sunglasses whose lenses showed black as her hair.

'In ordnung,' she said. The man made a circular gesture to four men standing quietly in the room.

'Pack,' he said. They had brought suitcases with them. Outside Wehmerweg 45 a dark blue BMW stood parked. It had arrived without the clockwork noise of Jim's Volkswagen but at four-thirty in the morning nobody noticed that. Along the road two more stood parked. And a silver-grey Mercedes. For a quarter of an hour people came and went. The man with the crooked shoulder stood out of the light

4

from the lobby, swinging Jim's house keys over his forefinger. Quiet-moving men carried out three bundles in blankets, four suitcases. With nurse's fingers the girl in dark glasses dressed the two smaller bodies in T-shirts, jeans, pullovers, arranged them in the Mercedes with their heads on a pillow. The bigger figure, sprawled in the back of the BMW, gave her more trouble, but it too was dressed in a shirt and trousers. In the shadows along the street a figure that had been half an hour in its sack had had a quick-acting hypodermic and was asleep, crumpled and sullen-looking, indignation on the curves of pale, freckled skin, straight dark-red hair drooping over the forehead.

The four motors of the neat cars purred in the stillness of a Hamburg morning early, before the autumn dawn. Five a.m.

The four cars slid down into Stellingen, to join the main road leading to the autoroute. They did not hurry; by the time they reached the autobahn junction at Netthöhren and turned to swing southward they were no longer a convoy. Four more cars travelling through Germany. Moving along at a good clip, without exceeding limits. Or no more than all the other respectable businessmen.

They stopped once to tank up. Nobody paid attention to people asleep in the back: such sights are commonplace. They turned off the autobahn near the Karlsruhe junction, and drove into the wooded hills near the pleasant town of Baden-Baden. It was in the middle of a dry, warm autumn day, frequent in this part of the world around grape-harvest time, that Jim woke.

He looked at his watch, and felt puzzled. It was the normal time. He felt normal. A slight headache; the kind one has after sleeping heavily, that will clear after a cup of coffee. Then he noticed his sleeve and frowned: he had not fallen asleep in his clothes? And what was this noise of birds? And there was a peculiar smell, not like the Wehmerweg. Not in the least like Hamburg! Jim remembered the sack and woke up with a jolt. He was lying in a low armchair. He started to climb out, and a polite voice said, 'Don't trouble.' Jim turned and stared. A thin man in youngish middle-age, with a small beard, a benign expression, reading the *Neuer Zürcher*

5

Zeitung, sat on a sofa before a stone fireplace. He had never seen this man before. Jim's mind began to work. Who had put a sack over his head? – this didn't seem a likely candidate. And why? And where the hell was this?

'All your questions will be answered. You slept well. A glass of champagne?'

Plainly a country house. The furniture, the low ceiling, the deep window embrasures in thick walls, sunshine outside and birds chattering. A copy of *Country Life* lay on the coffee-table, next to a bucket with a bottle in a napkin, and glasses on a tray. Jim had a trained mind. He could neither synthesize nor analyse; he had nothing to go on.

'I have a great many questions. And a headache.'

'That's normal; you had a sleeping drug. An aspirin will put it right. The champagne is a good notion, believe me. What you need then is breakfast. Brunch, if you prefer.' Civilized manner; fluent English; indefinable accent, not English or American: vaguely Latin. Jim took the glass, the proffered aspirin. Not *sekt,* either.

'One is enough: I don't take pills.'

'I know.'

'How? And for a start, who are you? As a preface to what the hell goes on.'

'I'm the Doctor. I know because I have studied your habits for some months. I have kidnapped you.' Spoken as though it were the most natural thing in the world. What did one make of that? He swallowed the aspirin, the champagne. Delicious; exactly what he wanted. 'The Doctor' smiled, leaned over, pressed a bellpush, poured another glass. He had slight deformity in the shoulders. Kidnapped? That had become a frequent occurrence. At present it seemed pleasant. Jim stood up, looked out of the window. A paved terrace, with climbing plants, clipped evergreens as a windbreak. Beyond, a garage. Beyond and behind, grassy hillside; trees. Well; one thing at a time.

'You have the wrong man,' said Jim, almost with regret: wherever it was it was comfortable.

Even luxurious. The door opened and a servant in a starched white jacket came in pushing a trolley with an electric hotplate, covered stainless-steel dishes, a coffee-pot, a good smell. He picked up the orange juice and drank it. Fresh! The servant said nothing, turned round, walked out. Jim felt no idea of violence or even protest: he felt flabbergasted. He stood like a tree.

The Doctor sat there placidly: working breakfast at the Hilton. Put a hand under his chin and looked at Jim as though he were a most interesting person. Tall, with pale, freckled skin. Dark red hair, poker-straight; a prominent mouth. A straight nose, well-shaped ears, a pale-grey glance with no green in it, the eyelids pink and swollen from work.

A slightly sore patch on his hip: they must have jabbed him there: his memory had gaps in it. Jim saw himself across the room in an old-fashioned looking-glass that showed him in south-easterly light, felt a fool, sat down. He was hungry. To appear at ease he took the lids off dishes; fresh bread, an omelette with grilled bacon and lambs' kidneys. Field mushrooms! It looked as good as it smelt: he began to eat. What else could one do? Nothing made sense, but the food, at least, was real, the coffee strong. Life flooded into him. He reached for the champagne, feeling voracious. The Doctor smiled.

'Splendid,' he said. 'No, I haven't the wrong man. You are Jim Hawkins, a name which has sometimes been a bad joke. You were born near Lechlade in Gloucestershire, in comfortable circumstances. You went to Stowe and to King's College, Cambridge. Bachelor of Science, a bright boy. Bright enough to go to Amherst as a post-graduate. You were a good learner and became a good teacher. Also a promising experimental physicist. You married Leora Ferrandini. Whom you met in the most banal way at Sun Valley. You are naturalized American citizens in good standing: I congratulate you both. Your last post was as associate professor at Michigan State. Not a thrilling job. Hamburg offered you a chance to make yourself known with some interesting work. Your children have inherited good bloodlines on both sides: I congratulate you again. You are able, balanced, imaginative – and you have a talent for mechanical design. And you have been kidnapped; is there anything further?'

Jim thought of several things to say, but had his mouth full. 'Where is my wife?' he asked, severe but vulnerable.

'She has probably finished her breakfast by now,' simply. 'She had the same drug as yourself but had more natural sleep and was less fatigued. She'll be joining us shortly no doubt – but I would' – apologetic – 'like to finish our business first. And to forestall you – the children are still asleep. But Marika is looking after them. You need have no worries on that account. She is a valuable woman, trained: she has experience in kindergarten teaching, a diploma in child psychology: she is also a nurse. You can have confidence in her.' Jim felt stunned by all this virtue.

'Kidnap!' he said in a high soprano. 'Fucking hell!' Jim was thinking that the biography was public property. Passport details, so to speak. But I like champagne, I don't take pills. That's not in the computer print-out. I've never done secret work. There's no dossier on me. And the C.I.A. may be obstreperous upon occasion, but they don't think of these games in Langley. He wiped his plate with a bit of bread, ate it, and bellowed suddenly:

'What are you playing at?' The Doctor looked as serene as a small child.

'Jim,' reproachfully. 'Don't shout. It's all easy. You've been kidnapped by terrorists.'

Clichés chased themselves through Jim's mind. The brain reeled, the mouth gasped, the mind boggled: und so weiter.

'Terrorists,' said the Doctor primly, 'vary. There are to be sure the violent, the brutal, the psychopathic, the exceedingly stupid. Try and accept that they are sometimes bright. Surely, you have only to look at me.' Accustomed to observing physical realities, Jim did not ask whether he was dreaming. He poured more coffee. As an afterthought, more champagne. The Doctor patted his pockets, found a packet of French cigarettes – Gallias with charcoal filters.

'You don't smoke,' he said blandly. 'Neither do I – save on a social occasion. Let me explain, Jim. I kidnap you. Your wife; your children. I have planned this for some months. As you see, simple, efficient. Not expensive, all things considered. Money is no object: I have plenty. In view of my design, we've done it for nothing.' He struck a match, lit the cigarette. 'What I want, Jim, is that you build me a bomb.'

'Well . . . certainly money's no object. Better start again: I'm not a chemist.'

'No. You're a physicist. I had a choice of several. I picked you because of your aptitude. Also for your equilibrium – which you are demonstrating. An atomic bomb.'

Jim burst out laughing, which might have been the champagne.

'Aren't you dramatic.'

'To be accurate – no. I detest drama. I loathe complications. I like things simple.'

'Then I'm afraid you've over-reached yourself. First I can't. Second I won't. Third it's impossible. Fourth I'm tired, I'm off balance, I'm in the land of Oz, call it what you like but I'm not a –' Jim looked for a word; ended weakly, 'paranoid.'

'No,' agreed the Doctor. 'That's exactly why I chose you. You can, you will, and it isn't impossible. The United States Government says it is, to be sure, but I don't believe it – any more than you do. Man, I have studied the subject, just as I studied you. In the garage outside there are all the tools needed. Also the textbooks. Also the material. That's all. Telling me it needs a whole Manhattan Project is the purest nonsense – as you well know.' All right, thought Jim. All right. I know a tiny bit about the subject. Enough to demolish you in two lines.

'Really?' said Jim. 'What material?' in the blandest voice imaginable.

'I have,' said the Doctor, for all the world like a clerk taking stock on tins of Campbell's Soup, 'thirty-seven kilos of material. That is something over the standard figure given for a critical mass if we start to think in practical terms. It is – forgive me, was, in the shape of uranium hexafluoride: you eff six, if I adopt the jargon. As we are aware, uranium in its natural form, only point seven per cent two-thirty-five, must be subjected to a complicated, expensive and secret process, taking a long time, in order to be enriched – laboriously – to separate out uranium two-thirty-five, what is known as

9

weapons grade. You are aware, Jim, working in the Federal Republic of Germany, that the Germans have accelerated this process. The technique is known as nozzle enrichment, and a pilot plant exists in the town of Karlsruhe. You are also aware that in the course of these processes it is extremely difficult to measure the amounts concerned. Jim – you can believe me now, or you can wait till you see it. We have not hurried' – the voice was equally unhurried – 'any more than with yourself. The material was stolen in packets of around a hundred grams at a time, over a long period. It is known to you that such quantities can be abstracted from any enrichment plant without the faintest risk of discovery. It is known to me: it is known to any educated member of the public. All that is needed is a bribe: I am in a position to pay generous bribes.' The voice was not even ironic. 'I dare say that you know, despite your modest disclaimer, that it is fairly simple to convert the UF_6 to metallic form. I have a technician who does what is necessary.'

'How?' asked Jim, bluntly. You must try and shake the bugger. He's too calm altogether.

The Doctor felt in his inside breast pocket and took out a sheet of paper.

'I anticipated your objection. I may say that this piece of chemistry, while Chinese to me, is available in a paperback book. Mmm ... let's see ... I'm instructed that there's no great trick to this. Heat hydrofluoric acid, producing hydrogen-fluoride gas. Mixing this at roughly five hundred degrees will produce water and uranium tetrafluoride: we've dropped two effs. We then make a firework. Powdered magnesium and potassium chlorate, the school children's familiar weed-killer bomb, are added, apparently to help generate heat. We heated, in a crucible, the tetrafluoride with these other compounds. We got to 600°. They ignited. In combustion – I am told – we were left with uranium metal, plus magnesium fluoride. It was allowed to cool. There was a lump' – the Doctor sketched with his hand – 'of metal.'

Jim looked at him.

'What kind of metal?'

'We have it in the garage. Rather like lead. Scratch it – I

10

may say one does that with great caution since it is highly toxic – and it is silvery. It oxidizes rapidly on contact with air – I'm quoting, but I have seen for myself – to a chocolate brown colour.'

Jim shrugged.

'It won't make a bomb,' he said flatly. 'Whatever you've got, it's nowhere near weapons grade. It might look impressive, and feel it – a bit hot from alpha decay – but it doesn't pop. It's about five per cent – it wouldn't even run your central heating plant.' The Doctor smiled.

'I am assured by a trustworthy source that the grade is a great deal higher than that.'

Jim had never jumped from a plane, but knew what it must feel like if the main 'chute did not open. Still got the reserve. Panicky fingers fumbling for the release. How did the man know? Wasn't it last week we were discussing this very point? Herr Trautmann stiff, holding the official line; it's utterly impossible. Kenneth Neilson looser, saying there were too many assumptions, that too many unlikely conditions had to be tacked together. Me saying it could be done. And it has been . . .

'Absurd,' said Jim, too loud. He tried it again and it came out a silly grasshopper noise, a feeble scratching.

'Far from it. As you have no trouble in seeing.' Jim found his reserve.

'Look, I don't know where this is. In the country somewhere. And you are threatening me; leave that aside. Tomorrow at the latest my boss will wonder what has happened to me. And the police start looking. It's only a matter of time.'

'Not in the least. I know him well,' cheerfully. 'We are going to write him a tiny note – your hand might be a scrap shaky, and that is attractively pathetic. You find yourself in urgent need of a few days' rest. Personal problems have created havoc. So you've gone to get straightened out and your wife is looking after you. He will feel momentary irritation, but a few weeks on compassionate grounds will be arranged without even filling forms in.' It is true, thought Jim dully. Some of these high-security places would jump

11

the resident shrink on you the second you tried that game, but DESY has never been fussy.

'Meanwhile we send a brief scrawl to confirm the authenticity – here –' casually producing another piece of paper. A memo-size letterhead. Doctor Roland Sebregt, Member of the Association of Consulting Psychiatrists. Basle: Switzerland. Jim wondered whether he really existed for only a second before being convinced that he did, and would confirm every particular. Swiss; creamy. Nothing could be more reliable and respectable. As for the little line in his writing, Jim knew he'd write it. This man hadn't made threats; threats weren't his style. But holding Leora and the children – the threat existed and that was enough.

Jim – be hardheaded. You pride yourself upon having imagination, but don't let it become over-active. You can't challenge these people frontally. Play along. Be subtle. Gain time. It sounds feeble. But maybe it's less feeble than it sounds. You are in their hands. But they, equally, are in yours. This is the weak point in their argument; that they can have a lunatic notion of building a gadget but you're the physicist. Maybe this man does have weapons grade U-235 in metallic form floating round his garage. And has he got it protected? What in the name of God is the critical mass for unreflected weapons grade U? Thirty-seven kilos is about right. It's not sitting there in one lump, is it?

His belly knotted till he realized that it couldn't be. It must be in two or more sub-critical masses, at least a couple of metres apart. But if you went in there with a scintillation counter the thing would go mad. If it's true, this is the hottest place in Germany.

Jim, who like all who work with radioactive material lived with a detector badge pinned fig-leaf-wise, since physicists like their sex life as much as any man, felt a cringing sensation in the scrotum. There's a neurological test, he thought feebly, akin to the classic Babinski reflex. Doctor Roland Sebregt would tickle my balls gently with an orange-stick. Mutti! Chattering glibly about chemistry, and we want a few metres of lead and concrete round that garage.

Jim got up again, stared out of the window. The garage –

say eight metres away across the terrace. Wistaria and clematis growing up a picket fence.

The enormity of it choked him. Loony scraps of phrase about justice, personal liberties, human rights, international law came up hot in his throat like vomit. He swallowed. On the other side of the flowers is the greatest source of energy we know.

'It is a pleasure,' said the Doctor amiably to the back of Jim's head (rather long, the hair, needs cutting there in the back of the neck), 'to confirm so quickly that you are an intelligent man, not given to tripping yourself up with trivialities.'

Telepathy is a commonplace. Jim put his hand up to the nape of his neck. Must get Leora to snip with her sewing scissors.

If I were going to be guillotined, there would certainly be a tough German NCO to flip me on the shoulder at morning parade, with their well-worn jokes.

'Get yer 'air cut, boy, or you'll blunt the razor.'

We're falling about, laughing.

Jim turned. Nice country-house living-room. Pine panelling. Beams pine, old or creosoted to look like oak. Stand of flowering hibiscus.

'Who are you?' abruptly.

'A terrorist.'

'Where do you come from? Palestine? Chile? Uruguay?'

'It has no importance, Jim.'

'Tell me. I won't say anything before I know.'

'No. Think what you like.'

'I have to know.'

'No. It is useless to say "What if I do not co-operate?" That only blunts the tools. I am a craftsman. I take care of tools.'

'I have the right to know.'

'You have no rights whatever. No more than myself. Sit down: it is irritating to talk to the back of someone's head.'

'That's as may be. I won't budge till I know more.'

'I am a professional, Jim. I aim for brevity, economy, efficiency. I treat a fellow-workman with respect. It should be

13

obvious, but most people are intoxicated by reading espionage fiction. I am civilized. Emphasize the professionalism. I have no use for brutality or sadism. I am compelled by circumstances, by the need for secrecy, to apply constraint to you and your family.

'Do not, I beg of you, cause stupid and gratuitous suffering to your wife and family. As for the other persons, the ten thousand-odd who may lose their lives in this – let's have no cant. People die, be it of heart attacks and road accidents or collectively of naked starvation. Malnutrition if you prefer,' cuttingly.

Jim felt floored. Specious, but examine that for sophisms.

'I refuse,' he said.

'Then you die. Your wife and children die. It has no importance. A hundred thousand a minute. I die. And then? You are a physicist, I a metaphysicist: let's stick to our own jobs.'

'I cannot cold-bloodedly prepare an atomic explosion. You cannot ask it of me.'

'You wish to die? – simply arranged. Start again. I have prepared this for some months. I was careful not to injure you, especially neither your hands nor your eyes. I put a sack over your head, to intimidate you, since you fear asphyxia. I wish now to treat you well, and your family. Your children will be cared for with affection. You will have privacy, air, exercise. You can live a normal existence with your wife: indeed I count upon her.' He sounded aggrieved.

'The surroundings were carefully chosen. So were you. I am neither a maniac nor a psychopath.'

Jim tried to stand his ground.

'I refuse to be bullied. If you have an offer, state it. What is your purpose?'

'My political philosophy need not concern you. Others state their wishes to me; I to you: let that suffice. You fulfil the wish. Means will be afforded; you provide the skills. You are chosen for that.'

'Upon what terms?'

'No terms. Are you interested in money?' contemptuously.

'You want an offer? A million dollars? In gold? You go

forward, you do your given and chosen work. That is all.'

'And afterwards?' desperately, 'what is supposed to happen after all this? After the explosion,' lamely.

'To you? The cover will be adequate, the reward adequate. The resources are adequate. You need fear nothing. Nobody will ever question it. Money is not lacking, nor are friends. For the moment you have my word, but I keep it.'

'And that's all?'

'And that's all.' He rang the bell, gestured to the white-jacket to clear away.

Jim stood rooted, staring at the man. Richard the Third, the villain hunchback? A myth he had never believed in.

The face was the same; sensitive and marked by pain. This man is a crude instrument of destruction and murder? One does not believe it of Richard, either. The evidence is all too blatantly cooked by the wretched Tudor family. But above all it does not fit the character. What one sees, knows.

A tired smile.

'Let's not be frivolous, Jim.'

Anything even faintly 'knowing' would have put him in a flaming rage. The smile had vivacity, brilliance. But strangely, the face was kind. That sounded ridiculous but it was a fact, and the effect was impressive.

He would try another throw for all that.

'And what's your suggested target – Israel?'

'No. Nor oil wells. That is a waste of time, Jim. Matters of race are trivial. We belong to a human race. We laugh, we sail boats. The phrase is Abelard's, a good one. *Homo risibilis, navigabilis*. We are in danger of a world in which we will no longer laugh nor sail boats. A world of ants. We are not ants.

'We live upon a planet, trivial and unimportant, but our own. The balance is delicate, of grass, trees. Even of land and water. A tiny movement of climate wipes us out, as ice did before. The ants are fiddling at that balance.

'Think as a physicist. What is required of you? An atomic explosion, physically trivial. A thousandth, a ten-thousandth of the energy in a natural phenomenon, such as a hurricane.

15

'You ask whether I am semitic or anti-semitic. These are trivialities.'

'As a political gesture, an atomic explosion is not in the least trivial.'

'Therefore I make it. And why is it not trivial? Because of cant. I can use this cant, for leverage. But it only exists among frightened men in over-populated areas. Ask an Eskimo his opinion of atomic bombs. Ask a penguin, in Queen Charlotte Land.

'Be grateful,' sharply, 'that I do not ask you to nourish yourself with plankton in the absence of whale-blubber. Very large numbers of persons get no protein, are consequently feeble. You and I, Jim, are not feeble. The proof is that I have a good cellar here. You are fond of burgundy. I have here a Richebourg '59. I have also a Margaux '45. You may choose which you would enjoy most, this evening, and I will give orders accordingly. Both are "rather nice". Isn't that the English phrase, dreading hyperbole?'

Again the brilliant smile.

'You are a prisoner, Jim. So am I. And we are both free men. Let us admire paradox, whereby the wealthiest Italian millionaire lives in terror of kidnapping. What a good thing, morally speaking. How admirable that his wife should turn her sable coat inside-out, and show a dirty raincoat to the world. How admirable that she should ride in a Fiat instead of a Ferrari. Be profoundly grateful, when you get a glass of wine in a toothglass, and find that it is a Richebourg. Be grateful too when you get recycled sewage, as long as it's in a Baccarat glass.'

The Doctor got up. Thinner and frailer when standing. That is an illusion. More vulnerable, maybe. I'm pale and tired, thought Jim: I'm beginning to limp.

'We'll look at the workshop, shall we?' They went through to another room.

'This will make a pleasant bedroom for you both.' Jim could not feel much interest in that just now.

Unbolting and opening the French window on to the autumn sunshine, warmer than expected, 'Rather a nice house,' said the Doctor, 'it belongs to a wealthy indus-

16

trialist. He only uses it in summer: I can't help feeling he is mistaken.'

He led the way down steps to the flagged terrace, through the gateway in the hedge to the garage.

From the roadway, it would be a broad low building, wide enough for three cars. Inside it was partitioned. The nearest part, which plainly had held a car, could do so again at short notice. It had been changed into an office, with a vinyl-covered sofa. On either side of the sliding door in the partition stood a neat stack of unopened cement bags.

'It occurred to me,' said the Doctor almost apologetically, 'that this partition might need strengthening.' Jim looked at him, and decided to say nothing.

It was well lit, by a large window facing south. Radiators made for a pleasant warmth. There was matting on the floor. Overhead lighting and a bureau lamp. Next to the drawing-board a range of shelving had been built. It held stacks of paper, drawing and writing materials. A pocket calculator caught Jim's eye and he picked it up. A Hewlett-Packard HP67 – quite a sophisticated model. Above was a row of books. *Basic Nuclear Science. Atomic Energy for Military Purposes. Explosives & Propellants. The Blaster's Handbook. The Reactor Handbook.* His hand shot out, flipped the title page. Yes, that was the right one – 'Volume III: Part A. Physics.' Well ... *The Handbook of Chemistry and Physics.* And paperbound stuff – standard maths tables, a couple of tracts on fast reactor theory, a Xeroxed copy of *The Los Alamos Primer.* It was all there!

He turned around disbelievingly to the Doctor, who was looking bland.

'No trouble at all, Jim. All freely available from any library. Shall we look next door?'

In the corner stood an ordinary metal box, like an ammunition box.

'Is that ... ?'

'Part of it. We split it up, needless to say.' He walked across, lifted the lid. Wrapped, to stop it oxidizing, but naturally it had oxidized on the surface. No longer the bright, silvery colour of freshly-cast metal, but the pleasant chocolate

17

brown that means uranium. Jim's mind slipped back to the physics laboratory near Emmanuel, in Cambridge. The lecturer's voice ... 'These small lumps are perfectly safe to handle, but don't scratch at the oxide, which is highly toxic in powder form. In the trade they are called "broken buttons". If they are enriched to weapons grade, and if you have enough of them, you have a bomb on your hands.' The simplest, the most fool-proof of gadgets. Since Jim had handled metallic uranium frequently he did not feel the hair prickle on the back of his neck, or anything like that. He felt empty. He had thought there would be a thousand difficulties to point to, virtuously. Now, he was no longer so sure. This quiet man beside him might have been a landscape designer, who finds an awkward big boulder on the terrain. 'Well, we'll shift that, shall we? Get a stick of dynamite for me, some-one. You'll find all you need in the office, in that box in the corner.'

Jim straightened up.

'You've no guarantee stuff like that will pop. It could as well be a lot of old iron.'

'Hardly,' said the Doctor, all innocence.

'Well all right, I'm exaggerating,' drawling. 'You'd stand clear, mucking about with it. Be some delayed neutrons. Some gamma radiation, obviously: you aren't just playing with meccano. But I very much doubt if you'd even get a fizzle.'

'I think we've the equipment to see – and measure,' said the Doctor, imperturbable, sliding open the partition door. Jim felt a fool, because he could not help catching his breath.

It was still a double garage, generously measured to be sure, for a man with a Rolls, and a Ford station-wagon for the shopping. Lit like the other with window and skylights. Floor of polished concrete, plastered walls. But Jim had imagined some greasy backstairs garage, with a scruffy bench and maybe a piddly lathe.

This one would turn 45 centimetres in diameter. There was a 48-inch Bridgeport milling machine. Automatic feed. Yes, thought Jim mechanically, unable to stop himself, one would need that. A small instrument-maker's lathe. Band saw.

18

Drill press. As for the ordinary garage tools . . . Everything spotless. Gas welder and torch: electric arc welder.

'Well, holy cow,' said Jim. That attractive naiveté, thought the Doctor, warmed. Good man, this.

'I admit we had a good start,' he said modestly. 'The owner has a factory concerned with metallurgical techniques, and likes to do his own experiments. Which is one good reason why we chose this place. Ideal, I may say, in other ways.' Jim was looking at the power supply. Three circuits of 25-amp triple-phase.

'Didn't it attract attention, putting all this in?'

'Most of it was there already. The local electricity people see no hindrance to obeying a wealthy man's whim: why should they?' Jim turned slowly to the shelving along the partition wall. An oscilloscope – the Tektronix 454. Like the pocket calculator, a serious tool. Not a toy. Some EMI and RCA photo-multiplier tubes. Much of the equipment he habitually used, for particle-counting, for monitoring. The mind was bloody well boggling.

Have to make an effort.

'One would need,' he said importantly, 'a proper quantity of scintillation plastic – NE 102.'

'Quite so,' said the Doctor. 'To measure radiation. Anticipated. Provided for. In fact, laid on. You'll find it in that carton.'

'And,' a bit desperately, 'proper remote-handling equipment. You think I'm going to bugger about in the same room as near-critical masses of metallic uranium, you've another think coming.'

'Naturally, Jim. In fact I don't mind saying that it gave me some worry, because we thought of it rather late. I spoke to a man with experience in the matter. I explained my difficulty. He was reassuring in a way that charmed me. The Germans, as you know, make admirable model train sets.'

Floored.

'Admire the oven, Jim. We're proud of it.'

Jim had stopped in front of it. A furnace – was it just a ceramics furnace? – but impressive. He did calculations in his mind. Forty by forty by fifty, roughly. What was the

19

melting temperature of uranium metal, anyway? One would need to look at *The Handbook of Chemistry and Physics.*

'It will go to fifteen hundred – centigrade, naturally,' said the maddening voice. 'I'm not of course an expert. I don't recall the exact figures. I remember that uranium melts at around twelve hundred. Beryllium at perhaps fourteen hundred. I am instructed, as the lawyers say, that it is adequate for our needs.'

Jim, staring at the furnace, was thinking that yes, one would need to cast the metallic uranium into a shape – no, he didn't want to think about it. But the size, for God's sake, the size ... Not bigger than a fair-sized grapefruit. Uranium is a heavy metal. Much like lead. Now a lump of lead the mass and weight of a critical mass ... How would you do it? Lost wax process, similar to casting a small bronze statue. Mutti; this furnace will handle that without the remotest trouble. Make a wax mould, model heat-resistant non-distorting plaster around. Cook the wax out over heat. Pour in melted uranium. You've a spherical or cylindrical core. Now just assume – assume – a gun-type gadget.

How does this man know? That I've spent time, much time, thinking about how easy it all is? Now that I come face to face, it's less easy. But I've *done* these calculations. I *know* it can be done. I know how *easily* it's done. I just haven't the figures by me, but let's see.

Fire a bullet into a hollow core. Never mind how that's done; that's a mechanical problem solved by a bit of high explosive and some backyard mechanics. Fire it fast enough, you needn't worry about predetonation or delayed neutrons. Delayed, ha: a milli-second. No, goddammit, fire your bullet fast and you've instant neutrons. And that means, if you've a supercrit mass, it will pop. Assuming you've a reflector, and the mass isn't Lady Godiva, that she's wrapped in steel, she'll pop.

No she won't. That stuff is nowhere near high-enriched. It just can't be. Suppose she's about fifty per. If you had a better reflector she might pop. Need maths.

It *m i g h t* pop. And in that case ...

Jim hit an air pocket, plunged 10,000 feet.

Cast a near-crit mass. The reactor handbook will tell you what that is. Put a high-class reflector round it, something better than steel or aluminium.

Just wait a moment. He mentioned beryllium a moment ago! Now how did he know that? He does know something about this subject! Perfectly true; need to look it up in the handbook but it would be a better as well as lighter reflector than steel. On the other hand there'd be technical trouble: the stuff is toxic and difficult to work.

'I'm tired,' he said abruptly. 'And above all, bewildered.'

'Yes,' said the Doctor, all sympathy and cups of weak tea.

'I can't even think about this now. There are more angles than I can count. And I insist on seeing my wife.'

'To be sure,' comfortably. 'You'll wish to talk it over together.' Ushering Jim back across the terrace. 'I'll ask you to excuse me as I've a lot to see to. I'll have that message given to your wife. And I'll look forward to seeing you both at dinner. Do ring for anything either of you need, and the servants will take care of it. The apartment is yours – your privacy will be respected. Within limits, the house, but we'll speak of that another time.' He drifted out with a little duck of the head.

A young woman sat with her elbows propped on a table, her hands folded into a fist or an attitude of prayer, the thumbs against her lips. She was dressed in trousers and top of gunmetal grey, in a knitted jersey material, severely cut and perfectly plain. She was well built, with a supple figure. Her hair, straight and dark, had been brushed loose and tied back with a red ribbon. Sitting straight, feet stretched out, shoulders back, in clothes suggesting an athlete's track suit, she could be taken for a tennis player; a crucial match in preparation, in a key competition. The stillness of her pose held both concentration and muscular détente.

Even the surroundings had a country-club look, though smaller and less impersonal. There was little furniture or decoration. There was a large fireplace, with hearth built out, in massive blocks of sandstone rough-dressed, and a picture

21

above it, the only one, of a river, the bank, men and women bathing.

The table was natural wood, the chairs tropical model of bent rattan. Floors and panelling knotty-pine board, clear varnished. In the corner a small bar, with a kitchenette behind: small sink, refrigerator, two-burner cooker. An electric barbecue stood on the bar.

To the other side and occupying half the big room was a fifteen-metre pool, its tiled surround ending in sliding glass partitions that opened to the patio beyond, to fresh air and sun. There was no sun at this minute: the view was of grey cloud above tree-clad hill, and outside was the short slippery grass, full of wild flowers, of an alpine meadow.

It took a time to puzzle out, before realizing that it was nothing more than a rich man's summer hideaway. The simplicity was elaborate, self-conscious. He had pointed to where the sunny upland meadow flattened out at the woods' edge, and said 'I'd like a shack there. To cover the pool. For when it's cold or rainy.' Guests weekending in the country would go up to the summerhouse for a swim, and stay to play, loaf, cook campfire meals. For larger numbers he could hold poolside parties.

It had stood unoccupied for a time: there was a close smell of sunbaked wood and varnish, which after the winter would be dustier and damper. The young woman had opened the shutters, and slid a door back to the terrace, to air the inside. The air of the pinewoods, loaded with life, was flooding in. Somewhere at the back a pump throbbed quietly like an air-conditioner: she was changing the pool water. The air is chilly in the hills in autumn, when the sun is covered, and she wondered whether to turn the heating on.

Scattered about, half unpacked, were materials looking incongruous here. Instead of adult rods or guns were children's pool toys of inflatable rubber. The dartboard and the 'pétanque' set of *boules* in stainless steel had been left perhaps behind, but not the blackboard, nor the boxes of colours. The projector for sixteen-millimetre movies, but not the school text-books. Classroom adjuncts; a globe, a dictionary, loose-leaf folders.

22

Despite the cool grey day the young woman wore wrap-around sunglasses with large lenses, so that looking her straight in the face you saw a handsome nose, a wide mouth, a round chin, but the upper face was as though masked. The black hair was parted on the left, dragged back too hurriedly or abruptly. She wore no make-up. She looked as though she would be pretty. You would be curious enough to want to find out, to tell her to take her glasses off. She never did: would she be scarred, by burns, an auto accident? You began to imagine some drama. An exploding flask in a chemistry lab? – there must have been something, for a pretty woman to mask herself so uncompromisingly. Her movements and attitude were otherwise perfectly unselfconscious, so that you hardly believed in a ploy to attract attention.

She stood up and went through the open door near her. A guest bedroom, done in the same pine panelling and rattan furniture. Two beds; one made up: the other with its cretonne cover, a suitcase thrown on it, a pile of clothes. If one were curious about Marika one would look at these clothes. She had a taste for the exotic, for Chinese or Indonesian things. Saris and shifts, bright batik prints on cotton or silk, dashikis. For colder days, autumn evenings in the hills, there was a llama jacket, a Peruvian poncho, high-necked sweaters in deep colours, red and brown. Plain things like her 'track suit', severe and buttoning high to the neck, as if against a hostile environment.

If you liked amateur psychology, in fact, you would start to play at diagnosing. What, all these defences, and camouflage! The eyebrows raised at the austere fortifications (a curtain wall as it were, smooth and offering no grip to besiegers), but shot up at the sight of an inner keep surprisingly ornate and luxurious. A renaissance château, if you were amused enough by the metaphor to extend it to Marika's underclothes! What, crêpe de Chine! Slips! And even cami-knickers! And flowers embroidered on them . . . One scarcely sees such things now. They are cut by hand, by French or Italian 'lingères'. Terribly old-fashioned. Costing a perfect fortune. Hand-embroidered, good heavens: pale grey with scarlet poppies; lavender with lilac inserts. Do you do them yourself?

There was in reality no one to examine Marika's clothes as she put them away, so indiscreetly. But a hypothetical girl friend idling there with nothing to do might have shrieked. (Marika had no girl friends, and they would not have been idle.) Darling, slips! And suspender belts? Peonies on them, like Victorian chintz? Sweetie – pure Jane Eyre!

It would not have been so very wide of the mark. Marika *was* rather Jane Eyre. Regency virgins, severely brought up at Lowood School, on bread and scrape and the birch if you were naughty. School-marms. Governesses. Nurses on isolation wards. End-product is Florence Nightingale, no doubt. Not far short of the mark. Marika did indeed make, and embroider, her own underclothes.

The young woman tidied the rubbish away. A lot, but the Doctor said it might last a month or more, and bring more than resort clothes, Rika, please. Even in the country, better than après-ski. Evening things, feminine. I want this man, and the woman too, perhaps especially the woman, to feel a sense of comfort, well-being. Your contribution will be vital, going well beyond the nursery part.

There was a movement, a restless toss from beyond the pool area, from the other guest room. She dropped shoes, and crossed the playroom swiftly. Mutter, of a child talking in its sleep.

Here both beds were made, and two little girls in them. She had undressed them again and put their pyjamas back on, to be more natural when they awoke.

The smaller, the nine-year-old, was asleep still and quiet. The big one, a sturdy and obstinate-looking eleven, was beginning to surface; flushed and throwing herself about. Marika went on her knees and began to stroke the forehead with her fingers.

'All right, darling,' she said softly. 'Only a bit of a dream.'

Jim sat there, useless as a Christmas tree on the sixth of January, with what passed for thought eddying aimlessly about inside, and the door opened without his noticing, until the silence struck him, so that he looked up and saw Leora.

He couldn't think of anything to say, but a smile of nervous relief at seeing a known and beloved person came across his face. She had nondescript brown hair, clear skin that showed the blood, pretty ears, pale grey eyes with no green in them, an odd bony nose, a slight figure that looked thin in a sweater, and corduroy trousers which didn't fit her very well.

There was a box of English cigarettes on the table. She took one, made a snort at *Country Life* sitting there, tore a piece off a house advertisement to make a spill, lit her cigarette, rearranged the logs in the fireplace, took the hearthbrush to tidy fallen ash, propped her behind against the arm of a chair and said:

'Where the hell are we – any idea?'

'In the country,' said Jim helpfully.

'Quite a way to the south, that's evident. And still inside Germany, I believe. They certainly brought us in a car: they'd hardly dare risk a frontier with us lying there doped like sacks.'

Jim gave a slight shudder at the mention of sacks but said nothing. Why add to the helplessness?

'I'd like to know who dressed me in these – one of these damned Koreans? Being stripped and manhandled while unconscious; well, it's the least of my worries.'

'Are they Koreans?'

'These whitejacketed persons that bow and say nothing – I call them Koreans. It was bizarre – I woke up in a frilly female sort of bedroom; you know, flowered chintz – and was stunned; I lay studying it. I found the needlemark on my bottom. There must have been a Korean looking through the keyhole. Came sailing in with a breakfast tray. I was thirsty as anything; that was the dope, I suppose. I ate, too; I was hungry. I found a bathroom and had a wash. I came out on the landing; the door wasn't locked or anything. Started down the stairs, and a Korean popped out and said politely you were in here, and here I am. I've found you. Where are the children – have they been stolen too?'

'Yes,' said Jim. 'I'm told we're not to worry, that there's a woman looking after them. Everything is just beautiful.'

'I'm going to see about that!' starting up.

'No – wait. I know a bit more than you. You haven't met the Doctor yet. I had better tell you straight out that these are terrorists.'

'Oh, I knew that straight away. Is DESY supposed to pay a ransom? – poor old Herr Schulmeister must be doing his nut. Or I was wondering,' Leora had plainly determined to keep a firm control of herself, 'that anarchist gang. Several of them are in prison. The idea might be to bargain our liberty against theirs.'

'Simpler than that, I think.' Jim was wondering whether to tell her or not. Sooner or later he'd have to. 'This Doctor – he seems to be the chief – we had a talk. All very polite.'

'What they tell us,' said Leora, 'doesn't have to coincide at all with what they're really after.'

'I believe it's the truth. He gave a demonstration – convincing! Not interested in money or in getting comrades out of prison. They want me to do a job.'

'This is bad fiction,' said Leora. 'Opening the safe, or engraving the phony banknotes? Kenneth will be in an uproar, old Trautmann in another, half Hamburg in a third.'

Jim told her why he thought that Hamburg was going peacefully about its business.

'But what on earth are you supposed to do?' Leora stopped abruptly: she'd had an idea. 'Oh no!'

'Unluckily for us, it's oh yes. And there's small point in wondering why me, and not some other boy out of some other physics lab.' Leora had gone very white. 'I thought of not telling you. But you're bound to find out. This Doctor – he'll tell you, I believe. His tactic is to be plain and businesslike. Show us exactly how thoroughly he has us sewn up. When I've seen exactly how little choice I have, I'll give him, he reckons, no trouble.'

'But he can't know . . . I mean like the other evening with Kenneth, when you were all arguing about whether it could . . . unless he had a bug in the flat or something . . . I mean, it must be bluff.'

'It isn't. In that garage thing across the terrace he's got all the tools, and a big heap of s.n.m. Sorry, that means weapons

26

grade stuff, or something near it. Enriched U. Pinched I don't know where. Little bits all over the place, probably. Munich, Geneva, France, England. Might not all be the same grade.'

'Or Italy,' said Leora, sceptical about security in her own fatherland.

'Does it matter?' asked Jim.

She had taken hold of herself; become again the practical Leora.

'He may be bluffing. You can bluff him. Tell him that whatever you said recklessly after a few drinks it can't be done. He may think it can, oh, from reading Ted Taylor or someone. But lots of people argue that Ted's bonnet is full of bees. It isn't like building a model aeroplane. These people can't have grasped how difficult and elaborate ... tell him you can't do it, and if he doesn't believe that to go fetch Ted.'

'I think he knows enough to check me out,' said Jim bleakly. 'The equipment and tools over there are pretty complete. I guess he'd say well, where's the snag? Doesn't go this way? Well boy, try it another. One can stall. But for how long?'

'And if he didn't know that,' said Leora softly, 'very likely he does now.'

'Oh Jesus. I hadn't thought of that. You mean ... ?'

'I mean if he has sophisticated equipment over there, what's to stop him putting a bug in here? He sounds like the person who'd think of that.'

'He is,' said Jim, not very happily. They didn't look at one another.

'What asses we are. The obvious ...! Well, shit. If he has it's too late and if he hasn't, there's no harm talking.'

'Talking about what?' asked Jim. The silence got thick and heavy, like bad rice pudding.

Leora lit a second cigarette, cruised around the room.

'Germany all right: most of the books are in German. French and English, too. I wonder who the house belongs to. Lot of history and biography – could be worse. And for you – a heap of crime thrillers. We can also play chess. Or cards. Can you play bézique? I can teach you ... Those flowers are nice. What's through here? Ah, bedroom. This is intended for

27

us. Two suitcases packed with a lot of junk one doesn't want
... Pretty cool cheek, this whole performance. And a little
bathroom that got built on afterwards at the back. This is an
old house. In other circumstances it would be pleasant ...
What am I supposed to do, I wonder? Knit? Cook? Or
twiddle my fingers and be a good well-behaved little hostage
... I'll tell that fellow one thing, and that's unless I get my
children back p.d.q. he needn't expect any co-operation from
me ... You're not listening: what are you thinking of? Look,'
gently, sensibly, 'don't brood. We face this in an equable,
empirical fashion. The situation doesn't call for brains, but
for common sense.'

'I agree,' said Jim. 'I was thinking whether it isn't perfectly
true to say that the notion is impossible. Even if this stuff's
what he says it is – and I've only his word for that – it would
need some very close calculating. Borderline the whole way.
In quantity, in enrichment. It would be a crude, stupid illiterate sort of gadget, and it wouldn't do more than fizzle. The
stuff is still full of junk – crappy cocktail of several isotopes.
Can't even calculate till I know what's there.'

'And how does one know what's there?'

'Only way I could think of would be to go right back to
what they did at the beginning of the Manhattan Project.
Assay it, and do a neutron count.'

There was a discreet knock at the door. A whitejacket
appeared.

'Would you like some tea?' Clear, if wooden, German.
'China tea or English tea?' Leora giggled and even Jim found
himself grinning. A very conventional, country-house week-
end, this.

'China,' said Leora, 'please. Out of a pot. The pot warmed.
The water boiling. Not too strong. Lemon cut very thin.'
The whitejacket bowed.

'And I am to say, please, that you are welcome to make a
promenade. Behind the house is woods, only please, on the
west side is a high fence, and not to go that way but any other
you like. And down the steps from the hall is a games room,
by the wine cellar, when you would enjoy to play ping-pong.
Supper is when you like and the Herr Doctor asks to suggest

a drink around seven-thirty, only Miss Rika will not be coming before maybe eight-thirty, because of putting the children to bed.'

Leora was thunderstruck so Jim said, 'Thank you.'

'Bitte, bitte,' with great hospitality.

What did one do – cry? Laugh?

'One has a nice cup of tea,' said Jim.

'And one puts in Oscar Wilde dialogue,' said Leora recovering. 'Like why do the servants eat all the cucumber sandwiches. Will they really let us go for a walk? As far as we want? Out of sight?'

'As long as they hold the children, and we don't even know where they are, I reckon they'll let us do anything we please,' said Jim calmly. 'He must know perfectly that we're not going through any fence. The threat is unstated. It's simply there. Here.'

Jim awoke early. At exactly his usual time, in fact. Creature of mechanical impulses, he thought crossly. I don't feel well at all; in fact I feel lousy. Exactly as though I had drunk a great deal. Nightmarish and liverish. In fact I had a glass and a half, like everyone else, and migawd, that Margaux: fantastic. If one has to be brainwashed by terrorists, this is the way to choose. Did the Doctor bring or buy this wine – or is this the cellar of the owner? Who is obviously an industrialist of wealth and originality, and taste showing itself in unexpected ways – the wine cellar like the metal-smith's workshop.

It's like jet lag, of course. Delayed neurophysiological shock. Take an adult man in good shape and balance, in what is called the prime of life. Shoot him in a capsule from San Francisco to Paris, and he'll feel hungover. Take the same man, put a sack over his head, shoot him with a dose of some powerful drug that will knock him out for eight hours. Isolate him so that he comes to in a new world, unsure who these things are happening to. Crowd him with new sensations and batter him with fearful threats – the more fearful because wrapped up in comfort, and even in luxury. And he'll wish to God he never left San Francisco.

Once more Jim had woken thinking he was at home, in Hamburg. An owl had been hooting, and in the Wehmerweg they were close enough to woodland to hear birds in the early hours, the hours Jim liked best. Even owls.

But here the noise was greater, because of the great silence. They were deep in forest countryside, that was certain, and protected by hills from the prevailing winds, which were westerly. One could hear the whispering in those tall dark pines. It was impossible to tell how high. The air was keen at night. Cold, as it is in Central Europe at over five hundred metres altitude in still autumn weather. In this pure air he had slept heavily, but had woken at the usual time, as he always did, somewhere between five-thirty and six. He knew that without looking at his watch, and he had not needed an alarm clock since being a student. Always to be up at six was part of his discipline: he did his best work then.

But knowing, subconsciously, where he was and what awaited him he had not wanted to wake. Stayed warmly rolled in a womb of blanket, feeling the fresh air on his face: he had stayed English and would never take a job with air-conditioning. He had heard the owl hoot. And strangely consoled he might have slid back into a doze for five minutes. And then the beast had come.

No buzzard, nor even eagle could scream like that. Lungs, surely, of something four-footed and furry, carnivorous and mammalian and lithely, muscularly heavy. 'Ahi, ahi-i-i.' Could that be a vixen? But that was no mating call. That cry would surely strike, and paralyse with terror, every small animal for a mile around. 'Ahi-i . . . Ah-i-i.' There again. Triumph in it, as well as bloodsoaked strength and ferocity. The cry was male, that of the hunter returning, telling that the hunt was successful, that a limp and vein-drained corpse dangled at a saddlebow.

There were no coyotes in Europe, for God's sake. There were wild cats but could a cat give that big full-throated mezzo-soprano cry? It would be shriller, thinner. Jim was carried back to his childhood, reading Thompson Seton. Just so had his scalp prickled when Yan says 'Boys, that's the yelling of a lynx'. But there was no lynx left in Europe? In the Pyrenees, perhaps. My God, is that where we are? Or in Rumania? Poland? In Russia . . .! Was it possible?

Jim was awake. He jumped out of bed. That's a nightmare, he said to himself. Leora was sleeping deeply; peacefully, as far as he could tell. He would make coffee, just as he did in Hamburg. He dressed, washed his face, brushed his teeth; things that stopped imagination running wild. I'll believe in a lot, thought Jim, but not in Russians kidnapping an American physicist in Hamburg and bringing him back to make a clandestine bomb for use on Peking. We left that fantasy behind with Batman.

In the living-room the fire was out, but a sharp and lovely smell lingered: embers from beech logs. Whitejackets had cleared the table, aired the room. The trolley stood invitingly. Rowenta coffee-maker and toaster. Coffee fresh-ground in a screw jar, bread wrapped in a napkin. Fruit juice in a vacuum flask. Eggs if he wanted, and a little saucepan to boil them in. Damn little wrong with the service! The eastern window was open; he went to close it. Dawn was growing over the trees on the hillside, beyond the garage. He stared at it for several minutes, watching the day grow into the pearly haze before sunrise. Going to be a lovely day. He leaned his hands on the deep windowsill until cramp in the forearms, and the smell of fresh coffee, struck through to his nerve-centres. He turned and put bread in the toaster. There was even Cooper's Oxford Marmalade. He would let Leora sleep awhile. He turned the electric ring on, went to fill the pan at the bathroom tap. The ring was glowing: he put the pan on, sat in an armchair, snapped on the reading light behind it. He felt in his inside pocket for the three or four pens that were always there, chose a blue ball-point. And where had he seen a pad of scribbling paper lying about?

The water was fizzing; he dropped an egg in carefully and looked at his watch. Methodical eggtimer is our Jim. Poured out his first cup of coffee. The toaster had popped up long ago but he liked it to cool. The butter had been put on ice-chips now of course water, but was still firm: the room was cool. Too cool – he got up and went to switch the radiators on. Egg was ready: he switched the ring off, lifted the egg out.

Jim, we are now organized. The expression 'working breakfast' meant a lot to him. He ate his egg and toast, solemnly; no mess, no crumbs. The mind went round in neat concentric circles. Drank his coffee. Blue ball-point went around, in the same circles. He dropped it, jumped up, went through to the bedroom, unbolted the French window, crossed the terrace. The flagstones, the flowers, the leaves, the grass: all beaded finely and exquisitely with dew. No time for that now.

The door of the garage was not locked. Jim turned on lights, rummaged on the bookshelf, found what he was looking for, bore it back in triumph, like the hunting lynx – was it a lynx? Noticed his footsteps in the dew. Shut the French window behind him. Leora was still asleep. Poured more coffee, with a sigh of satisfaction; man who has made a good breakfast. The carriage clock on the chimneypiece struck seven in liquid, sweet notes. Jim put the scribbling pad on his crossed knee.

i) Critical Mass of gadget 40% 25 in 25 – 28 matrix (% by volume) 40 kg

Jim scrabbled for a black ball-point with a fine tip, which he used for making calculations in margins. This went on for some time, then:

Critical volume in litres, 40% 25:5·51.

density: 18·95 / illegible scribble / cm^3.

MASS (TOTAL) $5·5 \times 10^3 \times 18·95$ scribble

= 104·23 kg

He looked at this for a long time, before realizing that his coffee had gone cold. He drank it angrily, and hunted for the red ball-point. In slow oblique strokes, he crossed out everything. Underneath he scribbled:

All right, suppose we've got 60% stuff.

The black and blue began to interweave in a formal dance upon the paper.

ii) CM of gadget, 60% 30 kg of 25 – 50 kg of total U.

crit. vol. crossed out and some black in the margin then.

critical volume: 2·64 litres. The bloody thing fits in a paint can. Steel as assumed reflector.

$V = \text{pi } R^2.\ 2R$ for height to diam. ratio $= 1.0$

multiplication factor for well-reflected system $= 1.015$

$\times 1.015$

$$\frac{2.64 \qquad \times 10^3}{2\text{pi} \qquad R = 7.5 \text{ scribble CM}} = r \text{ scribble } R^3$$

Point scribbled out. But I'm uncomfortable shooting a long thin plug. We query: mass of plug.

A long scrawl of symbols ended in -2.3 kg, much too small.

The gadget is ready to pop.

So we need different scribble height–diam. ratio.

Jig jig jig for height/diam. $= 0.5$

This requires 10% more s.n.m.

jig $V = 2.64 \times I. I = 2.904$ l.

jig $R = 12.27$ cm (d $= 24.5$ cm uh)

$H = 6.19$ cm

getting FAT.

Will need MUCH *TAMPER*/reflector

Jim tore the page off, ran down the steps to the terrace, leaving the French window open. He didn't look at Leora this time. To tell the truth he had forgotten all about her.

He had forgotten the scribbling pad. He took a fresh sheet off the pile in 'the office' and wrote 'supplement I' on it. Then he decided to make himself comfortable. Turned on radiators, arranged the angle of the lamp and the drawing-board stool.

Leora had been awoken by the scurrying to and fro. This, if nothing else, told her she was not at home. Jim, so quiet, neat and methodical in movement at work; disciplined mind co-ordinating a disciplined body; fine tuning of hand and eye; never made a racket in the early morning. When tired, to be sure, he bumped into things, but it was absent-mindedness. A tendency to pull at doors, and protest at their refusing to open, when all one did was push . . . gently. Complaints that one's pullover had shrunk in the wash, only to discover that one has put it on back to front. She rarely felt irritation. It meant that he had better things to think about.

This racing around and banging was a sign of anguish.

My poor Jim. He had a ridiculous notion that this was 'his fault'. That he had dragged the children and her into a horrible scrape out of carelessness or stupidity. Relief from anguish was now sought instinctively in something he could do, and do well; work. Had the Doctor, astute psychologist as he evidently was, thought of that? Leora thought it likely. But she didn't want to overestimate the little bugger's cleverness: that wouldn't do. It was playing his game for him. But she could not help admiring it.

Leora got out of bed, goosefleshed under her nightdress from the draught between open door and open window. Put the blankets to air and bolted for the living-room. Warm; coffee still fresh.

Jim had gone off to think about bombs. Being Jim, he would think about the moral aspect, but would instinctively refuse to get tangled in theology. A tool was a tool: it had bad as well as good uses. But Jim was not the person to argue along the lines of 'Adultery is bad: therefore forbid sexual intercourse.' His mind was trained to simplify.

To think of theology, to disentangle sophisms, to look at right and wrong and ascribe responsibilities; her job; that was the way her mind was trained. It was also her job to protect those vulnerable objects, a husband and children. Which job came first? She rarely hesitated. Right or wrong, one's daily work. Be it painting or writing, looking at stars or wondering about the structures of crystals. Now stop that, said Leora, catching her hand winding a spoon round and round in a cup of coffee that had been thoroughly stirred five minutes ago.

Be pragmatic. The Doctor is a clever man. He is a criminal. Therefore . . . no. The syllogism was wrong.

The Doctor is a criminal. He is criminal in clever ways. It does not follow that he is an intelligent man. He can be outwitted. And perhaps best by taking advantage of his cleverness. By judo, thought Leora, who knew nothing whatever about judo. Perhaps now is the time to learn. This is a prison. But a prison has a key, and there is a man who holds it. So far so good. Establish superiority over this man, without his being aware, for he thinks that holding the key establishes his superiority with no further effort. If, however, you are subjected to torture you do not find the trick at all easy. And it is torture. In small, clever doses.

You snatch people. With the injection of a drug you obliterate them, move them around like parcels, isolate and disorient them. You then treat them kindly, with excellent food and wine. All classic, so far; commonplace initial stage in brainwashing. You strip them naked with little humiliations, you create a dependence, by alternately offering and withdrawing indulgence. With a woman, for example, you take away her children. You put them close by, but just out of sight. Pleasantly, humorously, you reassure her that the girl looking after them is altogether admirable.

Leora, who was moving lumps of sugar around the table in patterns, like electrons wandering around their nucleus – or like a family – stopped it and went for a shower. I'm smoking too much, she said. I don't care. I am going to make myself ravishingly beautiful.

The Doctor had knocked politely at the door, around eight last night. Dapper, with a suit of raw silk (he tended to look made-in-Hong-Kong) and a bow tie. Towing behind him a whitejacket with a drinks trolley.

Talked about the house. 'I like these old farmhouses, don't you?' pointing out how skilfully the modernization had been done. Yes, thought Leora, and how skilfully microphones have been planted. If we make love he sits enjoying it. 'Did you have a pleasant walk?' Oh yes, and we noticed the fence that we aren't-allowed-to-go-near. Quite so, he said agreeably, but it's a sensible restriction. If the children saw you – why, that would cause unnecessary grief and suffering.

'Rika will be joining us for supper. A splendid girl.' Oh yes, Marika has done a child-psychology course, in Denmark. Worked at an *école maternelle* in Paris. Has a diploma too in nursing: the children are in exceptionally good hands.

Being, plainly, intended to loathe Marika from the bottom of her soul, Leora had no trouble at all in doing so. And then the little shock, doubtless foreseen, of finding that Rika was nice. Genuinely so, as far as one could judge.

Very pretty: stupid Jim goggling there the other side of the

35

table. Loathsomely tall; willowy, statuesque, similar annoying things. Glorious blue-black hair (natural) in a long supple rope, but no moustache; a faint shimmer on the fine bare arms. Great chunks of Assyrian curls up to her navel, thought Leora spitefully, but in justice we've no proof of that. A good plain frock of midnight-blue silk, long and straight, and suits her.

Is she really that pretty, when one can't see her eyes? Is she always going to be masked by those huge black glasses? But simple in her manner, unselfconscious, with a soft voice. Undoubtedly gentle, and affectionate, in the way she speaks of the children. Well poised – she's about twenty-five.

'Don't you want children of your own?' asked Leora.

'I would like to, very much.' Unaffectedly. And nice table manners.

Leora was proud of Jim. He had absent-minded ways of putting elbows on the table, waving forks dreamily through the air, or even chewing bread with his mouth open. Tonight he was polished, without being over-formal. A bit stiff and English. But there, the English had good table-manners. So different to the Italians or the French: Leora had been ashamed of herself, when first married.

Good dinner: simple food, but well cooked, nothing Arab there.

'What, no cous-cous?' asked Jim a bit acidly.

'I'm fond of it; we'll have it one of these days,' said the Doctor, imperturbable. 'And roast pork. As in England, done with the crackling on: quite delicious.' Touché, what?

And the famous Margaux '45. What could one find to say about that? With underdone roast beef, and *gratin dauphinois*!

'Talented cook,' remarked Leora.

'Oh yes, they have many valuable skills. Henry for example,' aside to Jim. 'He's your machinist – you'll meet him to-morrow. You saw yourself how spotless he keeps the work-shops.'

Some polite shop-talk about Jim's job, to show he knew all about it. And cheese soufflé.

'Now should one use Parmesan only, or should one have half Gruyère too? What's your opinion, Madame?'

'And you ask that of someone born in Venice!' said Marika,

36

amused. Everything so fucking civilized . . . Shove her face in
the soufflé, dark glasses and all.

A whitejacket came towing the vacuum-cleaner in.

'I'd like to do the bedroom myself if that's all right,' said
Leora, 'so I'll borrow that, when you're finished.' Very
politely; she was going to be polite always and for ever.

'Certainly, madam.' Equally so.

'1 brought their school books,' Rika had said to her, simply.
'You won't really see a lot of me, during the day. I didn't
think you'd want them to get behind. And I'm sure you'll
agree it's better that they have a completely normal routine,
don't you think so? They went to sleep at once. Tired, of
course. Naturally, they've been told there's nothing wrong.
That their father is overstrained, and has gone off for a few
weeks' quiet. And that you're looking after him.'

'A few weeks,' Jim had muttered.

'Why yes, Jim, that's about right, wouldn't you think?'
the Doctor had said equally. 'I should imagine six at the
outside. Perhaps less with any luck. You'll find Henry a
great help, and the design shouldn't be that complicated,
should it? An implosion system might be more delicate – no
no, I've promised myself not to talk shop at table, unless of
course you wish to,' courteously. Jim had filled his mouth
with salad, and mumbled something in Chinese . . .

'Generally we light the fire in the evenings,' said the whitejacket, 'unless you'd prefer it lit now.'

'Light it now,' said Leora. 'I'm all for Christmas cheerful-
ness and festivity.'

'And Miss Rika said that if you had a shopping list she'd
be happy to look after it. The car goes down daily.'

'Goes down where?' No answer. Well-trained servant.
'Thank her for me, and I'll bear it in mind.'

'I'll bring a basket of logs.' And Leora was left to queen it
in her drawing-room. A little music, dear Miss Woodhouse?
Just don't scream and smash things.

Children accept new situations, even abrupt changes, with
great flexibility. The placid acceptance is a trap, Marika
knew. One could not know what was going on in those heads

37

behind an apparent passivity. They could be distracted for a long time with novelties, and were. 'Ooh, a pool; can we swim?' A minute and detailed observation of every knife, fork, spoon, and cup, as well as what was for breakfast and why. So you're Rika, and you speak English with a funny accent, but you seem reasonably correct with us. Yes yes, but where's my mother? She had determined to face this as soon as might be, and head on. Nothing is gained by evasions; quite the contrary. They observe everything with great sharpness, and draw their own conclusions.

'You're wondering about it all. Why we're here and what we're doing. I thought I'd give you breakfast first, and let you see for yourselves. We've nothing to worry about, and that's all we need remember. But do you know that people have illnesses sometimes which are infectious? Don't fidget, Cass; listen patiently. You can look at it in a minute. Illnesses which are dangerous if allowed to spread.'

'Has my mother got one?'

'No, nor has your father. He met someone who did, or might have. So we take precautions.'

'Like polio. A girl at school got polio. She's called Bernadette.'

'Rather like that, yes.'

'We've been pricked. Cass howled, but I didn't. She had an excuse because she's tiny.'

'I never howled then. Tiny yourself, Harriet Fussbucket.' Got a slap and instantly did howl, quelled by Marika.

'Listen patiently. A man who has been in Africa can catch this illness. It's rare, and nobody knows much about it. It's called a virus. To make sure nobody else catches it we have to put you in isolation as this is called, instead of letting you go to school.'

'Are you a nurse?'

'Could it kill my father?'

'One at a time. Yes I am. No it couldn't because we watch over him carefully. But suppose he did have this infection, we have to be certain he couldn't pass it on to you. It's dangerous for children. That's why you won't be seeing him or your mother for a couple of weeks.'

38

'Is this a hospital?'

'What's it called? Funny kind of hospital.'

'Lassa fever and it can kill people. No it isn't. It is like a home for people who have been ill and come here in the hills to get their strength back.'

'Are there other people here?'

'No, because luckily these illnesses are rare. But it's important to realize that other people can't come here because of infection. Quarantine that is called.'

'Oh, I know. Dogs in England.'

'That's it exactly,' said Rika relieved.

'Months and months. Nobody allowed but you? Because you're a nurse?'

'That's right and that's why we have wire around, so that the milkman or the baker couldn't forget and come in with the groceries.'

'Is it a holiday?'

'A good place for a holiday, don't you think? But we must be serious. We must do work too, so that I brought your books.'

'Oh yah.'

'No oh yah, at all. One can't play all day. You don't want to slip behind your class.'

'What about my dance classes?' asked Harriet. Cass was already bored, or making the best of a bad job. Staring at the picture, plainly on the verge of demanding why all these characters were all naked. One bother at a time. They will have plenty of bothers. Let them get as many as possible off their chests now.

'We were going to the State Opera for the new ballet and we don't want to miss that.'

'We'll hope to be out by then but we mustn't take risks. One can't have everything. We have this huge meadow, and the pool. And the movie projector.'

'Why isn't there television?'

'In places like this people don't want to be reminded of horrible things. You know, like earthquakes, or floods.'

'Or terrorists with bombs.'

39

'Exactly,' with approval of this ready intelligence. 'Only upsets everyone.'

'But what about?' began Harriet who had a large and ready fund of what-about.

'Enough for now,' said Marika.

Jim was gibbering away on bits of paper.

Since we plan to use a conical plug, we will probably want to alter some things.

You see, this stupid thin plug, like a penis going into a vagina, that's all wrong. Stray neutrons, pre-detonation factor.

He stopped, appalled. Staring at his own scrawl. 'Since we plan to use . . .' I Do Not Plan To Use. What the hell is the matter with me? There was a scratching noise behind him. He turned irritably. A whitejacket stood there with downcast eyes, big scarred hands loose and quiet beside his body.

'Ah. You'll be Henry.'

'Yes sir.' Jim had not noticed, but Leora had already commented on 'how bourgeois they all are'. True that the white-jackets behaved like Uncle Tom back on the plantation. No nonsense about comradeship or brotherhood. It bespoke their discipline. It was meant also, she thought, as part of the softening-up. Intoxication, to use the jargon. Quite old, this one; grey-haired. Looked dependable.

'What can you do?'

'Foundry work. Metalsmithing – any kind. Precision. I was trained as a locksmith.' Not servile. That was the independence and obstinacy of a craftsman.

'Rare metals?'

'Yes sir. Goldsmith.'

Jim pointed his nose at the box in the corner.

'You did the chemistry on that?' A bit dubious: it must have been tricky. And there wasn't much equipment of that sort, here.

'I helped with it, sir.'

'Elsewhere?' in a friendly voice. It didn't wash.

'I'm not prepared to say.' Quite. Had his instructions. They had a chem. lab somewhere. Mm. Jim felt suddenly at a loss.

'Well, I've no particular instructions for you. Or not now.

Those machines seem in good order and clean. What else do you do?'

'I service the cars. Drive when wanted. Whatever is needed ... with electricity. Carpentry.' Like putting in microphones, no doubt.

'Well, all right.'

'I am to be at your disposal. At any time.' And went off. Sturdy, a bit stupid. But reliable. Make a good careful guard. No mistakes with doors or fences – the locksmith. The thread of Jim's attention had been broken: he fidgeted with his papers.

What Jim was doing was in essence simple. The basics of design in an atomic device *are* simple. It is fundamental, for example, that while plutonium cries out for an implosion system, metallic uranium is eminently suited to a gun-type device. The fast neutron chain reaction which leads to fission, and the abrupt release of immense energy, is brought about simply. Two masses of U-235, which held at a short distance apart remain subcritical, when joined go supercritical, developing great heat and pressure. They must come together very rapidly. Hence the 'gun'. A bullet is fired at a target, literally by a gun, using an explosive charge.

The first piece of design is the target, generally called the core. Jim was thinking of a cylindrical lump, fairly short and stubby.

Using a lump of bare uranium, neutrons would leak outward in all directions, so diluting the energy produced that no explosion would take place. The core must therefore be enclosed in a thick shield, of a material which is a mirror for neutrons. Steel will serve, or aluminium, if it be thick enough. The earliest gadgets were made this way. They were very large and clumsy, and extremely heavy.

Jim's first problem of design was thus to find ways of reducing the mass and weight. To help him he had a great quantity of published information about what constitutes a critical mass, and the fruits of several years' experimenting with different sorts of tamper, or reflector, as the isolating shield is called.

While thinking in general terms about this he had begun to wonder about the other piece of uranium; the bullet. It must slam into a pre-arranged hole or space made for it in the core. Jim's simile of a penis and a vagina is a rough illustration.

What bothered him was while a bullet goes very fast, neutrons go faster still. In the fraction of a second it would take for the plug to fit the hole neutrons would skip about and leak. When this happens the uranium heats up and melts, and there is a violent radioactive discharge, but no explosion. It is known as a fizzle.

This creates more complicated problems of design. The Doctor would not be able to build a gadget, however well he read up the literature. He might create an extremely nasty and mortally dangerous effect, but nothing that would bang. If he wants something to bang – to pop, as it is known – he needs a fellow like Jim. Part of whose skills in physics is to design apparatus that will work in the framework of a given experiment.

To release, and better still to control, the energy locked in an atomic nucleus is one of the most wonderful experiments known to a physicist. It is a means of passing the frontier of the known universe, and we are running out of frontiers.

Leora knew this. The Doctor knew it, or was psychologist astute enough to guess it. A person like Jim, isolated and made helpless, has little to do but think. He thinks of the problem put ready to his hand, a problem he has already thought about a great deal. His mind, trained to be concrete and exact, is not concerned with anything as abstract and imprecise as ethics.

To be sure, the energy released in this experiment is so appallingly great that there is great destruction. There will be loss of life. But that is not the point. It is the appallingness that is so interesting. By making the experiment one learns how to make it less appalling. And the interesting thing about any experiment is to predict the results. If we do certain things, in a precise, delicate, elegant fashion, certain effects will take place. Jim had thought even more than most people – because he knew more than most – about the dreadful things that happen when you pop a gadget. He hadn't the least intention of allowing it to happen. The threats to himself and his family if he refused to allow it to happen were very disagreeable to speculate upon. Therefore he didn't. He kept his mind instead upon a paper exercise. It was quite absorbing enough to contain his energies and curiosities. And also his fears.

Jim took a new piece of paper.

Try $h/D = 0.8$

$2.64 \times 1.02 = 2.693$ l.

Then $R = 10.233$

$D = 20.46$ (call it 20.5)

$H = 16.4$ cm

take a plug 10 cm in diam. & 10 cm long

$$M = \frac{\text{pi } d^2}{4}, \text{ h rho} = 14, 88 \text{ kg}$$

So we have the core

Big block: 20.46 by 16.4 cm. Hole cut out, 10 × 10.

Total mass: 51 kg exactly 1 crit. mass in steel reflector.

But this is more than 1.8 crit. mass in Be^9 (29 cm jacket)

Reflector mass:

rho $Be^9 = 1.82$ gm/cm^3

He made a little drawing, like a flattish cylindrical cheese:

rho V = a line of figures scribbled out

outjacket: 19.2 kg

each upper & lower slab: rho V = 10 cm × $(15.23)^2$ ×

pi × 1.82/1000

13.26 kg/slab

arrow total ref weight 45.73 kg just about 100 lb

total mass of core + reflector 213 lbs (96.7 kg)

Under this last figure came a long serpentine squiggle. At the end, in red ball-point, Jim wrote:

Uranium melts

Beryllium melts

He muttered and fumbled with the chemistry handbook and jotted:

1132°C 1278°C

A whitejacket knocked at the door and said, 'Would you like to come for some lunch, Madame says?' Jim stared blankly at him.

. . . . .

43

Kenneth Neilson, Jim's hierarchical chief and project director, was by seniority head of the group of American and other foreign physicists at DESY. He was, said one or two of the younger ones, 'best qualified by knowing no maths, no physics, and running extremely fast to stop anyone finding this out', but it was unjust. He did perhaps too often argue that 'all the damned paper leaves no time for work'; was a bit self-consciously the administrator. But he had valuable gifts; getting on well with Germans not the least.

The spry fox-terrier eyes, the wrinkled intellectual forehead, the greying sandy hair backsliding at the menopause, and irritating Indiana accent, that reminded sensitive juniors too forcefully of General Eisenhower, did not make him a charlatan, if they did underline mediocrity.

Herr Trautmann the Director, distinguished elderly party (sixtyish, silver hair, silver-framed glasses), was a lazy soul, mighty clever at delegating little jobs to Ever-willing-to-oblige Kenneth.

'Ah, Kenneth, this is sad; your boy Hawkins.'

'Well, it was sudden, Director, and quite unexpected; Jim really was the last person one had thought . . . I went round to their flat, which is locked. Nobody knows a thing about it. I've had to do everything, like cancelling the milk and holding mail . . .' The old man was quick to let no grievances develop.

'I know. You have this theory it's the wife, and that Jim's excessive devotion, yes, we won't let that bother us now. All is made clear; I've had this communication from a psychiatric person. I didn't really read it. All clinical and earnest. Whether he's off his rocker a bit, or she, or both; what came first, chicken or egg, bores me rather. You'll see that the shifts are rearranged on the accelerator, and you'll read young Hawkins's working notes,' as though it were a five-minute chore, thought Neilson. Should enjoy a good long nervous depression myself.

'Told Fraulein Magda,' went on the Director, 'to write a note of sympathy; we make allowances for family worries; we place the boy on sickleave awhile; hope not too long, all the same. You'll take steps, Kenneth, see he needn't worry

44

about completion of the experiment.' The hell I will; like your cheek. 'Not important though: really wanted to see you about this.' What's he on about now?

'Concerns you, as you'll see. Tiresome directive from those political people in Bonn, agitated at a confidential report that's circulating. Confidential, my eye; here, read it. Not all of it, man,' when Neilson made faces and riffled the sheets with his thumb, 'only security nonsense. Say-ee-ah no doubt.' Every time the 'political people' were a bother it was the C.I.A.'s fault, a favourite manoeuvre.

'No no,' said Neilson who was famous for knowing all the acronyms, 'E.O.D., that's Explosive Ordnance Disposal; Indian Head, Maryland.'

'I can't be bothered learning their new names: all Langley-Virginia to me. What have they to do with it, huh?, why come bothering me? People who dig up buried shells, disarm washed-up mines and such. Long way from the sea-coast, here: they think Hamburg's a fishing village; Gloucester-Massachusetts?' Deliberately dense; above all, lazy.

'Well, Director, one of their functions is defusing devices, as you justly say, and they naturally worry about letter bombs and such, booby traps, and they're concerned to stop that passing the gave. Their rough idea is prevention better than cure, no?'

'All this nonsense about I.E.D.s: they talk this jargon from Langley.'

'Improvised-Explosive-Devices, it's what I was saying –'

'Don't interrupt, mafias and mad bombers, sometimes, Kenneth, you Americans, with all respect, surpass yourselves in spending other people's money. Look at this nonsensical proposal, apropos of young Hawkins, security measures should include a consultant to give independent evaluation of personality problems and Floosh Floosh.' Old boy's personal acronym for jargon.

'Fellow evaluates, sends in his little bill, ja?' Who pays that?

'So I've told Fraulein Magda to send a rude letter back.'

He had an armoury, and a secretary trained to match the wording to the choice of missile. It could have been worse:

'rude' was relatively mild in his vocabulary, which extended to 'downright insulting'.

'Now, Kenneth, they'll be upset so what you do is this: you write a nice line to your dreadful people in Bonn, our security is fine, we're all searched at the door, we don't make explosive devices nor welcome any, we don't have any nuclear material, and go worry Karlsruhe who get a great deal more money than us. You understand me, it comes better from you. More tactful that way, allowing your embassy to justify their interference towards my masters. I won't keep you now. You might ask Fraulein Magda to come in on your way out; thank you, Kenneth, and don't worry about your boy. This Swiss fellow will have it all under control; sounds competent if boring. Two people like that in one day is really too much.'

Win one and lose one! At least Hawkins going off like that, without a proper word to anyone, had not created trouble. Which it well could have, were it not for turning a vulnerable flank to nagging about sloppy security.

He wouldn't write any letters! Saw through old Trout's game: that would amount to an admission that Neilson had not been properly diligent in supervising the personnel. What he could do was telephone Jimmy Repellini in Bonn, who was the embassy troubleshooter for matters like this. To say I'm a bit vulnerable and Trout is working up a fuss – no, not like that.

Memo: quiet chat Repellini, persuade him it's his job to keep NRC or whoever from being obstreperous. Neilson reached for the phone, mentally rehearsing his wording: conciliatory. Look Jimmy, you know how touchy Germans are; nothing treads on their corns like suggestions that they are casual about terrorism, so do avoid well-meant but heavy-handed stuff about IEDs while that interminable trial of the terrorists in Stuttgart is going on. Of course it will never end: that's the whole purpose of the operation.

'Come on in, come on in,' cried the Doctor with great hospitality. 'Have a glass of sherry. Or would you prefer a whisky? Properly cold sherry,' temptingly. It was good to come back to reality. 'So you've been calculating?' Good humour vanished at once.

'I have,' said Jim sullenly. 'Enough to show me the notion's impossible.'

'Impossible isn't French or so say the French,' without losing his joviality for a second. 'Let's hear it for the deaf man, Jim.'

'Theoretically possible,' shrugged Jim crossly. 'Great big monstrous thing. Heave it into a Volkswagen minibus. Nothing more than a fizzle, at that.'

'What seems to be the trouble?' like a kindly dentist. Seems as nice. Fatherly teacher, will now correct little Johnny's exercise-book.

'The calculations are all crap anyhow. Based on sixty per cent. What guarantee is there, but your word? I'm not denying your word, but you've taken some other guy's word. Not good enough. When it's a bit lower, you've a thing that will melt itself inside the casing, and poison an area the size of this estate.'

'No no – that won't do. What's your figure for crit. mass? Fifty-one kilos in steel reflector? Then we need a better reflector. Meanwhile cast a mass – Henry's standing round doing nothing – in two pieces, for the core, say, and make a neutron count. Give you a close enough assay for the enrichment percentage, surely?'

'Not as easy as that sounds. Henry ever handled U before?'

'No problem, no problem,' heartily. 'Now about this tamper. If steel's too large and heavy . . .'

'Beryllium. You mentioned it yourself.'

'Ah. How much?'

'A lot,' obstinately.

'Hum. A lot. That would be a problem, Jim. It's not so much the price. But it isn't stuff one can order from a chemical supply house without attracting attention, in large quantities. I wouldn't go as far as to say that it's as bad as uranium, but that's the general size of it. A small quantity – five kilos, say – would be perfectly feasible.'

'Then you're up the creek.'

'Have you thought about paraffin, Jim? Light. No bulkier than metal. I could get you chemically pure paraffin – not

47

just by melting old candles down. Those would absorb too many neutrons, wouldn't they now?' He knows a lot, the bugger. He knows a lot.

Lunch was simple and good as dinner had been: soup, spaghetti, carrot salad; cheese, fruit, the Doctor's conversation. Nothing was taboo except current affairs: there were no newspapers, no television set or radio.

'My dear Mrs Hawkins,' peeling an apple, 'nothing is easier than to argue that current affairs are only interesting when a few weeks old, when grains of genuine fact can be judged. News is a fraudulent commodity, blatantly manipulated for political ends; truism. The rest is ephemera: gossip and catastrophes peddled to feed morbid appetites. I could argue, without fear of contradiction, that an intelligent man could find all that he wished to know in a few literary or scientific reviews. We could find time, to discuss complex subjects like communications.

'However, I am asking you to take my prescription as you would a doctor's. You might be told, for example, to eat less salt. You find this troublesome for a day or two, but you quickly grow used to it, once you accept that it is for the benefit of your health.'

'I don't want to argue anything,' said Leora, feeling overcome with lassitude, 'with someone who at any moment can tell you to shut up and sit down. It would be like arguing with Stalin. I'd rather curl up with a book.'

'All argument is futile,' said Jim. 'The Latin name for knowledge is science, and that's no coincidence. Nine-tenths of conversation is paradox and playing on words, and the rest is opinion.'

'Accepting that to be so,' said the Doctor, 'what is going to be your afternoon's employment?'

'For the good of his health,' said Leora, 'and of mine, he's not going to do anything. He's off shift now. We're going for a walk, rain or shine. And argue with the hillside.'

'Laudable,' said the Doctor. 'I've no quarrel with your programme. Enrico Fermi, I recall, was a great walker. Don't make your walks too long. And always start by going up hill. It's less fatiguing coming down, in hilly terrain.'

'That is not in fact accurate,' began Jim seriously, but the Doctor was already talking to Leora.

'I receive by the way excellent reports of the children from Marika.' He folded his napkin and got up. 'We'll be English,' he said smiling. 'I'll expect you for teatime – I'm sure you'll need it after that healthy exercise.' Unmistakably, an order.

Where were they? Jim the meticulous, distrusting all conclusions when the premises were unsound, fretted at his ignorance of geography, geology, botany, in turn. Leora, Venetian-born, said there were hills everywhere, all the same and all boring, which irritated him.

'The Taunus would be more open – I'm not sure. Schwarz Wald, maybe – but there's plenty of choice,' ruefully. 'A Swiss shrink is the only clue. Somewhere towards Switzerland, but I think we're still in Germany.'

Jim's mind was on road maps. A stylized switchback shows a hill pass: the traveller, peering suspiciously at indicated mileage, finds fifty-five where it should be around twenty, and smells a lot of hairpin bends. Big hills, looked at from closer up, dissolve into a jumble of smaller hills.

They had expected to find a view, but around them higher hills stood, frowning, clothed to the summit in trees. The house lay in a shallow bowl, roundish, about two kilometres across, but from here they could see a bigger valley, some miles in width, he could not guess: in the higher, purer air the distances were deceptive. They might he thought be eight or nine hundred metres up. The hills were bumps in a bigger system, their valley an unimportant dip in terrain. On a road map it would not even be marked. Only an artillery map would show how the contours wound down to the valley floor, linking this land to the traveller's simplified picture of autoroute and urban centre.

From their hilltop, looking down forest clearings, they could see a little cluster of houses, a minute steeple: 'the village', perhaps five kilometres off. But in this microcosm of a mountain range, they might be twenty miles from a town, or a hundred. Whichever way you looked – trees. Move, and within five minutes you come to a hollow, and looking up to take your bearings, you lose even the local hilltops.

A large prison; agreeable, peaceful, even beautiful.

They tried to work over, above the 'forbidden area' where the children were. Leora with a wistful notion of getting close without being espied. Knowing them so near was an itch one longed to scratch.

But maddeningly, the terrain was impossible. A rocky slope, itself a painful scramble, dropping to a nasty boggy bit and rising steeply to a belt of tangled spruce. The wretched trees, striving for light, formed a choked mass of skinny trunks, half of which had died. Penetrable only with an axe; a tropical jungle would not be more difficult than this scratchy barrier. They tried, but did not try a second time. What good, finally, could it do?

On their own slope, barer and sunnier, they could climb. The trees grew wider, the dead trunks fell and rotted.

The top was a rocky outcrop, fortress of sandstone covered in moss. Bastions and keep and watchtower; in Leora's Renaissance imagination the robber baron's hold. Caves; clefts of chill humidity clothed in ferns. From the dry tower, a keyhole view down the valley.

'Which valley?' asked Jim with his practical sense. 'Where does it lead? Does it lead anywhere, except exhaustion?'

They scrambled back to the shoulder, open and bare. Woodcutters had felled trees here, carted them. Old moss-cushioned stumps: it was not recent work, but there was trace still of a bonfire, made as though by trolls; violent and dangerous forest denizens. Instead of a place of camp and fellowship Leora saw conquest and slaughter, a place of barbaric feast, with bones and skulls buried beneath heather, despite this vista of quiet, unsmeared by industrial pollution.

Beautiful; but one could not forget. Below the forest and the woodland undergrowth, below meadow grass and field flowers, was the wall, lichen-grey, and the faded red rooftiles of an upland farm, now a rich man's country house. A treasure lay there, guarded by Fafnir, a modern treasure; kilos of uranium. In the outbuilding.

'What was that garage, before?' Jim was good at this sort of thing.

'Haybarn. Stable below.' Small mountain cows; light, muscular horses; perhaps mules.

'Carthouse maybe.' Wagons narrow and lowslung: sleds in winter with high, curving prow.

'How did they live?'

'I'm no farmer,' said Jim slowly, thinking about it. 'Where I come from it's the plain; cereals and sugarbeet. Nothing like that here. But those valley floors are fertile; narrow but deep topsoil either side of the streams. Well drained too. The sunny side, vegetables, maize, tobacco maybe. Above that hay. No vines; it's too high. Too cold in winter. There'll be a lot of snow. Five feet deep; two or three metres where the wind piles it. On the shady side good grass; turnips, potatoes. Cherry, apple, pear trees. Good country, wonderful in spring and autumn, hot in summer. Too steep to plough much. They'd never get rich, but they were prosperous. Lots of water to turn mills, and they'd plenty of animals.'

'It could never be industrialized.'

'No. There might be minerals in these hills. But in thin streaks, nothing you'd call a vein. Difficult of access and quickly worked out. They might have mined. Iron maybe – silver even. Uranium there for all I know,' he added snidely.

'Now there's us. Deeply buried . . . Why is it all so empty, now?'

'Depopulated,' said Jim. 'The fields are too narrow and steep to work with machinery, the farms just aren't large enough; too much effort for not enough return. Long winters, isolated villages. And bad television reception – the hills block it. The younger ones had no use for that. They moved down to the flatter valleys. Big fields. The bright lights closer by.

'Only a few old ones left, who don't mind three months of icy roads. A few might go on still, digging, mowing the hay with a scythe, fattening their own pig, curing the bacon in the woodsmoke. When they go there'll be nothing.'

'It's a shame,' said Leora, 'letting it all die.'

'Yes. But the meat is too thin and light. Who'd pick the cherries? – not fat enough or early enough for the markets. It's by-passed. In these days they've nothing to contribute that would interest commercial circuits. What grows here is too sweet or too sharp for the towns, where they want food that's big, bland and tasteless. So it dies.'

'And then the town dwellers come back.'

'What?' said Jim.

'Don't you see? People come again, looking for what is real. So far, only the rich. Like this man who owns the house. He came, and said "How picturesque". Dose of comfort, the central heating and that. Summerhouse with a swimming-pool. Come up at weekends with a station wagon with servants and a crate of wine and thick steaks.

'The roads are too narrow and winding, perhaps, for weekend trippers much. But they'll get here. Isn't it lovely, isn't it peaceful. Quaints and cutes. Buy up the cottages, fill them with phoney furniture. Bogus beams and bogus wrought-iron. And the garden then, for fresh salad.'

'I see,' said Jim. 'Once the road is widened and the kinks taken out you'll have them racing up and down. And the wheel comes round. The transistor and the record-player, vandalism and the crime following the noise and the pollution. Poor old Germany. Vote right wing because there's too much socialism and taxes are too high. Discontented whatever happens. Secretly wishing the Russians would come, and sweep it all away. Rich, and miserable.'

'So bomb the lot,' said Leora bitterly. 'Save the Russians trouble.' They sat on soft moss. Leora plucked a spray of heather.

'Hemmed in, even here,' she said. 'There's so much intelligence against us.' She looked at her boots stretched out in front of her. 'He thought of bringing the right clothes.'

'Yes,' said Jim slowly, 'he's done his homework all right. Even on technical grounds – he knows too much . . . *Reactor Handbook*,' he quoted wryly, 'page 278. Figure 6.10.'

'Which is what?' not surprised by his startling memory for figures.

'"Effect of various reflectors upon critical masses of spherical highly enriched uranium in fast neutron systems",' said Jim. 'It's all there, in the damned book, for anyone that cares to look. Turn the page to figure 6.11, and you've the conversion of spherical masses to various cylindrical geometries. Everything but my own pointed head.'

Over them a steel-grey mass of cloud marched stolidly, leaving a patch of clear sky between two hills. The westering sun filled it with orange light.

'Cut and run,' said Leora. 'Tomorrow. Feint; I go up the hill, you go down. Village can't be far. I can gain a lot of time for you. I get back for tea, rather late; I say you're out on the hill with a sprained ankle and you're coming on more slowly. You'll have at least three hours, maybe four. They can't get away. If we're caught here, stuck in these atrocious hills – so are they.'

'You think I'd leave you – and the children – here at risk? If you can't leave them, do you think I could? He knows me better. And he's cornered, you say – you think he wouldn't bite? With a woman and two hostages of eleven and nine. American. Pretty problem for the German government. And for me.' The sky was beginning to redden. 'Come on; we'd better get back. Otherwise Uncle Sugar will be cross. Back for tea – you heard him.'

'So we're wrapped up?' said Leora, staring at him, not seeing.

'We're encased,' said Jim.

As they scrambled down the hillside, clambering and slithering, they had to dig their heels in, to brake. He could hear Leora muttering, in a rhythmical, chanting manner.

'What's that? Stop a moment – these damn pine needles.' They were clinging to his sweater. He was hot and sticky. 'Get our breath.'

'No. I wasn't singing,' with a vicious kick at a root. 'It's Auden.'

'Ah.' A poet Leora could quote the way he could the *Reactor Handbook*. 'One of your men.'

'Yes,' breathing deeply to get more oxygen, 'with a talent for horror stories.

"For, if he stop an instant there,

The sky grows crimson with a curse" – that made me think of it.'

'Can you go on?'

'Yes – "The flowers change colour for the worse,
           He hears behind his back the wicket
           Padlock itself."'

'Doesn't sound too good,' said Jim, with an attempt to sound humorous. 'It's beginning to get dark. Let's go on.'

From the top of the meadow the house looked welcome. Lights shone. Together, they looked over to the left, to the forbidden territory, where the high fence was hidden by a belt of evergreen.

'What can it be like?' she asked.

'Just another house,' said Jim prosaically.

'Rika told me they had a swimming-pool. The slope goes southerly – they'll get more sun. A summerhouse, maybe.'

Tea things were laid on the trolley. The fire had been lit. It was warm and cosy. There was no sign of the Doctor.

'I'm hot and sticky,' said Leora, 'I'd like a shower. But I'd like tea first.'

'I'd like a shower first. Tea after. Come on.' He took hold of her abruptly, slashed the zipper of her jacket open. Obedient, she let herself get propelled towards the bathroom, stood passive, got stripped, a bit wooden, thinking rather about tea. She got shoved under the shower, where she forgot about tea.

'We're encased,' she said, holding on to him tight under the tumble of water.

'Yes. And about to get tamped.' She kicked impatiently in despair, the way she had kicked impatiently at the root, at her clothes.

'Go on then – tamp me.'

She reached for a towel and started to laugh.

'The babes in the wood – had a good screw to forget their anxiety. And shall I give you another quote from Auden? Not a horror story.'

'If it's appropriate,' dropping the soap, not cursing; quiet now.

'It is, rather. "Thanks to your service,
                The lonely and unhappy are very much
                alive."'

PART TWO

'The Tamper'

'The woods stand round'

How much did the Doctor know? He went on being imperturbable. Jim could not tell. There were moments when he appeared extremely acute. There were others when he just seemed stupid. At drinks time, around midday, he came tapping – so politely – at the workshop door.

'This is knocking-off time,' said Jim sourly, 'not knocking-on.'

'I brought you a whisky,' with that brilliant, charming smile. 'I thought that if I glanced at the calculations it would help me – when we come to talk shop over lunch.' Almost apologetic, diffident. Not quite.

'Nothing here tells you much.' A jumble of squared paper covered the drawing-board. Scribbled figures and rough sketches, only the careful alternation of Jim's different-coloured ball-points showing any hint of a methodical mind. 'It's nothing, if that shit of yours isn't sixty per cent, it might as well be lead.'

'And if it's more?'

'Then it'll reach criticality earlier,' indifferent.

'And Henry's casting this block for a core?'

'Yes. Two slabs, upper and lower, like two millstones. Top one with a hole in it – that's for the bullet. Like this,' scrawling.

'I see. There's no danger in that.'

'In that much, bare, unreflected – no. Even if it were weapons grade – well, you'd take precautions. Lead apron. In fact, two lead aprons. And I'm going to want a lot of concrete around here. For Henry as much as for me,' taking

55

a slosh at the whisky. 'Henry doesn't seem worried. When I ask him he says he trusts you.'

'That's right. He does. You don't. Not that I blame you, of course.'

'I wouldn't even trust Einstein, if that's any consolation.'

'So you put these two blocks together to form a core, and you take a neutron count, is that it?'

'Roughly speaking. Get an informed guess.'

'But I don't want "roughly speaking" – I want it exact.'

'You won't get it. Apparatus for measuring neutrons with precision – it exists. Taken years to design. A lot more sophisticated than anything we've got.'

'I'm informed,' said the Doctor pedantically, 'that what we have is adequate.'

'I am not trying to deceive you,' said Jim. 'Shove some scintillation plastic into a paint can full of wax – literally – and we can see, if we're extremely careful, how near criticality we get.'

'And what's this?' tapping his fingernail on the papers, making a thing of controlling impatience.

'Oh that' – dry – 'is the bullet. I am a theoretical physicist and that is the beginning of a hypothesis.'

'And may I be permitted to take these sheets with me, to study them?'

'As long as I get them back,' drinking some more whisky. 'Do you mind now? – I'm pretty tired.'

'Of course, Jim, of course.' Henry appeared, eyes downcast as usual and hands at attention by his sides. Let them get on with it. Rain was spattering on the terrace. Jim walked across slowly, feeling boneless. They could hang him on a crossed stick and put him out in the field to frighten crows, and he'd be quite happy.

He let himself fall in a chair. He'd forgotten his glass: empty anyway. Leora got him another. She was knitting; he felt obliged to show interest, say a polite word.

'A jumper for Cass,' she said, counting stitches. 'I asked Joan Crawford to get me some wool and needles.'

'Nice colour.'

'She chose it. Winter will be coming.'

That Henry! One didn't know what to make of him. Standing there with his expression of stolid obstinacy, as though to say, 'You can't fool me: I'm wise to you.'

'You wear the lead apron, right? Two, even. This isotope is ... look, have you ever handled any of these rare earths before?'

'Thorium.'

Thorium! Where the hell had they got that and what were they trying to do with it? From 'Jupiter'? – the Jülicher Pilotenanlage for thorium element reprocessing? One could get full-strength weapons grade stuff out of that, but the chemistry would not be easy. Had they tried that and failed? What had gone on, before he came on the scene? But Henry was 'not saying'.

'Well, you're aware of the risk, in highly radioactive material. It isn't just a dose of clap, if you're careless. This mass will have to be cast, and machined. Watch the shavings.'

'I will recover all with care.'

As though the expense mattered. Jim supposed it was the training as a goldsmith. Still, Henry had done a competent job on the furnace.

Leora looked at him. In other circumstances it would be nothing she hadn't seen plenty of times. Jim concentrated meant Jim absent-minded. Going glassy at the table with his fork pointed at distant horizons, licking sauce off his plate with a finger. Childishly, and blushing when 'caught'. Not even knowing she was there, becoming red-eyed with potency when he noticed her.

Looking at him now her anxiety came racing in like a spring tide. She had spent the morning controlling it, learning to live with it. Like a fish perhaps, if one found a very big and powerful fish on the line. Pay out line. Reel in. Brake. Let him have line a bit at a time. It was all very well to talk of 'paying out line': the metaphor was treacherous. Was she playing the big fish, or was it playing her?

The Doctor came in brisk and hearty. 'Ah, there you are,' as though he had expected to find them somewhere else. 'Beastly day. I wonder what's for lunch. You know, Jim, I think I'll have another one too. Well ... Henry's going to machine that upper slab. A bit of polishing and they'll fit very nicely. I took a quick glance at our bullet – quite absorbing. Study that in detail this afternoon and let you have it back tonight. You're not going out to walk in this, are you?'

'Certainly.'

'If the bad weather digs itself in,' said Leora innocently, 'I daresay that White Jacket the Comanche Chief could get us loden coats. Couldn't he?' She saw the quick glance of suspicion before the Doctor controlled himself and said, 'Something of the sort.'

We are certainly in South Germany, unless it's Austria. She felt cheered somehow; the isolation was that tiny scrap the less. And Jim was having a third whisky. Overstimulated! She knew what would happen now, and was not surprised when it did.

'Pretty stuff,' said the Doctor helping himself to Russian salad, 'like silver when it's freshly cast.'

'Very,' said Jim, 'but undramatic. Unspectacular. Not like the Wages-of-Fear gag with nitroglycerine on trucks. Public thinks it must be dead harmless. Else Uncle Sugar wouldn't push it round the New Jersey landscape that casual way. Find nice names to call it. Industrial Effluent maybe. Do the same trick ourselves. Instead of calling it something pompous like s.n.m. we start calling it shit.'

'Jim,' murmured Leora, 'we're at table.'

'Nothing to spoil your appetite. Of course, we do exactly as you suggest; we don't think about it.' Eating heartily. 'No, I'm not being frivolous. Just consider sewage for a while.'

'Do we have to?' asked the Doctor politely. Jim was beginning to enjoy himself.

'We don't think about it here. All under control. No typhoid or cholera in civilized societies. Sort of disgraceful, so we don't talk about it in polite company. But here we're all in the family. It's only shit when all is said. What happens once it's past the pretty nile-green bathroom and round the S-bend? We don't bother about it then. Like me; I'm a physicist. If I were in pathology or parasitology it might interest me awhile. But think for a moment – won't hurt us.'

58

'Jim,' said Leora. He paid no attention.

'Gets turned into fertiliser, or ought to be. Hell, there are boys who work on these problems. Come up with a new building material – a plastic maybe; totally bio-degradable, wonderful thermal insulation. A plasterboard: extraordinary acoustic properties – never guess that was shit. Won't make it known; might build sales resistance. Step closer – don't be scared – smells of violets. Just think what it'll mean to industry. Don't say shit, say Magic.'

'Jim.'

'Yes, I'm building a fantasy. I don't know the first thing about it. I rely on the City Engineer. Shit is something Uncle Sugar looks after. Just like special nuclear materials.'

'Jim – please.'

'Oh all right, all right.'

They walked that afternoon around the valley, following overgrown woodcutters' paths, Jim silent again. Leora wanted to get him talking. It was line. If she could get him to run off with line she might find a way to hold him.

'Where did he get that stuff – was it really stolen in transit?'

'God knows – there's so much of it. Seriously, since it's medium-grade, likeliest is it was stolen from an enrichment plant and that could be anywhere. But suppose he'd taken plutonium – there's more of that floating about than there is shit – I was perfectly serious!'

'You had too much whisky,' primly.

'Look; the public knows nothing about nuclear material. Doesn't want to know. It is shit. Say you were interested in sewage, go to the Town Hall, after a couple of boobies who didn't know nothing you'd find a man who was interested, bright, and delighted to tell you. He keeps quiet about it, because the neighbours might snigger. At the local filling-station he's a municipal engineer. Not the shit-house king. You get it? Not classified, but nobody talks about it. This fellow's vital to our daily comfort and our freedom from cholera, more so than the Schools Superintendent or Hizzoner the Mayor, but nobody admits it. Shit stinks.

'So does plutonium stink. Barring fanatics, nobody wants

to know. It's controlled by the Nuclear Regulatory Commission, Atomic Energy Authority, a faceless bureaucracy. Supposed vaguely by the public to do good. Bringing the Peaceful Atom to Central Africa. In reality, of course, it sees that the guys who invest in expensive toys like reactors get a good return on their investment. That atom is there to be sold.

'So there exists a massive Circumlocution Office, devoted to saying everything is dandy. Ask questions and you'll be shown reports; ten thousand words saying it's dandy. Ask more questions and you get the glassy eye. Like the man in Dickens who said "I want to know". That's classified, they'll say, but don't worry, Uncle Sugar is taking care of you.

'And when we hear a lot of nonsense we say "oh, crap". This metaphor is like love, it grows by what it feeds on. We ought to say, "Don't shove all that plutonium in my ear." If you were in a business like fish-meal, or sulphuric acid, you might think they were superior varieties of shit. You've seen nothing till you look at plutonium.

'In the business there are a lot of isotopes, cesium this and strontium that, which aren't nice. Toxic as hell. Isolate them in deep water they glow down there with a blue light. Make your flesh creep. But it's still only so many cubic metres, say. There are a few deserted saltmines in geologically stable subsoil where you bury it and forget it. But plutonium is something else again. Hundreds of kilos charging about, all over the world. In oxide form it's a fluffy powder. Breathe one thousandth of a gramme, you're dead.

'It has other funny tricks too. After a calculation with this stuff – I won't dignify it by calling it shit – you don't take away the number you-first-thought-of: you add it on . . .

'Put it in a reactor to make power. By normal standards, of coal and oil or whatever, you'd make power, you'd be left with a percentage of ash. Here, afterwards, you've more plutonium than you began with. Known as breeding, exactly like rabbits; you've lots and lots of little ones.'

Leora had resolved to keep quiet, to let him spit it all out. This was no longer whisky.

'We use the simile "to breed like a rabbit". It's easy to think of rabbits as rather sweet. Nice furry things, which hop about and look inoffensive. They aren't of course in the least sweet, but they're reassuring because there are hawks and foxes to keep them in balance, and myxomatosis to fall back on in case of need. Rabbits aren't going to overrun the human race.

'Somebody wrote a book about how sweet they are. Now if only one could write a book about how sweet plutonium is. Uncle Sugar would give that fellow really impressive money. All the Nobel Prizes there are.

'You can't destroy it. Stable isotope; lasts thirty thousand years. Look, you'd see a sunset from here – if there was any sunset.' The sky was solid with marching clouds, a flock of dirty sheep huddled too closely for one to see grass, all the way to the horizon.

'Jim,' said Leora, 'are you really going to build this bomb? You'd be a mass murderer.'

The Doctor was reading, with a cup of coffee and a cigar. Relaxed and comfortable.

The core is 20·46 cm in diameter. Mechanically, we may safely take a projectile slightly larger in dia than we did before.

D proj = 15 cm

R = 7·5

$V = \frac{1}{3}$ pi R^2 1 which was 10 cm = 589 cm³

rho = 19·89 gm/cm³

so mass of bullet = 11·72 kg

Now to make room for the initiator, we shave off a very small part of bullet

3 mm

Mass of U removed appr. 1·3 gm. Which will not affect: totally non-critical at this point.

A lot of brooding there. Li-Po. And again Li-Po. As though a Chinese poet had made himself three millimetres tall and sat on the point of a cone. Then he changed his mind and buried himself head downward in the core where the bullet fitted in. The Doctor frowned and looked at the next page. This was clearer. Li was head down in the cleft. Po sat on top of the cone.

The Doctor permitted himself a smile. The perfect school-master, our Jim. All done on the blackboard, in front of a crowd of slightly dense children. Probably he always worked like that. The didactic mind.

Now: how much Po^{210} do we need?

We get $3 \cdot 7 \times 10''$ disintegration/sec/curie

We get $3 \times 10'$ neutrons/10^6 disintegration

$$So \quad \frac{3 \times 3 \cdot 7 \times 10'' \times 10'}{10^6} \quad \text{neutrons/curie/sec}$$

$$= 1 \cdot 11 \times 10^7 \text{ neutrons/sec}$$

It is sufficient to assure us that we get *one* neutron in the first 10^{-6} second after gadget assembled.

(The Doctor did a quick calculation of his own. One millionth of a second!)

My guess of $0 \cdot 1$ curie was quite exactly accurate. I be an S.O.B.

So we need to glue $0 \cdot 1$ curie to the plug. How *big* is this?

$\cdot 03\mu$ curies $= 6 \cdot 8 \times 10^{-12}$ gm

$$\frac{3 \times 10^{-8}}{6 \cdot 8 \times 10^{-12}} = \frac{3}{6 \cdot 8} \times 10^{-4} \text{ gm}$$

at appr. $9 \cdot 3$ gm/cc this has volume $4 \cdot 7 \times 10^{-6}$ cm^3

appr. $1 \cdot 6 \times 10^{-2}$ cm in radius!

Put it in your eye and lose it.

The Doctor picked up his telephone, dialled a long-distance number, asked for an extension, got a voice.

'Suppose I were to ask you for Polonium two-ten? Is that a problem?'

'No – within reason. How much? A gramme is a great deal, you know.'

'My instruction is zero point one curie. A speck, I gather, you could put it in your eye and lose it.'

'Except that it would kill you rather quickly there,' dryly. 'Can do.'

'And lithium? – wait: my note says a trivial amount. 0·45 gram.'

'No problem at all. Send it to you loaded on a Dinky toy.'

'Many thanks.'

Li had indeed got very small as well as upside-down, the poor fellow. Six point five by ten to the value of minus two cubic centimetres! And painstaking Jim had looked up the weight of lithium!

'Mass murderer?' Jim was saying, thoughtfully. 'Can't quantify that. How much mass? What's murder? This is an old problem. Oppenheimer had it; Teller had it. Harry Truman had it. Solved it.'

'That was war-time.'

'Yeah yeah. Wartime. All declared according to the Geneva convention and everything. And these people are terrorists; they're waging war, none the less.'

'A just war?' asked Leora. They were both very calm, very academical. A nice stroll in the countryside, and we'll talk about catastrophe-theory.

'What is just war? We don't know who they are, and I don't want to find out. They're Palestinian? We've precious little use for them, but I recall that when I was a boy and we had the Haganah, we in England thought of Jews as terrorists. They're Chileans or something, waging war against the C.I.A.? Or International Telegraph? Or United Fruit? Or whatever? There's money somewhere making war on money. Where's justice?'

'I'm saying that in no circumstances is it permissible –' He cut in abruptly.

'Quite. I'm a murderer whatever happens. I choose either to kill some Chinese, or alternatively you, my children, and myself. Do you think I hesitate, there? One or a thousand – I don't even know what his target is. It's the World Trade Centre in Manhattan or it's the local synagogue, what odds? We've all got to die some time.'

'So you're a terrorist?' she flung at him. 'Willing to die and you don't even know what for.'

'No,' said Jim flatly. 'For the good of the people some place. If for nothing else – maybe an atomic device used on a civilian target would wake the hypocrites up at last to the crude fact that they don't want to face – that the irresponsible proliferation of plutonium had better be stopped. Even if there's no more oil and we all go back to candles. I'm using paraffin wax, too. Joke.'

They tramped back down the hill in silence. Tamped, Leora thought. And worse, by sophisms. The fact is that my much-beloved, valued, treasured man wants to make this bomb. And will use terrorist arguments – any specious non-sense – to justify himself. Which is what, I think, our Doctor friend has been counting on. And I have to live with that.

She had heard the arguments before. Hadn't been married to a physicist for nothing, all these years. Jim had never been engaged on a security project, nor anything with any military application, but if you did any work on particles it meant handling radioactive materials, and if you had any intelligence you thought; you speculated. Even if Jim was sardonic – 'Nine tenths of physicists never think at all, except of course about money' – in the course of many evenings over drinks the conversation had come back, to what lay behind the jokes or the jealousies.

'Look; fire was also a terribly dangerous discovery.'

'How many times already have the prophets announced the imminent destruction of the world?'

'You know, when the first railway reached the utterly terrifying speed of forty-seven kilometres an hour, an extremely learned scientist said that man was physiologically incapable of resisting these violent accelerations.'

There were the attacks.

'Leora sounds as though she would have approved of burning Galileo.'

And the cynical.

'Leora, it's nice of you to want to beautify existence, but you remind me of the municipality of Rome, which planted a lot of bushes to make the place prettier, all of which were stolen inside twenty-four hours. You don't grasp that what's at stake is simply money.'

Oh, one argued, but in the long run, as Jim said, the argument was academic: there was no turning back.

The world was full of nasty things. Like anthrax, or botulism. Similar to the poison gases, remarked Jim. One wasn't going to use them because the wind might suddenly change. Who'd want to poison a whole country with long-lived radioactivity, when you might want the grain that grew there?

'Ever been through a hurricane, Lee? Or seen a tornado? Or an earthquake? You've seen Mount Etna erupting: you must realize that it's a potty little safety-valve for the energy that's there. What's a few megatons? – it's like striking a match.'

Leora had learned to keep her mouth shut. Who was she – grubby little Italian peasant – to quarrel with her bread and butter? She'd never been happy, but she'd stifled the qualms. Now it was happening to her. She was in the trap. Right and wrong existed. It was not just a notion of ethics, abstract concept. Physicists cheated, to her mind, or rather they evaded. They weren't interested in abstract concepts.

'We're physicists. Not metaphysicists.' She'd felt horribly frustrated. Surely the two were inseparable. What was the earthly use of wondering how things happened, when one never bothered to ask why? Nobody would listen to her.

'Might as well ask why is the moon not made of green cheese.'

'Better ask her why does she worry,' Jim said kindly. 'Look, darling, the system's imperfect, but on the whole it works well. People are pragmatic. They don't fuss about why floods or why famines – they look for means of controlling them. Nor do they go about poisoning the water supply of Washington D.C. That stuff is strictly for James Bond.'

'The world is full of moral imbeciles – nihilists,' she had said. 'People who will stop at nothing to further their own selfish ends.'

They shrugged. Physicists were conscientious people who took a great many precautions. Before trying out the fusion bomb, how many miles and miles of calculations had been made, to ensure that the earth's atmosphere would not go up in flames. Leora simply did not have a clue.

Physicists were kindly, civilized people, who loved Bach, and admired his mathematical genius.

Jim had been isolated, brought to his knees by the threat

of torture. His wife and children were held hostage. What had he left but his work, his skill? It was the one thing left of his maleness, his pride, his self-respect. My poor Jim, caught in the terrible dilemma of the physicist's 'I want to know'.

To know whether it would work. To construct a home-made gadget. Will it work? For years already physicists had been toying with this fascinating hypothesis. Some, one or two eminent, had predicted it would. Others – equally eminent – predicted it wouldn't. As far as was known the experiment had never been made. (If it had been made, fear of its being repeated would cause everyone to keep Very Quiet about it.) Of all the physicists in the world Jim had been chosen. Some tens of thousands, reduced to one, and that one, her man.

A fellow Jim knew, good physicist, wrote his United States Senator a letter saying 'What happens if'. The Senator, polite, wrote back saying 'I share your concern. I am enquiring. I asked the Authority to reply. I enclose their reply.'

Uncle Sugar, bland as hell, wrote eight beautifully-typed pages, entitled 'The Feasibility of Building a Crude Nuclear Explosive Device'. Eight pages of maple syrup. Oh no, it can't be done. But naturally we are alert. We are taking every precaution.

Jim had snorted loudly. 'Anaesthetic,' he said. 'Dearest people; beloved folks, sleep on your two ears. The Guardian Angels are watching over you.' It took lots and lots of money to produce prose that greasy. A real high-paid literary talent had composed that.

Jim was secretly happy at the chance to prove this Soapy Sidney a phony mouthpiece. To put a cracker under his tail.

Jolly, Leora agreed. But wrong.

She was sorry but she could not help herself. Whatever Jim felt, she was going to make an effort.

She chose that evening. By an unspoken agreement, a tradition had been set up. In the evenings, they were Civilized. The Doctor appeared in his nicely cut tropical suit of tussore or shantung, and a bow tie, a formality suiting his grave, balanced pose. Marika, pretty and smelling delicious, appeared made-up, wearing a long frock. Like a party. The

66

dinner was good, the wine good. Candles burned on the table. And they made, unconsciously, an effort to live up to it. Jim disliked suits, and rarely wore one (jokes about the Umbrella, the Calf Briefcase, the Bowler) but he did have a look of being English. His years in the States and in Europe had not effaced this. But he would take a shower and appear with his hair shiny, in pressed trousers and a spotless sweater. And Leora herself had fallen readily – if only to keep Jim from staring at Rika – into the habit of wearing a frock, doing her hair and putting on earrings. The very first day Rika had thoughtfully produced a whole shopping-list without being asked. Self-heating hair rollers, an aerosol can of lacquer. Little things a woman likes and wants, to preserve her self-respect in prison. Which increased one's helplessness that much more. So much worse, thought Leora, than being shut up in the 'Sexy House' in Santiago and tortured. Nobody strung her up, put an electrode against her clitoris or said jeeringly 'You think we'll rape you: well, we won't.' That would only shatter one.

The Doctor was cleverer. No neurotic little killer, this; no unshaved Palestinian in a dishtowel and a cartridge-belt. The Doctor knew that one must handle delicate tools with care. Keep them whetted, dust-and-dirt-free, with just a drop of oil. Not throw them about: not let them fall.

In two or three days, even the conversations had acquired a formal pattern. The Doctor talked to Jim about medicine or architecture. Marika would be confiding about draughts and warm underclothes for children, about confidence and self-reliance and taking-furry-animals-to-bed. About reading aloud, and drawing, about the things the children expressed in paint or clay. Madame Montessori. About anything as long as it was not terrorism, right and wrong, bombs. Leora was sick of shop-talk concerning devices, pops and jerks (how many million ergs made a jerk?) and the elaborate jargon of speed. How many milli-micro-seconds were there exactly in the 'shake of a lamb's tail'? Or Godiva – one of those sniggering jokes. Godiva was an experiment with a near-critical mass of plutonium. So-called because she was naked, i.e., un-reflected. Ha ha.

67

Grub first, then Ethics, she thought. Brecht.

Murmuring about the wine. Amazing how long it has lasted ... I mean only a ... Of course the year was exceptional ... One would take it for a Corton and it's only a ...

'Whoever you are,' said Leora, 'you're terrorists. Whatever you plan it's a terrorist act. You pretend to justify it. All right, do so.'

The Doctor put down his knife and fork. His smile was there for use, but he did not turn for it. He looked at Leora and said, 'Go on,' politely.

'Since we're associated we have a right to know. You don't care about rights so you push that aside. Say then that I want to know.' She switched to Marika abruptly. 'You talk about trust. That you're in a position of trust, that I can trust you with the children. You plan mass murder and you sit burbling about the wine and how pretty it is when it snows here. I like to look things in the face. I want to know.'

'Take things one at a time,' said the Doctor quietly. 'It is business practice to tell lies about everything. A commonplace, for example, in espionage is to tell an agent he is employed by the country where his sympathies lie. He remains in happy ignorance of his real employers being the very people he thinks he combats. I do not believe in this. I tell the truth, or I keep silent. Where we come from, who we are – it is better to keep silent. There are things that you can and shall know. First, understand your general position. Increased knowledge is not always the road to wisdom, an abstract remark; a woman thinks in concrete terms. Jim perhaps understood this quicker.'

'Can I have one of your cigarettes?' asked Marika, timidly. 'Try and think ahead. I don't mean to sound insulting. I'm sure I would think of nothing but the present, that I'd be missed from home, that people wouldn't accept a sudden disappearance. The director of the school for instance – Frau Prinzing.'

'Madame Putzi,' said the Doctor, switching on the smile. How did they know, Leora wondered, the silly names she had for people? Had even the flat in Hamburg been bugged?

'It's natural,' said Marika. 'Something will turn up. Like in

68

films; the villain's plans go astray through a tiny accident, and the rescuers arrive just in time. But we aren't villains, you see.'

It was said so simply that Leora was taken aback.

'Look forward, instead. We're not going to assassinate you, to cover our traces. You'll reappear, after a few weeks' absence, with a convincing explanation. It has all been worked out.

'You don't want to know much about us. It would be a threat to you more than us. You'd be embarrassed, handicapped in taking up life again.

'The children, I hope, will remember only a happy time while you were away. You need feel no fear. Or guilt.'

'At that moment,' the Doctor took up, 'where are you? Put painlessly back into circulation, as you were taken out. And where will we be? – you won't know. You will be compensated; we haven't discussed this yet.

'Money? If you wish; might be an embarrassment, hard to explain. A good job might be better. It's within my power; you have my word – seldom given. My power is wide; you've seen that. You are level-headed; you see that we are not assassins. We do not do wanton things. People trust us.'

'It's my turn to listen,' said Leora.

She was listening, but in two places: here and in Hamburg. No! She didn't want to be in Hamburg. A place where nobody would enquire after her. They were right: no one would even notice. A million people going about their business: not one would lift an eye to ask whether she'd been knocked down by a streetcar, won the Toto, contracted leprosy or become a nun.

Wasn't that the terrifying, the soulless thing? How many people could you remove from circulation, every day, without being noticed? A hundred? And keep that up for a week? A person herself nameless, the checkout girl at the supermarket, might say a week later: 'Strange. The little Italian woman in the red raincoat; haven't seen her for some time.'

Her own father, least complaining person she knew, who hadn't raised an eyebrow at his only daughter going to the States, or marrying an Englishman, had murmured 'Hamburg!' when he heard of the job at DESY.

Her eyes filled with tears. She wasn't a homesick girl, running back to Mum, whining about 'home'. Home was where Jim was.

But that instant Leora's feet were on flagstones in a square. She knew each, hollowed with years, filling after rain. Each centimetre of wall. Brick, stone, plaster: crumbling. Window blocked with wire or grille: rust. Balcony; flowerbox. Any time of day, any day or year, Leora could tell you the point where sunlight gave way to shade.

Seventeen steps to church porch; she knew the height and breadth of each interval. Call it ten years, four years old to fourteen, of skipping on the street.

Dreariest, least memorable of squares in Venice. Tourists came here because they'd got lost. Church of no merit, pictures of immense boredom. Venetian lesson; Tiziano too can be boring. Mawkish monuments. Well, greengrocer; merzeria, baker: two cafés, one Socialist, one Communist.

Dull. Everyone knew everything. You had given your geraniums too much water, your canary was off his feed. The vegetable you'd chosen for supper. The how and why.

The day Leora, aged eleven, put a scarlet blouse in the wash while her mother was at a funeral, and the family's underclothes turned pink, was remembered better than bombs. What would happen if a stranger, a foreigner, were to disappear? Without having seen him pack. The place would be as petty still, as trivial-minded as the day Leora, aged sixteen, shrieked that she wouldn't waste a day of her life longer here.

How many skipping rhymes do I know? Sixty? A hundred?

I see old Corrado, potbellied, turning wood. Uncannily rapid for all the wall-eye, for all the glasses of rosso coming out of his armpits. Winking at little girls, sly, spitting in sawdust, saying 'He that believeth shall not make haste'.

He smelt, and wore woolly slippers.

What am I doing here? wondered Leora. What is the purpose?

'Arrange the facts in order,' the Doctor said. 'There will be no trace. The special nuclear material was abstracted some time ago, in small quantities. Appears upon no inventory. Material unaccounted for; a catchall.

70

'The assembly ... You were both chosen for your skills. Flexibility. Nobody else is in this secret. There can be no leak.

'Now, the employment of this device ... You are right; we are not going to explode it in a desert. Hypocrisy would not earn me your respect. Yes, this is a terrorist act. Neither wanton nor indiscriminate. A political act, designed to change the destiny of peoples. In such a case each individual adopts a viewpoint according to his nationality, heredity, environment. Agreed? So we do not express viewpoints. Suffice it that this act will be found elementary justice, by people counted in millions.

'It is aimed at no people, or constitution. The target chose itself, after careful thought. There will be casualties, but not in large number. No damage to military installation, or even commercial interest.

'When it's to put your conscience at rest,' producing his cigars, 'I wish to take pains.'

'But an atomic device,' said Leora. 'Even if I accept all you say, you're a terrorist group, you plant a bomb. High explosive wouldn't make me happier, nor the act less serious. But an atomic explosion ...'

'Leora, there are two arguments. One: there are many terrorist groups. Some I disapprove of, for many reasons. But all have one thing in common: they use explosives. I don't wish to make a confused impact upon opinion.'

'Impact is a good word,' murmured Jim.

'Quite,' disregarding the sarcasm. 'The other is that explosions, even large ones, produce no result. They have a half-life, to use jargon, of a day in the world's Press. An atomic device will arrest,' the cigar circled. 'Start at Vladivostok, and go on round. A truckload of nitro-glycerine would not help us to that. Not to mention that truckloads of rubbishy explosive, in areas protected by even elementary security precautions, attract notice.

'Without being technical, the smallest device, a tenth of a kiloton, a pop and not a fizzle, is what we need. I rely on Jim and his silences. We'll discuss it at the appropriate time which isn't here, but I was struck, Jim, by the trick for quick neutron

71

release, the scrap of lithium and dab of polonium: was that your invention?'

'Paperback book,' laconically, 'by Ted Taylor.'

'Really! I thought the initiator was a closely guarded secret.'

'So had I. Seems not. Struck me at the time. I made the calculation – it works!'

Leora cut into the congratulations.

'All you've told me doesn't answer the problem. Is it right or is it wrong? I don't see how atom bombs can be anything but wrong. I fail to see how anyone could maintain the contrary. Don't talk to me about floods and famines. They are acts of God, force majeure. Don't tell me ends justify means; I don't accept it.'

'I do, I'm afraid, talk about force majeure.' Marika put her hand on the Doctor's sleeve.

'Leora, have you seen dead children? In large numbers? Did you realize that the horror of children who have eaten earth was not always a monsoon that failed or unforeseen drought. It can be deliberate. A cynical manipulation. Political, to create leverage, even commercial; stealing food to resell. I have seen that.

'That is the evil. That I am determined to combat. I am not evil. Nor is he. We are not mystics. We do not understand your metaphysics.

'There, tangible, is evil. I hate violence. But there is no other tool.'

Leora looked at her in silence.

Leora, naked, making love, thought of her grandfather . . . She lay shaking . . . Jim, accustomed to concentrate in silence, not a man to pant like a dog, stroked her closed eyes.

'Less bad,' he said, feeling her unknot. She giggled, startling him. A woman who never stopped surprising one. One got used to being surprised, but . . .

'He that believeth shall not make haste,' she said in the dark. 'It's in the prophet Isaiah.'

'Not, probably, in that context.' They had agreed from the beginning that even if there were microphones in the heads of all the matches, that was too bad for the microphones. It does not diminish the spied-upon, said Leora; it does diminish the spy.

'My grandfather used to say so.'

'Can you sleep, now?'

'Yes.' Before going to sleep she felt herself come back to life. That obstinate corner of her mind that refused to be helpless. Whatever they said, it was wrong, and nothing would persuade her . . . She would plan. Like the Doctor, like Rika, like Jim and the extreme care with which he fitted things together, she would construct a method. She had time; she did not know how much. But as the carpenter used to say when he set the circular saw going, he that believeth shall not make haste. He had two fingers missing, from his left hand.

Jim had created an atmosphere of his own in the 'office'. I could walk in anywhere, said Leora, and know he'd been working there. No physical signs, except an extreme tidiness; not a smell. But he imposes his personality in subtle ways upon pencils and bits of paper.

There was a tap at the door: the Doctor.

'No wish to interrupt you; wanted to give you your papers back . . . I don't find much bother about size. Weight, on the other hand . . .'

'Like I told you: beryllium is the only way to reduce weight.'

The Doctor shook his head.

'Can't be done. The bit you need to go behind the bullet, two kilos or whatever – yes, I realize you haven't calculated it yet – that can be done.'

'Twelve,' holding out another piece of paper. 'Must be twenty centimetres there, to avoid any risk of neutrons leaking back. And here, reflector fifty-three, bottom slab eighty-eight, top slab with the hole in it for the bullet, eighty, plus the twelve of beryllium, two thirty-three. Plus the core which is around fifty, that's two eighty-three. Not to speak of the firing mechanism and little etceteras of that sort. These are the roughest calculations, but however you refine them you're not getting below three hundred kilos. Heavy, but home-made bombs *are* heavy.'

'I realize,' said the Doctor mildly. 'What thickness are you at there, with the reflector?'

'With paraffin? Well, using beryllium we had ten centimetres thick. Have to go to twenty-five. That's a lot, but the handbook says that using graphite ten inches would be required. Might with paraffin get down to seven inches. That would give,' picking up the calculator, 'one forty-seven kilos. Work on one fifty.'

'Not too bad.'

'Cut down that far and you risk a fizzle, as you must realize. Look.' Jim took a fresh piece of paper and made a drawing of what looked like a can, inside another can.

'A thin steel jacket – say two millimetres – to enclose the core, leaving always a hole in the top for the bullet. To that we weld small struts to hold another thin can, uh, seventy and a tiny bit centimetres across. Fill the space between with paraffin – just melt and pour it in.'

'To all of which,' said the Doctor gently, 'you attach the firing mechanism. The "little etceteras of that sort". In calculating the diameter of your bullet, Jim, you must have given thought to the gun which fires it.'

'Yes,' calmly, 'I have. Getting it is your problem.'

'I noticed that you were working on a diameter of about ten and a half centimetres.'

'Well, you guessed it. A one-oh-five millimetre recoilless rifle.'

The Doctor smiled.

'Jim – you must take us for terrorists! That is not impossible. I have a notion,' rubbing his beard, 'that the calibres may vary slightly – according to provenance.'

'That's just a question of milling – your shop would take care of that.'

'It would be long and heavy. Adding considerably to the bulk and weight of our gadget.'

'That again is your problem. I'm just designing this damn thing.'

The Doctor walked the length of the garage, turned and came back again. Jim sat on the stool by the drawing-board, scribbling aimlessly.

74

'I don't want to keep you here longer than is necessary, Jim. I'll work on this problem. It may take a couple of weeks.'

'I've other problems. And they'll take a couple of weeks.'

'Henry's got his blocks cast.'

'Henry,' dryly, 'is going to be busy. Building a thick concrete wall. There,' pointing to the partition. 'The stuff must be assayed. If the criticality isn't right then your whole exercise in cores and tampers and bullets and guns stays the way it is. On paper.'

'Very well, Jim. Let's hear it.'

Jim threw his pencil clear across the garage. It fell to the floor and lay there.

'Understand me,' he snapped. 'This is a simple, but extremely dangerous experiment. The stuff you've got here kills. It would kill me. You. Us all.'

'Take it easy, Jim. I'm perfectly well aware of that. What I do not grasp is the need to make such an experiment here.'

Jim was breathing deeply, flushed, pointing a second pencil as though it were a gun. It took him nearly a minute to get himself completely under control.

'We are in a position,' he said, 'parallel to the early days of the Manhattan Project. We possess two masses of uranium. We have calculated that when put together they will form a critical mass. We predict that when put abruptly together, by this powerful crossbow mechanism we've been talking about, they will pop. But we don't know. We don't know because we are in fact uncertain of the exact degree of enrichment this mass has attained. We do not know how many neutrons will be released. Whether there will be sufficient flux to cause a fast fission reaction within the parameters that will create an explosion. Am I clear?'

'You are clear.'

'The only way to do this is an experiment known as tickling the dragon's tail. Because that is what it is.'

'I am not a child, Jim.'

'Aren't you? Well, learn to be one. This stuff spits fire.'

The Doctor had controlled himself, too.

'You move two sub-critical masses slowly towards one

75

another,' spelling it out as to a child, 'using remote-handling equipment. When they get close, you go slowly, softly. You count, most particularly, the neutrons emitted. The count thus obtained will tell you, after some not too complex calculations, whether your mass will pop. We need, by the way, more sophisticated monitoring equipment. The NE-102, you understand, is barely all right. It's cheap. If one can't do better. I'd like a NIM-bin, some fast amplifiers and discriminators, more high-voltage supplies and cables, and a goddamned four-thousand-channel analyser.'

'Jim,' smiling, 'I hope that our dear Leora with her exercise in ethics of last night has not infected you with a desire to drag your feet. It can only recoil upon yourself. I should say yourselves.'

'I'm serious. I've never been more so. If you don't want to listen – it's your life. As for the gadget – you know what a fizzle effect does?'

'I've studied the matter.'

'I'm glad to hear it. The device would build enough temperature and pressure to destroy itself. There would be a discharge of neutrons, gamma rays, several nasty things. Enough to kill anybody standing around. It would not, though, create a bang. And if I've understood you correctly that is what you want. This has nothing to do with Leora. It has to do with me.'

'I make no promises. I'll see what can be done, with regard to the instruments. I will instruct Henry that concrete must be poured. We'll get a little mixer. Willing hands make light work – I can provide those.' Jim's sense of humour, sometimes buried but never that far off, was tickled, like the dragon's tail. All the white jacket tribe wheeling barrows and busy nailing planks into a retaining wall. We will now build Hoover Dam. To keep the neutrons where they belong. He felt drunk. A sign that he could do with a jolt of whisky ...

On the surface, in these days – one lost count of time here with no reference to the outside world – nothing happened, so that nothing changed. Leora found she got used to the 'rest cure' with little effort. No shopping or cooking, with its boring routine of shall-we-have-lamb, or why-not-a-pork-chop. Why does one need three different kinds of detergent? Jim's warfare against the dish-washer. Uneconomical, noisy, and inefficient; I'm sure I could design a better one. Well then, why not show General Motors how to do it?

Nor was it the absence of newspapers: boring old *Abendblatt*. Jim ploughed through the dense texture of German politics (a good reflector of neutrons, surely) but she read it for the announcements of sales ... Or the *Herald Tribune*: did one have to get involved in the nervous skin-diseases of the Stock Exchange? Or even *Newsweek* – she did miss the book reviews. As for television ...

She hadn't gained weight. Lost a little, if anything, despite drinking a lot. Features sharpened, her skirt a fraction loose. Smoking too much. But she didn't feel bored. She fretted at first about the children: hated Rika solidly for a week. Rika sticking pins in her helplessness, Rika with her ghastly competence about meal fads or bedtime preferences and her chat about child psychology; the eagle eye on their underclothes and toenails.

Imprisonment was irksome. But the certainty of microphones everywhere weighed less heavily than she imagined. To be spied upon in bed or bath – but no, truly, she had determined to behave as though there were nothing there, and no longer thought about tiny antennae twitching when Jim let go an uninhibited fart. Maybe there was nothing there. They had no proof. The Doctor did nothing to show that he had overheard. Why not look? Leora suggested, out on a scramble in the hillside, feeling secure, unless there were a transmitter in the heel of one's shoe. To show we are undefeated. Hunt around. What Henry hides we can discover. What use is that? asked Jim: they could pester us in a multitude of ways.

The illusion of freedom, on these walks, was the worst feature of the tamper. The Doctor allowed them to range far afield (provided always they were back by 'teatime'). He had decided, apparently, that there was no risk. There was no harm in their knowing roughly where they were. South Germany; that much they knew. For though, in the wet woods and misty autumn weather they were generally alone, they did meet local men plodding along woodcutters' paths on Lord knew what pursuit: a people sourish; taciturn and withdrawn, who muttered a greeting.

Once a man carrying a shotgun, in leather gaiters and a cape. This inflamed her imagination. In a flash she crept up on him, stunned him with a dead branch, seized the gun, rushed back, stormed the citadel . . .

Why not accost these people, send for the police, rouse the countryside, phone Hamburg, yell and shriek? In that well-fenced country estate hidden among the trees there are fearful things going on. Are you going to stand apathetically by? We may look like anyone, but we are kidnapped hostages, held sequestered, attached by invisible chains. DO SOMETHING.

'I'd as soon take hold of a black mamba,' said Jim sourly, 'if I met one in the jungle, stroke its tail and say Pretty pussy. That woman in her dark glasses, holding my Cass, with a knife in the other hand. You think they'd hesitate? You want to try?' grimly.

No, Leora did not try. She could imagine it too clearly. Even if these wooden-headed peasants could accept that there really was a terrorist group there under their noses; if one persuaded them that this was a piece of blackmail bigger than ever thought of – 'Look, my husband is a nuclear scientist: I know, he looks like anyone else but he can build bombs and that's what they want: you don't believe me but ring up Hamburg, ask for DESY.

If they succeeded in getting the special anti-terrorist squad with snipers' rifles and infra-red sights, with tear-gas and loud-hailers – it would not attack. Not while there were two little girls inside that building. They'd give a free passage. Supply a plane, to Libya or Bolivia. To a safe haven where the Doctor, intact and undisturbed, would proceed at leisure with his plan.

Even the occasional hiker who tramped past with a cheerful 'Berg Frei' – no, one could not speak to these people; there was no appeal possible.

Leora had gone over and over the blithe ease of their own

kidnapping. There must be something in Hamburg to scream 'Alert'.

'What about the car? Mine was in the garage, but your Volkswagen, with its dented fender? The neighbours all know it. Left there on the street; it would be noticed, reported.'

'By who?' said Jim. 'How many car-thefts are there daily in a city the size of Hamburg? Some industrialist with a Ferrari roaring into the Altona police howling his motor's been pinched; yes, there'd be a search, albeit desultory. But a Volkswagen, for God's sake. They tipped it in the Elbe. No, they didn't, upon reflection. Might be found by some dredger – they unscrewed the numberplate and left it anywhere. Gets towed eventually to some police parking-lot because of obstruction. Nobody reports it; the cops shrug and do nothing. Just some teenager, joyriding. Where does it come from – Berlin or somewhere – who cares?'

'Kenneth. Surely he won't swallow a vague story about overwork. He knows you; you're friends. He'd ring up, enquire.'

'Sorry,' blunt, 'he and I aren't that sort of friends. He's the project director. I've overworked, or had family troubles. Yes sure, dear-dear. But it can happen to anyone. Jim's in good hands; impressive shrink, clinic in Zürich, he's well looked after. Leora with him and everything. If there was anything wrong, I'd hear. He'll be back in a few weeks, as good as new. Annoying, but meanwhile the machine keeps running and it's my job to see it does so efficiently – that's the way Kenneth's mind will work.'

'Isn't there anything – Frau Prinzing? She'll worry at the children absent from school, and she's conscientious.'

'So are they. Don't you remember the joke about Frau Putzi – they have it taped. If we're to believe them, and I don't see why we shouldn't, they've prepared this for six months. It took that long to get this quantity of U slipped out of the chain undetected, written off as m.u.f. To set this place up, with the material, and the tools, and all. They've plenty of money, friends highly-placed – who and what is to stop them?'

.   .   .   .   .

I am, thought Leora. She was sitting in the bedroom, in front of the dressing-table. There was a small hateful spot in the corner of her eyebrow. Drinking too much whisky, no doubt. I am going to stop them, though I don't know how.

One thing, and one only, was clear. She had to get the children out. She and Jim, alone, could do nothing.

But how? The children were more closely guarded than the uranium.

She had not seen or heard them; not a glimpse. She knew where they were. The steps to the terrace at the back went farther up the steep bank to a path through the meadow, flagstoned, lined with flowering bushes and trees. It led to a belt of woodland, where there was a high chain-mesh fence. Probably, said Jim, burglar-alarmed. This was the country hide-out of a rich man. He had Chinese porcelain, Picassos – the security surrounds were common form to satisfy an insurance company. Up in the high meadow was a summer-house. Built originally, perhaps, because this ancient farm-house was too deep below the protecting hillside.

The 'summerhouse' caught the sun all day, even in winter. It was a simple wooden chalet: a big room with guest bed-rooms attached, a kitchen, a verandah and patio, a swimming-pool. Had its own heating. That much had been pieced together. There was a gate in the fence. Marika, and presumably the Doctor, had keys. There were one or more white-jackets on duty up there. (Nobody knew how many there were altogether. Four had been identified.)

It looked hopeless. The children were sealed off. To rescue them . . . Any fool could escape on her own. To take the children with her was impossible. She couldn't com-municate with them.

Even with Jim's help . . .

Jim . . .

She did not count on him: he was, now, an unknown quantity. One couldn't count on a man with an obsession: he was unpredictable. And Leora knew that Jim was, to a large degree (how large?) obsessed.

So had it been, surely, in the world of sharpened sticks and round pebbles in a sling. The first fellow who predicted like any scientist that iron, if hammered out when hot to a blade, would hold its edge set a few contemporary Jims thinking. One had been silent and preoccupied for weeks. Making drawings with sticks of charcoal, muttering and smudging them out again: plaiting leather thongs together until they could pull a stubby bow: fixing that bow to a stock of wood with a butt-piece (a brilliant stroke).

Look, you can shoulder it, steady it, sight along it: aim it . . .

How much longer had it taken, puzzling, before he hit on a winding mechanism strong enough to bend the bow? And again, the most difficult of all she imagined, the trigger mechanism which would arrest, at will release the bowstring? Though that had been a question of mechanics, once the principle of propulsion was mastered.

Finally, he forged a few iron bolts like crude large nails, sharpened their points with water and soft sandstone, loaded his terrible contraption, and, alone with his heart beating, pointed it at a log of wood. Whang. There was the proof of his prediction that a missile could be aimed at a distance, which could penetrate a shield, and body armour, and the man behind it. He had brought it to the chiefs and said 'This will make you the masters of the world'.

No he hadn't!

People like Jim did not think of being the masters of the world. They thought of drilling wood, maybe metal, of building great ships and bridges and towers. It was some crafty politician, an inventor of nothing but excuses, boasts, and prevarications, whose tiny eyes lit up agleam with the notion of conquests. Patient old Jim, vague about conquests but already full of notions, how to tie a string, maybe, to the bolt, went off to think some more about making his crude engine accurate, reliable, portable.

Leora had never grasped what lay behind this fidgeting with atoms. Nuclei and electrons, yes yes, lot of billiard balls bonking about. Hydrogen had only one satellite – poor thing, rather pathetic. And uranium had ninety-something of them: well, lucky old uranium. There was a thing called binding energy which held it all together; quite. Why didn't gold explode, then, and was her platinum bracelet radioactive? Jim, exasperated, said she was a fool. Or no, not a fool, having evidently some talent beyond wiggling her bottom. But badly educated, mentally lazy, a stupe, a saboteur, an enemy of progress. Go on with your knitting.

She wished she had paid more attention. Then, perhaps . . . it was too late now. Jim had gone beyond her reach.

At the start they were together; felt together the successive stages of imprisonment. Despair, weariness, apathy, and then the slow regain of activity, becoming more feverish as it became increasingly frustrated – but with Jim it was not frustrated, because he had found a problem which fascinated him, which he had always wanted to tackle, which he had thought about and speculated aloud over. Often sullen and taciturn, but full, full of energy.

A tendency to grab her suddenly; leave her gasping and feeling her bruises. But that was good. He clung to her; they were bound together by an energy quite as strong, and much more pleasant than those boring atoms. They communicated. In the daily sessions of ping-pong (batting an electron from one nucleus to another) which had grown steadily more skilled, from awkward misdirected pats to fierce smashes which stayed on the table and gave such intense pleasure, they had been wonderfully close; breathless, sweaty, but above all laughing.

Jim had stopped laughing. When listening to music, as they did every evening – it became a tradition, after the Doctor left them and the dinner-things were cleared away – he used to look at her for long minutes, thinking about her, thinking about the music through her, sharing her with the music, sharing her. He stared now at things she did not share, things a long way away but drawing closer. When he came back it was abrupt and violent, because he found it difficult. Her body lacked flavour, and he had to sprinkle lots of pepper on her. Like that other day in the woods . . .

Ridiculous, and comic. Stupid Jim getting red-eyed all of a sudden in the pine-needles. She shrieked idiotically, ran away, was pursued with heavy breathing, caught, had her trousers ripped off – decidedly chilly and draughty, as well as bursting

82

two buttons. And she had certainly not enjoyed it, gazing around panic-stricken the whole while (idiotic, laughable) for the dirty-old-man she felt sure was hidden in the bushes, leering through binoculars . . .

That had been funny but being raped by a total stranger did not excite Leora, nor give her pleasure.

And the decidedly brutish manner of sitting there at supper glaring lecherously at Marika. She thought she understood: he felt guilty, vaguely, at his failing interest in herself.

It was a small boy swaggering about whistling in the dark. She was ready to bet that he took her, now, telling himself it was Rika. Lilith the temptress; lip-smacking crumpet in the dark glasses.

In fact the two women got on well together. If, thought Leora, she'd take off those zombie glasses and stop making like the Tontons Macoute, she'd be human. Prissy, school-marmish, but a good schoolmarm. Better than well trained, mechanically competent. Genuinely devoted to the children, to all children; quick, imaginative; loving to play with them, read to them, teach them. Leora knew that the children were absorbed, content. Missing her, of course. She ought to send them letters. They ought to send her letters.

Sitting at her dressing-table, Leora got an idea. Never mind speculating about Marika; why she wore the glasses and what would happen if she took them off. The problem was communication. If she could not reach the children, she was a dead stick and might as well go off and get drunk.

Leora stared around the bedroom. Her eye fell on one of Jim's scratch-pads that lay around everywhere, with his ever-ready ball-point pens. Finer points than her own fountain-pen. Thinking, fiddling with the objects on her dressing-table, she found her fingers nervously clipping and unclipping an old lipstick in a pretty, brightly-enamelled case.

To be sure, the whitejackets were forbidden in here. She wanted privacy, she had told the Doctor: she would borrow the vacuum-cleaner and do her own housekeeping, here and in the bathroom: he had agreed, bland as always. Him and his microphones!

But the French windows gave no protection unless shuttered. Jim might come clumping in for something he had forgotten. It was his 'short cut' across the terrace. Leora went into the bathroom, turned a tap to run on pairs of tights dumped in the washbasin, and sat down on the lavatory to think. She could clean out that old lipstick. She could tear off a strip of paper, write on it very small, roll it tight, pack it in the lipstick. A thing that might be thrown over a fence, put in a parcel, otherwise innocently conveyed. A thing like a toy, which would not attract attention. She could exchange information then, if Marika could be persuaded that the children ought, you know, to write letters to Mama and Papa now and again. She could write in Italian, which she had taught the children by speaking it with them, when they were little.

But there was no guarantee that Rika spoke no Italian, could not read between lines. And it took too long. A code was needed.

Leora got it in a flash – and the same moment burst into tears. It was hopeless. How to make the girls understand the code? How to make that first, vital contact? How to make them understand that in an old lipstick case (a projectile that could be fired from a crossbow) there was vital information to them only.

Disguised as a game, to be concealed artfully, in ways that children (bright, clumsy, vulnerable Harriet; careful, secret, pretty Cassy) were good at inventing. Tall, solid (Jim's build), corn-blonde (a surprise) Harriet. Finer-boned, auburn-haired (Jim's colouring), green-eyed (Harriet's were grey), silent Cass. Big noisy bossy-boots who knocked things over and was untidy, and small graceful faithful-follower, true and devoted, who never knocked anything over, was meticulously Jim-tidy, his pet and his poppet. One must love Harriet more because she felt unloved and neglected, and she was so pretty, so vulnerable, must be armed against a naughty world. She was far too open, too sensitive, too generous, too fatally bright: oh dear, send us good shteady shtupid girls; the bright ones suffer so.

Leora cried and cried, and then stopped, turned it off like a tap. Stupid women cried. Well, cried like they bled: one had to have a cry from time to time; it was meaningless; one just did it. Pay no attention to the imbecile bitch.

The Doctor wouldn't, she devoutly hoped. She was judged tame, castrated, deprived of ovaries. Spayed: fallopian tubes in a tight knot.

She turned off the other tap, which was splashing water about. Got her knitting and sat in the clean, aired living-room. Rang the bell and told the whitejacket to fetch her some whisky. Let them think she was a proper old drunk. Fuck Rika.

Yes. Maybe literally. I wouldn't be surprised if I found ways of getting Miss Dark Glasses to pull her knickers down, before I've finished with her. And fuck the Doctor too. More metaphorically, thanks. I would not hesitate, if I thought it would do me any good. He is not unattractive. Like Richard the Third, and 'I am rather inclined to suppose him a very respectable man' (wrote Jane Austen, showing, at the age of twelve, sound judgment).

Leora knitted furiously. The wool ran easily, the stitches not too tightly pulled, the needles relaxed and obedient: not the way they sometimes were, duelling life-and-death against one another like rapiers and the Cardinal's Guards. 'Don't fight with your knitting,' Jim said sometimes, in the time when he noticed such things.

I will carry that lipstick in my pocket. I will be alert. Sooner or later, the opportunity will come.

She took a big swallow of whisky. Suddenly she saw how it could be done.

It was the Greek alphabet, taught them as a game, when they caught mumps, and weren't ill, but restless and feverish, and demanding constantly to be amused. Alpha, I want a drink of lemonade. Alpha had been most used; Leora had made fresh lemonade, with brown sugar and peel, by the gallon; four litres at a time. Beta (in a natural sequence, quite as frequent), I am bursting to do pipi. Gamma, I will play with my dolly. Delta, I'd rather do a jigsaw. Epsilon, what time is it? Zeta, I want to look at the television (no, my eyes *don't* hurt): there'd been a lot of fights over that one. Eta, Theta . . . she had forgotten them now. But they'd easily be learned afresh.

She would use the letters as questions (on her side) and answers (on theirs).

Alpha: is Rika with you the whole day?

Beta: when she is not there (like when you have gone to bed) is there a man there?

Gamma: is this a man who does cooking, cleaning, janitoring? Is he old and quiet, or young and active? (One could use a double letter, too.)

Delta: are you locked in, at night?

Epsilon: if I give you this signal, you must be dressed and ready, because we are going to escape, when I give it. (That could be bettered. There were possibilities – a double or even triple letter. Harriet, quick like a knife, would understand instantly, and use the code inventively.) Leora's lips curved into a smile.

'Well,' said the Doctor, sailing in with his tuner set to 'bon-homie' and the speakers exuding geniality, 'it's your birthday, Jim.'

Mm: much as usual, the 'irony' button had been pushed in.

'That's nice,' said Jim scrambling up and dusting his hands: he had been sitting on the floor in a wilderness of electric cable, 'now let's see; what sign of the zodiac does that put me in?' And yes, there came Henry, in plain clothes like an off-duty cop, flatfooted and downcast as usual, bearing a heap of parcels but poorly cast as Santa Claus. Henry was never bonhomous.

'Your fancy high-fidelity set.' Dump bump; Henry in a bad mood was heavy-handed.

'Not all that high. Like I said, a commercial neutron-monitor . . .'

'And as I explained,' irony more pronounced than ever, 'I prefer not to draw conspicuous attention to our experiments in physics. But don't be disappointed: I have a lot of your electronic jiggers, including most of those you specified.'

'Umhum,' instantly absorbed, very much like a child with a new toy; at once like a nasty, spoilt child. 'An LRS amplifier would have been better.'

'Now now,' paternally benign, 'you asked for the Ortec

one. Also it was easier to get. The trouble I had getting that!'
pointing to the toy Jim was playing with, a metallic-blue box
with four sets of outlet points.

'Yes, well, the LRS stuff is better – my opinion. But this,'
picking up the red box, 'fits the standard NIM-bin – that's this'
– a larger, open box with no front and two handles to pick it
up by.

'Show me by all means; I don't pretend to any knowledge
of electronics.'

'I suppose that yes; it is a bit similar to a high-fidelity
set.' Jim was making a little drawing of a series of boxes
connected by a line.

'Start here, that's a PM – sorry, photo-multiplier tube,
those things we already have. Connected to plastic scintillator.
Sends signals here, to the amplifier, through here, that's the
discriminator, to here, the scaler.'

'The what?'

'The counting device. That gadget with the little numbers
on it which counts.' Now it was Jim's turn to play indulgent
parent, explaining to the small child. The Doctor selected the
'irritation' button to replace irony.

'Get on with it.'

'Very well,' said Jim, 'stop me if I use too much jargon. The
individual neutron light signals reaching the photo-multiplier
produce short avalanches of electrons, a signal which is
detectable as a negative electrical pulse at the last dynode of
the tube. This small signal is amplified to make it large enough
to handle. Small signals, often called grass – or simply garbage – are thrown out by the discriminator. Because we want
to know the rate at which neutrons are being counted, we
put in a scaler which can be started and stopped by electrical
timing signals and then re-set.'

'That's all perfectly clear,' with no irony at all.

'What's that?' Henry with bumps and grunts, indicative of
large package.

'Paraffin.'

'Yes, I'm not too convinced about the paraffin.'

'Beryllium takes too much time, even in limited quantities,
as I told you.'

'Yes; well, got to do a count on the bare elements of the core first, in any case: know more, then. Meanwhile, for lack of anything better as neutron monitor, here –' Jim made another little drawing, this time of a cylinder. 'That's an ordinary four-litre can – paint can. Fill it up with paraffin, leaving a hole of five centimetres diameter, and in there we put a PM tube, connected to a five-by-five chunk of scintillation plastic; right? PM is linked to our high-voltage source, in there. It'll all work, but,' with deep regret, 'I'd have liked a CAMAC system tied to a D.E.C. computer – the PDP-11/40. I didn't quite dare ask you for that.'

The Doctor began to laugh, with genuine enjoyment.

'If we had everything we wanted, Jim . . .' Irony button on again. 'Never mind, there are more toys to come.'

'Yes. But this is still an amateur arrangement.'

'Quite so, Jim – we are amateurs. Now here is the closed-circuit television scanner.'

'Right,' thoroughly dry, 'we're not giving the sex-education class. No rubber penis going into a vagina, but a bullet going into a uranium core. And we operate that from out here, behind all this concrete that's created so much mess. So that we view the sex act on television.' All these sarcasms are a bit heavy, Jim admitted to himself, but the bugger asks for it. 'What's this little parcel?' looking at the label, which said 'Gamma Industries'.

'Ah yes, of course.'

The parcel was heavy – lead-heavy.

'Neutron source of known strength: I want that, you see, to calibrate the instruments. And this?' A cardboard box.

'Having spent a great deal of money, I felt I could indulge in a real toy. But neither this nor the money are in the least grudged, Jim.'

He unwrapped the surprise. It was a Lehmann Grossbahn model-train set, the largest made. Jim gave a short laugh.

'Yes. As remote handling equipment goes it's hardly ideal. It's in fact clumsy and imprecise. But it's been used before, and can be again. We can use it to pull up this neutron source to where we need it, which is out of the lead and up to the paint can, and it could be used if I can find nothing better to drive – in the end – the critical assembly tester. We're not going to go Tuff-Tuff around the room, you know.'

'I had not supposed so.'

'What we'd do is take the shell off the locomotive, and solder the motor, with its wheels, to a flatcar. Then, let's see, we would take the track and cut the right-hand rail, the forward direction that is, through at intervals of about one centimetre. Power each tiny section individually. Anything continuous is far too dangerous. Our reverse on the other hand must be continuous, and instant. We might want it in a hurry.'

'How would you go about that?' interested.

'Connect each segment with a diode, permitting the current to run only one way; back of course and not forward. Connect each segment to a push-button – Henry the artist with the soldering-iron. The train rolls forward, and will push the penis into the vagina, but only discreet distances. Need to push the right button every time.'

'I see. Ingenious.'

'Not very,' shrugging. 'When we throw the reversing switch the entire track is at once live; the train takes off and retracts the plug. Controlled from back here, of course, and watched on the closed-circuit TV. What in fact we could do – have to do – is connect all this to our paint can: the monitoring system. The system can even be set to act as a security device: the moment it senses too high a neutron flux it will automatically throw the train into reverse. We're going to test all this,' twisting his hair, 'very carefully indeed.'

The Doctor said nothing. He was impressed, and indeed he looked it, though Jim, who was already wondering whether he couldn't do better than bullshitting about with model trains, didn't notice this.

Leora would have noticed it. She was, though, not present, being just then deeply absorbed in a security precaution of her own. Locked as it happened in the bathroom, experimenting on pieces of thin plastic sheeting pinched from Jim. An old lipstick case was barely rain-proof, and if she wrote on a paper in very tiny letters it was essential that nothing be blurred or spoilt. Taking pains, neat-fingered, patient, she went on working at heat-sealing plastic edges into a waterproof bundle, until she got it right. There was a horrid smell, and hardly any gas left in her lighter, but she did get it right. She did what she could about the smell, and hugged herself.

There was such a lot she needed to say, and not much space on a tiny roll of paper. Space enough for a message to an adult – but for children it had to be very simple, lucid, readily memorized. She was refining her alphabets, but she could only do this in the mornings, when she was left free, and then for short spaces of time. It wouldn't do to be caught by the whitejackets scribbling on bits of paper: worse still to be caught blushing, screwing them up and throwing them hastily into the fire.

Leora did notice, that very lunchtime, that the Doctor's attitude towards Jim had changed. It was Jim, now, who took command of this 'little amateur physics experiment'. He no longer sat dreaming idly over bits of paper. He knew, now, where he was going.

She went to call him at midday, for a drink. She was nervous at putting her nose round the door of the lab, or workshop, or whatever they called it. She called it the garage.

Narrower than it had been: that was the new concrete barrier. All the whitejackets busy as beavers for the last few days, trundling away with planks and wheelbarrows. There was a vast quantity of electrical work going on. The place was full of electronic gadgets such as she had seen in photographs, idly picking up the catalogues Jim left lying about. Bits of flex and screwdrivers were all over the floor, and on the floor sat Jim, trousers covered in cement dust, hair tousled, brandishing the soldering-iron.

'Under the pavement lies the beach,' joked Leora. One of the student slogans from the Paris riots of '68, passed into catchword vocabulary. Jim did not smile. He looked at her as though wondering who she was. She felt chilled through.

'You really look as though you could do with a drink.'
'Uh.'

'Mister, will you do something for my toaster which doesn't pop up?'

'Yes yes, I'm coming,' irritably. And as though seeing her for the first time. 'What are you doing here? I don't want you here.'

Even the Doctor had an unwonted air of excitement. And she'd noticed Henry, whose walk was a leisurely shamble like the Pink Panther, hurtling about like Speedy Gonzales.

'Must have an alarm,' Jim was saying, 'to ring bells or sirens or no matter what. Between the disc and the counter we put a splitter.' One hand was already feeling for a piece of paper while the other fished in his jacket pocket for ballpoints. 'Like this, a sort of Y-joint. One branch going to the scaler as before; the other to a thing called a current integrator, and thence to a charge threshold discriminator, and from there to an alarm.'

The Doctor was looking blank, as well he might.

'Well, as you recall the disc throws out all the rubbishy little signals, called for that reason garbage, and we're getting a count on the scaler. Now here we're running part of the signal off to something which, in essence, automatically tallies the count, over a hundredth of a second or any such number, and checks to see if the tally exceeds a threshold which we have pre-set as the danger level.'

'Absolutely,' said the Doctor, topping up with Noilly Prat. Hydrogen and helium, thought Leora. Carbon and cobalt. Those lovely elements. Arsenic and antimony. I wish I had a few critical masses of those around to distribute in selected coffee-cups.

As it sometimes does at the end of autumn, after the equinoctial storms of rain and wind, the weather turned perfect. Windless, cloudless days of rare peace and beauty, which are the most beautiful of all because fragile and brief. The winter is preparing, with such confidence and leisure that everybody knows it will be long and hard. In the forest country smoke climbs from the chimneys in a thin madonna-blue line, perfectly straight, and the hawks wheel in long spirals through a vast pale sky. On the upland meadows the sun lies amazingly hot, sherry-coloured. In the valleys the dense evergreens smoke with evaporation. In the hanging woods the beech leaves, clinging tenaciously to the tree, are baked crisp like brandy-snaps. The last blackberries taste of wine and dew. There are nile-green, lemon, lilac sunsets. The dew is thick and heavy as a bison. At night through the still woods you hear the deer belling.

The exploring stage had passed and they possessed six or seven practised and familiar walks: they paused to examine a recognized landmark with a new, severer eye, judging a rock or a tree uprooted in last year's gales (the twisting root-mass dried and stylized) for its lines and proportions; no longer a picturesque feature in a romantic landscape but a drawing by a minor master: sometimes an etching by a major master, a stump and a bramble as Biblical as Rembrandt's old women.

That afternoon Leora and Jim climbed through the beech hanger to the ridge they had discovered which gave the best view; in shirtsleeves, their anorak sleeves tied round their waists. They sat on old stumps split and silvered by the weather, in the clearing at the top. Leora took her boots off and toasted her toes: Jim studied the elegant parasols of mushrooms which might be amanitas. Small animals had nibbled them but to conclude, he suspected, that this made them safe for humans was a myth. They had made the climb in almost total silence. It was steep as a downhill ski-run; a slope of eight hundred metres as he judged over a distance of say three and a half kilometres. They were used to it by now, no longer arrived puffed and sweaty, but ready to rest for a perfect half hour. Everything that was mundane could be left behind. For five minutes one thought of nothing at all, save stretching and loosening the muscles, in shoulder, calf, abdomen. Then one could think. Not of mechanical details, but of things in their purity. Physics or metaphysics; where was the boundary, up here? No slop about transcendental meditation, no self-hypnotizing repetition of platitudes packaged as mantras. Look at patterns of things, observant, concentrated. Listen to Mozart and feel joy at things inevitable, predicted. Jim, most unusually, meditated.

How high are we – eleven, twelve hundred metres? It is late, surely, for butterflies. Are they an aesthetic flourish, a useless, therefore necessary generosity in a Japanese landscape (what makes it Japanese? The height? The clear air?), or can they have a biological use? Is there some Alpine plant that would be pollinated, impregnated at this season? Why do I know so little?

Did Mozart take an interest? Did he make scrambling walks on the hills surrounding Salzburg? Did he know it all, instinctively, when he put his hands on the keyboard or picked up that tiny, touching, child's fiddle? Tiresome Leopold, boring Anna. Miserable, frustrating existence. What was the line Leora quoted from her annoying Auden? 'Indulged in toilet humour with his cousin, And had a pauper's funeral in the rain.'

In those stuffy rooms were there pale mauve flowers with slender bare stalks, and thirty or more little white butterflies at a time? How did one look at such a person, to apprehend him? Why is Mozart? Why are snowflakes six-sided? Why do crystals? Here one did not worry. One trusted. Fulminating energy all about one. 'This energy we call divine.' Spinoza, he thought. Never read him. Doubtless, never would. Was that bad? Had Mozart read him?

What's creation? Is it the conversion of one energy into another? Why was there a curve in the energy of the elements' nuclei and electrons, so that the energy was greatest at the two extremities of the lightest and the heaviest? One had learned how to bring about the fission of a heavy one: it was quite easy, a simple experiment in physics, and he was going to do it. The fusion in a light element like hydrogen was much much more difficult. No Heath-Robinson messing in garages would apply, there. Perhaps, some day . . . With a simple, efficient implosion gadget, hardly bigger than an orange. What a tool we possess! And how little we do with it. Threatening to hit people on the head, which made as much sense as using a diamond to tip an arrow-head. Digging, at best, dim-witted holes in the ground.

Well, perhaps this idiotically clumsy bow-and-arrow of mine, for whatever futile purpose that diplodocus of a Doctor has in his tiny skull, will waken the sluggards out of their apathy. People are astoundingly crass! He wants to pop this gadget, on the top of Mount Palomar or wherever, with maximum publicity, for monomaniac purposes of his own. But that very publicity ... He hasn't thought it out. Neither have I. We've both got a long way to go. Beware of euphoria, on this humming, sleepy hill top.

'Good up here, isn't it?' he said aloud.

'Yes,' said Leora. 'One doesn't think about torture or blackmail or kidnapped children. That's down there in the valley.'

Jim gave her a look of rage. Tactless bitch, who'd never yet learned when to keep her mouth shut.

It was striking how accidents of contour could create a whole micro-climate within a few hundred square metres. A slope going the wrong way, so that only the morning sun reached it, struck chill at once. A crinkle in the hillside, no more than twenty metres wide, got no sun at all, and the undergrowth was swathed in condensed icy moisture. They were not only glad of anoraks but wished they had brought sweaters. Coming out into the sunshine and dry slippery grass of the meadow was disconcerting: they had the feeling they were 'home'. Living in the mountains gives these sudden small pleasures and pinches.

It seemed to have infected everyone. The ratty whitejacket who generally served dinner, the one with slicked-back grey hair on a funny round skull, made jokes in his stiff German: the Doctor was positively genial. Leora felt positively friendly towards the governess. Jim was positively talkative; all about stars. Leora supposed there was nothing surprising in this. She recalled reading that the phenomenon was frequent among people held hostage by terrorist groups for any length of time. A lot of information has become available on the subject, and the shrinks have wise explanations for it. Psychological dependance. She felt sure that the Doctor had read the reports, and planned accordingly. No need for brainwashing or abominable tortures. We all become pals.

The weather must have something to do with it, because

94

by unspoken accord between the four of them they moved out after dinner. The Doctor was the first to complain that the room was stuffy, to draw back the heavy velvet curtains and unbolt the window, and let in a great gush of the marvellous-smelling night air.

'I say,' with his strange accent that wasn't quite Oxford (Jim's theory was that he might have studied there as an overseas scholar or postgraduate), 'just look at those stars.' A tremendous blaze filled the entire sky. 'Let's see, now where's Orion? We ought to see him.' Suddenly he and Jim were like two schoolboys, excited.

'Down in the ping-pong room – you know, where the garden furniture is stored – get two deck-chairs ... I've no telescope alas, but I've a good pair of night-glass binoculars from Zeiss; I'll get them, shall I?'

'Yes of course, and a couple of old rugs – keep the dew off.'

The two women looked at one another and smiled, impulsively.

'Let's get our coats.'

Leora's 'winter coat': they had never been able to afford a fur. But warm wool, with a good classic cut; she'd rather that than a cheap fur. Didn't like pallid imitations of Anna Karenina ... Rika's was a striped poncho which looked Peruvian, didn't mean she was Peruvian, since one could buy them anywhere in Europe. Probably meant she was anything but, Leora said when she laid eyes on it (rather nice, in narrow stripes of orange, yellow and burnt sienna), to which Jim replied that this in turn meant that quite possibly she was Peruvian; didn't Leora agree there was Indian blood in the features? No, Leora didn't, crossly, and couldn't care less into the bargain. Anyway, she wore a long close coat of thickly-woven cotton, printed with a traditional Persian motif ('off the mosque in Tashkent or wherever') and in this she looked Assyrian ...

They had to change their shoes, too. By this time the men were installed on the side terrace, deck-chairs stretched to horizontal, swathed in picnic-rugs, passing the binoculars from hand to hand, muttering excitedly. Jim's voice had its blackboard-and-chalk note. 'Now count two spaces to the left and at ten o'clock that's Vega.'

The women climbed the steps around the corner of the house, up to the back terrace, where the rose garden was, another flight to the high terrace – sundial, herb borders – cut out of the hillside, backed with a stone wall, full of rock-plants. From here on it was meadow, steps constructed of spruce logs, cut to width and pegged at each corner. The staircase led up through the meadow to the evergreens; the forbidden territory. With a kind of tact they turned away from that quarter to look at the house, now below them; roof-slope and chimney-stacks outlined black against the blaze of a clear night. They agreed that it wasn't cold at all, that it might seem cold at this height, or that it was cold in contrast to the warm day. Maybe one wasn't accustomed to the hill climate, and when winter came, which it would, suddenly, soon now, it would be really cold. For sure, there would be snow in December. Those rose-bushes would need protecting from the frost. Rhododendrons and azaleas were naturally hardy, weren't they? Himalayan, surely. Social chat. A tiny silence.

'It was the most marvellous day.' Rika, timid. 'The children were out on the grass in swim-suits, quite without risk.'

'I've been meaning to ask you – I should write them a letter, you know. They'd think it very odd if I didn't. And I believe they ought to write to me: I hope you'll agree.'

'I'd thought about that. I don't think there's any great snag, though I'll have to ask the Doctor. I'm afraid I'd have to censor it. Look,' with a rush, wanting not to spoil the first natural moment the two enjoyed, 'I don't want . . . I'll ask you to choose your wording carefully, and leave the envelope open, I'm sure I won't have to alter anything. I can say it was enclosed in a note to me.'

'Now I think of it, they can write first. I'll tell them to-morrow. You'll know what to say then. I had to invent, you understand . . . details, why they hadn't seen you. Goodness,' wanting to change the subject, 'I'd like to spend a winter here. I'd be ready to regret' – subjective – 'that it won't be long now.'

Jim's voice, lecturing, floated up from twelve metres below.

'Rigel . . . Arcturus . . . Damn that hillside; cutting off a whole interesting area. Down there on the horizon – Mars.'

'I know Jim's getting on like a house on fire,' said Marika, wanting to sound light. 'I don't know the details, but the Doctor is pleased, no, that sounds like patting you on the head, forgive me. I know how hard it is – do please believe, I understand. Try and understand me. There are things I believe in down to my roots, I can't put them into words. I know you think me a lunatic, fanatic, but you must realise it isn't hardness, nor cruelty.'

Leora had her hands in her pockets to keep them warm. She clenched her arms and hugged her body tightly, with a shiver. Her mouth felt paralyzed.

'I shouldn't have spoken,' said Marika, 'and whatever I say sounds awful. Somehow I'm not sorry I did.'

'A black hole,' Jim was saying.

'I'm all right,' said Leora abruptly, 'and I trust you. Not only that I have to. Women are pretty tough, I think, tougher than men. I suffer, I feel pain. So do you. But I manage. It's Jim I'm anxious about. He's pretty worked up.'

'I know. It's natural I suppose – in a physicist.'

'I've seen something like it before. Never this deep. We've drifted apart – no, that's not the right way of putting it. A sort of chasm, not wide, but deep. This is earthquake country.'

'The split will heal,' gently, 'and it will all be effaced.'

'I dare say you're right. He won't tell me what he thinks. He looked at me with hatred today. He is much alone, and he's off balance. I want to say – my turn to sound silly – he needs someone to feel confidence in. Too much solitude – I can stand it; he can't. At present, and I say this without self-pity, he feels closer to you than to me. You must realize this; realize that I understand it, am not furious or jealous. Try and show him some . . . camaraderie . . . He's, you know, attracted towards you; physically, I mean . . .'

'I've noticed,' unhappily. 'I don't want to cause you more pain'.

'No, I've accepted it. I'm detached. I'm thinking in terms of – oh, I hate the stupid word – therapy.'

'Well,' uncertainly, 'I'll do what I can. You'll write that letter?'

'I'm getting chilled. Let's go in, and have a brandy.'

Something lingered through the next day, something Leora could not put a name to. Not peace, certainly, nor tranquillity beyond the still splash of sunlight. Not friendship nor comradeship-in-adversity: absurd by definition, as well as cliché. Conceivably a drawing-together; not of four people sharing a purpose or 'seeing this through together.' But masks had been dropped. Marika, and the Doctor, were no longer fiercely-painted witchdoctors that glared, unwinkingly menacing, from the edge of the clearing in the rain-forest; or dolls dangling, barring the forbidden paths of the sacred wood. But human beings, like themselves.

And so it was through to the morning, which was Sunday. Until the scream. Scream, the most abominable sound Leora had ever heard. As when a sheet of fabric is ripped across, but a living fabric, that of a living human being.

PART THREE

'The Core'

'The bolt slides in its groove . . .'

A memory struck Leora on waking: a Simenon book full of the special quality of Sunday. The air is different.

That was a platitude here, at the other end of the earth to Hamburg! It strikes one first thing, in the hills. The air is cleansed and filtered by the patient trees which swallow the vile smells of cities; diesel oil and frying fat, cooked dust and fermented garbage; and water so fouled that only the carrion eel will survive.

But the forest is a sounding-board for noise, and the far-off plane or helicopter as cruel as the chain-saw. The ear has no expensive discriminator, laboriously filtering the unwanted signals out of Jim's electronic instruments. In cities we have lost up to half of our hearing, in the woods we can no longer hear the small sounds, and the desert is no more a garden of Allah.

On a Sunday morning early the backyard of Boeing recaptures a pale ghost of purity. In the hills the air's fabric has something of the earlier vastness and frailty.

Here too there was a 'Sunday Observance'. Leora woke to a tiny church bell, far down the valley, instead of the thick murmur of a commercial flight that was regular at seven every morning. No army jets today either (there is cynicism in their vulgar names; Phantoms, Mirages). No lament of power-saws eating trees. Just occasional rifle fire from the week-end hunters, made trivial by moisture, as though a match was snapped across. Even the dyspeptic moan of the vacuum-cleaner would be spared them today: the whitejackets only tidied in a languid fashion, and when Leora came out yawning knotting the sash of her robe, alerted to breakfast-time by the crash of a basket of logs, the fire was lit, early

99

because of 'Sunday', crackling, sweet-smelling. And for once Jim did not shoot out at the crack of dawn to tinker at his horrible toy train. He deigned to have breakfast with her, although his beastly scribbling pad was handy by the plate, with figures and symbols of her private Greek alphabet (she felt cross, as though he had stolen it from her) mixed up indigestibly with marmalade. She preferred the old slide-rule days to that stupid black box, the calculator he always toted about, slung at his hip in a leather carrier, badge of office, like a country sheriff with a forty-five gun.

Sunshine tempted her out, to the back terrace. The mulberry tree, nearly leafless, still threw spangled shadows over the corner where in summer the picnic table stood. She took one of the star-gazers' deck-chairs that had not been tidied away, and a treasure of the owner's library; the bound *National Geographic* collections (she had reached nineteen-forty and there was a Ford in her Future, and Packard, Nash, Hudson-Terraplane. She was dallying with the pleasure of a flying-boat. Or perhaps the Blue Train?).

The Doctor waved to her with a happy smile. He was the landed proprietor today, in corduroy trousers and old leather gloves. The dew on the steps would soon be rime: he had pruned the roses, and she strolled over to look. He would take a barrow, he said, to the forest for a few sacks of leafmould, and cut armfuls of young spruce branches to protect the bushes from the frosts of December. He hoped for a good fall of snow early. That would keep things warm and protected from wind, and snow was 'the poor man's fertilizer'.

Jim, annoyingly, had played deaf to her suggestion that he come out into the Sunday air. Stretched out horizontal, holding up the magic box and ministering to it, grunting and taking ball-points out of his teeth and scribbling the o p e n s e s a m e that winked in the little windows. Very wrong and wicked of Leora, very regressive and reactionary to look at perilous seas forlorn in back numbers of the *National Geographic*. She refused to feel guilty. Let other pens dwell on guilt and misery: ah, clever Jane. Leora was drinking a pisco sour, a thing she had always wanted to try, on the terrace at Vina Del Mar near Valparaiso when the scream came.

She rushed fluttering to the corner of the house. The Doctor jumped down the slippery steps like a cat. Jim's face showed at the French window from the bedroom, looking like grey putty squeezed in the glazier's fist. He threw his arm at her.

'Get back. Get back.' They crashed in at the door of the garage. There was a horrible pause while she heard them shouting in indistinct mumbles and her heart flopped and lurched and tied to tear loose, a fish in a net, and suddenly a whitejacket stood holding her upper arm, gripping firmly. Bumps and thuds, a man in a coffin already nailed down, banging the skin off his knuckles, kicking the nails off his toes, buried still alive. The Doctor, livid, appearing in the doorway, a vein in his temple beating, his gardening gloves still on. He saw the whitejacket standing sentry ready for orders, stripped his glove, dived a hand in his breeches' pocket, came up with a shiny bunch of keys, tossed them through the air, jerked out, 'Get Rika.' The whitejacket caught the keys, started up the steps at once. The Doctor stared at Leora.

'She's a nurse. She can at least . . .' He checked, said controlledly, 'Go, my girl, go. Nothing you can do.' She stood rooted. 'Vanish!' he shouted in a hoarse soprano, ducked his head down between his shoulders, pushed himself back into the worskhop.

'Jim – Jim!' screamed Leora. At that moment he appeared, dragging the Doctor with him, holding him by both wrists.

'All right, woman, I'm not touched,' harsh and stiff. He let the Doctor go. 'I've got it right back – it's safe now. But he – God – the neutrons.' They stood together panting, two wrestlers. 'Help me lift him,' said Jim. He looked up at Leora as though over a gunsight. 'Fuck off,' he said. Leora, standing amazed, turned and ran.

Without knowing where she was going, instinctively, she ran away from the house. Up the steps, past the roses, up to the top terrace, up the far side, up the wooden treads of the hill path. Perhaps it was sheep-flight, since the whitejacket had run this way. Or was it the shelter of the trees? An instinct to run to Rika for reassurance? She stumbled on the rounded, slippery logs that were both tread and riser, she stubbed her toes – she was in soft moccasins that gave no purchase. She was among the maples, on the still, innocent hillside. She ran on like a deer but stopped in the evergreens, close cypress and juniper, a green wall. She caught her breath, swallowing hard against burning throat and bumping chest, tore off a branch of something resinous, fragrant and sticky; drank the pungent smell.

In front of her the stiff fence came together in a narrow rectangle; a gate. The interior of the rectangle was blank; the gate was open.

She scrambled, ran, was through, scrambled again, stopped. She was at the far edge of the dense evergreens. In front of her was a belt of fragile birch and larch, and grass. There was no more cover. Voices pattered down along the grass, urgent and excited. Leora jumped back among the cypresses, went on her knees, hid. The voices came on, went past; a language she could not understand. Nobody had noticed her. She stood up, stepped out on to the path, walked on. The path was levelling out now at the top of a rise. Leora crouched at the extremity of the bare larches, her fingers on sun-warmed flags. The flagstones ran between mown grass to a chalet of logs. To her dream-house. The house was set cornerwise; no window overlooked her; it faced south to the sun and the slope to the forest beyond, utterly private. It was not thirty metres away: she ran on tiptoe, silent.

At the corner she crouched again. Beyond was a terrace of smooth varnished boards, a verandah, half covered by deep overhanging eaves. Sliding glass patio doors to the inside, standing open. She felt nakedly exposed to a thousand eyes, but there was no one. Then there was a splash, and a child's voice. Harriet's voice. It said, 'Don't splash, cretin.' Querulous, rather sharp. And Cassy, small and put-upon (pretending to be, rather) saying, 'Well, you pushed.'

The children were there. There in the pool. Six paces away. Her heart no longer beat; her breath and pulse were suspended. She climbed on the verandah. Absurdly she looked for cover, like Gary Cooper after that first treacherous shot from ambush: instead of handy barrels she found a rattan armchair with canvas cushions and tucked herself behind it.

Make her invisible, keep out bullets. She laid a palm on the warm boards: the planking was smooth, tongue-and-grooved, designed for bare feet; it was comforting. The other hand touched a mass of something woolly, pricked itself on a spike. Startled, she glanced down. Rika's knitting . . . She felt in her pocket for the lipstick and clenched her sweaty fist upon it.

Was there a whitejacket on guard? Surely Rika had run off in too much of a hurry. The longer you leave it the harder it gets: she edged to the corner of the door frame, fearful of a cast shadow, of a child looking up and going wide-eyed and letting out a huge yell . . .

Water-reflections danced in front of her eyes, mixed with a small girl, body all stomach and no hip, in a bright-patterned swim-suit.

Now she could understand the architecture. The summerhouse was one big room. The whole thing was designed with a deliberately sophisticated simplicity. A 'camping' holiday for children . . . No furniture: some bar stools, and a few more of the rattan chairs. The simple cooking, the still simpler housekeeping, was done by Rika herself. With a whitejacket to ferry her daily supplies, life was easy to organize. It was meant to be: the owners had only come up here to swim, sunbathe.

Still, she couldn't tell for sure. There might be a flat-eyed whitejacket with a gun lurking behind that door.

'Children,' she said in a hissed whisper, making a frightful face, holding a rigid hand edgewise upon her lips, shaking the other like a demented penguin's flipper, to enjoin silence. They stood paralysed and stared with enormous eyes. It was their mother all right, but suddenly turned bright green.

'I can't stay long. She will be back. Don't stop playing: don't come near me.' She hadn't any speech prepared; she could only jerk out a disjointed gabble. They might not even understand. But it would sink in later. There was the message; there was the message . . . All in the lipstick, prepared for just this moment.

'We are all right; we're fine. But we're prisoners, just like you: I mustn't be caught, so I must be very quick. Here is a message – inside this. It says everything. Read it, learn it,

103

destroy it, above all don't let her see it. You haven't seen me: go on playing as though I'd never come.' You fool, stop gibbering: that's all in the letter. 'I'll try and write and then you write back.' God, she wished she could say something sensible, but she felt so naked here, stuck up on this verandah, visible like the Scarlet Letter from a mile off. 'No, don't come over, I must run, but we're there, we love you, we think of you always, we'll get you out.' We! What we? Me! 'I can't stop, a huge kiss, and remember – you haven't seen me or heard me, but it's all there. 'Bye . . .' She blew two kisses, ducked back, ran bent-legged off the verandah scuttling idiotically like Groucho Marx. But she heard the thrown lipstick. It rolled trundling across the planks and the tiled surround, rolled too far, fell in the pool with a plop. Damn, thought Leora, until she remembered that it was sealed with plastic against just such a catastrophe. There was no catastrophe. Nobody was here. The last thing she heard was the messy schlumph of Harriet diving into the pool after the lipstick. She ran madly back for the shelter of the trees.

In the blessed evergreens she pulled up panting, heart again thumping, and told herself what an idiot she'd been. There was no guard. Rika would not be back for ages. They were in a flat spin down there. There'd been a horrible accident, with those radioactive materials. She didn't know how, and didn't want to. It hadn't been Jim, it hadn't been Jim . . .

I could have taken the children right then – now – escaped now; this minute. No, I couldn't . . .

Leora dared not go back; she felt utterly paralysed. Cursing her own cowardice – Rika wouldn't be back for half an hour. Instantly she began to create excuses for herself. Rika had left the gate open in her haste, and she would remember, and come back quicker. She would not want to leave the children for any length of time, first aid or no first aid. One could not have escaped anyhow. It may seem sunny and warm momentarily, but in the world it's November, it's cold. One can't run around the place with two little girls in dripping-wet swim-suits. It would take far too long to dry them and dress them.

Suppose I'd been able to steal a car?

Some hope! As though they left cars standing about with the keys in the ignition-lock ...

But I may never have another opportunity ... You will, she told herself. You will. You'll make one. No prison is so tight. You've just had the proof.

Get out of here, you stupid cow, before she really does come whizzing back, and locks that gate after her. A nice pickle you'd be in then! She dragged herself up, knees watery, calf muscles twitching as though she'd just been racing on Nordic skis. Pay no heed, Leora. You've only to slip back and keep off the path on the far side. Just slide unobtrusively down the steep part, through the maple grove. If anyone notices you, well, your distraught look and dishevelled appearance is nothing too weird. You were frightened: Jim bawled at you, told you to fuck off. You did just that. You ran, and then you stupidly ricked an ankle.

Leora turned the corner of the cypresses and came slap up against the gate.

It was shut and locked.

Oh God. After all that. The cool bitch; the thinking, re-membering, level-headed, child-psychologist bitch. After all that.

Or the whitejacket – he'd had the Doctor's keys: he'd recalled instructions, he'd come back for the bars and bolts – and the switch for the electricity ... What did it matter anyhow? She was properly done for now. Leora sank down on her hunkers, in the wet undergrowth at the side of the path, and put her face in her hands. After all that ...

'Hallo, Leora. Are you all right?' A very quiet voice. Five minutes, ten, fifteen later; she couldn't tell, except that she was too stiff to get up and her bottom was soaking wet. Rika's voice. Gentle, not vicious; not exactly warm either, but with no cruelty in it. Leora looked up, wiped her stained face with her wet dirty hands, stared blankly, despairingly at Rika unlocking the gate.

Rika walked the two steps upward, bent, put her hands under Leora's armpits, lifted her to her feet, felt the seat of her trousers.

'You're soaked. You've been sitting there some time . . .'

'Yes,' with a last racking sob.

'All the time?' thoughtfully.

'I don't know. I think so.'

'I see. You were badly frightened. So were we all. It's over now.'

'Jim?'

'Jim's all right. He wasn't touched. But Henry . . . When I missed you I thought you must have run this way.'

'Yes. To be near the children. It's instinct.'

'Yes,' gently. 'Did you go all the way?'

'Only to those trees – to the clearing. And then when I looked – then I thought no, that I mustn't, that something horrible would happen to them, too.'

'Yes. That would alas be possible. Listen carefully to me, Leora. I mean you no harm. But this is very serious. Did you go to the house?'

'No. I was terrified.'

'Understand, I can't ask the children whether they've seen you. You're supposed to be many miles away, at Doctor Sebregt's clinic. But I will know, if the children have seen you. Or if you have spoken to them. Children cannot keep that sort of secret. And then it would be very serious – for you. Can I trust you?'

'Yes. I didn't go. I – I wanted to. But it was too great a risk. I saw you pass down. I hid in the wood. Then there was nothing to do but wait for you.'

'I see. I realized when I was halfway down that I hadn't closed the gate. I was . . . in a panic . . . too. So that I understand why you were foolish. But – you were wise again?'

'I couldn't do anything to put the children at risk – you ought to know that.' She started to cry again. Rika held her with the firm muscular body which smelt clean, but of fear and sweat. I must stink, myself . . . Rika comforted her for a second before saying: 'I can see you're telling the truth. Come on down now. I'll take you. I'm not angry. I'll explain to the Doctor. He'll agree, I hope, that perhaps there's no great harm done . . . He can be severe . . . still . . . what you need first is to get out of those sopping things and have a bath, or you'll catch a bad chill. I'd help you, but I must explain to the Doctor, and I must get back to the children. They were playing quite happily, but if I'm away too long they'll miss me.'

'Was the accident – I mean was the man . . .?'

'He was badly burned, yes.' There were moments when one reached behind the dark glasses, and touched this young woman, and then the visor came down with a snap and the armour was again total.

'Is he . . .?'

'Yes he is. I do not like to see pain. Nor will I willingly inflict pain.'

They went down the steps. Jim was nowhere to be seen. In the living-room the Doctor was standing by the window on the north side, as though he had been there some time, doing nothing; looking out, his face lit by the strong light. He turned as they came in, every movement controlled. He studied her.

'You added to our anxieties,' he said at last.

'There's something to be said further, perhaps,' said Marika. 'She's shocked, and I'd really like to see her in bed.'

'You've time?' He considered it. 'Very well, you'll find me upstairs.' He turned and went out. I suppose it's true, thought Leora, I am suffering from shock, I'm beginning to feel so numb and don't-care. But I'm in possession of my faculties, thanks. What I have to do is hold the woman up for as long as I can. Give Harriet a chance . . . Giddy-headed thing she is, but not dumb; not dumb. I'm soppy at the knees, but it hasn't reached my head yet. Lie down, said the executioner to Socrates, and the hemlock will take effect quicker. But we owe an offering, first. Let's try to pay our debts.

Marika piloted her into the bedroom and began undressing her with firm nurse's fingers while the bath was running, helped her climb in, which she did unsteadily, hemlocked to mid-thigh. I'll be back in a few minutes, she said.

Leora felt sleepy now. I don't have to fake a thing, she thought. I want to fall in bed and let events take their course. That man is frightened, and in consequence very angry. My life, perhaps, is going to finish here. And I don't care. I don't

107

care about anything any more. If I thought it would hold that woman up, I don't know what I mightn't do. I wish Jim were here.

Perhaps she did fall asleep for a minute, because she thought Jim was there, but it was Rika again, the glasses like two black lamps gazing down at her.

'Can you manage? Clasp your hands behind my neck.'

Hemlock to the neck, now. Head barely functioning. She got a grip with wet hands. Rika took hold of her, heaved, reached for all the towels she could grab without letting Limplegs tumble over backwards.

She caught sight of her face in the glass. Why is that stupid grin pasted on it?

Marika wound her up in towels and they progressed woodenly as far as bed. Warm, damp, ready to die.

'Sleep,' said Rika and left her alone. She was grateful.

She wanted to sleep, but couldn't; the hemlock refused to go further. She managed to unlock cramped legs and stretch them out. Breathe deeply, she told herself. In the stomach hard knots of fear. Rika would be back with the children, looking sharply at them, their behaviour. She would search. The towel was damp and knotted in a lump; Leora pulled at it until it came apart, pressed at the cramp where her ribs divided.

She won't; doesn't know what to search for. That there is anything to search for. I managed to keep that from everyone, even Jim. Now my life is in that man's hands. Even more, perhaps, in Harriet's.

Leora tried to make her stomach loose by rubbing in a circle with her palm. I wish Jim were here. He'd do this better than me. He's working somewhere, still functioning, not at the end yet of his tether.

Fantasy gripped her. Now had it been Jim there, hit by nervous exhaustion and delayed shock, he'd have been pleased to clasp his hands round her neck. So would she.

This is a stupid fantasy. I am not in the least lesbian and nor is she. She's a nurse.

Might it have been, despite all this, pleasant?

Stop that, you idiot. You wish Jim were here and he isn't.

I don't know what I wish, but I must get rid of this because it's ripping me up.

Mean miserable climax. As long as it will let me now go to sleep.

Lump of lead. Block of uranium.

Jim came in an hour later, plodding heavily. He closed the French window and bolted it, with a vague feeling of bolting himself away, or was it bolting away the most appalling moment he'd ever lived through? Didn't know. Didn't much care, any longer.

Leora was deeply asleep, in bed. Good for her! Or well for her, whichever it might be. She could sleep! He wished he could . . .

Oh well, poor bitch. She didn't know anything about what they'd gone through that day. She didn't understand the first thing. But she had been mortally scared and he understood – she thought that he was touched too, by the flash of lightning. It wasn't in the least like a flash of lightning. No bang, no smell – well, there was a smell, the too-famous 'smell of ozone', but that was a thing for journalists. Put a level of radioactivity abruptly over the top and a great many things happen very fast. One simplifies, for journalists. And one doesn't want the public – Leora, roughly – to know. Because if they knew . . .

It was long past drinks time. Past lunch time. He didn't want to eat, but he'd better eat something. Because he was now going to have a drink. Several drinks. No, don't be idiotic. One socking drink. Where was the Doctor? The Doctor had behaved well. He had had, maybe, a few drinks too by now. Didn't want to show it. And there was a disposal problem . . . Thanks, I don't want to know about that. I've enough on my plate.

The fire had been allowed to go out; proof enough if one were wanted that the whitejacket brigade had its routine abruptly jangled. Not that it was cold, since the radiators were on anyway, but he felt cold. His feet were like blocks of ice. He rang the bell, abruptly. A whitejacket appeared, the usual one, the 'house boy'.

109

'I want a very big whisky. Put a lot of ice in.' He didn't want it to paralyse him. 'And the fire's out,' irritably. 'It's freezing in here. Move your butt.'

'Would you like anything to eat, sir?'

'Yes. No. Yes,' bored with the question.

'Soup? A scrambled egg? The Doctor asks to be excused. But that is what he asked for, in his room.'

'Anything you please.'

Even under well-controlled conditions, in the old days (all professionals, now, surrounded themselves by a doubled and tripled barrier of security precaution, only too painfully aware of the lessons learned the hard way), there had been accidents.

Best known, here in Europe – it had been well publicized, and years after, when the public had been judged sufficiently informed to stand for it they'd even made a television documentary. Which he'd seen. And shrugged at. But he remembered it now. Accidental cock-up at a nuclear pile in Yugoslavia. Had been a glitch on some quite simple experiment of measurement. Quantifying something: details of that had been fudged, naturally, just as they'd fudged over what actually happened. They'd written it up as an instrument failure probably, whereas it had been much more likely a human error: somebody had been careless. Five men and a girl, if he recollected right, had been burned, pretty badly. Badly enough. They'd turned, sensibly, the affair into an 'errand of mercy' job: the hospitals in Yugoslavia hadn't the facilities for treatment. They'd flown them to Paris and operated on them there: the classic bone-marrow graft. Been pretty far gone. One had died. The others, less close to the source, had lost their hair (a polite gloss over a few other things; losing one's hair is enough to give the public the necessary creeps). Been just a good exercise in solidarity and a good medical effort. One of the French doctors, short of donors in that group, had given spinal marrow himself and quite rightly and well, the Yugoslavs had made a 'Thank you, France' out of it.

But he himself remembered, as did everyone who had ever worked in the States, the first 'classic accident' which had made history like Doctor Crippen. The Case of Louis Slotin. So similar to this. It 'couldn't happen now' – and yet it had, in just such another amateur, show-off, cocked-up way.

It had been long before his time, so that he knew little of the background, but it had happened in the 'forties, in the 'heroic', 'pioneer' days of the Manhattan Project. Before they knew Enrico Fermi was a gone goose from all the slow burns he'd taken. A technician – and a good one, surely. He'd done the experiment many times, the classic old tickle of the dragon's tail; the bringing slowly, ever-so-slowly together of two spheres of bare U, which would together make a crit. mass and boy, watch those needles jump. It had been some public relations job, probably for a crowd of Pentagon brass anxious to see for themselves, in perfect safety ha ha, how their new toy would pop. No no, it won't *pop*, have no fear. It'll just go not-quite-crit, and Lou here has done this magic parlour trick lots of times; he's the boy for this catchpenny little demonstration.

Call it what you please, a contemptuous vanity or self-sufficiency. So easy to make the neck-hairs bristle on a few of these bone-headed West-Pointers. Of course, there'd been a remote-control mechanism. But Lou had chosen to go ho-ho-watch-me-juggle; direct, by simply turning two screwdrivers.

One did not speak of him without respect, whatever his fault. Such a small fault, for so great an error. And the man had paid the biggest price he had. The two masses had touched. Slotin – no, one did not call that courage, one called that devotion – showed his worth. There were only clichés; crap like true blue. He interposed his body and separated the masses with his bare hands.

Nobody knew what Henry had done, because nobody had been there. Now – oh, now; that could be disregarded; that is delayed shock and nervous reaction – Jim was still trembling with sheer rage. He threw back the colossal whisky and poured another jaggedly on to the remains of the old ice, bottle bumping on the lip of the glass, muttering, glaring and grimacing like a chimpanzee smacked for bad manners at the tea-party. Fucking cretin.

Obstinacy? Stupidity? A bumbling wish to be helpful or clever or get a medal? Leave him quiet: requiescat in pace.

111

And yet – frustration swelling the veins in Jim's neck – he'd told the bugger clearly enough.

They'd wired up the toy train, used it to tow the neutron source. Jim had been quite flatly dissatisfied and said so loudly. It worked, yes, and whoever had told the Doctor that one could use it hadn't been that far off the beam; early experiments had used toy trains. But Jim had said loud and clear that it wasn't good enough for him. He'd thought of a way which would take longer, but be safer. The lathe had an automatic feed: right, they'd cut screw threads. They'd put the cylinder in the jaws at the right-hand end, and replaced the tool assembly with a mechanism to drive the plug. Meanwhile, of course, the advance could be worked by hand; they'd done just that using a dummy plug.

And this morning, while Jim was not even there, Henry . . . And in God's name, why? Henry was not given to excesses of zeal. Had he had some secret instruction from the Doctor? That seemed preposterous. And the Doctor had shown courage as well as startled horror. This lightning had struck out of a blue sky for him, too. Well, they'd never know. They knew one thing: Henry had put the plug of U on the lathe, and started driving.

No, they knew a second thing. When he'd been hit, he had flung the assembly into reverse. When Jim and the Doctor arrived, it was safe.

One took a few days to die. And it wasn't an easy death. Slotin had shown a fortitude still better than his gut courage. They'd offered to put him out quickly, and he'd asked to die slow, for that, he said, would give the doctors a chance to learn something valuable. So they had, they had, like don't-let-it-happen-again. Nobody played basketball with lumps of U, since Lou Slotin. Till Henry.

They hadn't wanted to gain valuable medical experience with Henry. The Doctor hadn't asked him questions, hadn't said anything about martyrs for the fatherland, used slow, precise German. All right boy, take it easy, we look after you, the docs will know how to handle it, Rika will be here in just a minute and she'll ease the pain.

Rika had taken time. Not her fault; they had to get her,

and she had to get her kit, and come down the hill. Jim had run for a rug and a cushion and water: he didn't know what the Doctor said to the man or what the man replied.

Once Rika did get there she had been good. No wasted words or actions. Exchanged one look with Jim; he'd shaken his head and mouthed 'not a chance'. One whispered word to the Doctor, who had not altered a muscle in his face. She was on her knees fitting a needle to the syringe, hand not shaking, breaking a capsule. In medieval days they gave a quick painless nick into the artery, and the loss of blood induced coma in a few moments. The advantages of modern methods were not that great. Less blood. 'Just a tiny prick to make you comfortable,' she said in her usual voice as she opened the shirt cuff. Henry hadn't said anything. Perhaps he knew. She raised her head, the dark glasses looked at Jim, and the voice said gently: 'Leave me alone with him.' He'd gone to check on the instruments, and left her there sitting on the floor, the man's head propped on her knees. Like a Pietà. He'd been ashamed; he'd turned away. He'd an impression that she talked softly to the man for a minute, before he went under. Himself he'd been the other end of the workshop, eyes shut and head ringing, because he had felt ashamed, and not least because when a dying man has his head on a girl's leg, and she is sitting on the floor supporting him, to let him pass easier, and it chances that she had been enjoying the sunshine in a cotton frock, you don't go looking up her leg to catch a glimpse of her knickers. Or not if you're Jim you don't.

What's the word – honour? Letting a man die clean? Honour must be something meaningless. A man dies. I will die. More will die. We conjugate the verb 'die'. This gadget pops, or even this gadget fizzles, the man here is only number one, promoted out of turn. Let him die honourably then, the way I'd want to. Yes, I know it's meaningless: the man can't possibly know I'm staring up a girl's skirt while he goes, and who can tell, the knowledge might help him go easier.

No, Jim, no. Honour has something to do with not being ignoble. You may not have the chance, yourself, to die well. You may be called to die in shit. If there is somebody at the

113

end to have a twitch of honour, it may help you even when you do not know about it.

And her; there is a beauty about her and I'm not sentimentalizing. She doesn't give a damn about showing her knickers. She asks you simply not to look or listen while she helps the man die. She asks that for another, accepting that she herself might die raped, bayoneted in the belly, and dragged out to die naked on the street, with the flies on her.

These, Jim, are theological arguments. They don't often take you that way. But not every day does a man die for your work.

Jim took a third, massive whisky. He didn't take a fourth because a) it would make him sick; b) there was only a dribble left in the bottle. He lay down on the sofa and went off to sleep.

Leora woke, looked at her watch. Tea-time! Well . . . she got out, unwinding towels that had rucked up with her twisting in sleep and formed ridges, and probably woken her. She dressed, fingers clumsy. Empty, shaky, but feeling a kind of triumph. They hadn't come to get her, the cold softspoken masked man, the impassive woman looking with the dark glasses like the dark angel. Dress; we're taking you outside.

'Let us honour if we can, The vertical man, Though we value none, But the horizontal one.'

The bullet in the back of the neck? Or the fatal injection?

She dressed in silence, rustling. Microphones, maybe, alerted the Doctor. She hadn't been in the living-room five minutes before he slipped in. She'd had time to poke the fire, to go down on her knees by Jim. Turn his head a scrap to stop snores and nightmares. He stank of whisky. My poor honest, honourable old Jim. Be true to yourself, my dear. You know the one way, being true to your work. That way you show truth to me. As I will show to you. It must seem stupid, Jim. And heaven knows it must seem very unlike Leora. But I am going to get you much drunker than you are now. Not on whisky. On a girl. Doesn't sound much like truth to you. But that's the way I'm getting out of here, and I'm going to break this trap you're in. You got drunk because you'd killed a man. If I knew how, I'd kill every person here. Sleep easy boy.

The Doctor entered quietly, went and sat on the sofa drawn up near the fire. Behind him, in conventional Ritz-Hotel fashion the well-trained servant came pushing in the tea-trolley. Neither of them paid any attention to Jim or to herself. She went over and sat opposite him, in her usual place by the fireside, the way she always did when they had come in from a walk. There was a cake, a nice cake. The cooking-whitejacket (she'd never laid eyes on him to her knowledge) made good cake. In fact the food here was the best thing there was. If it wasn't for all that exercise on steep hill terrain (a kilometre is worth three, on the flat) she'd be as fat as an old sow.

Leora felt extremely hungry, ate two pieces of cake, and was sorry for it: she felt sick. The Doctor drank a cup of tea in silence, and a second, still in silence. He was not really that small. The figure was slight, and one shoulder a little higher than the other; the face harsh and sad. Very like Richard the Third today. Leora didn't utter because she could think of nothing to say. After he had drunk his tea he stood up, went over to where Jim was lying on the divan between the two north windows, looked down at the sleeper – who had a contented look; his siesta doing him good – and out of the windows in turn. Grass grew outside those north windows, and rhododendrons, azaleas, bushes that liked the shady side. Beyond the path the slope fell away steeply, to a thick belt of evergreen planted there against the roadside, the way it was all around, to hide the fence and keep any indiscreet eye from prying into the privacy that the rich pay for.

Leora sat, and thought about such things as fatal injections of morphia. And how handy it was that there had been no frost yet. That ground under the trees was soft and friable. One could bury people in large numbers. No shortage of space.

He turned round and looked at her, the way he looked at one always, as though one were part of a landscape. He didn't want to rouse Jim. His voice was extremely quiet and perfectly audible.

'Life is fragile. Today you saw this. It can be seen any day but is unappreciated, owing to men's remarkable capacity for refusal to face facts. And for confusing the particular with the general.

'As a rule we direct our efforts towards supporting life. Withdraw that support: it is as with a plant from which sun and water are withheld.

'Sometimes we cut a tree, to allow more life to reach others near it. That is forestry. And sometimes lightning strikes. Today you saw lightning flash, close to where your husband stood. You were badly shocked: that was not your fault.

'After a storm a young tree may be partially uprooted. It leans, it may be a danger, it may damage others close to it. The forester decides whether to finish with it or whether it can be replaced in the soil. Will it leave an awkward gap? Will it put out fresh roots? Will it always be unreliable, certain to go again, the next time a wind blows strongly?

'I do not like to lose trees, ever. I love them. To lose two trees in a day is to me a great catastrophe.

'I understand that you lost your head, momentarily. I think that you regained it before others were placed in jeopardy. I must emphasize how fortunate this was. If you had gone too far, today, I could not answer for the consequences. Perhaps you have been very lucky. You met Marika and she gave you support. I too am fortunate in her swiftness and grasp. I owe her today a great debt. She killed a man painlessly. She spared his knowing that I would have to kill him, and she spared me: I should have been obliged to kill him in that knowledge. I pay my debts.' He walked slowly towards the door and paused with his hand on the latch. 'I ask you to excuse me for this evening. I should be poor company.' Suddenly he turned on the smile that had so much charm. 'I was shaken too by today's wind, Leora. To use severity to others, to be agitated, to assume a harsh, scolding tone, would point to my own hold in the soil being brittle. How shall I blame you for showing fear, before measuring the extent of my own? I have besides a melancholy duty to perform, I have much to think about, and small appetite.' He looked at her with kindness and with affection,

116

too. 'This isn't an easy time for you. I admire your patience; I respect you. You are looking tired and drawn. Get a good night's sleep; it is an admirable prescription which I will make use of myself. I'll tell Rika to give you a nembutal if you want one.'

She didn't know whether she was bereft of speech, or whether she had nothing to say. All she could think of was that she'd eaten too much cake. She just nodded.

'We are set down here for a small while,' he said, 'isolated from the world, a small group. This gives us particular responsibilities. To myself, who chose this, especially.' He slipped out and closed the door softly.

She looked for a cigarette and couldn't find one. He had left – most unlike him – his little tin box of Panthers on the table. She took one and smoked it. I suppose he's right, she thought. We're a sort of family, electrons and things bound to a nucleus. Beware of fission. Did it not strike him that in separating me from my children and splitting me from my husband he was doing something equally dangerous? Beware of the consequences. But not now; she felt too tired to move.

The silence woke Jim, or perhaps he'd been lying on an arm and it got cramped. He snorted a bit, sat up, yawned, scratched, looked at his empty glass with distaste, stared at his shoes, looked at his watch and said, 'I've had a sleep,' in a surprised way, twitched and grunted some more. 'Sunday afternoons ... I hate this tumbling into lethargy ... You don't feel like a walk?'

'I couldn't, sorry. My legs are like cotton.' He sighed, irritably, as though to say 'Fat lot of good you are'.

'I was sitting here all morning, up to ... well ... anyway, I want a breath of air. Fuggy in here. I'd like a game of tennis, something to concentrate on, only it'll be dark too soon. Can't you make an effort?'

'Sorry, no.' Fresh out of efforts. He looked at her crossly, decided there was nothing to do about it, and said, 'All right. I'm going to go chop wood.' It was a pastime he was fond of. He loved the logs that were brought in for the fire. The Doctor when asked was, doubtless deliberately, vague, but said that 'the forest service' sold wood. 'The locals' would

117

for a fee deliver it in the shape of sawn logs. These were sometimes quite large and needed splitting. Jim enjoyed putting them on the block and swinging an axe at them. Did his wind good, and his muscles. Sometimes the logs had awkward knots in them. You could try from either end, but even if you hit the log dead true, the axe would not split it. There was a whole shed full. Bought a year in advance and left to season, he explained importantly. I could get to love this living in the country; I've really got hooked on it. Think of when the snow falls. Can't understand why these lousy rich don't live here all the – oh I know, don't tell me, else they wouldn't be rich.

The fine weather has broken up, thought Jim, making his way in the dark along the back terrace, stumbling over Leora's deck-chair and feeling it do him good to curse aloud and give it a kick. He stopped to raise his eyes to the sky, to get them accustomed to the dark – the terrace lights were turned on from the 'dining-room' where they never went; forbidden territory, a kind of mess-hall for the whitejackets. The sky was paler than the surrounding air. Looked, he thought with memories of childhood holidays in Norfolk, like the North Sea on a blowy day, and those long streaming clouds sailing across were destroyers, low menacing shapes half-hidden by the waves. Now he could see his way down the steps – didn't want to break his neck – and along to the woodshed, an extension of the 'stable end' of the house, where they had kept pigs in the old days. Round at the end to the side to turn on the light: there was a flagged yard full of empty crates, dust-bins, and as usual a couple of parked cars. A square of yellow light showed where someone had forgotten to turn the scullery light out. Here was the frontier, beyond which they had been asked politely not to go, and they obeyed. What was the point of not obeying? There was nothing to see. Other senses took in faint clinks, a smell of cooking – ah, he was recovering an appetite – the whine of the accelerator in the central-heating plant and the suck-boom of the furnace where the cows had once been lodged. Hay-barn above, where now 'the staff' lodged: all this domestic economy had no interest.

But, for a moment, a fantasy possessed Jim – to take the

118

axe that hung neatly on nails with a hatchet for kindling and the cross-cut saw, to go charging into the kitchen swinging with it, to lay out whitejackets left and right leaving them weltering in pools of blood. Arm oneself with guns: these people surely kept guns handy. Smash through the house spraying bullets into anything that stood in his way, ending with a mighty swing on a chandelier that would send both boots crashing into the good Doctor's bland, neat features. Carry Leora out to the car. It would be enjoyable to smash the motor of the other, take their paddle.

Logs split most satisfyingly when he got them true, in the centre.

No, no pursuit; he'd leave them all lying in heaps: have to, because of getting up the hill for the children. There was the dark-glasses vampire on guard. He didn't quite know about shooting her down; a bit unchivalrous that, no? Heroes mostly didn't, because female villains generally went limp and clung, at the crucial moment, and got screwed instead of shot. Well, nothing much wrong with that scenario. Leora would know nothing; he'd left her in a picturesque state of faintness in the back of the car.

No no, please; the children. Regretfully, no screw; one would have to make do with ropes and sticking-plaster.

A log that had not been hit true jumped off the block and landed edgewise, extremely painfully, on Jim's toe. Why did that always happen? There it was: one might go scything through that scullery door red-eyed and axe aflame, and find oneself inspissated or implicated and generally infibrillated among the garbage bins while the nearest whitejacket whirled crouching with the fish-slice (Jim tried to think of some more potent, more dignified weapon and· couldn't), gave one an abominable welt over the eye and knocked one spinning into the vegetable blender.

It is, after all, the rule. He who throws a custard pie must then stand still and on no account attempt to dodge. Until retribution in the shape of the return pie takes him squarely in the chops.

'Turn me loose,' shouted Brer Rabbit, 'or I'll kick the natal stuffing out of you.' The abominable grinning black beast didn't turn him loose. Nasty thing; he hauled off and gave it such a clonk between its evilly leering tiny eyes – and stuck faster still. Jim could recall vividly the child's appalled horror at the vile embrace that paralysed all his four paws.

Who was it – Herblock probably; it was his style – who had drawn Lyndon Johnson writhing impotent in the grip of the Tar Baby?

As a child; eight might he have been, nine? – already possessed by the passion for establishing facts by prediction and experiment, he had tried for himself. Smell of meadow-sweet and dusty hedgerows on a burning day in July: smell of stone-chippings and the roaring terrifying dragon-wagon of Urban-District-Council's tar sprayer and a child planting its bare foot on the wet glistening black skin. Did the Tar Baby really grip when one touched it? Yes it did, most humiliatingly, because of the clip around the ear from the roadmenders' foreman, and being unstuck with an oily rag dipped in gasoline, not nice, and being marched home by a painfully held ear to mamma, who was properly shocked at one's behaving in a badly-brought-up fashion, and much mortified taking it out of one – 'making a public exhibition of yourself' – with a wooden kitchen spoon.

What was the intolerable fascination of the Tar Baby? Why did one touch it in the first place? There was a Kipling story, of the children making one with enormous amounts of shoe-polish and gazing at 'the black and bulging horror'. But, enquires one child, how come he looks so hellish? Because you've put your heart and soul in it, says the sophisticated member of the group. 'Tar Baby is Art.' Yes.

Jim gazed with pleasure at the pile of split logs, hung the axe up with his deltoid muscles enjoyably painful, got a fright on the side terrace from a shrouded creeping figure hovering about there in front of the dim portal of the cavern that housed the Tar Baby.

'Who's there?'

'Me,' said Leora's voice, apologetic. 'Only getting some fresh air.' He was sorry for her, so sad and dim, but his irritability overcame it.

'You're not even properly dressed.'

She paid no attention, went on flitting aimlessly, up the steps to the half-covered rose-bushes smelling of leafmould and freshcut resin-weeping spruce branches.

'No stars tonight,' as though punishing her. 'If you catch bronchitis, don't blame me.' And ashamed of his sharp tone, 'Smells lovely, doesn't it? There'll be some funny memories when we get home.' It was a stupid remark, but intended to be kind; well-meant.

'I don't care if I never get home,' she said. Snubbed, he went in. Delayed shock still, no doubt. Ought to be in bed.

He said as much to Rika, after a long lavish shower and comforting the bruised and reddened toe: hell, the nail would go black and he'd lose it. But feeling great, extremely hungry, tingling at the notion of a really good drink, comfortable in clean clothes, limping only the tiniest bit in toeless sandals.

'Quite right, she should.' They agreed. 'And she mustn't drink,' righteously, sitting down in front of a blazing fire, all-his-own-work. 'Where's the Doctor?'

'He's busy; he can't come tonight; didn't Leora tell you?'

'I forgot,' said Leora vaguely. 'I don't want to eat. I'd like to go to bed.' And allowed herself to be taken off passively, Rika making a comforting fuss, ordering hot milk, producing a nembutal, tucking her in as though she were Cassy. 'I'll read for a quarter of an hour,' like Cassy, clutching the *National Geographic*. Jim, in front of the fire, felt sleepy. Not having that! He got up, roved about, opened a bottle importantly. What had they given us tonight? A still champagne. A tart with an egg-and-cream sauce and fresh young spinach. A bowl of grated parmesan: would one or wouldn't one?

Rika was taking an unconscionable time and he was very hungry: he gobbled a lot of salt biscuits and consoled himself with the thought that there was a second bottle, brought as though there were four of them as usual. And Rika who was generally so frugal, making no fuss when he filled her glass, saying that she'd had a hard day too, and that Leora had gone straight off with the *National Geographic* still resting on her chin, and would sleep right through, twelve hours straight

121

with the nembutal, and that was what was needed, she'd be okay in the morning, and yes, she would take a bit more, she loved spinach, but no, no cheese.

Slices of salmon braised in something like this they were drinking, also leaves of sorrel with a clean bitter flavour, and plain steamed potatoes in their jackets – he knew how to cook, the villain, as well as throw his fish-slice – and a remarkable piece of Roquefort, and with it a glass of Sauternes, and together that was really something, and a basket of fresh figs and coffee, and Jim getting pleasurably widdly, and Rika not frozen-faced but laughing at the stupidest of his jokes. Even that terrible old gag of the physicists finding traces of new elements in the debris of Project Panda (the first hydrogen gadget) and somebody's proposal (turned down alas) to call the first one pandemonium – corny, but irresistible.

And in a moment of natural ease, a movement of un-fumbled skill (a magician who has palmed the card a thousand times in practice) he leaned across and took her glasses off.

No scars or grafts; skin as perfect as the eyes, which were clear brown as an ape's and without the sadness, but as serious. No reproach.

'Are you sure? That is what you want?'

What a silly question. Or else a question full of traps. But this was not a treacherous woman. She needed to know.

He didn't want to answer. But the answer was simpler than he had expected.

'Yes, I'm a bit drunk. Makes it easier to talk. Also to talk too much.'

'Is that harmful? To drink too much?' She reached for the bottle and filled her glass. 'What a stiff, what a wooden creature,' drinking. 'Wine is a good beast. I react well to things. I killed a man. I had a rigid, wooden reaction. Not human. This will help.'

'I felt respect for you. I still do. Now desire. Is that dishonest?'

'No,' laughing a little, embarrassed. Oh, deprecatingly; desire . . .

'I wanted it to come about,' said Jim. 'I predicted it. But it isn't facile – you understand?'

'No I don't.' Picking the glass up abruptly and draining it.

'Yes, she's there asleep, next door. It's not aimed at her,' he shouted. 'It's not a weapon.'

'Isolated,' she said in a whisper.

Why can't I stop talking? thought Jim irritably. What a lousy seduction scene. Irritably he snatched the bottle, refilled both glasses. She took a cigarette and lit it.

'The moment's right. After death, life. Why do I talk so much?' banging the bottle down.

'Then my only wisdom can be to say nothing.'

'She's there, yes,' he said desperately. 'But yes, you're right – we're isolated.' Can't the woman understand that I don't want to talk? Want to go to bed with her and feel too helpless to begin.

She smoked the cigarette down to the end, picked up the glass and drank it slowly off.

'I am a giver,' she said. 'If you're a taker, you will get nothing from me. Not even pleasure. But I don't believe you are a taker.' She got up suddenly and walked over to the window, turned and stood there, formal and hieratic, framed in the fall of the curtains. He looked at her, wishing he were anywhere but here, wishing he had not spoken, that he had not been drunk enough to take her glasses off. She stood there struggling, feeling pain.

'I don't want to let you undress me. I can't. I will undress myself. Don't put any lights out. I want you to see me.'

Feeling shame at the triviality, not wanting to look at her, he went over and locked the door. Everyone had gone to bed. But it was something to do. And then one had to undress. Such a bore. So humiliating to anyone with a sense of the ridiculous.

When he turned she was kneeling, upright, naked, on the sofa. A pose full of dignity. He felt an immense joy at this instinctive protection given him.

'You said life came after death. I want you to give me a baby. Make me ready, please.' Strained, taut. Not minding

123

the nakedness, but wanting to put her glasses on again. He was looking at innocence. And at the best, making love is such a painful business. One dies. Either it is only a threshold, or it is just a vulgar discharge of matter that might as well be pus. She gave him no physical pain. He was – inevitably it struck him – her first man. He thought about that. What is she – twenty-seven? He gave her no physical pain either. They gave each other neurological pain, walking slow and deliberate along pathways of the nervous system. But that was as promised, welcomed, undenied.

Pain, like pleasure, is a selfish business, difficult to share; she shared. There was no more vulgarity in her than vanity. She said nothing; breathed harshly against his skin. Knowing no arts, needing none. There isn't any love, unless a wish to give. There's respect, unforced and compelled. There is the joy of accepting pain, and the pleasure of receiving another's pain, freely given. She gave, keeping privacy, innocence. He made a present of the confusion and the fear; the guilt. The knowledge. The expertise. And a bomb.

We're no longer declining gadgetry. We're no longer conjugating the verb 'pop'. It is no longer trivial, or technique, or tactics. It is real. I am real. She gave the privacy and the innocence, and the woodenness, the rigidity, the death she had inflicted: all that she knew, and had: it was a great deal.

It was very, very hard to give herself. Release for a man is so easy. And for a woman, so difficult; and so painful.

She sat up, smiled timidly, looked around her in a startled fashion, not quite sure what this house was, what she was doing there. Asked for a cigarette, which he lit for her: it tasted good and he took one himself, a thing he only did 'at parties'. Well, what else was this? Both of them felt the light heart that comes from accepting another's pain.

She got up and walked about the room, playing like a child in the street, that must not step on joins in paving-stones; fitting her feet into the stylized patterns of the carpet, small diagonal dance-steps, precise and careful. She moved freely when naked, a rarity still, thought Jim: everyone he'd known had seemed flat-footed and knock-kneed. Preferring on the whole to be horizontal. But give her a piece of chalk and she'd start to mark squares out and hopscotch. Cassy skipped very well: Harriet, clumsy and over-eager, fell over the rope and got cross with it.

She wore her hair loose in the evenings. It got now in her way; she tutted at it, borrowed his comb to get untangled, stood in front of the glass and braided it up, deft and beautiful, a thing all naked women do well, so plastic that the hand itches instinctively for a pencil.

He wondered if he had given her a baby; made an effort, wiped the notion out. Vanity . . . leave the woman's womb alone. Leora claimed she had felt Cassy implanted . . . no, leave Leora in peace; respect her privacy.

She asked for a drink. Girl has hollow bones, thought Jim, and was startled to find that he was perfectly sober too. There was still a glass left, and still cold, of the Sauternes; he gave it to her. She came and lay on the sofa, stretched her arms above her head, wiggled her feet, said 'Play with me'. He was less clumsy than he would have been at hopscotch. She made room for him on the sofa. He studied the palms of her hands, her stomach, the backs of her knees. It was all exceptionally important. The base of her spine, her ankles, the soles of her feet. A well-made woman, well-knitted, well put together. The tension of days – how many days? – weeks – he tried to remember and couldn't. Time had had no meaning. But it had hurt him in passing. Now time passed without enmity. The clock in the living-room had a thin clear chime like a child's voice, quite unlike the deep liquid bong of the grandfathers he had known. How was it that he had never noticed that, before?

Pleasure ran up his leg and thigh as a small flame will run up a beech log. He pillowed himself on her belly; silky hair. Could anything be better than that curve, curve of violin or axe-haft, curve of clipper-stern, of rifle-butt? Better; those are very good curves, artist's curves, physicist's curves, but they do not have quite the plasticity of a naked woman. To be Leonardo would be fine; to be Giorgione would be better. Her lips dragged gently over the sensitivity of skin and membrane. I am anyone I please to be, he thought, and I don't even have to stop being Jim. He blew softly at wood embers, watching them glow from red to orange.

He fell perhaps asleep for a second. The small fluttering flames turned blue, became the lolling flame around the mouth and nostrils of the nightmare. He was hanging, naked, suspended by the wrists to a central-heating pipe in a whitewashed cellar. Marika stood in front of him, leering, her legs apart, fiddling filthily with her hand, the other hand holding an electric cattle-probe that stretched up towards his helpless body.

'Let's see you enjoy it,' said her mouth foully.

He shuddered, opened his eyes wide: hers stared into his. Drops from melting ice-blocks ran down his spine. He jumped up. Something had broken; she was again far away. It was over.

'We must dress.' She dressed awkwardly, as though her fingers had stiffened. When she put her glasses back on Jim had to laugh, a little sourly, a little sentimentally, self-pityingly. But he could laugh at himself, at least! The adjective, he told himself, is 'wistful'. All gone! as Cassy says lamenting, smearing her finger along the empty ice-cream dish and licking it . . . There would not be another time. Childish! Ten years old. Harriet thinks too that the entire world combines to do her down. When sent, finally, to bed, 'But I'm never allowed to look at the television,' she wails, with great choking pathetic sobs; what brilliant actresses all these little girls are! He held Rika's coat for her with elaborate English politeness – an exaggerated delicacy, as though the wool were a cheese-grater, rasping her skin like so much parmesan. She turned to look at him.

'There won't be another time.'

'No. I know.' They stood and gazed at each other.

'There's only one way,' she said. 'Crude and abrupt.'

'That's the way it is.' Imbecile cliché – he could do no better.

She lifted her hand and took the glasses off. Her face worked for an instant, leaving white lines on the skin that sprung out and disappeared at once.

'Take me again,' she said, with childish simplicity, quite bare of any 'how many times can you lay me' vain whoredom.

Useless to kiss that mask – he swung her round abruptly; it had to be brutal. She staggered a little and put her hands out to steady herself. Pure porn, if that isn't a contradiction in terms. Raping a young girl with bullying maleness, whisking her skirt up and dragging her knickers off tearing them, making her trample the rags loose, seizing the young girl's bottom and forcing her over: no, it is not vile; it is right. And go into her like an ice-hockey player bodychecking.

A hair's breadth off raping one's own daughter. But as a good actor said – married to a very fine actress ten years older than himself, 'all great loves are incestuous.' Or, as the actress in question said at the age of seventy-five, 'There are only two things in my life. Acting, and making love.' She has to run off like a raped hen with her glasses in one hand and her rags in the other. Deliberately, she left him that way, that he would recall her so. Bent over and screwed; houp-la. Not love; we're not talking about love; there isn't any love. Just a momentary effacement of helplessness and solitude. Of no importance.

Leora was sleeping, sweaty and tousled, hair in her mouth and the *National Geographic* of April 1941 under her ear. Face serene, look of secret satisfaction: almost one would have said a grin. Jim arranged her, so that she lay peacefully; crept off into the bathroom, took precautions not to make a vulgar racket, washing Marika off his body. Crawled into bed with care, not going to crack a single cobweb. She did not wake; was in a nembutal sleep, a woman who never took drugs and was knocked out by a good strong one. Sweaty, inclined to snore. Loved, though.

She woke with a slight nembutal-headache. Jim was long gone: the slave of disciplined, patterned reactions. The coffee was still hot, but stewed black, no longer nice. She wrapped herself in a dressing-gown, washed her face in cold water, combed her hair, rang the bell with an insistent flourish for a whitejacket. The room was tidy, fresh, anonymous: ashtrays emptied, hearth swept. The old dead embers were carefully kept, in a neat pile for a fresh start.

127

'I overslept. Can you grind me some fresh coffee, and relight the fire?'

'Certainly, madame.' Politeness in place, showing no crack or flaw. Like a good detective, she searched the room for clues. Tiny marks. The upholstery for example, for telltale stains. If my poor silly Jim did not last night fuck the almighty ass off Babylein then Leora has a very poor eye for a man. She found what she was looking for with no great trouble. Firelight, boys, is a famous aphrodisiac. Her headache cleared by magic. She felt no satisfaction or amusement. A grim nod. Inspector French. Not that in his day cops looked for sex stains. Dear me no, that would be badly-brought-up. We make all our deductions from train-tickets.

But undoubtedly, certainly, a sense of reinforcement. I have found the crack in the crust, I am no more the prisoner in the opal.

She had breakfast, showered, dressed, did her housekeeping; all as usual. All was as usual. Jim is deep in contemplation of his core and his bullet. Babylein is hoping there are no bruises on her throat. All your screws are loose, girl. The Doctor, possibly, has a very good notion of what's been going on, unless he was out late raking the dead leaves with great care around those recently fertilized rhododendron bushes (how beautifully they will bloom next spring, and everyone will wonder why, but nobody will give credit to horticultural Henry). And as abrupt as a balloon deflating, euphoria left her. She didn't feel popped. More that trick the children had of blowing the balloon up with a great deal of suck and spit, and then holding the moist neck dragged apart, so that air escaped with a whining blubbering noise: beastly children with their vile tricks. But it comforted her now instead of deadening her, to think of them. She was draggy baggy Leora, who can't screw, can't even menstruate – long overdue, and spotty-faced, bulgy-bellied, dank-haired, feeling just shitty. But powerful, girl, powerful. It didn't give any pleasure, feeling powerful. An illusion. You aren't powerful. You're a manipulator, a cheat and a fraud. And to your own husband.

She went out into the open air; it would be less stuffy. The cold was beginning. A dank northwest wind was stripping the

128

last leaves off the maples. Air with the wetness of rain that can turn to sleet. The Doctor was finishing his rose-bed, strewing leafmould and overlapping spruce-twigs. He straightened up, put his secateurs in his pocket, looked kindly at her. She hoped he wasn't being sorry for her. But it was an advantage, it gave leverage, to look a wreck.

'Autumn ends. Winter begins,' stripping his gloves and flexing the stiffened whitened fingers.

'You're very conscientious: do you like gardening?' He gave the crooked, one-shoulder-down smile.

My dear Leora . . . A little sorry for her, the way they were these days.

'My dear Leora; gardens are my passion.'

'I'm sure it sounds both rude and naive, but I didn't know you had one – outside politics that is.'

'And without wishing to sound rude, you thought my ideas about politics unbalanced to the point of mania. Being a nice person you feel at certain moments quite sorry for me. Well, one passion can balance another – but wouldn't you agree that it is the apathetic person, incapable of passion or blunted to it, that should really excite pity. Gardens are my passion.'

'Which you indulge – isn't it a demonstration of something unbalanced?'

'Come, let me show you. Are you warmly enough dressed? Have you strong shoes?' He took her arm in a friendly fashion and let it go at once. She had done no more than stiffen a tiny bit, inside as it were. One had to give him high marks for perception: it was as though he had committed some unpardonable familiarity.

'I am a Doctor – that very German title. I should prefer to be Commendatore – Condottiere perhaps. More suitable – however . . . The doctorate is in natural sciences and my subject was in fact botany. It was in England that I leaned to look at trees while learning English. A tree, says the poet Alexander Pope, is a nobler object than a prince in his coronation robes. How much truer that is today.

'The owner of this property is to be commended. He has not really taken it seriously, has not made drawings, not

129

made proper thought for the future. It is all rather amateur. Of course he does not spend enough time here. But he is to be congratulated upon good will, a lot of natural good taste, some feeling for trees. It is a pity that he thought first of acquiring and preserving privacy. He planted too many varieties, but of course the variety in this district is rather poor. These wretched spruces that invade everything; a forest of spruce is a forest of boredom. Though there are some fine beeches over there. One cannot prevent the local people from chopping them for firewood. It is no crime to burn wood: all plantations must be thinned.

'Too thickly planted, many of these. Some should come out, like teeth. And he has yielded to the common amateur passion for showy little things. Those snake-bark maples: the big grouping of reds was excellent in conception. Now why will people insist on using old nylon stockings to tie young subjects to supports – nothing could be worse. Some notion of not injuring the bark. One sees savages who use steel wire. Some nurserymen think of nothing but money. In the noblest of professions one finds grocers – pill-pushing doctors, concrete-car-park architects. A fundamental distortion in the mind. Dress-designers who hate women. Productions of Shakespeare in which you cannot hear the words.'

'People who drop bombs.'

'To be sure.' Cautious and cynical again at once, head on one side, beady-eyed.

'What's the good of loving trees, a thing of course I approve of and applaud, if one hates human beings?'

'My dear Leora, I really thought your powers of reasoning would have taken you further. The moment is ill-chosen to speak with intensity, about the passionate idealisms of a man such as I was twenty years ago. We are 'Showing the Garden' as the lamented Ruth Draper used to. Let me try, though, to answer you seriously, without breaking our context. That by the way is the sweet gum, the liquidambar; is not that a beautiful name? And that the liriodendron, the tulip-tree. A wonderful thing, and particularly valuable in heavily polluted areas. To you a lover of language and a Latinist they must have a significance beyond their botanic qualities. No, I do not evade your question: I am thinking. When I was in England I became interested in language. Doesn't it go together? – a love and feeling for plants, and a rich and flexible language? Truly a favoured people. The collections at Kew are beyond praise. Is one not tempted to say that the English rule of that vast Indian sub-continent is of little account, save enabling so many notable plant collectors to explore the foothills of the Himalaya? And yet I care for all those scruffy millions of wogs scratching incompetently at grains of rice. Paradoxical. So many things can only be expressed in paradox. I should like to have a world in which poets were given their true value.'

Leora stopped and stared at him, not understanding. He was absently caressing the twigs of a small tree. His eyes followed hers; he laughed.

'It's a child. About seven years old. Glyptostroboides, the dawn redwood. Neither a true redwood nor a swamp cypress. Chinese. A thorough little beauty. Should do all right here. The winters are cold, but the summers warm. You are attached to your poet, Auden. Don't look so astonished.' She was gawking, mouth open.

'I learned to read, too,' he said dryly. 'You quote him, sometimes. What did he say about himself loving Eden, and his enemy the technocrat wanting a New Jerusalem? He saw a fundamental opposition. You must recall it. Between his and mine no treaty is negotiable – something to that effect.' She recognized it, but was too flabbergasted to say so. The Doctor was enjoying her discomfiture.

'"In my Eden",' fluently, '"a person who dislikes Bellini has the good manners not to get born; in his New Jerusalem a person who dislikes work will be very sorry he was born." The tragedy of people like myself is to find ourselves caught between the two.

'You're at sea. Let me give you another example. There is a fine story by an English master, of a soldier who comes back from the war of 'fourteen-eighteen in a deplorable state, a nervous wreck. He has visions, he hears voices. These voices tell him to go about the countryside; his phrase, as I recall it, is that he has received orders. To go about and plant flowers, for, I quote, "Such as have no gardens." He is of course thought to be mad. You think me mad. I have much in common with that man.'

They were both silent: he looked around the valley, with something like the eye of the buzzards one often saw wheeling in the sky above.

'Filthy spruces,' he said. 'They grow fast. So do larches, poplars, willows, trees of infinitely more purpose and value. The forests of oak, such as once clothed this continent; those doubtless are irrecoverable, lost with our innocence, a biblical Eden. But can we really do no better than the deserts and dustbowls which are the signposts of our failure? The person for whom I have contempt, Leora, is the bland, smiling optimist, the man who thinks mankind is perfectible, all by himself. The liberal humanist. That is the target I wish to strike.' He turned, and walked away from her. Leora gawped after him.

'You must forgive my interrupting you, Jim, but I bring you a present which is more than opportune.' Whitejackets lumbersome with a long crate. Jim scarcely looked up. Face pale and papery, a stork on its untidy nest. All the calculations done three – thirty – times. The uranium recast, machined afresh. Alone: not even Henry. One missed the narrow bat-eared head, the sad oblique eyes permanently downcast. What had he got this time? Him and his 'presents' . . .

The Doctor had dismissed the whitejackets with a peremptory flip of his hand. He had taken the big screwdriver and was levering the crate open.

'This, my dear Jim, is the current pattern of U.S. Army recoilless rifle. The M-40, A 2. Calibre one-oh-six millimetres, which your new bullet fits. A barrel of three point four metres. We'll be cutting that down. The present weight without the mounting, since this normally rides on a jeep, but we aren't going to go riding around in jeeps,' indulgently, 'is two hundred and twenty kilograms. Rather a lot: we'll have to try and economize.'

'What are we going to go riding about on?'

'For the present, just our dear old familiar Mercedes sedan.

132

No trouble. We might stiffen up the rear shock-absorbers a bit. When it comes to the point – I am thinking of a simple Volkswagen or Renault delivery van. A forklift trolley – no problem in any of that; it's there already. But we've too much length: this barrel will have to be cut.'

After all the theoretical jabber over reflector thicknesses it was a relief to have a practical problem.

'How much does it have to be cut down? The bullet has to go fast, as fast as possible. What's the muzzle velocity of this, as it stands?'

'Something over five hundred metres a second.'

'Get by with halving that, maybe. Needs working out: start cutting the barrel and the speed of delivery shrinks very rapidly. Weld on a flange, bolt that to the cased tamper. A metre of barrel anyhow, to take care of predetonation risk. Bound to be a big awkward parcel. How d'you propose to conceal it?' The Doctor smiled.

'That will be my little contribution to the exercise, Jim. A large pack of computer paper. Just see what you can do with that.' And Jim looked after him, mouth slightly open. What was it he was proposing to pop? Somewhere that used large quantities of computer paper . . . It didn't tell one much. Everybody did, nowadays.

Leora was composing her own bullet, hoping that the rifle would be recoilless. There'd been no echo of suspicion about the children, unless a trap had been set for her. Well, she'd burned her boats. It was weird to find the enemy so . . . well, kind; sympathetic, behind the mask. But that was the core of the whole matter. It alters nothing.

'Darlings,
'I feel bad at not writing earlier but it cheers me up to know you are happy and having such a good time. I was ill with a virus, and we were afraid you would catch it. All rather sudden wasn't it! but it's dangerous for children and one can't vaccinate against it; you know, like diphtheria or something. We are glad to know you are being well looked after, and you're behaving yourselves, we hope.
'I am much better already. So is Papa, but he was very tired

from work and not having a holiday, so he takes longer. He sends a big kiss to "his girls" and says not to worry. We're in a sort of clinic in the hills; it's quiet, and lovely air. Rather like where you are, in fact! We're allowed to walk in the woods around, but have to follow the treatments each morning. What I like best is not having to cook the dinner!

'Remember the alphabets we used to play the time you both had measles, gamma and mu and the others? Zeta meant you wanted a drink of water – that used to appear all the time on the notes you wrote! Write us letters, with lots of drawings, to bring you nearer!!

'Now I hope Cass is good and remembers to Brush her Hair every night. What was that? – oh yes, theta, surely. Theta theta! – and you too Harriet, do please be very careful to do your teeth and fold your clothes tidily and have everything ready for the morning always. Sigma tau; you see, we've been playing it too!

'So, my darling old alpha-beta, be patient girls, and it won't be long now. Lots and lots of love from your own Greeks,
Mu and Pi.'
P.S. now-now, or nu-nu? And what about poor old Xi?'

All this she embellished with as many of Jim's coloured ball-points as she could lay hands on; arabesques and whirligigs of all sorts to show – she hoped – how the 'reading between the line' ought to go. As long as they'd understood all she'd crammed into the lipstick. Still, Harriet had always been good at learning things by heart, and Cassy, while slower, was more retentive.

The Doctor, while withdrawn at lunch, perhaps regretting his outburst of spontaneity (the mask had slipped a bit) was jovial over this communication.

'Oh yes, they'll enjoy that. Who's poor old Xi?' smiling.

'Oh, he was a smelly old dog we had then. Horrid beast really; got ancient and cranky and had to be put down. They were heartbroken, of course.'

'Well, I'll pass this on to Rika. She told me of course about your suggestion. I find it quite sensible.'

'Plausible enough?' asked Leora, humbly.

They didn't make much of a walk: it was raining a lot, and Jim was sullen and irritable. Bad conscience! thought Leora, transparent as hell, as he always is. Having done me those dirty tricks there is now a great parade of it being all my fault. But I must admit, in honesty, that I provoked it to a large extent.

'Bloody rain,' kicking a dead stump, sending sodden touchwood flying and trampling on a thick bunch of diseased-looking toadstools. 'Can't breathe properly; all this foggy mess hanging about.' Indeed it was unpleasant, when the clouds hung so low that to climb even a little meant that one was right in them. Back at the house the living-room chimney was not drawing properly, and there was a stuffy smell of smoke and sodden loden coats; they had stopped repelling moisture and begun absorbing, and hung heavy and tickly, smelly even out of doors. On top of everything else, he was over-tense. Leora didn't know for sure, because she hadn't been told, but could piece things together. With Henry's disappearance (polite euphemism) he had to do a difficult and dangerous experiment with no one to rely on. As well as all the potty chores of soldering and machining. Now a very great strain indeed.

'Just when I need her support,' he grumbled in a pretended aside that she was meant to hear, 'not help, but at least not creating scenes, she turns on that stupid trick of hers of not being all there, going about like a mental deficient.' And gave the door an irritable push with his foot, slamming it. 'For God's sake don't shut that window; quite stuffy enough as it is. What the humidity level is – isn't there a hygrometer somewhere?'

'Terribly good for the rhododendrons,' she said irritatingly. What did he care about the rhododendrons!

At supper there was a bad atmosphere, because the Doctor was preoccupied and irritable. His face showed annoyance at the tetchy bickering, at Leora's sarcasms and little female cattinesses. What threw this into relief was that Marika – another one with a bad conscience, as much at having failed in self-discipline as being traitorous to Leora – was talkative in a strained fashion, and unhappy at the sullenness of the other three.

'The children were thrilled with your letter,' over-brightly. 'It has been quite a time of course; natural for them to be missing you. I was expecting that they'd get a jolt from it, a rush of homesickness wouldn't have surprised me, but they were very cheerful: I left them busy writing back, with lots of drawings. And of course your alphabet: they told me about the time they'd had mumps, eating all that ice-cream when their throats hurt.' Leora was not going to show how much this news excited her.

'They only had me to look after them then, of course; nowhere near as much fun as you give them.'

'Well,' placatingly, 'a busy time for you as well as anxious, with the shopping and housekeeping.'

'That's right. Of course I had a husband then who used to come home and read to them, as well as looking at me occasionally and even showing interest in whether I was alive.'

'Oh, shove it,' muttered Jim.

'Look, Leora,' said Marika, embarrassed, 'we all sympathize. We have to get this time over as smoothly as we can. Since the tragedy with Henry, Jim's having a rough time and he hasn't lost a day; I think it's terrific.'

'So do I – be even more terrific if you were there to stroke his forehead and be sorry for him. He'd enjoy it too, looking up at you with big cow eyes.' Jim swung his hand to give her a resounding slap, but the Doctor caught his wrist and said, 'Stop that,' in a voice harsh enough to pull them up.

'That's gone far enough, Leora. If I'd known that writing a letter would upset you so much I wouldn't have permitted it. Very well, I have permitted it, and you'll get an answer to it since that is already written, but I'll only allow it to be delivered if you behave.' More of a threat than he knew . . . Leora caved in at once.

'I'm sorry,' she said. 'I'll apologize to you all. But don't humiliate me, Jim. What you said was wounding, you know, and you've been mumbling insultingly all day.'

'That's fair enough,' said the Doctor. 'It is unpleasant when I am obliged to arbitrate a quarrel between you, and intensely so for Rika who does her best to make you both happy. I am intent – and I address this to you both – on treating you as my guests, the civilized way of handling our entire problem. I am loath to intervene in a squabble brought about by the weather and the nervous strain. But I can't allow you to involve either of us in these domestic spats. You must take that responsibility during our stay here. I do not wish to be obliged to speak of discipline, as though you were school-children.'

'"Our stay" is good,' said Leora. 'Our imprisonment, you mean.'

'Quite so, Leora, since you use the word. I remind you that we also suffer imprisonment. We control ourselves, and endure.'

'You chose that; we didn't. Nobody listens to you with microphones or kidnaps your children,' said Leora.

'Preposterous – nobody spies upon you. I am also account-able for my movements and actions: do you suppose I am alone in this enterprise? Now, I've said more than enough. I've accepted your apology; please accept mine. The con-straints are imposed by security; that's an end of it. No further reproaches. But I am surprised, Leora, at your sulking at Jim at a moment when he needs your comfort.'

'He doesn't want my comfort.'

The Doctor quite certainly understood the meaning of this remark, but chose to ignore it.

'Be that as it may, I don't intend to see the work hampered by tantrums. It is not in your interest. Another glass, my dear? And a toast, Jim, to old Fafnir. He snored away quite peace-fully there and didn't breathe any fire.'

'Pretty well,' said Jim, making an effort, sitting up and putting his shoulders straight. 'I gave him three sharp prods. Got more or less the same instrument reading each time. Nothing wrong with his knee-jerk.'

'Or his blood count?'

'Well, I haven't got that altogether quantified. But soberly – he's not anaemic. There's a certain amount absorbed by the paraffin; not more though than I'd expected.'

'And the leak-back from the bullet?'

'The beryllium takes care of that. The reflector's adequate.'

137

'It even occurred to me that the paper – I mentioned it to you – might add to the reflector's containing power. Is that wide of the mark?'

'We'll make a physicist of you yet,' said Jim with a faint grin. 'I don't want to talk about that, though.'

'Neither do I,' decidedly. 'No shop at table. Leora my dear, try and forgive me, I look at you with a paternal eye occasionally. You have a harder time than the rest of us, because you've the least to do.'

'Yes. I do suffer – from the inactivity. It's true.'

'I realize. And we mustn't let the strain get out of hand. I'm thinking of getting our friend Doctor Sebregt up here to take a glance at you. And if necessary make a small prescription.

'I'm not particularly anxious to discuss my physiology at table,' said Leora, alarmed by this development.

'But I see perfectly,' answered the Doctor, with oleaginous tact.

The crack had not been more than papered over. Leora slept badly, and woke feeling ill and miserable. She roamed about for a while, with no appetite and a horrible sensation of black doom pressing on her stomach, and an uncontrollable wish to scratch, the kind that when you scratch one place, starts up instantly in another. For an hour she felt abominable torment; despair, frustration, anxiety and wanting to vomit without being able to. She had a drink, ashamed of the frightening quantities of whisky she'd got through in these days, telling herself she'd think about that tomorrow. After two she felt able to eat an egg and a piece of toast, and felt better. She stopped roaming about, told herself that the more one scratches the more one wants to scratch, that this was just nervous anticipation, that the hell with it, since she had no guarantee whatever of her plan working now or any time, and the rest was just imagination.

I am a comedian, Leora told herself, an actor who can't be funny without being miserable first. Simpler even than that: pretend a rôle, start acting it, you begin living it. Act neurotic and you become neurotic.

138

But the rain had cleared up. As long as it doesn't start again, because if it's raining I haven't a prayer . . . However, whether or not the whisky helped she didn't give a damn. She went back to bed, and to her own surprise fell fast asleep, and woke only at lunchtime. There were shocking great rings under her eyes, but she felt fine.

With Jim there was a truce. It was plain that he felt unable to choose between sympathy – he glanced unhappily at the rings, seemed about to comment, thought better of it – and irritation with her. At the moment when he himself was frantically rechecking calculations, on the edge of success in a hair-raising experiment (one says confidently that yes, one knows perfectly how to do that, but actually doing it, under very difficult, badly-controlled conditions, biting back the spectre of known consequences; oh, the crevasse is deep and sharp. One hesitates long on the brink. In the end one has to jump). This was the moment Leora had to choose for gynaecological nonsenses.

Unbeknown to Leora, Jim and the Doctor had had a little chat. The one all tact, the other gruff and curt, but obliged to accept the logic of the argument.

'My dear man, far be it from me to go nosing about, but my duty is to guard against trivial mishaps. I make so bold as to ask your help in a simple diagnosis. Am I right in thinking female physiology is being a bother to her?'

'Haven't been following her into the bathroom, you know. But since you ask, I think yes. Ratty as hell; seen it before though never as bad. Acts on her that way. While we're that far into private life, puts a brake on me. Acts touch-me-not; I'm not going into details.'

'No no no. My dear Jim, I'm not that insensitive. I'll say no more than – well, Rika confessed to a peccadillo, and I reassured her. I stick to the purpose that unites us here, Jim. Having reassured her, I should like to reassure you. I repeat what I said at the beginning of our acquaintance: I'm a workman who looks after his tools well. And keeps them sharp. We're at a crucial stage in our experiments – I hardly need to remind you. One must know when to be rigid, and when to be flexible. Let's put it this way. Gynaecology, where

139

Rika is concerned, is no worry to me. Well-balanced person. As for Leora, I don't believe we need worry exaggeratedly. If a touch to the rudder is needed, we possess a good source of counsel. I've given Roland Sebregt a buzz: he'll be up this evening. He can take a glance at her. Poor girl, it's not her fault. Just let's be patient, Jim.'

At lunch the Doctor produced a letter from the children, as a peace offering. Leora looked at it with a show of indifference, wept a tiny bit, apologized to everyone, said she knew she wasn't quite the thing, but that it was nothing but a slight pile-up of nervous tension, that she didn't want to be troublesome, and only asked to be left alone a bit and not noticed. Everyone was sympathetic.

It had blown clear, and the wind had dropped: a high steel-grey sky with a few smudgy traces of a darker grey. Quite definitely not a rain sky. Might turn cold: the temperature had dropped a few degrees. A prelude, possibly, to easterly weather. Ground frost could be expected.

Leora went for a walk that afternoon. Tactfully, the Doctor had proposed a game of tennis to Jim, on the hard court where he and Leora played occasionally. Jim had set up 'a system' there for his beryllium when it needed to be machined. 'That's hellish toxic stuff: it's a simple job, and if pushed I could make do with a couple of vacuum-cleaners and a silicosis mask, but I'd prefer it in the open air' – this was finished, and the men agreed that 'the physical effort does us good'. The Doctor was not such a weedy specimen as one might expect. Crooked shoulder or no, he played better than Jim did. Well, Jim told himself, I dare say Richard the Third was a hot tennis player, too.

Leora was grateful to be in fair shape on the hills by now. It was not too steep; a wood-cutter's trail up to a col or saddle, beyond which they'd never gone. The path branched in several directions at a big tree, and there was a wide view. Maybe an hour's walk farther across the watershed and down the glen, one could see the steeple of a church and a few roofs. Ten kilometres perhaps, in all, from the house. The road that the whitejackets took with the car led much more directly to a

140

village no more than, she believed, two or three kilometres off. The daily 'bread and milk' run ... And down that way one came to civilization; a main road, a town, a railway perhaps. She didn't 'know', but it stood to reason ...

There had plainly been a fight over who should write the letter. Harriet had won it, as she won most arguments, and only a neat and slightly pathetic postscript stated 'Cassandra drew the pictures'.

'Good old Ma!!!! And perhaps feeling this was slightly cheeky, a formal 'Dearest Mama' underneath.

'We miss you a lot. We have a swimming pool. I can do lengths under water with my eyes open. We do lessons with Rika. We are very well behaved; she does not ever smack us though Cass deserved one for drawing with her lipstick. Nu nu nu!!! was it dithpheria we had? I miss old Xi. He would have liked it here. He would be company, sometimes at night it's a bit lonely he was then a good gard dog. We are embroidring handkerchiefs for you Cass has drawn the patterns (not very well, and she made hers dirty) but they are pretty with flowers and leaves. Of course I remember the alphabet, you forgot sigma it was the bell for when we needed you during the night and tau was our dressing-gowns!!! We have a nice room the walls are all made of wood. Rika's room is the other side so she is quite near when we want her but Cass dossent have nightmares any more and if she did I know how to look after her. Give our love to Papa and tell him to nununu and we hope he's better very soon because its nice here but we get bored though Rika is very kind I cook very well we have marvellous barbeque food and lemonade fresh not fizzie. It it cold at night Rika says its quite high in the hills but phi phi, we have lots of warm things.

We are looking forward very much to hearing from you from your loving daughter Harriet Alpha and Cassandra Beta.'

No guard at night, no whitejackets. Only Rika. My bright Harriet; she'd got on to poor-old-Xi and his importance in these circumstances in a flash.

Leora did her best to imagine what these paths would be like in the dark. Not too terrible, if there was light from sky or moon. They had been made in the old days when people depended upon these forests for a living. Sloping across the

141

hill contours, in spider-web formation, so that slow, sturdy horses could haul carts, timber-tugs, sleds in winter. Wide enough, not too crooked, the surface rutted (they used tractors now, of course) but passable. What she was most afraid of was taking a wrong path in the dark and getting lost. She made notes on a piece of paper brought for the purpose. She hadn't an electric torch, and didn't know where to find one. If there was no wind, one could make do with a little flame, she thought. She got back, and had tea with the others, and took her boots off, but 'couldn't be bothered to change'. When she was left to herself she put on clean socks. Nobody would comment on her wearing trousers and a sweater at supper. She wanted a drink badly, but bit back the need.

Doctor Sebregt arrived before supper, in a very nice Lancia car which he left in front of the main door, giving Leora wild notions of pinching it, because she was looking out of the window, and saw that he left the keys on the dashboard. It wouldn't do – she could be chased then officially, for thieving.

She wasn't frightened any more, by Doctor Sebregt. He had been assimilated into the plan. And, too, he was Auden's favourite kind of doctor, partridge-plump and broad in the rump, who'll leave you all your favourite vices. 'But with a twinkle in his eye, Tell me that I have to die.' He was cheery and full of jokes, and drank a lot of burgundy at supper. The Doctor called him 'My dear Roland'. The psychiatrist from Basle! This was the man who covered the whole operation. Officially both Jim and Leora were at his clinic in Switzerland. She wondered how far it was.

But he was certainly the ideal man. Nobody would disbelieve him, and she could imagine the cheery, joking, ever-so-reassuring and so trustworthy phone-calls he must have given to Hamburg. A shrewd eye behind all the twinkles: she was glad that all her symptoms were real! He would see through fakes. He had brought an overnight case with him, was lodged in the guest-room upstairs next the Doctor, and made much of the joys of country living.

'Ah,' with Tarzan delight; one could see him swinging from creeper to creeper, 'The good air! I am jealous, lieber Freund.

142

Bouh, the stink of Basle.' Talkative and fluent, in German, in English and French. Very much the cosmopolitan sophisticate.

When they had all had coffee comfortably together after supper ('Marvellous cellar our mutual friend does have, my boy – we are all "wie Gott in Frankreich", eh?' – the Bonnes Mares had been brought out in his honour), he turned chuckling to Leora.

'Well, my dear young lady, so we have a few tiny miseries, as I hear? Nothing to worry about there. But we'll take a look shall we? And Jim here! – ach, tja, a useless precaution. But we'll just take the blood-pressure, afterwards.'

'I'd prefer to go upstairs,' she muttered in some embarrassment.

'Of course,' with easy tact. 'There now,' shutting the guest-room door. 'Let's hear.'

'It's just that I feel upset, all round. Period overdue and sleep badly, don't always digest properly, get diarrhoea, drink too much and smoke too much; feel in a tangle.'

'Tut, that's nothing. Fix it in no time. There now, let's listen; top half's fine: tja, a pill. Blood pressure maybe a scrap too low. The tangle's no more than nerves. Much as I expected: I'll write you a chit. We can go down again if you like.'

'I don't want to go down,' squawked Leora. 'All looking at me reproachfully and thinking what a drag I am. I don't want to face it; I just can't.' He lit a cigarette with a deft flick and considered her.

'There now,' gently, 'I understand. Dramatizing a bit, as you'll agree when you've had a chance to unwind. Building it up, let's call it. Maybe a bit stiff and suspicious of me. We'll have to give you back your confidence. By all means stay here if that's what you'd like. I'll have a chat with the Doctor to hear how things stand. As I see it you won't be here much longer, but you might feel altogether happier – if we put you in care for a week. Meantime you curl up and have a snooze; here's a thing to help you sleep,' pouring out a glass of water and lifting her feet on the bed.

Leora had spat out the gelatine capsule before it had time to melt, before he had got down the stairs. At once she was at the door, listening. When she heard the two male voices in the hallway she slipped back and tucked herself in; was breathing regularly when the door again opened.

'There you are; out like a light. Leave her there; it's of no consequence. Can always move her later, and if you prefer we'll give her a prick, and I can take her back in the car, keep her in the clinic till you're ready. Let's go into your room and I'd really enjoy a little glass.'

'I'll tell the help to go to bed, then. Leave those two downstairs in peace. They provide their own psychiatric treatment,' indulgently.

'Och,' came the voice with the slight Swiss accent, 'it's no great matter. Look at it from a purely medical standpoint. Reliance.

'That's a fine girl, your Rika. Do your man a power of good. And this is a good girl, but she's been driven in upon herself. A nuisance, I agree. There are limits to administrative convenience, you know. He'll feel much happier if she's well cared for out of his sight: at present she's a constant reproach. And a bother: surreptitious assignments, what. Leave her in peace; Rika can help me put her to bed in an hour or so. And now I'd like that drink. These weeks have been for me, too, a time of anxiety. No kickback from Hamburg, but I had to keep on my toes.'

Leora locked the door, stayed there until she heard white-jacket come up with a slight clinking noise denoting a drinks tray. A polite mutter: creaks on the landing, on the stairway up to the attic, overhead, a thump of a whitejacket thankfully taking its shoes off. She slipped out on to the landing. Soft jovial voices rumbled from next door, a faint smell of cigar smoke. Doctor Sebregt enjoying the fleshly pleasures and country air: he'd had an anxious time. She crept down the stairs, her hand in her anorak pocket clutching the table-lighter she'd pinched off the living-room table. Through the door down there a faint murmur. Leora did not much care whether they were making love or virtuously chatting – on the whole it would be preferable if they had one another's clothes off, she thought viciously. The essential is an hour before discovery. That, she thought, she could guarantee.

144

In her socks she fumbled in the pockets of Marika's coat. Keys ... She crept into the 'dining-room' and opened a window on to the terrace. Heart thumping fiercely, she lost precious minutes doing up her boots, thankful for fresh socks, for quantities of adrenalin spurring her muscles. Quietly she flitted up the hill.

To turn off the switch of the current and the alarm on the fence was easy. To cross the meadow and climb the verandah and unlock the sliding patio doors was no problem. Within the summerhouse there was no trouble, since Harriet had said that they would be ready. Harriet woke easily. Cassy was cross for a moment, but had been warned: this anxious hurried ghost in the night was only Mama; instantly feelable, smellable, hearable as not being kind Rika, only rough, abrupt, strange, but still familiar, Mama.

Whipping them into trousers, anoraks, boots without a panic of hurry, without disturbing their confidence, was no bother. They had expected it. Had Mama not said that they were imprisoned, would escape, that she would come in the night, that they would have to walk in the dark ... it had all been in the code. Been learned by heart, exactly like a recitation for school. With Harriet marching light- and sure-footed in front (Bossy-boots firmly in command) and Cassy's paw clutched in her own, Leora cut across the hillside, struck the path she had mapped that afternoon, and they set themselves to breast the long dim rise to the col in a steadier, mountain-march rhythm. With those two small figures beside her Leora felt no anxiety or fear at all. We are free. We are free.

Jim stayed behind, stickily in the spider's web. But Leora's blood jumped. She felt certain that within hours (what to do with the children? – but she would think about that in the morning), she would have the situation in hand. Quietly, tactfully. Whatever is done, it must be very tactful. Otherwise they'll put a pistol to my Jim's head. There is the danger. We must go very cautiously, very easily. Three cobras there. Sweet, gentle, fanatic Marika (when she realized how she had been foxed she would be a female cobra). Dear, good, tree-loving Doctor Thing; Richard the Third cornered, and the fiercer, colder fighter. Fat, comfortable Swissy-Sebregt. Frightened, a poisonous biter. Furious at being wool-over-eyed, at his professional judgment being set at nought by a silly, hysterical, neurotic stupid little cow like Leora.

I have fucked the lot of you.

Free.

PART FOUR

'The Bullet'

'The sudden swift emergence'

Cassy was tired, by the time they reached the top of the hill. Leora could not take her in her arms: dared not try put her on her back. Harriet was very good, brave, trusting. Leora couldn't say so, but she was horribly frightened. They'd got to the summit of the saddle, and now it was downhill: easy. Overhead, the night sky had been pale, shed enough light to see quite a lot. They hadn't tripped over stones or tree-roots: they were here at the top. Leora herself had never been this far. She had to push along the now bitterly tired, sleepy, whiny Cass. Encourage the stout-hearted, faint-hearted, cross and jagged Harriet, whose nervous energy, at first such a comfort and support, was now a wail of bad-mouth nagging. And herself, terrified because she could see nothing, shying at every clutching shadow. Are we even on the right path? That village is somewhere in the valley, but I can't see it, don't know it's there. And even if it's there: there might be spitting cobras. Paths and roads blocked by Mercedes cars. White-jackets expressionless and competent. 'You must be tired, madame. I'll make you some hot milk.' Doctor Roland Sebregt no longer jovial, his busy little hypodermic needle glittering. 'Take the bitch's trousers down,' and vicious the ice-point into her bare buttocks. The Doctor, sad and hollow-eyed, very tired, still able to control himself. 'You've again given us trouble, Mrs Hawkins. I did warn you. This time, I have no hesitation. I am sorry for you. I'll do my best to see that it won't hurt. But this time, you join Henry under the shrubbery.' Or Jim. 'Christ, you stupid bitch. You put my life at risk and all right, that's nothing. But put my work at risk, that's you know the one thing I'll never forgive. Go on,

Rika, give her the morphia, lethal, she'll go out quite pain-lessly; I'm fond of the bitch, she bore me children, don't be cruel with her, just let her snuff out with respiratory paralysis.' She was so frightened. They could be absolutely anywhere in the hills. That path could have wound and twisted treach-erously. But follow the one rule there is. If lost in the woods, go downhill. Follow water. The water will lead you.

Well, she had, legs like lead, aching from hairline to toe-nail – God, she'd done ten kilometres and more this afternoon: now she'd done twenty, and that village was all the while around the next bend.

It was so dark. The children so tired. Herself so at the end of her tether.

The woods had not been hostile. The stiff dark trees had always drawn apart to let them pass. No stars, and no moon, but the sky had never been so dark that the path became indistinguishable: a track had always shown itself in a black-ness still less black than that of the trees. The strain had been to choose tracks: there were always more than Leora re-membered. Others came branching in that seemed not to have been there by daylight, and she felt more than any other terror that of losing her way. The marks she had chosen on her reconnaissance of only this afternoon were no longer recognizable: such a tall tree had mysteriously shrunk or receded, or there were tall trees pointing blandly to every direction. Such a large stone, uncompromisingly white by day, not in the least like the others, had shrunk into the same anonymity. Go up hill – yes, but which hill? A hillside which in light is a clean slope, by night is a formless confusion of bumps and folds. She told herself sternly that the path, being made by men and by day, would not depart from the logical contour of the hill's flank, but it was a blind faith.

Once or twice there was a noisy rustle in the undergrowth, scaring her out of her wits; what wits she had. The children saved her by not being in the least frightened. 'Deer,' said Harriet with perfect calm and assurance, Leora with thudding heart and hoping to God the child was right.

'If there are wild boar,' said Cass, 'will they attack us?'

'Little silly,' Harriet all contemptuous superiority, 'wild

148

animals never do unless they are frightened. And they aren't. They know perfectly when it's children.' Until she got too tired Cass chattered on in a long fantasy about bears and badgers and eagles and wild cats, Leora not listening, making mechanical cheerful interjections about the wives and children of aforesaid badgers and bears, glad of the small loquacious voice that stopped her terrors. Of imprisonment they had little to say, which did Miss Dark Glasses credit, she supposed. They hadn't had a horrid time. Prison to them meant a frightful dungeon in a picture book, with Gothic bolts and bars, and witches or maybe ogres.

When they got tired it became worse. There had been, at least, the immense relief of reaching the top of the col and recognizing it. They really had been on the right track! But the village was invisible in the shadowed valley: there was no speck of light, and the track henceforward unknown, unexplored. Leora could only trust to the downhill slope, down the long glen.

If one had even a torch ... But she had no torch: the best she had been able to think of was the table-lighter off the living-room sideboard, stolen that evening and stowed in her anorak pocket. It was useless, a flame bright enough to dazzle one's eyes but unable to illuminate the pitchy blackness rising twenty metres high around them.

The worst moment of all was after nearly three hours of march, and still no village. They had been going down a long, long while, and the ground had become level, and the track suddenly opened to what seemed a wide amphitheatre. Tractors had been at work, carving deep ruts in the ground, so that one kept on stumbling. Tree trunks were piled, heaps of rubbishy branches and stripped bark. One could see absolutely nothing. The sky was perhaps a thought paler, but Leora knew that this could only be false dawn. She sat the whimpering Cass on a log, and sat herself in limp dejection. At any moment there would be torchlight, and the confident, amused voices of the pursuers. Harriet was snivelling too, feet blistering. Leora staggered up and tried to summon three-in-the-morning courage. She fell twice over logs left diabolically strewn about to catch her, barking her shins and muddying her hands. The glade, she discovered, was a 'star', a roundabout of forest traffic. There were six different paths ... Three led back uphill, could safely be disregarded. But the other three ... On trees were mysterious markings of paint, white that showed up, reds and blues that could only be distinguished when one held the lighter up as high as one could reach. Foresters' marks? Or the signs left to guide walkers out hiking? It was twenty minutes, and seemed a lifetime, before she found a little painted signboard set stupidly too far back and half obliterated, but one could distinguish a symbol, a tent or hut – but definitely meaning a house – and some blurred lettering, perhaps, '... rberg.' She had seen such signs before. Jugendherberge: a youth hostel.

Then she couldn't find the children, and was afraid to call, and tripped on a dead branch and fell full length in cold mud. Then she heard Cassy crying in exhaustion and fear. When she got back to them it took another ten minutes to get Harriet to put her boots back on and get them laced, and halfway the flame of the lighter (at least a sort of comfort) died. She flung it in the bushes and sobbed a moment stupidly without tears. The air seemed much colder now. She comforted Cass, and piggy-backed her for a while, once she managed again to find the path that led at least to a house, and people in it. She soon had to put the child down again, in terror as much as exhaustion, because they seemed again to be climbing ... But they went on, for Leora had staked her last effort on this path and could not go back to the glade, though it seemed in retrospect to be a place of peace and comfort, with logs to sit on and a smell of fires where the foresters had burned cuttings in their midday pause over beer and sausage.

In fact it was what in the hills is called a 'false level' and was in reality the lip of the lower glen. Suddenly the woods ceased and became fields, and in the same breath Harriet said 'House!' in an excited squeak. They stopped in a kind of awe. They were out of the woods.

In the clearer light of the false dawn (they had lost a half-hour in that beastly glade) could be seen a group of three or four houses, and a roughly-metalled roadway. It was the village. It was four in the morning, and the village was asleep,

150

and instinctively they hushed their footsteps and kept silence. The pursuers might be waiting here, laughingly, gloatingly. There were dogs and people. But the dogs slept, and that crouching threatening mass when one reached closer showed itself to be a parked car.

The village was a straggling affair, no more than one untidy street down the widening glen; the houses at the top (humped little cottages with a vegetable patch and a scratched piece wired round for chickens) isolated in the fields, farther down huddled closer and into some sort of line on either side. They limped wearily down, but the notion of civilization, however primitive, had put heart even into poor Cass, and she marched courageously without complaining, holding tight to Leora's scratched muddy hand.

The road widened into a vague 'centre'. A little church with a tiny cemetery, trim and cared for. A stone slab had carved upon it the twenty-odd pathetic names of the village boys dead for the Vaterland in '14–'18. Presbytery perhaps, there next door, but the uncompromisingly closed shutters stopped Leora from knocking. What explanation was she going to give for these three dilapidated apparitions that a sleepy bewildered country priest could grasp? And it wasn't spiritual comfort they needed most right now: material: very material.

Suddenly Leora saw the first gleam of light. The children dragged back on her arms, frightened and unwilling, but she marched them on.

It was a shop, like the other houses closed and shuttered, but distinguishable from the multitude of tatty notices tacked to the facade, advertising ice-cream and frozen foods, unmistakeable – and surely, thought Leora, they will have a phone, and I can get hold of policemen, staid country cops.

The light came not from the shop but a window next it, a kind of annexe. There was a doorway beyond, but it led to a junk cave of rusty oil-drums and stacked beer-crates. She tried the shop door; surprisingly it opened. Inside was a stuffy smell of sardines and knitting-wool and safety pins. Light streamed through a crack in a doorway, and there was a noise of machinery turning. Leora stumbled over

151

cabbage-crates, pushed the door to the light. It was the village bakery. Of course, she thought stupidly: that's why there are people about at four-thirty of a morning.

A man stood supervising the dough-mixer, smoking a cigarette, happily disregarding hygiene in a dirty sleeveless undervest with bunches of hair in massive armpits. He slammed open the door of the proving oven, slid out a trayful of pale risen masses of dough, swung the lever of the big baking-oven, hitched the tray into place with a casual practised push of his big floury belly. Sensing a presence he turned, showing no surprise from small currant-black eyes in the big floury face.

'No bread for another half-hour,' he mumbled round the cigarette which dropped ragged ash on his belly as he spoke; he brushed it off with a casual flick of the bare forearm. 'Rolls in ten minutes if you want to hang on.' Clank the machine threw him up cut lumps of dough, which deft fat hands turned and patted into loaves with amazing swiftness: with rapid flicks scored obliquely with a knife, slamming the proving oven open with a knee and heaving in another ready-floured tray of loaves. Bread: staff of life.

'Haven't you a helper?' asked Leora mesmerized. The hands juggled like a cabaret magician, lighting another cigarette, pouring out a glass of beer, flicking out loaves without stopping.

'Lady, you innocent. Living in the middle ages. No boys will do this now. Too hard work. 'Nother ten, twenty years, no more bread. Some automated factories, maybe. No real bread.' He seemed to see her for the first time. 'Hey, where you come from? You been in the wars, by the look of you.' Why the baby-talk? Perhaps he always talks like that. And what does one care, anyhow? 'You get lost in the woods?' 'That's right,' said Leora, completely relieved. It seemed to be all part of the day's work to this slightly drunk-happy and friendly person.

'Often happens. Times we had to make up search parties. Townspeople got no sense. You now – got out by yourselves.'

'By ourselves,' she repeated mechanically.

'Kiddies too,' wagging his head at this manifest imbecility, 'out all night.' The heat and the light were beginning to make her head swim.

'Can I have some of that beer?'

'Sure – here, you're all in. You sit a bit. A minute, I get these rolls out. You have one, 'n' a cup er coffee.' Her teeth were chattering on the edge of the glass. 'Cops looking for you?'

'I don't know. Like to phone them.'

'I'll do that for you. Husband worried, ey? Lucky it wasn't colder. Here.' Clank; a trayful of rolls held together in regimented rows by their little suction-pads of still-tacky dough. He broke off three. 'Careful – hot.' His speed fascinated Leora. He moved around the tiny machine-crammed space like a boxer in the ring, belly and all, with flat sliding steps to the fridge in the shop for more beer, to the kitchen behind for coffee.

'Hold up dear; there.' She took a big gulp; thin and bitter but near-boiling, and cleared the haze a bit. You're all right, love.' He raided a shelf and came with two tablets of chocolate. 'Grab hold, sweeties.' The children were sitting on the cabbage crates and leaning up against each other were nearly out of the world: he chucked them under the chin jovially. They bit automatically into the hot bread and whispered, 'Thank you.'

'Got four like you, meself. I know – Coca-cola?' They'll be sick, thought Leora vaguely, not much caring. Or maybe it'll do them good – glucose for energy.

Flick – crash. Keep the mixer a-thumping, get the proving oven refilled for the second batch, clank out another tray of rolls.

'I got a better idea. Joey be here in a minute, and he'll drive you down. Comes for the first bread – right too, there he is,' as a gleam of headlights flicked across the window.

Joey was a thin, saturnine person with a leather jacket over greasy overalls. What his calling in life was Leora never learned. He did not utter, listened with no surprise or comment while waiting for his bread, nodded, jerked a thumb at the waiting car.

'Thank you so much,' Leora managed to say.

'All right, love: think nothing of it,' said the baker.

153

She felt a vague astonishment, that there was a real world, and real people in it, who were kind.

The motor was running, to get the condensation off the screen. The car smelt of oil and stale cigarettes. The stuffing was coming out of the upholstery and one sat on knobbly objects. Leora dragged a stillson wrench out from under her behind. It was a place of great peace and comfort. Joey still did not utter. While driving, fast and expertly, he took bites off the crust of the hot loaf. Leora closed her eyes but did not have time to sleep before Joey jogged her elbow. The car had stopped.

'You're awfully kind.' He just shrugged. What, kind? He was going that way anyhow.

They stumbled up the steps of the Landespolizei bureau. Safe now at least, she thought mechanically, from the doctors and the morphia needle, or the bullet in the back of the neck. She was still half expecting Richard the Third to rise off the bench where he had been waiting for her, with his thin crooked smile, but there was nobody there. A bare wooden counter, a tidy polished look, several cherished green plants. Country cops are all serious gardeners. One sees them off duty, in breeches and shirtsleeves, weeding strenuously.

A little radio was playing gently syrupy music. There was nobody. Leora arranged the children on the bench: still chewing stickily on the last of their bread and chocolate. They huddled in a sleepy, comfortable fashion. The air was warm, fresh, smelling of floor polish and deodorant spray. Very German; the police were excellent housewives. The music changed to something pop, angular and thudding. This went suddenly away and a deep sweet caramel voice said 'Sud-West-Funk-Zwei. Five-thirty. Good Morning.' The pop came back, vanished again, and a male voice said, 'Good morning: can I help you?' and Leora realized that this meant her. She woke up. She felt filled with energy and ready to go. The duty cop, seeing a customer, had abolished his plastic cup of Nes and the remains of a ham sandwich.

'I'm sorry; I'm afraid I have a peculiar story. I'm Mrs Hawkins, I come from Hamburg. I've been in the woods all night. That's why I'm so dirty and sort of dishevelled. Those

154

are my two children. I want to make a report, and a complaint, and I want to get to higher authority very urgently.'

He was gawking. 'Hamburg?' Like meaning well, what the hell you doing here down in the south? 'What's the nature of your complaint?'

'Kidnapping. Holding for hostage. I have escaped.'

'What was the name, again?'

'Hawkins. I'll spell that for you.'

'Ah. Now I know. We've had phone calls about you.'

'Yes, I dare say you have. The thing is, they aren't necessarily true. That's what makes this complicated. And very, very urgent.'

'That's all right, madam, take it easy. You've had a rough time. You're not too well, you know. 'S all right now; we'll look after you.'

'Please don't interrupt me for a minute. I've been up all night, scrambling round in the forest in the dark and I know I look dirty and queer. As you can hear from my voice I am perfectly calm, rational and sensible. So please don't make judgments in advance. Wait and hear me out.'

'But look, madam, I know about this. No need to explain. Your doctor was on the phone. You're all right. I can get an ambulance.'

She had known all this. While marching along the paths in the dark, she had prepared for it. Incomprehension and official bloop. She had rehearsed carefully everything she would say. A triumph of lucid, crushing logic. The trouble was that she couldn't remember any of her lines.

'Look, I'm very sorry but that's all hearsay. Anyone can ring you up and tell you tales. None of that is supported by any evidence. I want to ask you please to listen carefully to me, because this is important.'

'But it's perfectly straightforward; we've had the reports. It was sensible of you to come in like this. The cars are out looking for you.'

'Will you please LISTEN? I'm not budging from here and if you try to coerce me you'll regret it. I'm an American citizen and I want the consulate. Where is the nearest big town? Munich, is it?'

'Look, you're confused, madam, you don't even know where you are.'

'Quite right, and so would you be. Get it into your head, you wouldn't know where you were. You've been kidnapped. Kept shut up in a country house. Look, I must talk to your officer.'

'He won't be on duty before six-thirty. You can leave this to me quite safely, madam: I'll see that you come to no harm.'

'We have different definitions of the word harm. I don't just mean warm and comfortable and a cup of coffee. I mean safe. Safe from pursuit and capture.'

'Well, ma'am, if you've got complaints to make about the treatment you've received I'm bound of course to register them. But that's not really police business, you know. These are medical matters and I –'

'I'm not talking about medical treatment, I'm talking about a CRIMINAL complaint. Every citizen has the right to make it, right? And see it forwarded to the Public Prosecutor, correct? So get cracking.'

Very dubiously, he turned to the piles of neatly ranged printed forms on the desk behind him. Deep uncertainty, chewing the lip.

'Listen, when your officer gets here, I'll talk to him. He'll get the message. If he then finds out that you refused to acknowledge a reasonable complaint, you're in trouble.'

'Look, ma'am, have you got your papers? Can you produce proof of identity?' Leora was afraid that at any minute the door would open and ambulance-men in white coats come charging in full of zealous kindness. If I can only get it down on paper there must be some official reaction. But she had planned for this much, at least. She unzipped her anorak. She had emptied her handbag, collected a few things at least in the inside pocket.

'I haven't my passport. I left home in a hurry and against my will. I was drugged. I do though have my driving licence, and a credit card, and some more stuff. I'm the wife of a scientist working at a government research station in Hamburg. He was kidnapped together with my children and myself. You can easily check that.'

He studied the pathetic heap of paper with immense care, studied her face, went back to the papers again.

'This is a pretty queer story, ma'am.'

'Look, you'll agree I'm rational. Calm, consequent. Maybe a bit impatient; that's understandable.'

'That's not for me to say,' embarrassed. 'I'm sorry but – I mean – I better ask the doctor to come up and make sure you're okay. I mean, you've had a night in the forest, that's exposure and shock and fatigue. Well, sorry ma'am, but my instructions are that there's a person of your description, and the identity is correct from these papers you show me, who's been under psychiatric treatment, and that it's urgent that you should not suffer from the lack of the – the continuance of the . . .' Leora had only one card left.

'I understand,' she said very quietly, 'that that's the way it looks to be. That's the information you've received. It's unsupported, right? I give you other information, and that too is unsupported. And until you get adequate confirmation one way or another you've no right to make a decision. So pending that we'll wait till your superior officer gets here. And if he's not satisfied with my word he can call an expert medical opinion on my health and state of mind. And we'll see then if I'm compos mentis, and to protect me, that examination, which I'll submit to, will be carried out in the presence of witnesses and a United States Consular official. Right?'

'Well, ma'am,' sufficiently stunned, 'that's all quite proper.'

'And now if you've no further objections, and since there isn't exactly a rush of customers this early, and since we've an hour to wait, will you please register my criminal complaint in formal terms which I will then sign?'

'Now good – yes ma'am. Would you kindly come in, and, uh, sit down? And uh – what about the children?'

'They're asleep. It's warm here. They'll take no harm. They've had some chocolate. And I've had a cup of coffee, from a kind village baker. Can I have some Nes? And I'm afraid I interrupted your breakfast. Perhaps we could both have some?'

'Why . . . sure. A pleasure.' He said, 'A moment' dubiously, vanished. Leora sat, looked at the table, covered in forms being typed up. The one nearest to her said, 'Whereas deposition has been made of a complaint by Herr Schenk, Joseph, born the . . .' Her head went whirling in slow spirals round the room. She steadied it on to the wall. Notices. Calendars. A large photo of a young girl laughing, in ski clothes, with very beautiful teeth. Signed at the bottom in good firm handwriting, legible; with character: she hoped she could do as much. 'With my sincerest regards and love to you all, Rosi Mittermaier.' Suddenly the amplifier of the short-wave radio on the side table, which had been humming placidly, like unagitated bees, crackled, coughed, spat, and said 'Car two to bureau. Car two. Over.' Her anxious pal came clanking in, in as much of a hurry as he could manage carrying two brimming plastic mugs, flicked the switch. 'Go ahead, car two.'

'Vagabond on the railway line. Flight and evasion. Apprehended. Possession crowbar. Bringing in for verification. Checking railway premises, okay? Ends.'

'Acknowledge: okay: stand by. Both cars: come in one, come in one.'

'One, on railway bridge at Breitestrasse on seven-four-five. Some frost on bridge, a semi-articulated skidded, some material damage, no corporeal, taking measurements, traffic unimpeded, ends.'

'Acknowledge. Okay, both cars, stand by: message. Suspend search on woman reported missing psychiatric clinic. All right, got that? Subject here at bureau making statement. Acknowledge or do I have to repeat?'

'One acknowledge.'

'Two acknowledge.'

'Okay till finish of tour: ends.' He released the mike switch, said 'They were looking for you, see?' pushed across the plastic mug, said, 'Bitte, bitte,' and started hunting for carbon papers in the drawer.

'Whereas,' said Leora, sipping and making a face.

'Moment. Married name. Maiden name. Date and place of birth.' Leora hoped she could remember all that.

'And whereas complaint has been deposed before me, Heinkes, Christian, Agent Second Class . . .'

'Well, briefly, I was seized in Hamburg in the middle of the night . . .'

'What date was that?' Lord . . .

'Can I look at your calendar, please?'

Leora sat in the office of the Landespolizei lieutenant. He was freshly shaved, and there was a strong smell of Aqua Velva. She didn't care to think what she smelt like. He was at his desk. The typed 'procés-verbal' of her tale – three forms full of carefully corrected typescript – lay neatly squared in front of him. He was smoking a Peter Stuyvesant, and so was she. He was a dark round-headed Bavarian with a heavy chin, blue despite the shave, and a small mouth which pursed. He had it pursed now. He was about three kilos overweight for his uniform. Leora didn't know whether she liked him or not, but thought there was a good deal to be said for him. Damning with faint praise, that. There had been a great deal to be said for Heinrich Himmler; he was likeable, too. But this man was going to be honest, she thought, and that meant a lot. He was not stuffing her down the chute into the nearest rubbish-bin in order to dispose of her, despite a civil servant's evident terror of sticking to a Tar Baby.

He'd begun by bullying, of course. She'd stood up to that fairly well, without bursting into tears or letting her voice get fish-wife. Then he'd become soapy, which frightened her a lot more. Fear made her aware of how incoherent it must sound. His hand had gone out two or three times to the telephone, and then drawn back. Now he was looking wise and paternal.

In fact his mind was full of vague metaphors about nests: wasps' nests, mares' nests; fouling one's own nest. The woman's story was perfectly preposterous, and he didn't believe it for a second. It could be checked, of course, but it just so happened that he knew about that house up in the hills. Been a thing once about burglar alarms. Wealthy fellow, the type who has friends in political circles. Been peremptory; made it clear that he didn't intend to be bothered with pettifogging regulations. One needed to know exactly where one was going with such types; not get dragged out of your depth. Above all, not to find yourself getting told off

159

like a schoolboy. And the woman was an American woman, and if there was one thing to be avoided it was a fuss with the State Department, or the Pentagon, or ... or whatever (he wasn't too sure which was which). They'd all be extremely sensitive about some neurotic civilian working maybe on a military project, and maybe secret into the bargain. Then he'd get told off by the security services. And he didn't want that!

One would go up there, preferably alone, and maybe out of uniform, and be formal. Covered, then. But get rid of this woman as fast as one could.

'Now good. This will all have to be gone into. There are some aspects that don't come within my competence. To provide care for yourself and your children is plainly a matter for your consular officials.'

'But what –' began Leora. But he put his hand out, palm forward, peremptory.

'Now please, I beg of you. This is all in hand.'

She couldn't make out what was going on. But she was kept busy with the children, awake now, cross and inclined to wail. There was a lot of bustle. The lieutenant remained sealed in his office, where a typewriter banged away. A doctor, curt at being brought out at this time, putting his consulting hours out of gear, appeared, looked her over without enthusiasm, had an irritating way of not finishing his sentences.

'Mm, yes, slight shock, touch of exposure, fatigue of course ... nothing there rest wouldn't take care of ... state of tension: you're wound up, unnaturally tight, aren't you? Don't want to talk about that? Well, I've been asked to see that you're not physiologically damaged. And uh, able to give a coherent account of yourself. Shouldn't be travelling, but not my rôle to insist upon that ... Give you mild sedative. Don't drink alcohol, keep warm, drink tisanes. Get some sleep; best thing for you.' He went off in the belief she'd had a road accident. 'That's what happens,' shaking a finger, 'when people drive too far at night. However, no bones broken.'

At last a cop appeared with a large official envelope. The forms had been filled in at last. He touched his cap.

'Got a jeep outside, ma'am, if you'd like to get the children settled.'

160

'Where are we going?'

'Police Headquarters, miss, in the town. 'S all I know; just been asked t'see y'get there safely. All aboard? Sorry, not very comfortable; best we can do.'

The noise and movement soothed her. She felt safe in a moving jeep, with two large stolid uniforms up front. She put an arm round each child, and fell into a doze. She woke for a moment when they reached the autobahn – too late to see the signs: stupid, she told herself, I still don't know where I am. Must remember to look out for the next set of directions. But her eyelids closed again.

A different noise woke her, as well as cramped arms; another rhythm; the stop/go of city traffic, the ting-ting of trams, the lurch of shifting into low gear.

'Where are we?'

'Town, miss.'

'Yes,' feeling foolish. 'But what town?' The uniformed shoulders turned to take an anxious look; was the woman all there?

'You've had a good sleep,' kindly. 'Stuttgart, ma'am. Here we are; end of the line: this is where we get off. They'll look after you.'

A big concrete fortress; a bewildering complex of glass and plastic, municipal notions of interior décor, where she tagged along after the polizei's boots, towing children who were numbed. Could have been the Chase Manhattan Bank for all she knew, but for the uniforms everywhere of city cops. The peelers as Jim called them – what was happening to Jim: what was happening to Jim? Waiting-room with comfortable benches where she plumped down dully among more people waiting with patient sadness to be disposed of by authority.

'Mrs Hawkins? Sorry to give you a start.' Quiet voice. A person younger, brisker than the lieutenant. smartly dressed. Sober suit, quite Chase Manhattan, but brilliant tie, blue and grey and sand colour. 'Aschenbach, Criminal Police; let's go in my office shall we? Bring the children. They'll be all right. I'll find something to play with,' smiling, ruffling Cassy's hair cheerfully. Leora felt wide awake, rested; much better.

161

Up in a lift, along a passage. 'The office' was only one in a row of boxes, but it was sunny, smelt fresh. It was all very encouraging. There was a stainless steel and imitation leather chair that was comfortable. The young man smiled, muttered something, went out with athletic movements. His desk was neat: on the blotting-pad lay what Leora recognized as 'her complaint'. She felt a sick foreboding at the sight of it, but the young man was back, cheerful, hands full. A glass of tea with lemon, some paper and pencils for the children (on the backs of the sheets were neat drawings of traffic accidents, which fascinated them at once), two packets of chewing-gum, and a cardboard box full of model cars. 'Borrowed from my colleagues in the Traffic Department,' engagingly. 'Oh yes,' sitting down, 'here's your doctor's prescription, which those clods forgot to give you. So, Mrs Hawkins,' tapping the papers 'this is all nonsense, isn't it?'

'Oh no,' frightened, 'not a bit.'

'No, I beg your pardon; I expressed myself badly. I meant that this is a stiff legal expression of what is evidently a story with more behind it. You feel up to telling me? Suppose we forget about this,' turning it over, abolishing it, 'and start again from scratch. By the way, I've phoned the consulate. They're sending a Mr Smith, whom I don't know. Some legal adviser, I dare say. Not that you're in any trouble – let's say that I've got to sort out your position with our civil and police authorities here, and Mr Smith I've no doubt will handle any points germane to your nationality, and – well – I daresay he'll take it from there. But right now ... what I want is a large general picture of these adventures you seem to have been having.'

Leora felt so heartened that she was at a loss. She sipped at the tea, accepted a Milde Sorte ('All I've got, I'm afraid') and said; 'All of a sudden, in Hamburg ...'

The fire was out. Marika had changed into trousers and a sweater. The Doctor looked much as usual. Sebregt's face was puffy with fatigue and fear.

'I can't risk bringing him across the border. My face is known at all the frontier posts.'

162

'Very well,' the Doctor said. 'You shall have the honour of conveying some heavy lumps of metal. So eminent a medical man; nobody would look inside his car. They'll have finished dismantling the device. You'd best be off, if you're sure to show yourself at the usual hour. You'll give Rika the drugs she may need. Ring the bell.'

Leora was repeating her story quietly and mildly, in the office of a young inspector of the Kripo called Aschenbach. She claimed it was a criminal complaint: very well. A relatively junior and inexperienced officer but nobody – he had been told rapidly – was likely to take her very seriously. Here is the 'procès-verbal' of her tale to the Landespolizei. Take another complete report; type it up. Bring it up to the Prosecutor's office. He can, if he judges fit, order a psychiatric examination. Unlikely – the discrepancies between the two tales, the confusions inherent within them, will probably suffice. Get her on to the Americans as soon as possible: Consulate's been given a ring. They're sending somebody around, some *Knabe* called Smith, that's right, like Schmidt. Follow-up? I'd be most astonished. The Prosecutor will likely instruct the Landespolizei out at wherever-it-was to check it up. Find a private clinic of sorts – as far as we know the doctor had reported her missing, asked that she be picked up, handled gently; acutely paranoid, schizo, what-do-I-know. Oh and Sepp. That French cop who came about the left-luggage-office corpse. Tidy that up with him. Nothing to it, just make sure that he signs all the forms discharging our responsibility for stale French corpses left lying around German railway premises. There's a good chap. And don't come worrying me with dotty women: I'm going to be very busy all day.

Herr Aschenbach agreed with Leora that the tale might not be suitable for children, and they were taken to play in the office of a female colleague next door. Who was out: all those juvenile prostitutes, he explained.

She was glad when he dropped the joky manner. Been assumed, she guessed, to put her at her ease. And very likely himself as well. Alarmed, no doubt, at the prospect of her going suddenly acutely paranoid, pulling a knife and saying she was Abraham and he'd make a good substitute for Isaac seeing there were no rams caught in thickets much around central Stuttgart.

Mr Smith came sidling in half way through. Leora had been bothered lest the consulate send somebody impossibly dense, the kind of foreign service officer whose ass would be best employed in briefing pygmies on Lake Chad. But he was all right. Quiet, sallow, Boston accent, around twenty-seven. Looked bright. It was perhaps his second or third post, and he'd be equal to an emergency a scrap more acute than a lost passport. He tilted his chair against the wall, dangled one foot, said, 'Don't let me interrupt.'

Herr Aschenbach was all right too. A bit German. Kidnapped scientists – yes, that would happen in Hamburg. Provincial place, that. Wouldn't occur in Stuttgart. But he made no comments; his questions were put briefly, in a quiet, neutral voice. Leora began to feel rested.

'An atomic device,' said the policeman, writing it down as unconcerned as though it were weedkiller. Mr Smith kept his face that of an attentive listener, but couldn't stop his eyebrows going up and down.

'Polite disbelief?' asked Leora.

'Not at all, not at all.'

'There must be proof. I've no doubt but that it's all been cleared away in a great hurry, but this man Henry. He must be buried around there somewhere.'

'No doubt.' A thoughtful expression began to appear round Smith's face that might have been anticipation: wait till the old man hears this one . . .

There were polite expressions at the end. About confidentiality: Herr Aschenbach quite agreed. Prosecutor's office, yes. Contact. Liaison. Quite.

'You have my card; that's my number. I have my car right outside, Mrs Hawkins. I only hope the Stuttgart police haven't put a parking ticket on it.'

'But I thought diplomatic cars didn't pay parking tickets,' said Leora stupidly.

'That's right; they don't,' smiling affably.

.   .   .   .   .

164

Mrs Day was blonde, buxom, full of small feminine attentions, and, thought Leora, a bit overwhelming. But immensely kind. However, if everyone keeps on repeating, 'Now don't you worry a scrap,' I shall begin to get seriously worried. So far, I haven't made a good impression; that much I can see. That German was far too smiling and unperturbed, and this Smith . . . Never mind, it's the first step on the ladder. After a wash, and doing something about my hair, and with a few more always provideds, like as long as I don't fall asleep with my mouth open in the middle of a phrase, or start weeping uncontrollably, I might do better in the next round, further up the hierarchy. I'm having a weep now, but it's controllable. And maybe it'll vaccinate me.

'Sorry to be weepy. But I'm worried about my husband.'

'Of course,' said Mrs Day kindly. 'Who wouldn't be?'

'Jeesus,' said the Vice-Consul. The Consul was away that day. Somehow, Consuls always are away, on the admittedly rare occasions when one wants them. 'Who's got her now – Day? Good: well when she's had a tidy I'd better have her. No, I won't want you yet awhile: after, to go over the tale for any inconsistencies. I mean obvious glaring inconsistencies. Meanwhile, you'd better do all the checking you can. Hamburg first: get on to the director at this DESY place, find out whether she – or he – had been showing previous signs of instability. Or anything else, I mean uh, like gambling debts. And who's our man in Basle – just verify this psychiatrist for us, without contacting him yet.'

'And Bonn? They're not going to be very pleased.'

'I'll do that,' none too happily, 'when I've heard her tale for myself. And, I guess, when I've some idea what the Germans think – though that . . . well, wait for it. Okay, if Day thinks she's presentable, shoot her in.'

He stood up politely.

'Glad to meet you; won't you sit down. MacNamara; kind of unfortunate, but I survive. I don't want to oblige you to go through all that again, and I understand that a written résumé is on the way, so perhaps we can start with informal conversation, and then take it from there?'

165

'And play it by ear?' said Leora, smiling she hoped attractively, looking at his hand which was sketching small embarrassed gestures in the air above his desk. The hand had a ring on it; a massive, ornate gold ring set with a ruby. 'Stanford, I see. Class of nineteen –' Both hands came up to stop her.

'Hey, hey.' The face beamed. 'The number is classified. And you?'

'It so happens.'

'Well,' with a big delighted laugh. 'And your husband?'

'Massachusetts – Amherst. But I met him out there on the Coast.'

'Ah, this is great.' And lucky touch, thought Leora. We're both from Stanford and by a logical conclusion I pass.

'I'm not demented, you know. I'm a little less dishevelled thanks to your kind Mrs Day. And I'm perfectly compos mentis.'

'I don't have the slightest doubt of it. So you came over with your husband to this place up in Hamburg – DESY, right. And before then?'

'Michigan State – associate in the Physics Department. East Lansing, you know?'

'Sure thing – Oldsmobiles!' They were old friends already. 'And so you're in Hamburg. And your husband's working on this thing they have there; a cyclotron, that's right? And you?'

'No. I gave up work till the children should be older. I'm not a Mzz, I'm a Missus.'

'Good for you.' Suddenly he recollected what they were there for. His mouth made a horrified oh. 'Then it's all true?'

'Yes, it is, I'm afraid.'

'Jesus. The Consul's away. Just as well, perhaps.

'Yale,' as though that explained everything. She nodded; she really had been lucky. 'And he really can make a – a – what's it called?'

'A device. A gadget.'

'And . . .' This was embarrassing again. 'Has he? Uh; I mean . . .'

'I don't know for sure. He can. I think he has, but I can't be certain. It's well on the way; I am sure about that.'

166

'He couldn't refuse, you mean? With you and the children held as hostages? But now that you're free? I mean they can't threaten him. They'd need him too badly, surely?'

'I don't know how to explain this. I think it's too late. He did resist, as long as he could. One needs to be a physicist, to understand . . . I'm married to one. You see, secretly, it's what they all want to do. It's the most exciting, eye-widening . . . look, I don't want to be personal, but hypothesize someone like you. Foreign service official. A good job. You've got tenure, bright, ambitious, still young. But it's middle management. And then hypothesize a fantastic dream. Sorry, I am being personal.'

'No, go on. I think I begin to understand.'

'All right then – hypothesize that a hand comes out and takes you by the shoulder and says Bill, you're tapped. As of now you're Under-Secretary-of-State: it's not just the German desk we're giving you, but the whole of Europe, and you'll have a free hand, and unimpeded access to the top. It would be a bit like that,' she concluded lamely.

'Jesus,' said Mr MacNamara for the third time. 'I see: I don't, but I see how I could. God, I have to get on to Bonn. This thing might already be usable. Not just a pipe-dream? Or a few bits and pieces? I knew nothing of the subject. Isn't it supposed to be far too difficult – need a whole team, need all sorts of special complex information?'

'I don't know. But I know it could be. Because before this even started there used to be arguments. Physicists – there are differences of opinion. But there's a consensus that the official line, as you've just quoted it, is rubbish: that it can be done, quite easily, one man. Jim always said it could. That's an aspect: he was so sure it could. Made up his mind that it should. If only to prove, beyond doubt or denial.'

'Yes. And you? Do you think it can? I don't mean on technical grounds: that's outside your province and mine, but on general grounds; human, political grounds. And then – there's been a lot of fuss about that recently – the nuclear material? The plutonium. We know it slops about now in staggering quantities: they say it's secure. But is it? Have these people pinched some?'

167

'We're graduates of the same university. You mustn't pin me down. And I – mustn't say anything that isn't evidential, that I can't vouch for. Some is hearsay. There was – no, damn it, there is – a garage next this house, which was converted into a chemical or metallurgical workshop. I was never allowed in it: I don't know what's there. But sometimes things were spoken of openly, in front of me. They were sure of me, you see. They can say I am mad, that it's all delusions and imagination. But it isn't. There is uranium. It's in a critical quantity. They brought it together to prove the existence of a critical mass. If I cry or become hysterical I beg you not to pat my head. It was done without proper precautions and a man they had, a technician, was terribly burned and he died. They killed him, to stop him suffering. God . . . sorry. But it's real, it's there. Machinery of all kinds, technical equipment: they discussed it stage by stage, and I was there. They have it; I've heard them say it will pop; that's the jargon. It would explode. An atomic explosion.'

'Hold on. Here, have a glass of water. Take one of these.' MacNamara lifted his hand with the ring on it and wrenched it across his facial muscles. 'Come to Marlboro County where the Flavour Is.'

'Sorry. I am, yes, inclined to hysteria. As a Stanford graduate, trained in detachment, I'd say the woman is trying to convey a very serious situation. And my man, my husband, is now a mechanical relay in the system. Telecommanded. And he's mechanically very apt. DESY will tell you so. So will East Lansing. He can do it, he knows how: he does.'

'I'd say you needed a drink. And it's only ten a.m. in Central European time, but so by God do I. I'm going to get a whisky for the two of us. You sit tight, hang on to your hat.'

Leora hung on to her hat, and wondered where the wind would blow her.

There was no wind in the Bonn Embassy, and no enthusiasm.

'Who's MacNamara? What are they putting up the chimney now – this place smells like a street-car. Oh, that MacNamara . . . Who's Hawkins? . . . oh, one of those. If that air-conditioner isn't working in thirty seconds somebody's going to be sorry. What's the name of the place? Daisy? Well, get them on the line. The Project Director, whoever's in authority there. It's a scientific establishment, there are Americans working there, I want to speak to whoever has personal and professional knowledge of these people . . . This MacNamara, that's all very well, but my experience tells me that the more plausible they sound the more paranoid they're likely to be . . . it's got to be checked; have Repellini come in here if he's around . . . You have? Then put him on. Berkeley here in Bonn. We've a query here on a man adrift from your establishment; one of our consulates is showing concern. You've an explanation? Yes, that's what we thought . . . Just give me a picture in brief terms, of the background. Security all right? Not engaged on secret work, was he? Now there's a further query on nuclear material. No, I mean of military application. Weapons grade, that's right . . . Karlsruhe . . . Jülich . . . very good, I'll check with the Germans. Right, that's exactly as I'd pictured it. Woman writing dialogue to her own screenplay . . . All right. My office will be in touch if need be. Thank you . . . Yes? Have him come in.

'Jimmy – take a seat a minute. What's the name of that woman, writes spy stories? There's always an innocent abroad, a professor of sorts, and a lovely young blonde girl and they get kidnapped by the Commies, and this real clean-living boy from the house in Langley has to go in there after them. You ought to be like him, but you aren't.

'No, it's not MacNamara, but no matter. That's our boy in Stuttgart who's been reading her. Here's the scenario: a physicist is over the hill from DESY in Hamburg, and his wife with him. No sweat – absent a few weeks with some kind of breakdown, being treated at a clinic in the Black Forest run by a Swiss shrink. They seem to have got it a bit ass-front-wards, by the way: turns out the wife is the one who's schizo. Maybe both are. Leastways, you know these clinics, they don't lock you up. She escapes, and turns up in Stuttgart at the consulate, all distraught, and she's tearing up the pea-patch with a tale of terrorist kidnappers holding her to ransom, and the big deal is the fellow's being blackmailed into building a home-made atomic device. Which is pure Batman stuff, am I right? Of course I'm right.

'So first, thefts of nuclear material, you're our expert, impossible, right?'

'No, not impossible; wrong. Unlikely, but not impossible. I'll explain. The accounting systems aren't accurate. Now and then they take stock. There's always a slight imbalance. Written off as unaccountable. Thing is, how big is the amount missing. Some confusion exists over what constitutes a significant quantity. General definition is that if it's under twenty kilos, which is sort of a vague figure for a critical quantity if the stuff is fully enriched, then it's not significant.'

'So there might be that much, or nearly that much missing and nobody sounds the alarm?'

'Back in Tennessee, maybe. This is supposed to have taken place here? Less likely. They're pretty careful. If they lost some, they wouldn't be likely to tell us. Who'd know would be Charley Korngold. Sort of tightlipped. He's their man, not ours. I know him a bit.'

'Well now; if this was just in the family . . . But this woman's flipped her lid, made a big grandstand accusation to the cops there about kidnapping and terrorists and blackmail. If they get agitated, and she's an American citizen, then they come screaming to us. That has this MacNamara set aflame.'

'You want I should go down to Stuttgart, maybe take a look-see?'

'You put your ear to the ground.'

A half-hour later Mr Repellini was on the telephone.

'Buz? I rang Charley Korngold. Who ought to be in Frankfurt. And what do you know, he's in Stuttgart. Investigating a peculiar rumour.'

'You get your ass over there. I'll have a chopper laid on for you. And ring me, right?'

The Landespolizei lieutenant had stamped out irritably, got into his car, driven up the hill. Fastening his seat-belt he became aware of a small hard package pressing his thigh. Colour-slide film, to go to Kodak for processing: put in his trousers' pocket to remind him to drop in at 'Foto-Binder': well, that would do on his way back.

The Doctor was apologetic.

'I'm so sorry you've been troubled, Lieutenant. We're distressed. My associate, Doctor Sebregt, has had to go back to Basle. She was responding well to treatment. These sudden crises do occur, alas. We liked to see her walking happily in the woods. She was under no restraint of course. We felt sure that rest here in the countryside – this nice house – our friend Herr Maier whom you know. Mr Hawkins – that's perfectly correct, yes a research station in Hamburg: oh, the usual; overwork, overstrain, without going into clinical details, an anxious over-meticulous personality. Very upset about his wife: we think he'd do better without these painful associations.

'What? That's just the point, my dear man. He was worried about his wife, who's been showing disquieting symptoms for some time, and that added to his tension: the one problem fed the other. We'd hoped that with activity – Herr Maier is of course a skilled engineer, in that highly technical field, semi-conductors, the properties of metals in electronic circuits. He has the garage fitted up for experiment and our friend was amusing himself with a physicist's interest in magnetic fields: no, hardly – therapy's not the word really: more a pastime. A toy train, well . . . I'll show you, shall I? It's no trouble . . .

'And this unhappy girl . . . There again, the medical picture is confidential as you'll appreciate. But they do combine schizoid features – very roughly it's a syndrome wherein they lose contact with the real world – and a nasty paranoia which can suddenly become acute, as we alas see.

'Oh, again roughly, a conviction of persecution, giving rise to fantasies of gangs and kidnappers. Quite common alas.

'They don't see visions, or not as a rule, but they get mysterious messages from imaginary persons, which tell them of threatened dangers and so forth. And she builds all that up, poor girl, into – have you still a minute? I realize these explanations are wearisomely technical. You'd care for a drink, while you're here?

171

'She'd been worrying too about her husband's work, where he has occasion to handle radioactive materials. Yes, exactly, there we have the seeds of the atom-bomb fantasy. I'm not the specialist; my background is in general medicine. I called in to see them and note progress. We hadn't thought she'd enter an acute phase. I'm afraid as a consequence she's lost confidence, regards us as hostile, wishing to entrap and imprison her – part of the syndrome.

'It's a great pity you encouraged her fantasies to go to Stuttgart. Still, I've no doubt she'll be in the proper hands and will be given the treatment she needs: oh yes, to anyone qualified it's quite obvious. Another little glass? I'm most disappointed: a crisis like that sets her back for months. Oh, she'll get over it. That is to say we hope so. They don't, sometimes ... She needs clinical care and supervision: rest alone won't do the trick.'

The lieutenant dropped in at 'Foto-Binder' on his way back to the office. He was a keen amateur photographer and was anxious to know how the Ektachrome-200 would reproduce the extremely interesting effects of light on water he'd been shooting.

He asked for Stuttgart Police Headquarters on the phone. 'Woman I sent down to you this morning; who interviewed her? ... ah, Herr Aschenbach, Landespolizei here – man, I wasn't to know. Melodrama, claiming protection of the U.S. Consulate, what else could I do? I've followed it up: I've just come from seeing the doctor who's been treating her. Not the Swiss shrink but this other – hell, I don't know; in Hamburg I suppose: what affair is that of mine?

'He tells me she's suffering from a syndrome. Schizo, and paranoid, that's the persecution bit. Oh yes, very plausible, that's characteristic. And this crap about bombs, that arises out of the husband's work, see? All hangs together. Americans are always consulting shrinks, let them worry about it. So she lodges criminal complaints? – can't you see, that's a symptom. They imagine terrorists and Doctor Fu Man Chu, that's typical: he explained. She ought to be under care he says, but he can't handle her because in the acute phase she

172

won't trust him now. Well, that's your bad luck ... Yes of course, I looked at it. A country villa in the hills. I know the place well, belongs to that big electronics factory in Munich. Maier, he's called: they build parts for rockets, radar or whatever. Fellow's a hot engineer, has a laboratory in his garage – no, in the country house; I've seen it. The husband was playing about with trains and stuff. You don't haul atomic bombs about with a toy train, do you? Well then ... bullshit, the woman is nuts. Chat her up, tell her yes, you're investigating, blah blah, and tell the Americans to wrap her up and care for her. The husband is over the edge, too: they've got him quietened down: he was in a state about her, but they've taken him off to Zürich. The shrink would be in touch. It's a classic. We all get had this way from time to time. I expected as much, woman with a James Bond tale of escaping from gangsters. They'd thought her stable enough to take a walk if that's what made her happy, and she suddenly goes critical on them.'

Herr Aschenbach cradled the phone and sat immobile for some while with his hand still on the instrument, making faces. He gave his head a shake to brush off cobwebs before turning without joy to a nasty dossier containing a rather stale corpse.

Leora was sound asleep. Mr MacNamara, kind man, had driven her to a hotel with ice-water, sanitized lavatory seats and a swimming-pool, booked her in as Frau Schmidt.

'Now you'll want clothes and things, I'm sure.'

'I've got my credit card.'

'Great. And Mrs Day says set your mind totally at rest where the children are concerned, she'll see they've everything they need.'

'By the way, Leora,' using her name with a little diffidence. That is rather touching, she thought: he wants me to know he's an ally. 'I want to ask you to stick around awhile. I know, sounds a bit like the sheriff warning you not to leave town, but we're meeting, how to call it, a bit of incredulity in higher spheres. Can't really blame them; they're able to think of nothing but the President arriving – there's this disarmament conference in Geneva, you know, and afterwards a heart-to-heart with the German Chancellor, and they're trying to set up a Russian summit in Berlin the same week. So you do understand, they're all in a fuss over nonsenses like security and protocol, and they're not particularly anxious to take Leora Hawkins and her problems all that seriously right now. OK? Count on me; I'm on your side.'

It all went over her head rather. She'd accepted it limply. She was even surprised how limply.

She'd made up her mind that she would not let the children out of her sight, and now . . . it was extraordinary how worry fell away from her: even worry about Jim. Jim had become part of that outside world about which she had not thought for weeks. Newspapers; radio; television – how unimportant it all seemed. She had to think about buying clothes, getting her hair fixed. She was suddenly hungry: she had an omelette in the coffee-shop. While eating she picked up a paper that had been left lying, and looked at the headlines, feeling that she ought to show some interest. But the world was jogging along, it seemed, much as before she went away from it. The usual quota of accidents and disasters; the usual rows about common-market food prices; the usual international conference, disarmament in Geneva. All very dull. Feeling too sleepy to stand on her feet she went up and fell into bed without even bothering to use her new toothbrush.

Mr Smith was hard at work. Day had taken those children home to her flat, to 'get them what they need, and take them to a movie maybe', so he had to fill in for her, do whatever couldn't be shelved, and still do checking in Hamburg. All pretty peculiar . . . It was wildly improbable, as everyone agreed – Bonn had been sarcastic about 'reading spy stories down there'. Yet contradictions abounded. He'd spoken to a couple of fellows who knew the pair well, and been taken aback. Hawkins overworking? – why, sure, been putting in a lot of time, but that wasn't unusual. No sign of unusual strain. Not as though he were an intense burned-up-inside type: Jim was relaxed. But there it was; nervous breakdowns happened – everyone knew of cases when a collapse came without warning. The general attitude once initial surprise passed was, 'Lucky old Jim; could do with a holiday in the mountains myself.' And Leora had gone off to be with him and look after him; natural enough, why wouldn't she? Didn't have a job of her own. Leora? – sweet girl – no, no, nothing queer about her, no fancy love-affairs. Not over-neighbourly, kept to herself pretty well, but good friends with the circle. Shy, quiet kid, sensitive yes.

'Leora's gone nuts?' – incredulity. Still, yes, could be, poor kid. That is more the introverted bottled-up type. Hyper-nervous; well, ye-es, you might say that. Putting it a bit strong. Why, sure we'll look after the children, we know them well – sweet children. Just send them up and we'll pick them up at the airport; no sweat. Now that is pretty odd, now you mention it; both Leora and Jim gone bust like that, a real close couple – well, that might be the answer – very devoted; maybe there was such a thing as too devoted. But while they hadn't thought about it much; mean-to-say, this Swiss psychiatrist had rung up, had confirmed by letter: nothing very serious, but a few weeks' rest was indispensable. After that nobody had given it that much thought. What was there one could do?

Right, thought Mr Smith. What was there one could do? Phone this Swiss, who was perfectly legit. He'd got the clinic: Doctor Sebregt was away that day but yes, yes, it was all under control. Mr Hawkins was in care, they'd give the phone number. He'd gotten the associate there in the Black Forest. 'Yes, yes, rather tragic. His patient was suffering from acute fatigue, but the sudden collapse of the wife was a grave set-back, and he must be left in quiet and unworried. She – well, he was not a specialist and preferred to leave diagnosis to his colleague, but could say she had shown signs of disorienta-tion, and there might be a schizophrenic syndrome in view of this abrupt flight from reality. Undoubtedly she needed care, but to take it easy. Don't alarm or worry her: let her rest, sleep, try to make the worries less acute. The Doctor didn't feel there was much he could do to help, in the circumstances. Try and get her to consult another colleague, of her own volition, that's most important, of her own volition, not to coerce her. If she seems unco-operative above all don't force her, let her come gradually to herself. 'If I may give a word of advice, Mr Smith, I realize that the Consulate's responsibilities do not extend further than natural concern for a fellow citizen. It is good, though, that she feels reassured and comforted by the presence of sympathetic compatriots. Don't put pressure upon her. These systematic fantasies, why, they're only a symptom. Not to take them too seriously. Neither encourage nor contradict them. If you contradict abruptly, you risk her reacting brutally. Go along with her, but don't of course be taken in. I'm glad to know she's in good hands.'

The atom bomb stuff, the most absurd of all, had been explained by the group director in Hamburg.

'Oh yes, I know. The Embassy in Bonn's been on the line, a Mr Berkeley. One of the bees in old Jim's bonnet: it doesn't surprise me all that much. Jim always had this theory that some terrorist group would steal some s.n.m. – oh, weapons grade fissionable stuff – and kidnap a physicist in order to build a home-made gadget. He had it all worked out. You know, those inconclusive arguments that do take place in shop discussions. In the light of this – what's it? – well, neurosis – I suppose it's normal. A neurotic suspicion that it's as he thought; self-justification. Poor old boy, he's been brooding too much on the subject I take it, it became a fixed idea and now he can't get rid of it. Leora's a sensitive girl. Maybe she's taken on this fantasy and become impregnated by osmosis with it. Try and get her to come home here; she's among friends. No difficulty getting a good opinion and treatment right here, I'm sure. Give her my best regards, and thanks for ringing.'

Day agreed. Before she went off, taking the children with her, they'd had a brief word in his office.

'I've been playing with them. It's only hearsay, but you'd better mention it to Mac: the children's remarks confirm it all. They are all right. Fatigued from being up all night, puzzled and confused: they don't understand why their mother was so frightened and nervous. It's all as she says, but it's her interpretation that's open to query. I mean they were taken off in the middle of the night – they were given some sedative, I'd guess – and then they were cared for by a kind woman, professionally, by the sound of it: some nurse. They were in a chalet affair in the hills, annexe to this clinic or whatever it is, and were told perfectly sensibly that their parents weren't too well. They played, and did lessons, and had a holiday, no strain at all, and then they were alarmed by Mama appearing suddenly in a distraught fashion with a peculiar tale written on a bit of paper and hidden in an old lipstick. I'm afraid she is over the edge even when she seems normal now. I've heard that paranoid types act convincingly once the crisis passes. She came creeping in the middle of the night, rousted them out of bed, and took them on this absurd trek through the woods. Obsessed, poor girl, with the notion that they're being persecuted. Whereas anyone can see that the children were kindly and affectionately treated. It's a great shame. They're quiet, but we'd better see that she doesn't get hold of them and start pouring out these fantasies. She's plausible, I admit.'

'She was at Stanford: you can imagine, that got to Mac: he went overboard for a moment. He'll regret that. Buz Berkeley up in Bonn was sarcastic about it. The Germans have been in an uproar but that'll die down as quick, I have no doubt.'

'Where is he now?'

'That's just it,' grinning a bit maliciously. 'Got a call from the Public Prosecutor's office. German Security Service buzzing, saying what the hell is all this nonsense. So he's gone off with a long face, to eat crow and admit he was suckered by a hysterical woman because she happened to be a graduate of Stanford.' Mrs Day laughed, sobered, made a face.

'Well, I got her parents' address. I telephoned. They'll take the children. Her father will be here as soon as he can make it.'

Leora slept.

Stefano Ferrandini, his daughter liked to say, was a man of few words, few actions, and few ambitions, but those to the point. (Jim liked him very much. 'And I'm glad my father-in-law hasn't one of those names like Achille or Cesare. Wouldn't

177

suit him. Not flamboyant.') He was an engineering draughts-
man. He walked to work, and enjoyed it; smoked ten cigarettes a day, and enjoyed them; had never owned a car, and
enjoyed that. All his married life had been passed in the same
large, but unpretentious flat in a poor quarter of the city: 'I
see no need for a change.'

Quite typically, instead of taking a taxi he bought a street
map, studied it carefully, and walked from the tramstop to
Mrs Day's flat.

She was charmed by his conversation.

'Coffee?'

'With much pleasure. Black, if I may.'

'How lovely to live in Venice.'

'It is detestable, but no more so than anywhere.'

'Is the uh, instability a worry to you?' Tact, with Italians . . .

'We are used to it. Minestrone Ministeriale, government by
Vegetable Soup.' Mrs Day pealed with laughter. 'You must
not think me original: the phrase belonged to Mussolini.'

'Gifted man.' One learned tact in the Consular Service.

'As a journalist much talent, yes. Unfortunately he thought
that enough.'

'What good English you speak.'

'But little. I grew up in the twenties. It was felt that the world
should speak Italian. A great handicap to us.'

'Leora and the children will be here in a minute. They're
just washing their faces.

'Uh, Signor Ferrandini,' said Day, self-conscious about
saying anything in pretend-Italian; such a dreadful number of
vowel-sounds it did take. 'Uh, I do hope you won't take it
amiss if I say something personal.'

'By no means.'

'Well, we had hoped, of course, that Leora, I mean it would
be such a good thing, wouldn't it, if she were to go quietly
home with the children to your house.'

'I had hoped she would,' with simple dignity.

'I mean, we're only too happy to have her. I mean I'd be
very happy if she'd accept to stay here awhile with me. I
mean, I'm divorced you see, and I live by myself. But obviously, I'm putting this very badly I know, it would be infinitely

178

preferable psychologically if she went home with you. Will you forgive me, I'm really embarrassed, if I were to say that on the whole we'd prefer it if you know, she kind of stuck around here in Stuttgart for awhile? That's sort of official, it's an instruction from Mr MacNamara, that's the U.S. Consul or vice-consul to be perfectly accurate, but let's just say it comes from up top. They want Leora to stick around till her story's sort of checked out. She's very generously accepted that. It's not that we disbelieve her, you understand; I'm putting this very badly. She's not in any trouble, and she's not under any pressure from us. No surveillance, to use a bum See Aye Ay sort of jargon, but we'd be happier. I only mention it so as not to hurt your, well, to avoid your being kind of disappointed.'

Stefano smiled faintly.

'I'm a believer in independence, Mrs Day. I've never complained about my daughter's actions. She married an English fellow, she became a United States citizen, she set up housekeeping wherever the job seemed right. No complaints or grievances at this end. It might seem to you cold-blooded, but I brought her up to know her own mind and take her own decisions. She knows this. She knows that if she wants me to look after her children but not to ask questions, that's a right I gave her as soon as she could reason. So set your mind at rest. Leora knows that with me she doesn't have to give explanations. Nor will I ask for them. I am anxious, and I am curious, but I know that she trusts me not to ask you for explanations. What she wants me to know, she will tell me.'

'Oh that's just great.' Day could have kissed the old boy. 'I can only say I wish our American moms understood that.'

Mrs Day had braced herself for a distraught scene, with floods of voluble Italian, and was much relieved to find Stefano 'more the courtly Doge type' (as she admitted to Mr Smith later, who replied crisply 'Stop talking in clichés, Day').

The meeting was very good; Leora determined not to let the family down. Her father stood up, gave her three formal kisses, turned to the little girls and did exactly the same by them. This sobriety took possession of everyone. The girls cried a little, blew their noses, said they would be good.

Papa was good too. He asked no questions whatever, least of all to Leora, least of all about Jim. It was the very opposite of what Day had dreaded.

In fact she fell into the trap herself, in an embarrassed desire to make conversation, and floundered in maternal detail.

'I'm afraid the children's clothes . . .'

'My wife will see that they have all they need.'

'Of course. Little girls' clothes are so pretty, in Italy.'

'They will feel at home.'

'Of course. And they speak Italian, don't they.'

'They can learn the Venetian dialect. We regard that,' smiling, 'as being much more important.'

'Oh, of course. And the museums,' slightly desperate: Leora was staring out of the window again.

'Come, children.' There were to be no wordy unnecessary adieux.

'So soon?' said Day stupidly.

'We have exactly forty minutes for our train.' She produced a large box of chocolates.

'Your kindness, Signora, will not readily be forgotten. They are not for the children. I do not allow them to eat sweets. But we eat much fruit.'

'Your wife, perhaps.'

'She will be very pleased and touched. Harriet, Cassandra, you will please thank Mrs Day for her great kindness.' And both little girls, falling absolutely naturally into this antique formality, curtseyed and said the right phrase. Everyone is magnetized by the man. Like Mussolini, thought Day idiotically.

He walked unhurriedly down the street, holding a child by each hand because streets are dangerous. Nobody looked back. The children had their heads turned up to him and were already talking excitedly, unselfconscious, utterly confident. At the street corner, before turning to disappear from sight, all three turned and waved formally, with the abrupt Italian jerk upward. The children in the identical pattern: they had already become Venetian children. A magician, thought Day. Talent, not just as a journalist.

180

'My father has done that all his life,' said Leora quietly, standing with her at the window. 'Every day, on his way to work, at the corner of our square, he turns so and waves to my mother. If she were not on the balcony he would do so just the same. But she always is, even when it rains.'

'He's a remarkable man.'

'He is stable, you see. Not like me. But I am obsessive.'

'Would you like to stay here, with me, Leora? I've lots of room, and I'd love to have you.'

'You are very kind,' sounding just like Stefano, 'but even for American hospitality – you have done so much.' She turned suddenly and held her hand out. 'For my children, I too wish to thank you.' Day embarrassed again. 'It's nothing, nothing,' she mumbled.

'It's everything. The children are the most important of all. With my father they will be happy: they always are. And for me too, thank you. I trust you completely. But I'm better off alone, in my hotel. And I have so much to do.'

'But it's what we're there for. You need not worry: if you trust me as you say, you must believe me. We'll do everything. Mac is very good, and so is Harold Smith despite that priggish Bostonian manner, believe me.'

'I do.' Leora took her by the shoulders and gave her an abrazo, the abrupt formal kiss on each cheek, just like Stefano. But with real affection, thought Day, much touched.

'I'll drive you.'

'No. I'm like Father, I'm quite happy with the street-car. But I'll keep the raincoat if I may for a day, till I get one.'

'Of course. It's a bit wide in the shoulder is the only bother. An umbrella?'

'No thanks. Truly I'm fine. I'm fine. Truly.'

Day watched her down the road; springy Italian walk. Feet very well placed, she thought. It's not just the shoes and the gloves being so well cut; one always notices the hands and the feet. And the neck, the carriage of the head and shoulders. The real ones have fantastic style. She's not pretty, but her walk turns suburban Stuttgart into a calle. Now stop being sentimental, Day. You better give Mac there a call.

Good survivors, Italians. What had the old man said?

(Old, nonsense, sixty and youthful for that.) Vegetable-soup government, economy a plate of boiled spaghetti, but we are supple, we are bowled over utterly, but we quickly again become upright. He had looked at her directly and said, 'The children will take no harm,' with a very clear articulation. It had been the one and only reference, even oblique, he had made to current circumstances . . .

Now for mercy's sake dial Mac and tell him that, at least, has gone off with no hitch. Poor old Mac. Worried; this business, and especially this damn Repellini character, is sending him off his nut: as he says himself in the phoney German they all used when they didn't want to be taken too seriously, 'I'm fair dunderkopfed.' A bit cute, but graphic. They all were, and what went on in the head of Leora nobody cared to make a guess about.

Sepp Aschenbach banged in at the door of the Kommissionar despite having been told not to, but got an unexpectedly sympathetic hearing.

'It's just that however crackers she appears we have surely the moral duty to check it out, no? Costs us nothing just to look. There's no instruction not to. And that dunderheaded Landes loo-tenant – he'll do nothing. If there's a body there we can find it.' Slap went the glasses in the middle of the blotting pad.

'Listen, m'n junge'.' A pause. 'You're a Wurtemburger aren't you?'

'Badener from Karlsruhe.'

'No matter, you understand this town, you know who runs it. Now I've just the one piece of information you need to turn the key. You know who owns that house up there? Maier Electronics in Munich. Put that in your mouth and chew it. And now for your information, something which is none of your affair and which I'm not in the least obliged to give you. The moment I heard of this affair, reading that report, I stretched out my hand to the far-speaker, that's this,' suiting the action to the word, as to a backward child, holding Sepp with watery but alert blue eyes, 'and rang Charley Korngold in Frankfurt. You know who that is?

The commissaire for special services, with Federal responsibilities and special powers. This is not a job for us, boy, but a job for him. Charley is a man I went to school with. He is thorough, tenacious, and just in case you were wondering, he's also bright.'

He put his glasses back on, sign that the interview was at an end. As Sepp was at the door he looked up again.

'It's good though, boy, that you cared enough to worry. That'll do.' This particular thaddledo, though there was one in identical tones that simply meant Piss Off, was shorthand for 'I think about it too, and even if I do nothing it's being taken care of'.

At the Public Prosecutor's office – the Staatsanwalt is an Attorney-General, who examines and if need be furthers complaints made under the Criminal Code – a conference was taking place amid long faces. Present were this official; Mr MacNamara, defensive and somewhat prickly; a high security official of the Federal Republic, who had driven from Frankfurt, cross at a peremptory call from the Attorney-General. And a quiet man, a Political Officer from the U.S. Embassy, vaguely a security type, who C.I.A. or not, was on the lists of all the left-wing papers, and who was 'watching' eventual United States Government interest. You never knew, in the case of a nuclear scare. Nothing in it, but suppose the Press . . .

'We must *not* let the Press get hold of this. Should this woman try to make a Press scare, it must be made plain that she's irresponsible.'

'And suppose she isn't irresponsible?'

'Now sorry, Mac, no hard feelings, but as far as we're concerned she is. You've heard what Charley here had to say.'

A right pair they make, thought Mr MacNamara spitefully. Jimmy Repellini isn't a bad guy, even if he does look like the Mafia hit man on late-night television; an advantage probably: if you look that much like a stage gangster nobody's going to believe you're a security agent. But this Korngold . . . Like a comic-strip robot; metallic, square,

183

bald, broken-nosed, globular-eyed, with a voice off a poor-quality tape.

'Our standing instructions,' said the lawyer smoothly, 'are that with any deposition containing allegations of terrorism, and by the same token a bomb threat – I leave this nuclear thing, which is patent nonsense, aside – any deposition, I repeat, not obviously motivated by malice, neurosis, self-interest or advertisement, the security authorities shall be contacted immediately. That is exactly what we have done. We receive an apparently logical and consequential tale, with a note by an experienced police officer that the author is on the surface collected and coherent, and that her tale is not shaken by the standard interrogation. We receive confirmation from the United States consular officials that the woman in question is indeed the wife of a scientist engaged in research upon radioactive materials. That is good enough for us, with no further pretext for intervention. The story had to be checked. Myself, I'm prepared to shelve the affair sine die upon word from the gentlemen of the security services.'

Korngold frowned and growled.

'Don't push me into corners, Herr Stellvertrehter.' He sat with big shoulders hunched, big hands jammed in jacket pockets. 'I have a formal assurance from Karlsruhe and all other establishments handling highly-enriched material that there are no discrepancies in stock and no reason to suppose a breach of security. That's as far as I go, but as far as I'm concerned it's the end of the line. I don't know what happens in Tennessee,' with a snide glance at Repellini.

'Anything can happen in Tennessee,' said the Embassy man easily.

'Seem to have our cart in front of our horse here, Charley. We're talking about if a group existed, and if it happened to acquire some hot material, and if it happened to kidnap a physicist, could it then create a nuclear blackmail situation. Well, how about premise number one; does such a group exist and what are its aims?'

'Horseshit,' said Korngold. 'Of course there are such groups in every spectrum of political opinion extreme enough to preach violence as an instrument. Left, right; upstairs-downstairs. So they got opium dreams about a nuclear threat: the very idea is a measure of trivial and unstable thinking. They couldn't do it, and couldn't keep it secret if they did.'

'Oh, you got that official handout too from the Nuclear Regulatory Commission?'

'We seem to be losing sight of the point at issue,' said the lawyer, 'which is the credibility of this woman. Quite evidently, the police were not asked to make a formal enquiry. They were asked to verify. It seems plain that the woman has been under psychiatric care, that she has a tendency to fantasy, and these fantasies, by the nature of her husband's employment, are coloured with nightmares about an atomic device. Has anybody anything to add? Mr MacNamara will you sum up for the defence?'

'Certainly not, and I accept no innuendo that I am encouraging irresponsible tales. It was clearly my duty to bring this matter to the attention of the legal authorities and to our Embassy. The presence here of Mr Repellini and Herr Korngold testifies that I did so. This woman produced a coherent tale. What facts in her tale are verifiable I don't know; it's not for me to judge. There seem to have been a few phone calls. It would be a very poor terrorist group that couldn't produce a cover story. Is she really schizophrenic? This Swiss doctor says so, but who's he? Come to that where is he? Come to that where's her husband? Fellow was treating her, she escapes from care – seems to me he should follow her up, continue caring for her.'

'As I understand it she was a voluntary patient; he had and has no right to restrain her. He says, quite properly to my mind, that if she deludes herself into a hostile view of him he cannot continue to treat her,' said the lawyer.

'Maybe her hostile view has some justification.'

'That is a point which can only be established, I should think, by an independent medical examination. We have no power to order such or to compel her to submit to such, since she has committed no offence.'

'If she thinks she has an important point to make, Mac,' said Repellini grinning, 'you might try and persuade her to submit to such.'

185

'Spoken like a true s.o.b.,' said MacNamara, laughing. 'Get her to go quietly home, where she has friends, is the consular duty as I read it.'

'We might like,' said the lawyer, looking at Korngold, 'to know a little more about this house and its ownership.'

'You can leave that to me.'

'Very well. My duty is clear. Formal complaint has been laid both with the district Landespolizei and the criminal police here, and I can't dismiss that out of hand. I therefore call an adjournment, either until medical opinion is available upon her state of mind, or until facts come to light which call for further enquiry. I think that's all for now, gentlemen.'

Leora was woken by a telephone tinkle.

'Frau Schmidt? – Herr Schmidt is here for you in the lobby.'

Leora was about to say that she knew no Schmidts when she recollected herself and said, 'Put him on.'

'Thought I'd like to ask to take you out to dinner,' said Mr Smith politely. 'Mac's tied up, he's sorry, asked me to say. Thought maybe I could fill you in on developments.'

'That's kind,' profoundly grateful she had had her hair fixed and bought some clothes. 'Be right with you.'

'Sure. Wait for you in the bar.' And indeed she found him a pleasant, considerate escort. She did her best in turn to talk easily and naturally, but could not rid herself of the knowledge that it was a duty assignment for him, that he was trying all the time to weigh her up, to puzzle her out. And what he had to tell her, laboriously clothed in drinks, dinner, a bottle of wine and lashings of tact, was a ball and chain. I'm going to get nowhere with these people, she thought, and when she excused herself as very tired – 'It's been a long day for me' – she could see he was glad to be rid of her.

Day dawned cold and pouring with rain on the city of Stuttgart, which smelt of wet umbrellas and the peculiar plastic compounds the Unterturckheim factory puts inside Mercedes-Benz automobiles. Sickly, bland, nauseating smells of instant-coffee, of cigars, of cabbage, of plastic flowers. Even the real flowers smelt artificial: Leora caught a whiff of a pretty bunch of freesias and caught sight simultaneously of her sallow face in a glass, and felt like throwing up. Mr Korngold and Mr Repellini, breakfasting together half a kilometre off, ordered schnaps to go with their third cup of coffee and looked at one another without enthusiasm. In the hills the rain was mixed with sleet. The lieutenant of Landespolizei, in receipt of a tiresome instruction – always the same these people, saying neither yea nor nay; why couldn't they either shit or get off the pot? – looked bleakly out of the window. The phone rang.

'Foto-Binder here. Thought I'd better check with you: we've a slight problem. I've just had Kodak on the line about your Ektachromes – seems they're fogged up, and since you asked for special trouble to be taken they're asking whether you really want them all processed.'

The lieutenant swore. Fine way to start the day.

'What do they mean, fogged up?'

'Well, foggy. Pinkish-blue haze they say on every slide, extending to the unexposed areas.'

'What the hell is that in aid of? Can't be the camera.'

'Well the only time I've seen a similar effect was from a security check at an airport – were you on an aircraft? Or did you have an X-ray at the dentist's or something?'

'No, of course not.'

'Odd – well, I'll tell them to cancel, shall I? Sorry about that.'

The lieutenant swore again, and looked out of the window some more, and suddenly got a horrid thought. Such a horrid thought that it took him a minute to decide what to do. He lifted the phone unhappily.

'Get me Civil Defence – no – no, cancel that. Get me Security in Stuttgart.' His embarrassment was considerable and his explanations vague. Stuttgart listened in ominous patience, and then said curtly 'All right, all right. We'll ring you back. Stand by for instructions.'

A phone rang on a refrigerator full of bottles of fruit juice: a waiter answered it, threaded between tables.

'Mr Korngold? Phone for you.' He was back in a moment.

'Something's come up – let's get over to the office. You want to ride with me?'

'Lieutenant? – Korngold here, Federal Security. Now listen; keep this line open. Using your other line, ring this house. Polite, non-committal, ask permission to come up, mm, take us an hour or more, say around lunchtime, tell them anything, just for a chat, to check up a few loose ends. Right? I'll hold on, here . . .

'Phone doesn't reply? Okay. Now the owner of this house is Herr Maier, right? And that is Maier Electronics in Munich, right? Good, I'll be up around lunchtime, with a technical squad. If the house is shut, so much the better . . . What are you telling me? Burglar alarms? So what? They ring in your office, don't they? Don't worry about that, man, the responsibility's mine, and I'll have authority from the Attorney-General if need be. Expect me in a couple of hours then . . . Worried about legality,' with a smile crinkling metallic areas in the square flat face.

'Maier Electronics.'

'That's right. Gentleman who has interested us from time to time. Wealthy, so quite a big shot in Bavaria.'

'Right wing, surely.'

'Oh, that's right, quite right. Very right.'

'So a bit sensitive.'

'In Bavaria. We're not in Bavaria. But what do you know – a camera film that got fogged, and a fellow who'd told the Kodak technicians to be real careful with this one. Isn't that something?' chuckling. 'Mad as hell he was, until he suddenly remembered he'd paid a visit to this dump where a physicist was playing with a toy train. What's Herr Maier been playing with in his home-workshop, hey?'

'And what does the independent medical opinion say about Mrs Hawkins' paranoia?' asked Repellini. 'Let's give our local MacNamara a ring . . . Mac? Jimmy here. We think a piece of evidence might become available that could, I say could, lend credence to your dippy dame. What have you done with her?'

'Done? Done nothing. I had Smith brief her last night. Took her out, explained things. Tried to get her to agree to an

188

independent psychiatric check. She didn't say yes, or no: she was supposed to come in this morning to discuss that. Hasn't shown.'

'Well, suppose you have your boy Smith bring her in – we may want her.'

'If you say so.'

'Why,' drawled Mr Repellini, 'I do say so.'

Getting a technical squad was no great problem.

'What are we supposed to be looking for?'

'Stuff pretty high-enriched. U-235 maybe, maybe plutonium. In largish quantities.'

'Jesus. Well, all right, need a beta-gamma monitor, a neutron monitor, boron-tri-fluoride. That's okay, I guess: we'll lay that on.'

But the Attorney-General wasn't having any.

'That's as may be, Korngold, but it's clearly unlawful search and seizure; I'd have to account for that in court. You want to secure a conviction?'

'Strikes me I want to stop a leak that might lead to nuclear blackmail on Federal Republic territory – that what you want?'

'You don't convince me. I grant you may have got hold of a scrap of evidence, but that's thin. There are plenty of places using small quantities of low-grade nuclear material, any of which would be enough to fog a film.'

'You know any electronics engineers keep stuff like that in the garages of their country house?'

'Yes, well, this Maier has a lot of political influence. That naturally does not affect the independence of the judiciary; quite so. But I'd still prefer to follow the rule-book.'

'Right, you want to do things the hard way. Let's get this Maier on the line and see if he wants to defy the federal security authority. We're losing time, that's all.'

'Herr Maier is on a business trip,' said a secretarial female. 'São Paulo, or maybe Brasilia.'

'What did I tell you?' said Korngold. 'In that case I'm going to ring the Federal Minister of Justice, get a blanket authorization on security grounds. That satisfy you? I want in, to that dump.'

'That will satisfy me,' said the Attorney-General blandly.

'All right, Lieutenant, we're going to break and enter. You take full notes, and make a legal deposition, and I'll countersign it all, and we're all law-abiding, and nobody's civil liberties are threatened, okay? Right boys, in.'

The technician carried a yellow box by a handle. A telephone coil connected to a probe, a chrome tube some twenty centimetres by three.

'Never mind the house', said Korngold, 'this garage interests me.' A cop produced enormous bunches of keys; they stood around while he fiddled and muttered.

'Positive,' said the technician. 'Something here, all right. Background reading – one millirem.' They passed through. Korngold grunted and pointed.

'Fresh concrete – in large quantities. Go on through.'

'Christ on a bike!' The needle had hit maximum. The technician switched the meter from low to high-range reading. 'Five hundred millirem an hour!'

'Sweep around the area.'

'Look for yourself.' The probe was under the lathe. 'Near maximum – this is on high-range.'

'You got your lead jockstrap on?' enquired Repellini.

'Place has been cleaned up,' said Korngold, 'but there's metal shavings and dust down there in the crevice. Sample kit please.'

A lead box, glass-lined, was produced. 'We've got what we want. It's got to be formally proved. That's evidence.'

'It's U all right,' said the technician, 'and pretty highly enriched. Mass spectrograph will tell us how high. To get it assayed we'll have to go to the Tech. University back in town. Their Geology Department will give us a mass spec. reading.'

'Yes, but what quantity did they have?' muttered Korngold.

'Significant?' He straightened up. 'You realize, all of you, that this is secret. A whisper from any of you, and it's your ass. Clear?'

'Let's get the fuck out of here,' said Repellini.

'No no,' said the technician kindly. 'No immediate danger.'

Leora had sat for a long while in the coffee shop, wondering how insane she was. Kind, tactful Mr Smith! Thanks though, but one brainwashing at a time is enough for me. So go back to Hamburg, dear, where there are kind friends or home where Mama will be happy to have me. And leave Jim, my poor Jim, happily screwing Marika until the moment they've got their machine ready. And then . . . and then . . . 'Ein Stoss!' The knife-blade going in. Just as soon as we've got the grave dug . . . But where had they taken him to?

'Fetch me a whisky,' she said to the waiter.

There was something in her mind, and she was trying to think back. Had it been that moment on the landing, shivering in her socks with her boots clenched in her hand, listening agonized to the casual, cheerful, conversation between Sebregt and the Doctor? Something about Switzerland, had she imagined that? About taking them to Switzerland? Sebregt came from there; he had consulting rooms in Basle, and a clinic somewhere out Zürich way. Unless she found out where Henry was buried, which could be anywhere in the woods, there was no evidence, even if these Germans were willing to look. And they weren't. Didn't want to rock any American boats. And the Americans didn't want to rock any German boats! No wonder the Doctor had not bothered to pursue her.

She was about as much use as an ice-cream cone here. Switzerland was large. They could be skiing in Gstaad, bob-running in St Moritz, skating round and round in Davos. Counting gold napoleons in Montreux. Driving peacefully down the pass towards Lake Como. Or making speeches in Geneva: people were always making speeches in Geneva, to which nobody ever listened.

Leora jumped up, said, 'Get me another of those,' to the startled waiter, went over to the newspaper rack, got a *Herald-Tribune* and a *FAZ*, and a *Süddeutsche Zeitung*. Yes, there was a report there in all three. There was an International Conference on Energy. One of those resounding, totally empty exercises in public relations. 'Discussions at the highest level' – blah blah – 'on Thursday and Friday the Chiefs of State are due to address the Assembly.' 'The intervention in the debate of . . .' – skip that. 'The high spot will undoubtedly be the day when the President of the United States, the President of France, and the Shah of Iran will in turn . . .' 'Among the heads of government present the Prime Ministers of Sweden and of the United Kingdom will be heard with especial attention' – blah. Is that possible?

At the very beginning – it seemed deep in a dim past now – she had speculated, 'What on earth can their target be?' And Jim shrugging. 'What interest has that? The important thing for them – or for us – is that it goes off at all. They could be planning to blow up the Vatican for all I know and it would still be irrelevant.'

Yes Jim. But it's no longer irrelevant.

'Half-measures!' – she could hear the Doctor's ironic voice at the dinner table. 'Half the world starves. The nations poison themselves in their greed for ever-increasing profits. An intoxicated populace sits goggling at the petty misdeeds of lunatic oafs flinging grenades. Now what, Jim, would force a whole ego-centric universe to pay attention for once? A universal catastrophe? The pop? What is the biggest megajerk ever detonated? Compared with an earthquake, it's an old woman pissing in the sea. And who cares for earthquakes? Tut-tut, send the International Red Cross with a few blankets and some typhus vaccine; the day after, it's forgotten. Who in Europe even knows where Guatemala is? No Jim, quite a tiny pop. But strategically placed.'

Leora got up.

'I'll sign my bill. Bring it out to the desk: I'm checking out.' She went over to the porter. 'Will you get me a self-drive car? Something quite small. Have it brought round in front, and as soon as they can. Ask the desk for the account. Don't bother about luggage; I've only an overnight bag.'

She walked along the shopping street. Surely yesterday she'd passed . . . yes, there it was. Hunting horns, silver brandy flasks, Tyrolean hats with feathers, loden capes. Nothing lethal that might tempt juvenile delinquents to break a window. But an armoury.

'I want a gun.'

'Certainly, madam. For your own protection? A pistol? You have a police permit?'

'No. A hunting gun.'

'Certainly, madam. Rifle, or shotgun?' She thought. 'What kind of game did you have in mind?'

'I'd be no good with a rifle. Shotgun. A repeater.'

'Certainly, madam,' puzzled, but it's the profit that counts. 'Manual repeater? Pump or bolt action? Or an automatic? Twelve bore – or sixteen?'

'I've no idea whatever – advise me.'

'For a lady of your height and build – single-barreled, and automatic, I think. Five shots without reload – this is a Beretta, very nice. Or Husqvarna?'

'Anything you like, as long as it works. And a box of cartridges.'

'Number Fives? Six?'

'A heavy pattern.'

What on earth is the silly cow planning to shoot at? And what do I care? Going out to shoot! Doesn't know whether it's deer or partridges – a lot it matters. Just you be dressed for the part, dear, because nobody will bother as long as you're willing for a good screw in the heather.

'Shall I have it wrapped, madam?'

'No. Just show me how to load it.'

As long as I'm not around when you pull any triggers.

'May I see your credit card, madam? Perfect. A tiny moment, to make the photostat . . . A beautiful gun; excellent buy, madam. You'd like to take it with you?'

'I'll drive past. In about a quarter of an hour.'

'I shall look out for you, madam. Save you the trouble of parking. Many thanks, madam, that is all in perfect order.'

Why should I care about money, thought Leora. Jim's monthly cheque will have been deposited in Hamburg, and isn't even touched.

And another monkey was bowing slavishly at the porter's desk. The usual Opel Kadett. Go anywhere with that and nobody will notice you.

'Can I leave the car in Hamburg? I'm going for a bit of a holiday. Berlin maybe?'

'Anywhere you like. You've a German licence? And may I see your credit card? Sign here, if you will. Many thanks. Guten Tag und gute Fahrt, gnädige Frau.'

'I'll just go pick up my parcels.'

The porter rushed to open the car door for her. They'll do anything for that discreet crumpled bit of paper. Touch their hats and grin.

'Good day to you, madam, and thank you, and have a nice holiday.'

'Thank you,' said Leora with a beaming smile. Nice, eager little car.

'I'm so sorry, I'm afraid Frau Schmidt has checked out. Just a quarter of an hour ago. On her way to Berlin, I think she said.'

'It's of no consequence,' said Mr Smith. Heavens, the woman's committed no crime. Can't have the cops running after her. The girl's confused. Needs a break, that's all. Glad to have missed her, really. What could I say to her, beyond banalities? That we're glad to be shot of her?

PART FIVE

'The Initiator'

'The Scissor-Man'

Was it a dream? It might well have been.

Jim dreamed that he woke. He opened his eyes: it was dark. Dark swirled about him in thick coils of mephitic vapour. Winding around him, threatening to tighten, to crush the life out of him. An appalling terror took hold of him. He closed his eyes again. That was better. He felt sweat on his face, signalled to his hand to come and wipe it off. The hand obeyed, but with an alarming lethargy. I am drugged, thought Jim.

Since his eyes were no use he tried his ears. Auditory mechanisms seemed no better than the visual. He could hear nothing, not even the familiar tick of the alarm clock. The silence came in thick sluggish coils like the dark. He wished to get up, to turn on the light, to look at his watch but the thick lethargy of his limbs told him that this was a task too great for present strength. After a while he thought that this was a half truth. It was more accurate to say that he was afraid. Terrorstruck by whatever was there in the dark, just outside the radius of his breath. In any case, he was convinced that any movement of his head from the horizontal would bring on a crippling huge wave of nausea and dizziness. I am drugged; it has brought about a sense of physical disorientation. Am I floating in a bath of some warm oily liquid? Perhaps glycerine? My head seems to be facing upward, my body lying on its back. But can I be sure? The only thing I can be sure of is that I'm hallucinating. This kind of drug-induced disorientation can produce strange illusions. But I cannot be floating head downward, surely. I should be unable to breathe.

This is a pillow I'm touching? Am I even sure of that?

I am lying on my back, breathing through my nose. My breath in my nasal cavities is making an enormous amount of noise. Am I snoring? I mustn't snore.

With a heavy, floundering effort, bogged by the leaden blankets, Jim turned upon his side. His hand went out to explore this pillow, so-called. It touched hair, sending an electric thrill through him. Someone – someone strange; that was not Leora – was in bed with him. He moved his hand down. Go very lightly indeed, explore very carefully. A shoulder, a back. A softness of behind. A woman. A naked woman. Marika, of course.

That was, he supposed, nice, but how did he come to have a naked Marika in bed with him? Better not ask. It was a very strange bed. If you ask, something horrible will happen. He was in any case too tired to ask, or too lethargic. You are drugged, boy. This is nightmare. She is not there at all. There is no bed, no pillow, no naked woman. You are dead. You are a decomposed corpse floating somewhere in the sea, buoyed up by decomposition.

'You are hurting me,' said Marika's voice.

He came awake with a jolt.

'I am? But I was scarcely touching you.'

'You were pressing very heavily into my neck; it hurt my spinal column. I am here; be reassured. I am real, alive. Touch me, explore me. I am quite naked. I belong to you.'

He did. The sensation was pleasant. One was pleasantly suspended between waking and sleeping, running fingers up and down a woman's spine.

'Is that better?'

'Better. Not so heavy. No, still too heavy, and too stiff. Play a piano, or a violin, or anything. Get the fingering right. Better. I am awake, wide awake. You are awakening. It is slower. There.' He explored her behind, rolled her over. There were relapses in which his hand became enormous, his fingers as thick and stiff as immense shiny sausages in some horrible butcher's shop hanging in a stupid dangling line. But it got better; he wanted her, he took her, as far as he was able to judge, competently.

196

He rather thought that he fell asleep again for a little while. When he woke again the dark was still intensely dark. But not thick, not strangling; he was no longer in risk of asphyxiating. She was there, comfortably resting on his collar-bone, breathing quietly; awake, alert.

'Who are you?' he asked curiously. Her voice was quiet and clear in the darkness. Sometimes it seemed to come from far away, but still clear and distinct. The drug has not yet worn off. But it is wearing off. Jim decided that he did not want to know where he was nor why she should be in bed with him.

'I am Marika.'

'But who is that? Who is the person?'

'It is not a person. It is a woman, warm and alive, in your arms, whom you have taken, whom you can take again, whom you will take as often as you desire. If you do not, rest quietly. Talk if you feel like it. Sleep if you feel like it.'

'I have slept. I want to talk. About her, the woman, about Marika.'

'Marika is not a person. It is a people.'

'What is this people?'

'You wish to know? Perhaps you should know. She will tell you. A people invaded and conquered over and over again. But never subdued, never reconciled, never accepting bondage. Slowly changed by the bondage. Brutalized by the brutality. It suffered very much, very long, very slowly.'

'What is this people?'

'It is of no consequence. There are many peoples like this. Many Indian tribes. This is a very old people. I do not know where it came from. From other countries. It found a land, a good one, fertile and watered. Plains and hills. It lived there in peace. It became civilized. Then invaders came, strong and terrifying. It wished to live in peace, but this was not possible. The invaders were fierce, energetic, greedy, heavily armed. Too strong. The land was conquered. At first the invaders lived quietly, content with their gains. But they pushed steadily further, disregarding treaties, greedy, wanting more. They took the whole land. They held it. We rebelled. The rebellions were put down with fire and bloodshed. Worse, with genocide.

We were driven into barren inhospitable regions. Our women and children were shot with bullets, cut down with sabres, killed by any means. Cold, starvation, pneumonia. Violence often. Children taken by the feet and swung against stones to knock their brains out. Women raped until they haemorrhaged to death. Any means was good. We were an ignoble remnant, an inferior race of dirty diseased savages, to be exterminated.'

'What are you? Navajo? Zuni? Cheyenne?'

'It does not matter. All over the world there are others like us. Remnants of us survived, in spite of everything. There were even moments when we multiplied. Hard to believe. We had become the savages they said we were. We forgot our customs, our religion, our language.'

'I have heard you talk that language. What is it?'

'It does not matter. When we grew, despite everything, too strong or numerous laws were enacted against us. Penal laws, harsh and oppressive. We were forbidden movement, forced to obey curfews, no gathering or ceremony was allowed us. We became the savages they claimed we had always been. Sly, crooked, treacherous. Sometimes we assassinated isolated individuals or groups among the conquerors. We even waged battles, though we were always beaten, as much by our treachery, our incompetence, as by superior force. We had no solidarity. We distrusted one another. Plots and cabals undermined us. Our lands were gone. We lived in such poverty that we became subhuman.'

'Mexican? Peruvian?'

'All those peoples. Famine was inflicted on us. When by chance we found food we could not digest it: it did not nourish us. After famine came typhus. We fled and wandered bewildered, knowing nothing, understanding nothing.

'At last they wearied of persecuting even the wretched remnant we had become. They left us alone. A piece of the ground we had once owned was allotted us. We had become so barbaric, so backward that we could not administer even this. We fought among ourselves. Our numbers dwindled further.'

'Paraguay.'

198

'I tell you for the last time, it does not matter. We accepted the economic stranglehold of the conqueror; his laws and customs, his currency and systems. We pretended that we still retained traces of our own individuality, but these were feeble and silly pretences. We spoke his language, we obeyed his codes, we drove his cars, we sold him our animals when we had nothing else to sell. Ourselves we had sold long before. We are crooked, illiterate, barbarian, all that they had ever said we were. Our men cannot build, our women cannot cook; they no longer know how to breastfeed a baby. They say we are independent now. It is not true.'

Palestinian, thought Jim: it must be.

'By some obscure trick of genetics I was healthy, straight, intelligent – even pretty. I went out into the world. I tried to educate myself. I tried to understand. I met more people like myself. Everywhere, behind the civilizations like France or Germany, the United States or Britain, I met suffering, oppression, apathy, hypocrisy. Nobody cared. Nobody would move. Resolutions were passed. The United Nations made speeches. All rubbish. Yet we were a people once. We have contributed to the world, to civilization, we have played a role in dignity, simplicity, honesty. You could go from door to door of our people and never meet a thief. We were open and frank. Hospitality was sacred. Go among our people now, and you will find nothing but lies, litigation, cheating and chicanery. We can never struggle back. Disease and despair, famine and plundering, breaking and stealing have worn us too far down.'

Argentine Indian perhaps. Intermingled with Spanish blood and Basque. That language, unlike anything I have ever heard, could perhaps be Basque. Remnant perhaps of the Spanish Civil War? Emigrated to Argentina? Oh hell, what does it matter? She is right.

'I can do little. I am helpless. I am not a Judith or an Esther. But I have met a man whose ideas were mine. To-gether we will do something. With you. You have come to help us, to rescue us. You are a good man. Hold me. Love me, again. I am lonely and unhappy.'

.   .   .   .   .

199

Afterwards, Jim thought he fell asleep again. Was it all a dream induced by heavy dosage of hypnotic and soporific drugs? Some of those things had weird side effects.

The air was different.

Less cold; less invigorating. A change in the wind? A true southerly wind was a rarity. Something enervating about it, not truly a scent but carrying a memory of mimosa and umbrella pines, so different from these stiff wet northern spruces. They were a long way south of Hamburg. Perhaps in springtime here when the south wind blew one could imagine the smell of sun, on the rocks of the Esterel. A lazy feel; a holiday feel. His head was heavy, his veins filled with lassitude.

The light was different. Darker than it should be. That was it; he'd woken much earlier than he should. The wind had changed; it was much warmer; there were too many blankets on the bed. He had been dreaming, sleeping too heavily. One woke in the pitch darkness from that deep pit, and lost all sense of orientation.

He remembered – they were no longer in Hamburg. He still wanted to sleep. His head felt heavy. Arms and legs ached. Body sweaty. Touch of flu. He could not be bothered looking at his watch. He didn't care what time it was. He was ill, and tired. Jim rolled over sluggishly, heaved his pelvis – even that ached – into a more comfortable position.

He'd been dreaming again. He was lying in bed, in the dream, lazy and not concentrating. And Leora was sitting up – right on her half of the bed, in sloppy pyjamas, hair tousled, shaking a finger at him crossly. 'You must learn it,' she was saying, 'you must get it by heart. If you don't, you'll be punished. It's very important. Repeat again after me. We are, I know not how, double in ourselves. Got that right? Now: we believe, we disbelieve. Come, it's not difficult. Again. We believe, we disbelieve. Good: last phrase. We cannot rid ourselves of what we condemn. We cannot rid ourselves of what we condemn. Come on, waken up. Now the whole again, right through. We are, I know not how ...' The voice was Leora's in a bad mood, sharp and scolding. The face was somehow not Leora's. And why did she have long black hair suddenly? Was it her, at all?

The smell was different. The house should smell of wood. Smoke, and things that went with wood. Varnish and floor-polish, linseed oil and resin and through the window the strong invigorating smell of trees soaked in rain. The smell here was altogether wrong. And the light was wrong; he'd overslept, for it was much too light. He sat up with a jerk and looked to the window.

The window was different. In the wrong place. He stared in disbelief; was the window barred, and why were the bars a funny shape? Nonsense, of course there were no bars. That was a wrought-iron balcony. A German rococo of the late nineteenth century.

The bed was different. It was too wide, too soft, the eider-down too fat. No wonder he'd slept heavily. And where were they, in heaven's name? Leora was already up: her half of the bed was hollowed and still warm but empty. And there was something odd because the bed did not smell of Leora, but of an entirely different woman. He snatched at his watch. Daylight, eight o'clock. He looked at the window again, knowing now. The light was wrong for eight o'clock, and there was no grass outside the window; there was only sky. And he had been in bed with Rika! He looked again at his watch, in disbelief because there was something wrong there too. It should have said Monday. It said Tuesday! And the heavy ache in his bones, somehow connected with Hamburg in his mind, was not fever but opium. He had been drugged again . . .

He looked around the room in idiot astonishment. A conventional bedroom, furnished in German Biedermayer with much mahogany and flowered chintz; wavy blue tendrils and flabby pink roses: the carpet was a faded sky blue. His greatest shock came from the dressing-table mirror. His hair was not the familiar dark red. It was black, as black as Rika's. The eyes were bloodshot. Only the face, needing a shave, was still Jim's, however pasty.

If they were imprisoned in a different house, and he'd been dumped unconscious in this puffy bed, and – migawd – sharing with Rika – where the hell was Leora?

Sunday night . . . she'd gone off distraught and hysterical, demanding to sleep in the guest room. That Swiss had been there. She had created an uproar. What had happened to her? Had they killed her?

He must control himself. He took great breaths, went over to the window to breathe better.

More disbelief. A steep slope with pinewoods, but a different sort of slope, and different pines. There below was a road. There below was the sea! Were they on the Mediterranean? The sea had a funny look. There was a mist on it, and a sun struggling to pierce the thin, clinging sea-fret. He was high enough to see over it. Large masses of cloud – those were not large masses of cloud. Those were montains. Those were Alps. This was a lake.

Not a lake he'd ever seen. He'd seen Como; this was not Como. Not an Italian lake anyway; it was the wrong way round. The sun was slightly to his left, so he was looking from north to south. A Swiss lake. Or maybe Austrian? Surely none of the Austrian lakes was this big? Nor a French lake, surely. What Swiss lakes were there, this big? There was Constance, and if he were on the north shore this would still be Germany. There was Zürich, and there was Neuchatel. There was Leman, of course, and wasn't there Lucerne, or was he muddling that with Lugano, Locarno? The place was full of goddam lakes; one couldn't remember them all.

The immediate geography was foreshortened. Couldn't see much. It was a second-floor balcony; one couldn't go out on it; no room for more than a window-box. A pretentious fake. Typically Swiss–German, mentality of a nineteenth-century butcher who'd made his pile, to build a high villa on a steep slope! There were three floors, maybe attics above. A place for lots of servants, to show off. He could not see straight down; the real balcony got in the way. Beyond was the roof of a car, a white Mercedes. Fussy flowerbeds full of geraniums, too bright in colour. Gravel. Tops of trees. Beyond was a road dropping steeply down to the wide lake-shore boulevard. It gave one vertigo. Where was Leora? He decided to have a bath, a shower, something. Needed a shave. Needed to clear his head. Needed something to eat. No appetite, but felt hollow in the stomach. Many things were needed. Jim, pull yourself together. For weeks you've been a zombie.

Outside on the landing he found a bathroom. Also on the landing a whitejacket, familiar depressing sight, pottering with a vacuum-cleaner. Who looked at him with a flicker of a grin, half-contemptuous.

A horrible bathroom, at once cramped and pompous, with huge porcelain objects. There was his razor, his toothbrush. Nothing of Leora's. He felt afraid.

He went down the stairs slowly, belly knotted. After showering he'd filled the bath and lain trying to lift the black cloud, but it had not worked. Sour stale lassitude.

The first-floor landing had already been vacuumed; the sand-coloured staircarpet appallingly clean. The hall was prim, narrow, full of pier mirrors and little tables. On one side was a door which showed him a drawing-room, fake Louis Quinze in cream and yellow satin. The other side was right; a smell of coffee.

'Come on in, Jim,' said the Doctor's calm voice. 'Make yourself at home. I'm afraid this coffee is stale: we'll have some more.' He picked up a brass bell off the polished mahogany of the dining-room table and tinkled it. Imitation cow-bell: all had a Swiss smell, a musty propriety – Switzerland in the eighteen-eighties. The sun had eaten up the mist and struck boldly through the windows in lozenges of red, green and yellow; Victorian stained glass. The Doctor was freshly-shaved, in a dark suit, *Neuer Zürcher Zeitung* folded to the Stock Exchange page, exactly the rentier who had built this house. A whitejacket appeared.

'Some fresh coffee. Jim? – you must be hungry.' Some dim inheritance from early upbringing, middle-class shibboleth; no personal matters in front of the servants. The effect of the house, redolent of bourgeois attitudes. Jim wanted to say 'Where's Leora?' Instead he said, 'I can't eat, yet. Maybe later. I want something to drink.' The Doctor's eyebrows, composed as ever, did not flicker.

'A bottle of white wine. One glass. I'll ring again, for the coffee.' Jim sat, on stiff imitation Chippendale. The picture on the wall was not a steel engraving of the Monarch of the

Glen, but a near-Swiss-miss. The Doctor's eyes were blood-shot too, and his face – hard to tell in this light – paler than usual. He smoked his little cigar and turned to the music criticisms. A premiere of *Don Pasquale* at the Scala had his total attention. Whitejacket brought a silver tray. Greenish bulbous glass. Bottle of fondant. Jim clutched at every detail, to keep a grasp on reality.

'So we're in Switzerland.'

'As you surmise.'

'And that water down there is?'

'Lac Leman.'

'I like to know where I am even if I've lost the habit.'

'When it was necessary I concealed it. It isn't, so I don't.'

Placid Jim . . . Leora said he does not ignite but has to be detonated . . .

'Where's Leora?'

'Right this minute? I'm not altogether certain.'

'All right, mate; now you can stop fucking me about.'

The Doctor folded his paper neatly and laid it aside.

'I've been waiting for you because there are explanations to make. I understand your nervousness; I've been under strain myself. Control it as I do. I have admired the tenacious instinct which kept you concentrated on your work in a time of stress. Our task is nearly finished, but not quite. A man's work will save him from every sort of folly.'

'No longer good enough.'

'The flaw in our system was that we all had tasks, except Leora. Enforced idleness has been her undoing. The chimera fills a vacuum thus produced – classic, and I blame myself for not perceiving it. We must also give Leora credit for being an adroit actress. Gave us the slip neatly,' with ironic admiration.

Jim, who had been ready to shoot out and take the pip-squeak by the throat, pushed back in his chair. Slow, he told himself; work it out first. He poured himself a glass of the white wine with a hand that shook very slightly, so that he wondered whether the Doctor noticed it.

'Go on.'

'Off she went in the middle of the night. Ran to the police, ran to the local consulate, created a noisy fuss.'

'So you're blown, sky-high.' Jim's voice, gloating at discomfiture, was full of relief. Straightforward situation now. Terrorists holding hostages. Those idiots had learned to handle that, one hoped.

'Not in the least. A slight emergency, I don't deny it. We decamped in a hurry. We had to drug you, disguise you a little, for which I apologize. We've left our friend Sebregt a quantity of explaining, which might embarrass him, but there . . .' He chuckled; it was rather funny.

'I don't see what you're laughing at. Every security authority in Europe is looking for you by now. You'll be in the net within hours.'

'You ought to know me better, Jim. You know I planned this. Do you imagine I gave no thought to premature leakage? Nobody, for an instant, will credit Leora's tales. Assume that some nervous security man wonders about them. He will check half-heartedly, without conviction. He goes to Sebregt. He would discover – assuming the interrogation thorough and professional – that she knows nothing. Neither where we are nor who we are. Nor exactly what we are doing. Nor why.'

'You forget one thing.' Jim poured out his second glass with a hand now firm. 'Leora might not be believed. And when people ask where I am, that's of no great moment; I agree, they won't much care. But when people ask where the children are, that will be taken seriously. A good weapon against me, I agree, but you will find it double-edged.'

The Doctor stood up, walked over to the sideboard, rummaged in it for a glass.

'I believe I'll join you after all. The children, you say. You needn't worry about them – she took them with her.'

Jim got to his feet. I understand the manoeuvre, he thought; he's put the table between us. Go slow. He started to walk around the table.

'So that means,' in a drawl, 'that I'm the only hostage you've got left.'

The Doctor turned around to face him, unbuttoning

his jacket. In his waistband showed the curved butt of a revolver.

'Don't let's be melodramatic, Jim.'

Charley Korngold and Jimmy Repellini – 'Migawd,' said Mr Berkeley in Bonn, making a personal report to the Ambassador, 'I've difficulty taking that pair seriously; they sound like trombone-players left over from Woody Herman': – were driving down the autoroute to Basle. They didn't have much to say to one another.

'If we'd been left alone,' muttered the one.

'Too many people got into the act,' said the other, two kilometres farther.

'We're Laurel and Hardy. After you, Stan, after you, Ollie. We try to get in the door together. This Sebregt holding his sides.'

'What has happened to that woman?'

'Disappeared. The Berlin story is a blind – no record of her at the border crossing.'

'What does my esteemed colleague in Berne say?' asked the Ambassador sulkily.

'What would you expect? – that he has trouble quietening the Swiss. The Swiss say in high indignant tones that they do not welcome interference in their affairs, that their security is watertight, that Germans of all people had better mind security leaks, that this reminds them of German generals telling Hitler it wasn't their fault: alternatively of Nato generals explaining to the French that Popular Front governments are bee ay dee, bad: alternatively of American finance ministers telling Italians that the lira needs to be disciplined: briefly, what you'd expect: stiff and taking a dim view.'

'And I've got the President arriving tomorrow for consultations with the West German Government.'

'Yes, well, Washington now thinks it would save embarrassment if he flies direct to Geneva, and by the time the energy thing is over we're supposed to have this tidy.'

'I've got it closer still,' groaned Repellini ten kilometres further. 'You ever read Tintin? The French comic strip?'

'Yes. Read them to my children. Yes: the two detectives, the identical twins – what are their names?'

'Dupont and Dupond. They aren't quite identical. If you look closely one's moustache is a little longer and more ragged.'

'Is that me?' asked Korngold cutting out to pass a large tanker with 'Frischknecht' in huge blue letters on a vermilion ground. 'They both have accidents with their bowler hats.'

'The Swiss are going to love us both,' said Repellini, and relapsed into a sour silence.

'Now just let me recap,' the Ambassador was saying, 'there was a neurotic and hysterical tale by the wife: we agree to give that no weight, since she's vanished. Right? Now factually, is there anything to go on beyond a report by some technical institute in Stuttgart? They found traces of uranium where the woman said they would? Is that reliable, by the way?'

'Yes, it's reliable as far as it goes – it's a reason-to-suppose. Quantities, nobody will say how much, of enriched uranium. Enough to build a weapon? – nobody's saying that.'

'And the Germans,' querulously, 'are saying it's impossible, is that right?'

'Not quite impossible, Ambassador. Impossible to have stolen it from them, they claim. There have been leaks back in the States and this report from Senator Kennedy says the explanations of the Nuclear Regulatory Commission are bullshit.'

'Yes yes yes,' irritably, 'but that's Senator Kennedy's baby and not ours. Furthermore there's a physicist missing, who might or might not, nobody willing to give a definite answer, be capable of constructing a weapon. And he's over the hill. Or off his nut. Which is it?'

'Jimmy Repellini in liaison with the German security people is checking that up right this moment.'

'Well, he'd better have a definite answer or his ass will be back checking leaks in Tennessee.'

'One moment,' the young frontier guard at the border post outside Basle. 'Herr Korngold, right? There's a gentleman here enquiring for you.'

207

'I knew it,' pulling the car in. 'They're putting us on the leash.' A youngish unsmiling man in a gaberdine raincoat nodded through the window, opened the back door and got in, bringing a smell of menthol cough lozenge. 'Hammerfest, Federal Security. Herr Korngold?'

'Repellini, United States Embassy, Bonn.'

'Um. My instructions are to afford you gentlemen guidance and assistance. I gather there are ambiguities concerning a patient of Doctor Sebregt's?'

'More or less.'

'Good. We take the first to the left at the lights. I'm bound to say Doctor Sebregt has a clean bill of health in our office. We ask you to be prudent. Go easy on the unfounded speculations, okay? If he were to make a complaint . . . let's say, we wouldn't be very happy. Follow the boulevard, and a right turn two sets of lights from now. That is, at the second,' pedantically.

Jim looked at the little man. There was melodrama in the pools of coloured light. Or it was the white wine on an empty stomach. That stuff made one reckless. He felt lucid. There were better ways of doing this. He sat down at the head of the table, in the chair with arms, where Victorian heads of families carved roast beef and dispensed moralities. Mr Barrett of Wimpole Street. He reached for the bottle, poured more of this agreeable Swiss plonk, made himself comfortable.

'No, I wouldn't want you to shoot me with that cannon. Let me tell you that you'd be helpless if you did. Leora walked out under your nose and took the children with her and you've lost your leverage. Where are the fine plans now? You think you've a bomb? You haven't. You've two lumps of U that will make a critical mass. It has no trigger mechanism. You're going to drive around the countryside with a recoilless rifle in a truck. I could build you a mechanism. Who's going to make me? You? What with, that gun?

'Leora has a weird tale and they don't believe her. Maybe not, at first: I can understand that there'd be a certain incredulity. But they're going to check on you. They go to that house and find that machinery, and they ask questions.

Jim's been there, who's supposed to have gone crazy. What's he been playing with, lumps of lead? Ho ho. They fetch someone who knows the difference. You think that stuff leaves no traces? It's been machined on a lathe; there's dust, that garage is hotter than anything save your ass. A few more hours there'll be half the Swiss Army with monitors looking for that lump of U which signals its presence a kilometre off.'

The Doctor remained calm, looking and listening. His pale face had become suffused with dark blood.

'A large speech,' he said. 'I shouldn't have let you have that bottle on an empty stomach. You fool, do you think these things stop me? I and those with me?' He mastered himself, took a glass from the cupboard. The flush faded. He poured a glass of wine and sat at the far side of the table. He lit a cigar. He took the revolver out of his waistband, cocked it, laid it on the table.

'You have been treated with humanity. That has led you, apparently, to regard me as inept. A mistake.'

He put his finger inside the trigger guard of the gun and swivelled it till the muzzle pointed at Jim.

'I dislike melodrama as much as you do. These Smith and Wessons have a very light pull. A small movement would blow your head off.' He swivelled the pistol through a hundred and eighty degrees. It was pointing to his own stomach.

'It's a thirty-eight, a police calibre. Nine millimetres. At this range, it would blow me in half. If that served my purpose I would not hesitate. Either way. You or me. It would make no difference.' He picked up the gun. 'A cocked revolver is a dangerous object,' he said in his pedantic voice. He uncocked it and laid it on the table. 'Even like that. The safety is off. Not a thing to treat lightly.' He picked up the glass and took a sip.

'We don't know one another yet, Jim. Through no fault of your own, you have not shown yourself. We have admired the other's technical or organizational talent. What we are really made of – that remains to be seen.

'I made a mistake. I allowed your wife to remain alive. It was foolish, and I have paid for it. This has compressed me.

209

'Perhaps there are advantages. It might help you see me under a different light. I am not in this business for money, Jim, nor for power, or ambition or advantage. It is what I believe in.

'You are mistaken, Jim,' playing with the glass, the pistol, twisting them, 'in thinking my freedom of action compromised. Put at its simplest, I am not deprived of information. What does Leora know? – nothing. What do the German or Swiss authorities know? – nothing. All of them fumbling around in the dark, bumping into one another, hampering well-meant activities. They know neither the time, nor the place, nor the circumstances in which I propose to detonate my gadget.

'We, Jim, whether we like it or not, are not merely associates. We are bound together in an enterprise larger than both of us. You need not take my word for it. You will judge for yourself.

'You think perhaps that I would torture you. You know that such procedures are abhorrent to me, that they are the contradiction of everything I struggle for, the degradation and brutalization that I attack, that I see as my worst enemy. I would not hesitate, if that were the only course open. I have others.'

The face remained pale, the features did not twitch, the mouth did not stumble over syllables. The eyes had become injected with blood.

'I have powers of action, and I receive information. You have seen that I am well served. These servants are my associates, often my friends. We are bound by strong loyalties. You have seen that, I believe, with Marika. All know something of my project.

'I am well informed. I know now where Leora is. She is in Stuttgart. I know where the children are. They were cared for by a Mrs Day, a United States consular official. Leora's foremost wish was to protect them. She thought of her parents. Her father wasted no time in coming and taking them back to Venice. A man of decision. You see that I knew of all this at once.

'Leora made an interesting choice. In removing the children from my control she thought she would break the grip I had

210

upon you. In a sense she was right. It was a hold that prevented you running away, writing little notes, talking unguardedly. She decided at all cost to break that. She abandoned you. She has left you. She realized perhaps that you had made up your own mind. She gambled.

'She has failed. She has convinced nobody. She is causing worry, and embarrassment. It is no secret. These are kind people, who try to help her. They thought that the children if left in her care would be exposed to grief and strain. They persuaded her of that. It was easy to learn all this.

'I could threaten you. I could show you a long arm as well as good ears.

'This was a mistake,' playing with the pistol. 'A melodrama. Like you, I yielded to a silly impulse for a moment. I make mistakes, which is why I never do anything in a hurry. The threat is not only horrible, it is unnecessary. In leaving you, Leora showed that she had finally understood you. But Marika had understood long before.'

'What was the threat?'

'I don't want to speak of it. A bullet from a pistol much smaller than this,' picking it up and putting it away, 'could lodge in a person's spine. Paralysing it. Even a child.'

'Are you making this threat?'

'No. You are one of us. Marika, in deciding to trust you, showed much quicker understanding than I did.

'Let's have breakfast Jim, shall we? Ring the bell, if you would.'

'Ah, that's nice . . . put the tray in front of Mr Hawkins . . . many thanks.

'I've made myself clear, I think: I'm not going to labour the point. We know the evils into which the technocrats are leading us, and always for motives of greed. Actions can only be judged in terms of history. It is given us to write a page of that history. Future generations will owe us a debt. Your children among them.

'Now time's a-flying, and we've still a lot to do. I've something for you,' pressing the bell-push. 'This should have come to us in Germany, and it gave me some trouble to have it diverted . . . Bring that American parcel, would you? After

211

we discussed this, and you explained the complexities, I spoke to a fellow who is skilled in these problems of radio control and this, he tells me, is the right thing. Comes from Daxon Electronics in Vega, California; transmitter, receivers and servos all in one package . . . thanks; put it on the table and unwrap it, would you?'

'Not enough,' grumbled Jim reluctantly, 'need more.'

'We've got more,' tranquilly, 'there are three of them.'

'The Herr Professor will be with you in a moment.' Tone of hushed respect, making Repellini want to laugh. Only doctors and banks achieve this muted luxury. These girls in their beautifully starched and ironed white would be the envy of any hostess agency.

A large modern office building, full of the creamiest consultants. Very handy; one could skip straight from the fiscal counsellor to the shrink if he made you feel at all psychotic. And they could cash your cheques without leaving the building. Building full of tricky kinds of glass, looking like silver, like bronze, like porcelain, even like glass from time to time. Glass doing clever things, like admitting light but not sound; with mirror finish, Florentine finish, pearl or opal finish. Maybe the girls' overalls were made of glass. Maybe the girls were, too.

All very soothing: a Haydn quartet purred away just above the limit of audibility. One wouldn't know whether Sebregt evaded his taxes, but he sure had good fiscal advice.

They were alone in the waiting-room. Patients never laid eyes on one another here. The security was excellent.

'I am sorry to have kept you waiting. Do please come in to my room.' Ho, nice desk he had; white marble, about the size of the Lake of Zürich. 'A cigar? You may speak with perfect confidence – nothing goes outside this room . . . To be sure, Herr Hawkins.

'Your earlier enquiries failed, for a very simple reason. We deal a lot in pseudonyms here. People do not always want it known that they consult doctors . . . I did not see him here, nor in my clinic. He is not under my care. There seem to have been misapprehensions . . .

'I was called into consultation by my colleague Doctor Wallner – what? From Hamburg as I understand: my dear man, I don't know every medical practitioner in Germany! I am frequently called into consultation in the region, in Munich ... I was given to understand that an American physicist had suffered a breakdown and that it was desirable to treat the matter confidentially. A small matter, straightforward. I saw no need for clinical tests; a brief examination confirmed my colleague's diagnosis. Fatigue, the most commonplace of our century's woes ...

'My dear man, I gave it no further thought. Why should I? He was plainly in excellent hands. A few weeks rest, country air, walks, a bit of tennis. No call for drug therapy ... I did not meet Doctor Wallner: I hadn't especially expected to. A busy man, no doubt; most doctors are ... I met a nurse, charming young lady. He seemed as I say in excellent hands ...

'A country house as I understand, lent by a friend. Now, to abbreviate, I was called again quite recently by this young lady. Not very convenient; it was in the evening. A pressing message that Frau Hawkins was behaving in hysterical fashion; gave rise to some anxiety. I was able to make a superficial examination, and no clear diagnosis. She was certainly disturbed, and hostile. I said a few words to calm her, told her I would be happy to see her and prescribe for her next day, gave her a sedative, and told the nurse to have her brought here the next morning. I have been told that she has discharged herself from my colleague's care ...

'What she suffers from, and what treatment would be appropriate I have no idea. Not to put too fine a point on it, she'd had a good deal to drink. Not the best conditions for a diagnosis.'

The smell of cigar smoke would not hang about in these rooms; sucked out at once by silent and efficient air-conditioning. Nor anything else. No hint of ether or alcohol, fear or anger. Even the red roses on the white marble had no smell at all.

'A few questions if I may?' asked Korngold.

'But of course.' Repellini had to pinch back a grin. Charley

Korngold, a good hand at the blunt question and the forth-right remark, pussyfooting!

'It's to get things clear in my mind. You came to see this woman, simply on the strength of a phone call?'

'I don't altogether follow. It interested me, naturally, to follow the progress of my patient.'

'Who'd made a good recovery?'

'Who seemed well. I suggested that he come in with his wife, for a check-up. I should dislike,' a little stiffly, 'to make a diagnosis or to pronounce upon a person's health without studying him at some length in good conditions and making a physical examination, with such tests as might be indicated.'

'Of course. You'd rely on the indications given you by Doctor Wallner. But if I've got it right you've never actually met him.'

'If I've got it right,' with a smile and a shrug, 'he's in Hamburg. I spoke to his nurse. She showed me the usual letter with a request for an opinion, such as a colleague writes.'

'With a letterhead? Did you keep it by the way?'

'The usual memo sheet with a printed address. Hamburg somewhere; it's not a city I know well. But are you casting doubt upon Doctor Wallner?'

'Oh, there's a real Doctor Wallner in Hamburg all right, but he's never heard of any of this.'

'I fail to account for that. But why should I doubt it? One is frequently sent patients by colleagues in general practice. My secretary would be in touch eventually with details of my opinion, and of course the administrative and financial side.'

'Oh quite.'

'I am to conclude from this visit of police officers that I have been the victim of a charlatan?'

'It looks like it. Can you give us a description of this nurse?'

'I paid her no particular attention. Youngish, prettyish, darkish. I looked at the patient ...'

'Of course. Can you tell us about that?'

'Much the usual. Complaint of nightmares, irrational fears, disorientation, imaginary catastrophes. The familiar

214

symptoms of an incipient depression. They are afraid of crossing the road, feel isolated or lost, unable to speak coherently, terrified of being asphyxiated. In between, apathetic, rambling, unco-ordinated.'

'Could such a state be induced by drugs?'

'It's conceivable, but there'd be signs which one would recognize.'

'One last question in the form of a hypothesis. Suppose a man were kidnapped by force and held sequestered; might he act as you describe? To a superficial examination?'

'Rather an odd hypothesis. Not within my experience. It seems far-fetched; I take it you've reason to suppose something of this sort? She was under no restraint. I'd be inclined to put it the other way round. In depression they have all sorts of irrational terrors: I hear things you'd scarcely credit.'

'So that if she'd complained to you of being kidnapped?'

'Oh, I shouldn't have been surprised at all. Commonplace. They fear assassinations, intrigues, being poisoned, anything.'

'Thank you very much for being so helpful.'

'Not at all. Command me if I may be of service.'

The local security chief was called Herr Dorschner. Like most people in the business he was a succession of clichés: plump, dapper, placid, baldish, a long nose, sandy hair. And sceptical.

'Summing that up, Korngold, it's a load of nothing. What would you say if I came to you with this moonshine? What are the alternatives? That this is as the man says – a nervous depression accompanied by fantasies, and there's some misunderstanding about this Doctor Wallner. That this is a genuine terrorist operation, and that Sebregt was involved in order to put a sheen of respectability upon the doings – all rather unlikely, though I suppose it wouldn't be too hard to fake the symptoms of nervous depression. And the third – which perhaps you haven't considered with enough care – that this woman is faking the entire tale consciously or not, in order to create panic or confusion. Find her and interrogate her.'

215

'I'm more interested in this large quantity of uranium that's floating about.'

'Very well: assuming this woman really was held as a hostage and escaped. That there really is a terrorist operation. That there really is some crude atomic device. All three seem to me unproven, but say it's so. Good, they've been interrupted, their cover's blown, they're lying low somewhere. What's the point of the whole thing? A blackmail threat? A ransom demand? We've received none. Neither have you, or so you tell me. Mr Repellini here tells us neither has the United States government. So it's moonshine.

'Give me something to act on. If there's a terrorist group what are its aims? Is it right-wing, left-wing, what? What object does it seek to serve? Is there a threat to some target? If so, what is the target? Fussing like a lot of old women won't help. We've this energy conference, with a lot of heads of state present. Not my sector, but I'm told the usual stringent security operations are active. We've the United States President scheduled to visit the Nuclear Research Institute: ditto, same sector. I'll talk to Geneva, but I don't see how I can help you here. You've a Berlin conference with the Russians coming up: if there's a blackmail threat on the cards that sounds a likelier job. Isn't this woman supposed to be there? However, that's your pigeon.'

'What the hell?' grumbled Korngold. 'Swiss! They might know all about it, wouldn't tell one. Trouble with them is they're always in the goddamn right, and don't they let you know it. We've no guarantee where Hawkins is, or even that the fellow Sebregt saw was Hawkins. Is he part of a gang? Has he built a crude gadget, assuming that's possible? Too many assumptions. If that Maier is involved, since they were using his house, then it's a right-wing group, and this Swiss stuff is a red herring; it's Berlin that we want to look at. Imagine telling the neighbours that there might be a bomb, and we've lost it!'

'If you have a bomb,' said Repellini, 'and you have to move it, what's your problem?'

'According to what we're told, it's so big you'd need a truck.

216

You see a truck, loaded with weapons grade U, being ferried across at Helmstedt? Knowing the neighbours, I don't. Unless they're at the bottom of the entire thing.'

'Comes in from the cold, Charley.'

'Yes, that's ridiculous. I'd like to have a nervous breakdown myself. Go to Doctor Sebregt with my irrational fears.'

'Pretty dodgy story, that tale of his.'

'Right, but what can we prove? Until we lay hands on this clever guy who says he's Doctor Wallner from Hamburg, but forgive the Viennese accent.'

'Or has he a Libyan accent? I wish we could find this Hawkins woman. Consciously or unconsciously, she knows more than she's said: I'm convinced of that. I'll talk to MacNamara.'

'Some dimwit let her slip. Unless she changed number-plates – how many green Opels are there driven by women with brown hair? A thousand?'

'Well, one good thing. Washington's just going poopoopoo. I don't have that smell of scorching cloth telling me my ass is afire.'

'I'm not too sure,' said Charley Korngold.

Herr Dorschner's colleague in Geneva was on the telephone.

'Grusenmayer here. The Americans are on at me, with a ridiculous tale about a bomb: Berne tells me you know about it.'

'Yes. The Germans are fussed about an ex-SS type called Maier, has an electronics factory in Munich. Got a house up in the Black Forest, where they tell me they've found traces of uranium. The story is consistent up to a certain point.'

'You mean the atomic scientist from Hamburg who did or didn't have a nervous breakdown?'

'That's right. Covered by a local doctor. Nothing wrong with him. Pompous. Makes too much money. Treats a lot of Arab sheiks. I don't see anything in it. I mean he might or he mightn't, but what are we supposed to do?'

'No no, but there's one thing. The feedback on this woman with the self-drive car. I've got her signalled in Montreux: you want to tell the Germans?'

'Why? Charley Korngold's looking for a pretext to involve us: why give it him? You picking her up?'

'What for? A woman with a self-drive car, doesn't even bother changing it – not very much like a terrorist operation, ja? Keep an eye on her, right? Do nothing, unless she does? If there's anything, she leads us to it. Just thought I'd let you know.'

The noise of a car motor, followed by the brief skid and spurt of gravel as the car braked, awoke Jim from apathy. He went to the window as the doors slammed. Already the note of the motor, no longer the familiar Mercedes sound, had roused him. As the Doctor climbed out, perky as an early morning blackbird, and shook the creases out of his suit, Jim's fatalism deepened another notch. You had to hand it to them! The intensive comings and goings in this sleepy lakeside suburb, full of old ladies, were not going to draw attention to that garish fleet of cars with German plates. A nice executive Peugeot, a very proper car for Vevey.

The lady of the house came out of the front door, trim in charcoal grey trousers and a white shirt, altogether the efficient secretary.

The two conferred in the late afternoon sunshine, hereabouts warm enough to comfort old ladies at this time of year. They glanced up at his windows. Have no fear, the mouse is in the cage.

Lots and lots of activity. Whitejackets unloaded parcels from the back of the Peugeot – as usual when returning from a shopping expedition the Doctor was bringing 'presents'. What would they be this time? While he watched, a Renault Estafette van with plain panels came up the slope and whisked around to the back of the house. It had been coming and going all day, delivering flowers, or cream cake, or whatever the old ladies of Vevey thought they fancied. Coffins, maybe. Jim went downstairs, air of weary nonchalance, magnetized by curiosity. He'd been thinking all day about teleguidance systems, looking out at the lake and chewing a pencil. There hadn't been anything else to do.

The Doctor, plainly in high fettle, was in the living-room

218

untwisting the wire of a champagne cork. Marika stood in the bay of the window, watching the sunset over the lake.

'Right, Jim boy. There it is.'

'There what is?' sulking deeply; everybody enjoying the party except that poor little shy boy in the corner.

'Never mind; a glass of this will put you right. Let me explain rapidly. My esoteric knowledge, I admit, is borrowed from friends with hobbies. Herr Maier, for example, is interested in metallurgy: handy when it came to things like furnaces and the melting-point of beryllium. And a friend in the United States sends the enchanting toy you saw this morning. It wasn't really designed for us, because Herr Maier is not in our confidence to that extent. It was for his associate Franz, who is the engineer heading up his electronics division, and who has the pastime of building model aeroplanes. Like this - I am told there's more than a hundred and fifty hours work there.' The beautiful thing, with its wing-span of over a metre, stood on the coffee-table.

'These aerodynamic passions leave me cold and I scarcely care whether the thing would ever leave the ground. However, I am assured it does. It is kept on a fairly strict lead, of about a kilometre as I understand, so that it remains in sight. What interests me more is this box, containing these little switches. Like all true enthusiasts,' pouring another glass, 'Franz was delighted to demonstrate. They have as a rule five controls – now let's see if I recall. Retract under-carriage, ailerons, rudder, climb and dive – but what can the fifth be?'

'Speed of the motor,' said Jim, drinking the glass of champagne without noticing. 'Let me.'

As long as it were something precise. Discussions about philosophy or political science, the etymology of Linear-B script or whether a Cretan bull-dancer really could grasp the horns and vault over them – they were interesting but there was always a sense of dissatisfaction. One could not predict . . . But here he was on ground that he knew.

'We'll fly it over the lake,' said the Doctor. 'A suitable pastime for a retired ethnologist thinking of settling in Vevey.'

'Be serious,' said Jim, slapping down the empty glass.

Always an excellent listener, the Doctor: stopped at once.

'The package,' said Jim, 'has to carry a clock timer, three radio receivers, and a transmitter. Before we seal the box we must know at what time and date it will be delivered.'

'That is now established.'

'All right. Clock set inside. Alarm clock, if you care to visualize it that way. Until this timer announces the arrival of delivery time all other circuits are dead.'

'I don't want to interrupt, Jim. Isn't this a luxury of complicated precautions?'

'Look, there are two overriding requirements. Apart from the package being safe to handle. It's got to go off on command, right? And it's not to go off except on a specific command. How many elderly gentlemen, or little boys, are playing with aeroplanes around the lake shore? Do you know? Neither do I!

'Okay, it is not possible to fire the bullet, or indeed for the gadget to receive any signal at all, until it is delivered and in place. That's "A" time. After that, we send a specially tone-coded signal. Meaning in fact two distinct signals transmitted simultaneously at different audio frequencies. That will arm the device.'

The Doctor was still, serious.

'Meaning?'

'It closes a preliminary circuit – turns on the twin detonator receivers, transmits a special signal back so that we know the tasks have been accomplished.'

The Doctor made no comment. He gave a semi-circular look around the room, as though wishing to make sure what was included in the term 'we'.

'This reporting is called telemetering,' said Jim in his school-master's voice. Looking unconsciously for the black-board, chalk all over his jacket. Where was Leora, patient with the clothes-brush?

'The gadget is alive, waiting for our signals. One could . . . in fact . . . booby-trap it if desired. A probe of the box could cause it to go off . . . from "A" time onwards.'

Jim poured himself a second glass, thinking. Absent-mindedly he dipped a finger in the champagne and dabbed a drop on the shiny nose of the model plane as though baptising it. The drop trickled slowly down the finely-polished skin of metal. Titanium perhaps? A highly sophisticated model. Franz had the resources of Herr Maier's metallurgical laboratory at his disposal.

'When we select a time to fire,' said Jim slowly, 'when we push the button . . .' he was unconscious of the two immobile figures looking at him, of breath held for a second and let out quietly . . . 'another tone-coded signal is sent to the box. When picked up – by the second receiver – it starts an oscillator running, at about one megaHertz. And the third receiver comes on, looks at what is coming in, on its frequency, and reports back if it hears anything. Little boys, for example, flying model aeroplanes.'

The dragging words had become mesmeric. Nothing was heard in the room except the minute explosions of bubbles in the glasses. Jim twisted his glass round and round and round. Rika looked at him as though he were the prophet Isaiah. The Doctor took cigars out of his side pocket.

'Now after the clock oscillator ticks off precisely two-oh-four-eight cycles; that's two to the power of eleven, which is why I chose the number: binary powers are easiest to work with in this case . . . It opens a logical-coincidence-gate in the third receiver.' Sure. Franz would understand at once. Herr Maier wouldn't understand, but would purse his lips and nod. He was the boss, after all.

'The 2048 cycles take just over two milliseconds. The gate opens for exactly two more milliseconds. During this time receiver number three must get a final tone-coded signal which fires the device. If the signal doesn't arrive the clock oscillator is turned off and the scaler set back to zero to await another push of the firing button. If the final signal arrives within the two milli-second gate then the bomb will explode. That is to say a relay closes, power flows to the firing solenoid, the bullet's powder charge, which is simply the shell of the recoilless rifle, is fired. That's clear, I think?'

The Doctor, simple-minded retired ethnologist come to rest his backside among the old ladies of Vevey, could contain himself no longer.

'Jim,' faintly. 'Pushing buttons microseconds apart . . .'

Jim looked at him, with pity for the dinosaur's walnut-sized container of grey matter.

'A complex series of tone-coded signals cannot of course be transmitted by a hand pushing two buttons point zero-zero-two-oh-four-eight seconds apart.' Naturally, chilling.

'We put a duplicate of the clock-oscillator in the detonator and make an automatic sequencer which takes over the work of sending the signals, once the button is pushed.'

'It has to be built by tomorrow morning, and further refinements on the instrumentation this late in the day . . .'

'Simplicity itself,' said Jim pityingly. 'The oscillator is a multi-vibrator affair using a couple of integrated circuit chips and not much else at all. As for the alarm clock, any electronic watch will do. You need only look at the signals which go to the display and tell the time and the date; a matter then of waiting till the right combination of display elements is energized. Simple.'

'Your point is well taken,' said the Doctor, scribbling on a piece of paper. 'That can be done locally before the shops close – no risk in that.'

'Get your whitejacket in here,' said Jim, 'and I'll tell him what to ask for.'

'Very good,' taking a sheaf of notes from his pocket. 'Now when we discussed this last week and you suggested a model aeroplane frequency I got on to Franz, who was properly mystified, but promised to help. Worked out nicely, since we could get the equipment from California. Franz, simply, thinks we're going to fly his plane.'

'So we are.'

'Exactly. Now let's see . . . there are ten radio control channels centred around 72 megaHertz. The transmitters run a few milliwatts with an extreme range of a couple of kilometres. Now that's not enough – we've got to reach right across the lake.'

'I'll deal with that in a minute,' with crisp authority. 'Go on.'

'Yes. The signals are transmitted as "digital-proportional coding" – hm; that doesn't mean a lot to me.'

222

'It does to me, though,' striking in ruthlessly. 'Now listen. We retain the notion of tone-coding, and we combine as follows. Digital control signals will be multi-plexed on two separate pilot tones. This would be beyond the needs of a model plane but provides us with the margin of security we need. I asked for the Daxon control job because it's a good one. I was prepared to use Swiss or German models; you've got three and we've no problem. We take one, strip it apart, add the tone-multiplex section to the receiver; we set the other two on different channels, add the control section to the transmitters as needed. The multiplex system works much like the coding for stereo in an FM receiver – no problem to the local electronics shop.'

'I admire the range of your hobbies, Jim,' with something of the old irony.

'Nonsense,' impatiently. 'Radios, model aeroplanes; it's simple electronics. Any competent physicist knows something of that – part of the job. Don't interrupt. You're absolutely right: there's a problem of range and power, and I've thought some about it. Now what is it – five o'clock? Want to get down to the local radio shop.'

'Can't risk that, I'm afraid. I'll go myself.'

'All right, I'll make this fast. Not only must the transmitter reach across the lake – it has to get into the building. Model transmitters work from a battery and have one watt or so of power. We'll power ours off the accumulator in the car and have perhaps twenty watts. We couple that with a directional antenna – buy that too – and it'll certainly punch through. Naturally, we add a final-output amplifier to the transmitters – write it,' finger stabbing. Humbly, the Doctor wrote his shopping-list. 'And let's have some more champagne up here. And if you go out shopping, get lots more. And some oysters if there are any. I'm like a pregnant woman, I fancy an oyster.'

The Doctor was delighted. Oysters, he thought, that's a final-output amplifier.

'We use the model aeroplane frequencies,' Jim went on 'because they're the best. Could use ham-radio frequencies around one-forty megaHertz but we have to test these

223

electronics once built, here at the home base. Don't want some snoopy monitor listening in and wondering what's the strange signal. The model aeroplane band is safer because fewer people use it, they have much lower-powered transmitters, and they wouldn't listen to signals coming in. We get less interference too. Anyway it's admirable cover. What are we doing sitting in a car by a lakeside with a directional antenna? We're flying this model plane. Why I suggested it, in the first place. And we use the model plane servo actuators – your stuff there, for height and direction – to control the closing of the relays which actually fire our gadget. We need a couple of six-volt lantern batteries – write them down – in the package. I'd like a car battery for lots of power, but there's always that problem. Might get inverted. This package is plenty heavy, going to get handled with a fork-lift truck. Want it to be okay, no matter how the package gets stacked. All right – better get moving before that radio shop shuts.'

'Not to speak of the oysters,' murmured the Doctor.

Throughout the entire conversation Marika had not said a word. Waiting, one might have thought, till somebody closed a relay and activated her transmitter.

Buying a watch in Switzerland . . . One has to be tactful. It wouldn't do to ask for a Seiko: the Swiss not thrilled about Ja-pa-nese electronics. A radio shop has no such inhibitions, is thrilled with the shopping-list, delighted to stay open over-time for this wealthy and eccentric customer, a change from the old ladies of Vevey whose Bach and whose bite are a pest. Leaves an eye-witness, thought the Doctor ruefully, but after tomorrow one will no longer care. A slight deformity is not a handicap in life: it is the thing an eye-witness, inaccurate about the colour of eyes or hair, remembers. That is too bad. After tomorrow, it is unlikely that one will again wish to visit Switzerland. What annoyance the police forces of the world will be henceforward to model aeroplane fanciers. But today we're happy, and drink champagne, and eat oysters. It is two days from now that the hump-backed villain's purchases of transistors, shellfish and a Timex watch will acquire significance.

Extraordinary folk, these scientists. There was something mechanical about them. Arrangements broke down? They become sulky and rebellious? One set their scaler back to zero, and the oscillator began again to tick. They disliked the rhythm altered, that was all. A psychology that one had to understand – simplicity of mind. Nothing would go wrong, as long as one conveyed the right electronic instructions.

The same point, at the same moment, was under discussion in Bonn. The Ambassador was holding – for lack of a better phrase – a council of war. Grouped informally in his office was as weird a collection as he wished to set eyes upon. Buz Berkeley, his chief political counsellor. Jimmy Repellini, liaison with that embarrassing fact of life, the CIA. This physicist from Hamburg who worked with the man Hawkins.

There were also three pests. On the evening flight from Washington had appeared three faceless personages who were 'sensitive'. To whom one could only be rude up to a point. A real CIA man, straight from Langley. A terrible individual from the Nuclear Regulatory Commission, who had already distinguished boringly between the feasibility, the possibility, and the probability (underlined) of building a Crude Nuclear Explosive Device. And – the most ominous – a Presidential security officer. A guy who's got his fast draw below five-eighths of a second, whom the Ambassador squinted at, because this was the advance-man for the Martians. Not little tiny green men. Big Brown Men, with horribly resonant voices, and a Texas accent. The Ambassador's mind drifted back to the classic story of Lyndon showing visitors around the ranch, and lobbing his pecker out for a leak in the bushes.

'Not scared of rattlesnakes?' asked some bright boy, like he'd been cued.

'Shit,' said Lyndon, 'it is part rattlesnake.'

What could a diplomat do against these frightful people walking about with pecker erected to show you man, that's machismo, and letting you know he had small use for diplomats whose machismo was mostly in a glass of melting ice-cubes?

So far he hadn't opened his steely lips. But, thought the Ambassador with deepening gloom, when he does there'll be no stopping the sister-fucker. Among the diplomats one had known from a boy, only Averell knew how to handle these people with machismo. This man Neilson from Hamburg had a soft voice, thank God.

'Jim's a good physicist, a good chemist, a good mechanic, a really good improviser. Sure: given a few kilograms of high-enriched U two-three-five, he could build a gadget. Has he been given it? – not my province; leave that. Would he? You need to grasp the psychology of the man, not the skills of the mechanic. Jim has a rigid and orderly mind. Told he'd gone overboard, I wasn't that much surprised; he's the type. Jim's – sorry – I'm going to use a metaphor: say Jim was the manager of a football team; it's playing badly. Jim, from the sideline, full of technical knowledge and tactical skill, would like to call the play. So he equips his quarterback with electronic aid. But this quarterback acts from instinct. He'll kick, he'll pass, or he'll make a break, intuitively, without intellectual analysis of the play. Jim's sitting on the sideline raving. Go left, you imbecile. Quarterback, on instinct, goes right, fucks it up. Jim gets mad. But who do you sack? Your quarterback, or your trainer? But a good physicist, good man. Just – if they told Jim to make a bomb, he's the boy who would do it. Has he made one? I wouldn't know. Has he got the materials?'

'Repellini . . . you're not happy, but spit.'

'I got nothing. This gadget exists; it doesn't. Hawkins is there; he isn't. This woman is crazy, or she's telling the truth. All right, where is she? My opinion, Switzerland, since Charley Korngold's a careful man. The Swiss are worried? They say they aren't: all right they aren't. Then why should we be? They've ten heads of State to worry over: we've one.'

'But that one is the President of the United States.'

'And then? These Germans are good, don't mistake them. They're alert – if they have terrorist groups, what aims do these have? Right wing, left? If there's a group here at all, it's far right. Not going to try hanky in a place like Geneva. What opinions are worth – mine or the Germans'; no matter

– this is a bluff, It's the anti-nuclear-power-station mob stirring it up. If they can stop the President of the United States visiting CERN, the Nuclear Research Centre for Europe, making that speech about the great leap forward, great. That's to them the essential: a propaganda victory. You heard what the gentleman said from NRC.'

'Would he like to comment on that?'

'He would,' in a harsh Kansas voice. 'It is theoretically possible to design and build a relatively simple nuclear explosive device. The probability of such a device being fabricated for unlawful purposes depends on at least four important conditions, that must be resolved not only affirmatively but simultaneously for there to be a finite probability . . .'

'We're seeking a concrete conclusion,' said Berkeley, who caught the Ambassador's eye saying 'Save us from the Meat Grinder'.

'Even if successfully assembled and delivered, any crude, untested device will remain an uncertain tool in the hands of its creators. It may fail to detonate or it may fizzle.'

'Or it may pop.'

'It is an exercise in probabilities,' glaring.

'Quite. Mr O'Kelly?'

'We think in terms of two main types of weapon which could be used for an assassination attempt. Long-range and short. Short meaning, in general, a weapon that can be concealed about the person such as handgun or grenade. This falls into the category of long-range, right? Experience shows that we can never totally rule out either, given sufficient determination or preparation, but seems to me we can rule this particular weapon out of consideration quicker than most. On the grounds of sheer size. We are continually assured and I've heard it confirmed in this room that a crude nuclear device, even built by a highly skilled man, is going to be very bulky and very weighty. Correct? So our task is simplified. We make a thorough sweep of the area within the perimeter. Once that is monitored and accepted as clean no vehicle not previously checked will be permitted inside the perimeter. If only all our tasks were that easy.'

227

'Mr Grayson.'

'If we took all the crackpot threats we hear as serious, we'd have to keep the President in Fort Bragg, with a regiment of paratroops on permanent stand-to. I agree with the speaker who mentioned a balance in probabilities. We've three specific duties scheduled for the President within the coming week, and thus three specific targets. Our task is to decide whether we recommend that all or any be omitted from his schedule on security grounds. That is to say we look at each scheduled appearance. One, the United Nations. Absurd. A meeting of heads of State. Can't duck that, and any such proposal would be unacceptable to the Swiss, here, and opinion at home. Two, the conference in Berlin. Equally. Negative suggestions would invite an overriding veto from on top. On the consensus of opinion reached here, anybody recommend that we chicken out? I thought not.

'That leaves the speech slated at CERN. On the face of it the most likely target – if there is any target. Technical difficulties concerning nuclear material and monitoring same. I'm advised that the President wants it and is prepared to go through with it. Has some political sensitivity and we don't want a backlash in an election year. We need considerable grounds for apprehension before we recommended cancellation.'

'All right. Buz? – you take the temperature of the meeting.'

'One further point,' said Berkeley. 'If the anti-nuclear-power lobby could force us or frighten us into cancelling a scheduled appearance of the President and a slated speech on policy, it could claim a massive propaganda victory. It strikes me, struck me all along, and is also the German authorities' stated conviction, that this is the aim of the group. We can't ascribe any political slant to anything known about these individuals. We don't know that they've a bomb, or even whether they've seriously tried to make one. We're pretty sure that they want us to believe in a fictional bomb, and frighten us into withdrawal.'

'What exactly have the Germans discovered, Repellini?'

'A house where experiments were being made. Traces of enriched material. No means of knowing how much. Expert opinion is that at that grade of enrichment a considerable quantity would be needed. Even with heavy pressure on this man Hawkins, and accepting that he has the skill, was there enough to make an explosive device? Doubtful. Furthermore they were interrupted, had to decamp suddenly. Conclusion; even if they have the stuff, they're not ready. Will be detected before they can be ready. They've confused the trail cleverly but they're being followed up. They haven't a prayer. They've had accidents. The Germans have found a dead body close to this house. Autopsy shows death due to acute radiation burns, accelerated by an overdose of morphia. It isn't easy to build a nuclear gadget, and it's mighty dangerous.'

'Full circle,' said the Ambassador. 'Any comment on that last point, Mr Neilson?'

'Perfectly true. It's a very difficult undertaking, and I wouldn't care to undertake it. That Jim Hawkins might undertake it – I've given my opinion. That given enough time and favourable conditions he might carry it out – maybe. But in the time available, with these difficulties we've heard about, in imminent danger of discovery – virtually impossible.'

'Korngold tells me there's a major police operation afoot. Once they identify this dead man – curtains.'

'The wife?'

'She's in a psychotic state. Wandering about somewhere. Not in Germany; she hired a car and there's no trace of it. Could be in Italy – she'll turn up. Nothing to do with the others, and she had the vaguest idea of their project. Unreliable as a witness. Some time was lost because her tale lacked credence. Disregard her.'

'That's all then,' said the Ambassador. 'I think we could do with a drink.'

In days around the turn of the century, when *nouveaux-riches* built lake-side villas and stuffed them full of servants, the kitchen was in the basement. The kitchen was still there, though it had not been used as a kitchen for many years. It was full at present of cardboard cartons, and an astonishing quantity of paper. It was still full of servants. Computer paper comes accordion-pleated and tightly-packed, and cutting through it in bulk is a job to daunt even whitejacket tribes.

In the middle of the kitchen stood a large box. It was 1·8 metres long. Its height was a metre, its width the same. When, with much expenditure of sweat, a clumsy metallic contraption was stowed inside there was an 'Ouf' of relief.

'Even after measuring,' said the Doctor, 'I was a scrap uneasy. I had only rough notes to go on – a diagonal of 2·2 in order to have twenty centimetres of paper all round . . .'

'I wasn't bothered,' said Jim placidly. 'There's going to be a slight weight discrepancy. I hardly think it'll matter.'

'To wit?'

'Well, a box that size filled with paper would weigh about sixteen hundred kilos. Getting it on to the truck,' tranquilly, 'will tax our muscles. No problem the other end of course, but we could do with a forklift here. Now our gadget is around two hundred. The amount of paper we've hollowed out to form the cavity weighs more than that. We'd need to add some lead to bring it back to the right level. Funny,' said Jim. 'I cut the reflector down as much as I dared. I realize now that I could have added another couple of inches. We'd still have over ten centimetres all round of paper.'

'But the length . . .'

'Oh, we've zero-six in barrel length, zero-eight in breech mechanism . . . seven and a half centimetres more – it would have fitted. Too late now.'

'But it'll pop?'

'Oh yes. Small pop. But adequate – for the purpose designed.'

Day had come. A man Jim had never seen, with a powerful local accent, climbed into the truck's cab. A whitejacket – without the uniform – got in at the other side.

'Couldn't have been heavier,' said the driver, 'if it were gold bars.'

'It very nearly is,' said the Doctor. The motor caught and turned. The truck coasted down the slope, turned on to the lake-shore boulevard.

'There she goes. And what, talking about gold bars, would that cost you, from beginning to end?'

230

The Doctor assumed his quizzical look.

'If I were to tell you, Jim, as a rough figure, five hundred thousand Swiss francs – would you be happy to accept that?'

'It's meaningless – not my kind of figures. I say you'd better use your gadget to blow a bank vault.'

'Francs,' said a voice behind them, 'have neither meaning nor importance. Gold twenty-franc pieces with a label saying Napoleon. You push them to and fro with a shovel, and the poor stay poor. That,' Marika pointed after the truck, 'will change things.'

'So here we stand,' said Jim. 'By the shores of Lac Leman. The hooded woman. The hump-backed surgeon. And the scissor man.'

'I don't altogether follow,' said the Doctor.

'Oh it's nothing. Poem. Meaningless.'

'We have a day to get through,' said Marika, staring across the lake.

'It's a fine day,' said Jim. 'Let's fly our kite.'

Traffic was normal. As from eighteen hundred hours this evening the *Journal de Génève* announced, traffic will be restricted in the vicinity of the Palace of Nations, procedure surrounding the impending conference on World Energy Resources, which opens tomorrow in the presence of numerous heads of State. Eagerly awaited will be policy announcements of the President of the United States, the President of the French Republic and the Shah of Iran who are scheduled to address the assembly on this day. Further important interventions in the debate will include . . .

'Skip it,' said the driver.

'Nothing but official cars after that time.'

'We're in front of it.'

At the entrance gate there was a conglomeration of uniforms.

'What you got here, soldier? Let's see your manifest.'

'Computer paper. Special delivery.'

'What, all that? What do they do with it – eat it? Open up lid then, Jack; let's see. All parcels checked. Janey, so it is. Mother of God, twenty-five hundred civil servants printing

231

stuff on that what nobody will ever read. All right, soldier, check with concierge once inside.'

The concierge was even crosser than usual.

'What computer paper? What, more computer paper? I've ten tons of it stuck in each ear. What next? Fifteen hundred-weight of pencil-sharpeners, no doubt? Why can't you imbeciles have it in manageable packages? Go get the fork-lift ... How should I know? They had it at the canteen: there was fifteen hundredweight of cabbage there a moment ago. Put it in the office-supply store, and watch that freight-lift; it's only tested up to two thousand. Every time I sit down there's another security man looking up my ass-hole. Go on then, get it out from underneath my feet,' signing the manifest in a Hitlerian scrawl.

In the corridor two security men were having an argument. One carried a yellowish box, and in the other hand an object like a tube of chromed metal, attached to the box by a tele-phone coil.

'You finished on this floor? Get a move on, then.'

'Sure sure: radioactive typewriter ribbons. All right, Jack, mind my feet then, with that gadget of yours.' Making way for the truck, nobody was struck by the meters.

Stefano did an unheard-of thing that day. He left work an hour early. Offering no excuse, saying nothing. At work, everybody was stunned, and stayed stunned twenty minutes, which is in Italy a very long time.

They would have been more stunned yet if they could have seen him in a bar along the quayside, perhaps a hundred metres from the Rialto bridge, which he habitually crossed. It was to be sure raining heavily. But Stefano was equipped with the usual Venetian accessories – to wit a capacious, old-fashioned loden raincoat, the sort with a huge pleat in the back, and a bitterly modern umbrella of transparent plastic. He hadn't gone to take shelter. Nor to read the paper, which was full as usual of earthquakes, bombs, kidnappings, terrorists (called in Venice 'terrs' or just 'risti'), price rises and an international conference in Geneva: I doubt if you'd find one single person in all Venice who knew or cared what about.

Nor had he just gone for a drink, surely. But perhaps he had, a grappa in front of him, and actually drinking the stuff. Alcohol! A glass of wine at meals, though never more than one. A beer, or a Campari with a friend. But alcohol!

He said nothing, he did nothing, he appeared not to think; he studied Venetians, and the quite large number of tourists still in the city, who passed in a steady stream; the water-bus stop was almost opposite. Rain drummed off the canopy, people pushed past with barrows and odd-shaped packages, with cameras and gondolier hats and great bags stuffed with rubbish. A waiter sweeping up knocked his neat, well-polished shoe with the broom, and apologized.

Exactly an hour later he rose and paid: he'd had three drinks. He gave a generous tip. 'See you,' said the waiter. 'Goodbye,' said Stefano, startling him.

He walked home by the usual route and at the usual rhythm. The rain had stopped when he reached home. The square was wet and shiny, with pools in the hollowed stones. Stefano stopped at his habitual small bar. Signor Reali greeted him, untilted a chair, wiped water off the table, and brought him a beer, which he did not want and did not intend to drink, but he did not want his wife to smell grappa on his breath. That would be like coming home late, giving her a totally needless anxiety.

Harriet appeared, roller skating clumsily but with speed. 'Hallo Pops,' she said affectionately. 'You are not to call me Pops,' he replied. 'Right,' said Harriet. 'Can I have some beer?' 'You may have some beer,' with careful pedantry: she must learn proper Italian.

She drank half the glass in a gulp, scandalizing him slightly. It would be hypocrisy to complain: he wanted to get rid of it! She skated off; the younger generation. That was where one put hopes.

He went in. Cassandra, with pieces of material pinned to her, delighted with herself, capered like a clown.

'Stand still,' said his wife, through pins. All was well. It had been a nightmare. By a tacit agreement, nothing had been said since he had brought the children back. He sat down, heaved the satisfyingly solid small female behind on his knee.

'Don't encourage her to wriggle.'

'What is for supper?'

'All sorts of things you like,' said Cass. 'Guess.'

'I can't guess.' He could not hold it back any longer. 'Did Leora ring?'

'No,' pushing in a strategic pin. 'I was expecting her to. I don't know why; I stayed by the phone all day. Harriet did my shopping.' He gave her a warning glance over the child's head.

'She's busy, I dare say.'

'Do you want the paper?'

'No thanks, little cat.'

'Do you want the television on?'

'No.'

'You still haven't guessed: do you give up?'

'Yes. She's been in my mind; all day.'

'Artichokes!'

'Good! I'm fond of those.'

'Come here, Cass,' said his wife, 'till I unpin you . . . Mine, too.'

'She'll ring, I've no doubt, this evening. Switch the thing on Cass; I've changed my mind.'

'And octopus,' triumphantly, 'the white kind. I like those best.'

'What you can do,' said Stefano producing a paper handkerchief, 'is give my glasses a clean.'

Lac Leman, it is called in French, sounds more picturesque than the Lake of Geneva, but the reality is the same and dull. When the weather is fine it looks as gaudy as on picture postcards. When bad – there can be sudden violent storms – it is dramatic, but it was not the season for storms. It was stuffy weather, with a pall of cloud looking like industrial pollution. The sun struggled out now and then, without enough force to swallow the mist over the water, which was dirty and lifeless. On the south side, which is French, they tell you that the Swiss are polluting the lake, and that there are no fish any more. On the Swiss side they mutter about the French, who lower the tone of the neighbourhood. Both sides are depressing.

In November the summer activities are in abeyance: most hotels are shut, boats have been hauled out of the water, restaurant tables brought in for painting, gay cabins, selling ice-cream or lollipops, shuttered. The winter sports in the mountains around have not begun yet. When it rains you can walk disconsolate for long stretches along the shore, and scarcely see a soul. It did not rain, and there was no wind, but everything seemed exhausted.

Leora changed her base daily, so as not to attract attention. Everywhere was the same: dank rooms needing airing, and indifferent meals sloppily served, lazily cleared away, and overcharged for. She drove along the lake, languidly, feeling all energy oozed out of her bones. She met nobody but old gentlemen with dachshunds lifting their legs with no enthusiasm. When it got unbearable she went to overheated patisseries where overpainted ladies took off their furs, arranged their large bosoms and stared at her. She could digest nothing; she had no appetite, hardly ate, and what she did eat lay on a sour stomach blown up by gas. She smoked all day and drank a great deal without even getting drunk. Just another stomach-ache. She didn't know what she wanted. She didn't know what she expected to find.

She didn't even know whether she would recognize what she was looking for if she saw it. A Mercedes car? A familiar face? Your needle is in a haystack a hundred kilometres long. She tacked along drearily from Lausanne to Rolle, and Rolle to Nyon, and Nyon to Geneva, and back again to dreary Montreux, and saw nothing.

She acquired a follower. For a quarter of an hour she thought it was a pick-up (though who'd want to pick that up, looking at the face in lavatory mirrors?). But no! Cops. Only cops behaved like that. They changed from time to time, but tagged gloomily after her, neither obtrusive nor unobtrusive, looking at her, when they looked at all, with puzzled boredom. Were they Swiss, or German? She didn't know and didn't care.

Nobody arrested her, nobody even accosted her. The self-drive car, she supposed, identified her. It was in her name; she'd paid for it with her credit card. They seemed content to do no more than keep a fatherly eye. Showed no anxiety. She crossed the Rhone, to the French side, and spent an afternoon tagging aimlessly along to Evian and Thonon. The French border guard didn't stir out of his little hut, looked at her fishlike and waved her on with a bored thumb. On the way back a customs man in his red and blue trousers gazed at her with momentary interest but made no move to interfere. Driving back through Vevey to the warmth, and at least pretence of activity, of Lausanne she caught a sudden tiny spark of light on metal over the lake. She lifted her foot off the accelerator in the hope that something – anything – would relieve the monotony. Curiosity for the sake of curiosity. A model aeroplane! Just the kind of idiot pastime one would expect of old gentlemen who lived in Vevey and had valuable stamp collections, or ivory netsuke, or erotica.

Yet obstinacy kept her on the lake shore, just as the irritable restlessness forbade her to stay still. Even at night, gnawing at her own impotence, aware that it was hopeless, futile, stupid, she drove all the way down to Coppet – a name that meant something; was it Voltaire? Madame de Chatelet? Or Madame de Staël? – for a meal that was certainly no better than if she had stayed in Lausanne. In an attempt to digest it she went for a walk along the chilly shore. She heard a car stop and reverse, and the motor die. The follower! Much good might it do him!

Yet something is going to happen in Geneva . . . She felt certain of that. She read the paper. A whole heap of political carnival-giants (huge papier-mâché faces bobbing and grinning above the crowd) was coming to Geneva. And at the European Centre for Nuclear Research the President of the United States will make a speech about a Great Leap Forward. And he was going on to Berlin, to talk to Russians.

It wasn't Berlin. She couldn't say why, but a dozen wisps of conversation back in the prison in the hills told her that it was here. Without ever being able to bring her certainty home, and say why she felt sure that here, not far away, on this lake shore, were the sinister trio; the scissor-man and his two acolytes. On the dirty, muddy-smelling little beach, kicking aimlessly at a pebble, she was half inclined to turn and find her shadow – who was somewhere there in the shadows, wondering what the hell the crazy woman was doing – and shout at him that there was going to be a catastrophe, that she knew nothing, could do nothing, but she knew, she knew, she knew . . .

What was the use? Those Swiss would look at her and say soothingly that she must not worry her little head, that she was very tired, that in Lausanne there were swarms of dotty old ladies and there she would find soothing persons in lovely peaceful comfortable clinics, with starched white jackets and attentive manners and a pharmacy full of splendid peace-pills.

You going to go and face that indulgent voice, you with your dirty stained shirt that you did not bother to change, your stumbling mouth smelling of alcohol? Walk wearily back, kick the motor of that beastly car wearily into life, drive back to the sour bed and the psychotic dreams. Leora cried wretchedly, hardly able to squeeze out a tear, but that hot and burning like acid.

Something about a dog going back to its vomit . . . She looked dreadful and even the dragfoot slattern chambermaid who brought indifferently her indifferent coffee noticed it: looked at her with a vicious pleasure at finding somebody even more miserable than she was herself . . . Get again into the car: there is nowhere else to go: take again that road for there is no other road . . . A remnant of sanity was telling her to get out of this. Go over the border there into France at Ferney, or better still cross the autoroute and the border there up to Divonne, get your hair done and go gamble in the casino or something: enjoy life.

It was on the dreary stretch where the lake narrows, between Rolle and Nyon. There it was again. A big, shiny model aeroplane on the roof of a grey car, parked down near the smelly so-called beach. As she turned her head vaguely a figure got out and lifted the big dragonfly, its wings wider

237

than the car, off the roof to set it tenderly down on the ground. A figure she had seen a thousand times without ever paying attention to it: a flat-footed figure with domestic movements, a feather duster flicking at pewter on a chimney-piece . . . a whitejacket . . .

The car was idling along, in top gear but doing scarcely forty under Leora's slack scuffed toe. When she trod full force on the brake the little Opel did not skid, but stopped as though it had run into a wall. She had forgotten to press the clutch. The car jerked and shuddered; the motor stalled. Frantically Leora twisted the ignition key. The motor screamed. She wrenched the gearshift into reverse, careered backwards, lurched off the road, curved in a wide unco-ordinated backward arc. A thicklipped sticky crunch of the rear bumper against the shiny chrome of the Peugeot's front end. The three people sitting quietly inside the Peugeot were concentrated upon the small box with shiny switches that activates a model aeroplane's controls, and a dashboard clock saying two minutes to ten, while a few kilometres off, in the Palace of Nations at Geneva, polite conventional applause greeted the uprising for speechmaking of the President of the United States. They looked up with a startled jolt.

The impact sprung the door of the Opel open. Leora, who had not bothered to fasten her safety-belt – let the Swiss police stop her if they had a mind to – had only to stoop, throw aside the plaid car rug. Scoop up a brand-new, sweet-grease-smelling Beretta shotgun. For three days it had loitered dangerously, loaded, cocked (very bad for the firing spring) and not even a safety on. A flagrant disregard of rules for the handling of firearms. And she had no excuse. As a child she had been told by her father. 'Never never let your gun, Pointed be at Anyone.' Hadn't paid any attention. Irresponsible, unforgivable woman.

She didn't think at all. Jim was there and she didn't want to hit Jim, but she didn't think about that; she levelled the gun at two metres and pulled the trigger. She hadn't any thoughts. The windscreen of a modern car, triplex safety-glass, will not of course splinter when hit. If violently struck by a loose flint catapulted at speed, it will go opaque, starred into ten thousand crazy fragments which do not disintegrate.

The Doctor tried to rise out of his seat. No easy thing in a car. Especially sitting behind the wheel. Even if you were a gunman, trained to draw from your waistband in three-fifths of a second, the wheel would hamper you. Even if you got your gun out you wouldn't see anything. Not through a windscreen that is knocked opaque by a shotgun blast. It blinds you. You have a gun, but you can't see what to do with it.

Jim had seen her, in the instant between the shock to the car, which jolted the box from his hand, and the shot that smashed the windscreen. Instinctively he reached down for the box. He shouted 'Leora, Leora.'

Maddened, seeing nothing, she was so close, she screamed. Their hands could have reached out and touched, but for the milky barrier between them. Leora screamed 'Jim, Jim.' She slammed the barrel of the shotgun into the windscreen. It collapsed in one piece, like a curtain torn away. In front of her face she saw the Doctor's face, intolerably distorted. With her second shot, at a range of fifty centimetres, she blew him to pieces. The features vanished, into a red haze.

Jim was trying to get up. Untouched, intact, still grasping the box. She could see him, he was there; she could touch him if she held out her hand.

Marika had been thrown backwards, on the back seat, by the impact of the car. Then there was an explosion and she could see nothing. She struggled up into balance. She stretched her hand out. Part of the blast that tore the Doctor into shreds touched her, scoring the forearm so that pain ran along like a flame. She did not flinch. She knew what to do. The Doctor's revolver fell from his right hand between the two front seats. She concentrated upon it.

'Jim,' called Leora. Jim was struggling to rise, brandishing the black box in triumph. Marika jammed the barrel of the revolver into his left shoulderblade and fired three times. With her left hand she seized the box. There was blood running all over her right hand.

Leora's face stared at her in the picture frame of the broken windscreen, open-mouthed, aghast. Marika carefully wiped the blood off, and snapped the switch down. There was a delay of just over two milliseconds; the oscillator ticked two-oh-four-eight-cycles. Leora, leaning forward, put the barrel of the shotgun against Marika's temple and blew her head off.

Whitejacket, paralysed, had not moved at all. He still stood there with that beautiful model aeroplane clasped in his arms. Afraid to let it drop.

Three hundred metres behind, the Swiss security man, who had been following Leora for the last two days, woke up as her brake-lights jammed on. That bitch is totally off her trolley, he thought. Utterly mataglap. He braked to a careful stop and sat open-mouthed as her car reversed with a stupefying clonk into a brand new Peugeot. He saw the model aeroplane lifted off the roof, he saw the shotgun. Cursing, with a hundred metres to run, he saw the blast blow the windscreen silly. Running, jumping, ricking his ankle, cursing the pain and his own bad luck and the stupidity of it all he wrenched his pistol, only a seven-sixty-five, from its holster, ran, tried a shot, missed by a mile. He was shaking all over. The shotgun fired a second time. Answered by a fusillade. Deliberately, a third. On the worn dead grass of the road verge he stumbled, went down full length, held his breath, tucked the pistol barrel in the crook of his elbow, aimed for her knee, fired, and saw her fall. He stood, scrambled, ran.

Two people obliterated, holy Jesus. Where was blood, bone, grey matter, grey and red upholstery? There was nothing left. The third had coughed his life out in blood, hadn't lived two seconds. (It was not quite accurate. Jim, hit in the heart, the lung, and the portal vein by three nine-millimetre bullets, took nearly ten seconds to die.)

It took that long for the shockwave to reach Nyon from the city of Geneva. The sound arrived, the picturesque colours arrived, the fireball rose in a purple and gold sun rising irresponsibly, impossibly in the south-west. The Swiss security agent looked at the ridiculous things that had happened under his nose. The ridiculous things that were happening on

240

the outskirts of the city of Geneva. He couldn't believe his eyes.

Leora, with a smashed femur that was just beginning to hurt, lay writhing on the dead muddy grass, and vomited, and saw nothing. But she lived, she was alive.

That was something: nearly five thousand people lost their lives. She only lost blood, mind, husband.

Epilogue

T minus zero seconds. A President took his glasses off, to help him speak. Another President put his glasses on, to help him listen. Each knew what the other was going to say.

The auditorium hushed, and the Secretary-General, enthroned on high, looked around as though to say, 'There will now be no coughing,' though this was perfectly unnecessary. There was silence.

In the silence the first radio signal arrived on channel one of the model aeroplane band, placing a key in a lock. A long, long time later, the longest interval in the chain, time for the President to open his mouth – to be precise it was 0·027 seconds – a second signal arrived on channel seven: the key turned.

The President's mouth was open; ear tuned.

The bias voltage on the base of a transistor dropped to zero and current flowed through the coil of a solenoid actuator. A sound began to form in a nasal cavity, on the way to translating itself into a labial; the beginnings of the letter 'm'. The firing pin of a recoilless rifle bit into a fulminate cap and the 'm' started to echo in the eustachian tubes. As it reached a further bony cavity, that of the palate, several hundred grams of nitro-cellulose ignited. The 'm' gathered resonance in the mouth and the lips shaped into an orifice to expel it. One two-hundredth of a second later, which was an eternity, but time for the 'm' to reach the lips already contracting towards the vowel 'i', a small cone of uranium slid into the matching cavity in a larger block of the metal. A microscopic speck of polonium kissed a morsel of lithium. The teeth were not quite closed in the President's mouth; a sibilant was being prepared but had not left the throat muscles.

It had no time to reach to teeth and begin an 's'. The first neutron, half a millionth of a second after, emerged and was

242

absorbed harmlessly in uranium-238 a centimetre or so away. Not very much later, perhaps a millionth of a second, a second neutron emerged from the initiator. The 's' never had a chance, for this neutron lodged in a nucleus of uranium-235, which promptly fissioned.

There was energy in the auditorium. Muscles moved, sweat glands secreted, heat was generated. For instance, a sibilant formed and yawns began. This became trivial, for the energy released did not reach two hundred and six million electron volts per atom: the uranium nucleus downstairs did. There were also two radioactive daughter nuclei and three more neutrons. Two of these three neutrons found their way to additional nuclei of uranium-235. The chain reaction had begun.

It sounds fairly rapid. But finite, measurable. Rather laborious in comparison to – say Mozart's Requiem. That only took time to write down. Or to hear. If you like to think of infinity, time becomes a singularly trivial affair.

Another small amount of time – nowhere near enough for the transmission of complicated messages, like reading this, or forming a sibilant – and the uranium cylinder became a sphere of uranium gas, expanding, surrounded by a larger ball of X-rays, gamma rays, and neutrons. A thought, so far; as trivial as most thoughts.

The physical result, becoming perceptible to the senses, is less trivial. Half a metre from the centre the X-rays interact with the atmosphere, igniting it and heating it to a thousand million degrees: whether you are counting by a Fahrenheit or Celsius scale will be of no importance.

The air burns. Purple initially: cooling to yellow, at last to red, some seconds later as the fireball forms.

The blast wave, which only travels at the speed of sound, lags behind the pulse of light and heat. But together they lift off the roof of the building and enter the cellar, scooping up steel and concrete, mounting in majesty. It is only the Palace of Nations in Geneva. Architecturally not one of man's better efforts. But there are men inside it, even if these are only presidents and kings, ministers and delegates, journalists, bodyguards, simultaneous translators. Civil servants. There are also waiters, cooks, the concierge. Firemen. But there was no order of precedence for entering another world.

The funeral march of Beethoven's third symphony, now occupying the world's radio and television channels, is a march. It is frequently played as a dirge: an error. Marching were three presidents of Argentina, France and the United States; a king, of Persia, and a considerable train of folk. In step.

The air over Lac Leman was saturated with water vapour, and the suction wave following the blast cooled the air to below dew point. A hazy white sphere of cloud surrounded the fireball and the mushroom. As these things go, only a very little bomb. Only a very little bomb as such things go. Minimal loss of life. Certainly not ten thousand. The official government communiqués will mention under five. A large building has been totally levelled. Some particularly sturdy columns will remain standing until otherwise disposed of: they are unattended by floors or ceilings. Office-buildings some blocks away have lost a lot of glass: a few fires were also started. People up to a kilometre away were flash-blinded and badly burned by radiation. Flowerbeds were destroyed. Trees in the botanic gardens have suffered considerably.

Across the lake, where eccentric persons had been playing with a model aeroplane, and an unbalanced woman fired a shotgun, there were three extra fatal casualties. A federal security official became aware that even if he could get through on the telephone nobody wanted to listen to what he had to say.

In Evian a French cop, despite difficulties with the telephone, had finally got through to the Préfecture of the Haute-Savoie. The Prefect was absolutely firm about his responsibilities.

'Déclenchez le plan Orsec.' Roughly, the dam has broken. Policemen's free time is going to be abruptly curtailed.

It will take a long time, a year at least, before the increase in pollution of the waters of Lac Leman can be measured with any accuracy.